Outstanding praise for Larissa Ione

"Ione has the amazing ability to create intimidating, powerfully sexy and utterly compelling heroes."
RT Book Reviews on *Eternal Rider*

Outstanding praise for Alexandra Ivy

"Captivating, sexy, and with a sinful bite like rich, dark chocolate, *Beyond the Darkness* kept me riveted! The Guardians of Eternity series is highly addictive, the dialogue clever, the characters woven with subtle complexity. Alexandra Ivy has made me her fangirl!"
Larissa Ione, *New York Times* bestselling author on *Beyond the Darkness*

"Delivers plenty of atmosphere and hot-blooded seduction."
Publishers Weekly on *Embrace the Darkness*

"*Darkness Unleashed* is oh, so hot and wonderfully dangerous. I can't wait for the next installment!"
Gena Showalter, *New York Times* bestselling author on *Darkness Unleashed*

Outstanding praise for Jacquelyn Frank

"I love this book!"
Christine Feehan, *New York Times* bestselling author on *Jacob*

"A stunning new talent!"
Sherrilyn Kenyon, *New York Times* bestselling author on *Gideon*

"Enter a world of adventure and sensuality."
Lora Leigh, *New York Times* bestselling author on *Ecstasy*

Outstanding praise for G. A. Aiken

"Sexy and outrageous humor!"
RT Book Reviews on *Last Dragon Standing*

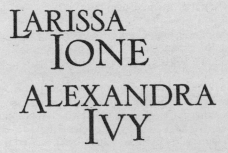

LARISSA IONE
ALEXANDRA IVY

Supernatural

JACQUELYN FRANK
G.A. AIKEN

ZEBRA BOOKS
KENSINGTON PUBLISHING CORP.
http://www.kensingtonbooks.com

ZEBRA BOOKS are published by

Kensington Publishing Corp.
119 West 40th Street
New York, NY 10018

All Kensington titles, imprints, and distributed lines are available at special quantity discounts for bulk purchases for sales
promotion, premiums, fund-raising, educational, or institu-
tional use.

Special book excerpts or customized printings can also be created to fit specific needs. For details, write or phone the office
of the Kensington Special Sales Manager: Attn. Special Sales
Department. Kensington Publishing Corp., 119 West 40th Street,
New York, NY 10018. Phone: 1-800-221-2647.

Zebra and the Z logo Reg. U.S. Pat. & TM Off.

ISBN-13: 978-1-4201-0988-7
ISBN-10: 1-4201-0988-X

First Printing: September 2011

10 9 8 7 6 5 4 3 2 1

Printed in the United States of America

Contents

Vampire Fight Club

LARISSA IONE

Chapter 1

Blood. Violence. Sex. Cheering crowds.

None of it fazed Nathan Sabine anymore. If someone had told him a hundred years ago that he'd be completely numb to the gladiatorial battle taking place in the hockey rink-sized arena below his VIP booth, he'd have ripped out their throat with his teeth.

Hell, that still sounded like a good plan.

Instead, he was watching a hyena shifter rip out the throat of another hyena shifter. Should have been the same-old, same-old, but one of the males hadn't shifted out of his human form.

Which was why the male had been at a serious disadvantage, and why he was now bleeding out in the sand.

Nate didn't give a shit why the guy had wanted to fight this battle, but he had to have known he couldn't win. The fool. No amount of money was worth dying for. Nothing was worth that.

Turning his back on the bloodthirsty roar of the spectators, Nate strode out of the private viewing box reserved for club personnel and wondered if it was possible to hate himself more than he did right now. Doubtful. He might be anesthetized to everything outside his body, but inside, he was a seething cauldron of self-loathing. Sometimes he thought that if he wasn't a daywalker, a rare vampire who could tolerate natural light, he'd step out into the sun and end it all.

And wasn't he a hypocrite of epic proportions, given that he'd just wondered why the hyena non-shifter had given up his life.

He took the stairs down into the commons, where people sought refreshments and placed bets while they waited for the next death match. At one time, the sour stench of their excitement and greed had turned his stomach. Now it was like any other unpleasant odor the nose learned to ignore. Lately, though, the stink was stronger, the result of a command from the big boss to step up the number of fights—and the brutality—in order to maintain pace with the unrest in the underworld. Fade was desperate to keep paying spectators coming to the club instead of enjoying the violence elsewhere for free.

The crowd parted for Nate, some whispering his name as he passed. An ugly-ass, gray-skinned demon male near the pit railing asked when Nate was going to fight again, and Nate swung around, his black hair snapping about his shoulders, his fangs bared.

"You volunteering to get in the pit with me, demon? Because I'm itching to put another set of antlers on my wall."

The normally inaudible beat of music from the dance club upstairs rang clear enough in the sudden silence to identify the artist.

The demon cleared his beefy throat as Goldfrappe *Ooh La La*'d its way to the end of the song. "Another time, perhaps."

"That's what I thought." Nate hadn't been in the arena in nearly seven decades, and these morons still wanted to see him fight—as long as he fought someone *else*. No one ever volunteered to step into the pit with him.

He sliced through the throng and slipped past the two guards who kept the general public out of the tunnel separating Gladius from Thirst, the respectable half of the club complex. He'd only gone about ten yards and taken the first corner when he heard footsteps behind him.

"Boss."

Nate stopped but didn't turn around. "What, Gunnar?"

"The body, sir." The hulking werewolf's voice was little more than a rumble in the shadowy hall.

"Why are you asking me? Where's Budag?"

"He went out."

Budag, who had once been Attila the Hun's right-hand man, was the only person besides the club owner who outranked Nate, but the asshole was hardly ever around. Nate had no idea what the demon in human clothing did in his spare time, but he certainly seemed to have a lot of it.

Exhaling on a curse, Nate looked up at the flickering fluorescents on the ceiling. "The male is a shifter. You know the rules."

Usually the dead were fed to the creatures that were kept either as bait for training or for actual gladiatorial matches, but a few species, including most shifters, could bond so strongly to a mate that after death, the surviving partner would be driven to find them. The club couldn't afford for some grieving, pissed-off female to track down the male's remains and cause trouble.

"Yes, sir."

Nate continued down the hall and up a flight of cement stairs. A casual observer who arrived at the narrow landing would see only a monitor mounted on a textured black wall. Nate checked the grainy screen, and after he'd ensured that no one was inside his office, he pushed on the wall, opening a hidden doorway.

From the office side, the door appeared to be nothing more than a sturdy wine rack, and it made a whisper of a click as it closed. Only Thirst's top management knew that this was one of two entrances from the dance club to the fight club. Most of Thirst's employees weren't even aware that behind and underneath the most popular vampire bar in North America, was the most popular blood arena in the human realm.

Nate had known for over a hundred years. He'd known, and he'd planned to take it down. And he would, when the time was right.

Self-loathing slithered through him again, because he'd been singing that tune for decades. So many right times had come and gone, and he'd done nothing. His interest had been as dead as his heart.

Cursing himself, he slammed out of the front door of his office and into another hallway, this one brightly lit, the walls plastered with gaudy murals depicting scenes of various underworld creatures getting their grooves on under disco balls. His shoes sank into the plush crimson carpet as he strode toward the club's public area. The music grew louder as he walked, throbbing through him like a pulse and granting him the illusion, at least, that he was alive.

Once he went through the swinging door at the end of the hall, he was immediately assaulted by sultry heat, glaring, colored lights streaming in the darkness, and all the erotic sounds that went with a place like this. The lower level was a mass of writhing bodies—people dancing, sexing, feeding. At the tables and on the couches lining the walls on the upper and lower levels, there was more of the sex and feeding. Cocktail waitresses delivered drinks under the watchful eyes of bouncers who ensured the waitresses went unmolested.

That had been one of Nate's changes when he'd been promoted to manager—a rule that no one touched the staff or he'd maim them. Period.

"Yo, Nathan." Marsden, Thirst's vampire chief of security and Nate's second in command, shoved his way through a gaggle of males eyeing three scantily-clad females leaning over the railing on the upper level. "We have a situation." Marsden's hazel eyes shifted to the medic station near the restrooms, and Nate sighed.

"Injury, overdose, or overfeed?"

"Overfeed. Vic is human."

"Shit." Bad enough when a vampire got too eager with an underworlder, but humans were a lot harder to treat, keep alive, and dispose of if they died.

"It was the perp's second offense," Mars said, as they moved toward the medic station. "He's been given the boot."

"Hope that boot was up the nightcrawler's ass."

Mars, the only soul on the planet who knew about Nate's daywalker status, didn't take offense at the dig at regular vamps. He merely grinned, revealing the latest in vampire fashion; gold-plated fangs studded with jewels. Feeding must be a bitch for both him and the victim.

"Boot went far enough up his ass that he lost a couple teeth."

Excellent.

Inside the thirty-by-thirty room set up as a medical station, John, a human EMT who moonlighted here on weekends, was monitoring the flow of blood through an IV inserted into a red-headed woman's freckled arm.

"She'll be fine," John drawled, his twang betraying his Texas roots. "This ain't her first rodeo."

True enough. The woman, whose name Nate thought was Allison, lay motionless and pale on the table, her silver tube top barely covering breasts made too big by a surgeon's scalpel, and her black micro-mini skirt definitely not covering what it needed to. She was a regular here, a swan who gave herself to vampires for blood, sex, or both.

John carefully applied a bandage over the punctures on her neck . . . a neck that was scarred from hundreds of feedings.

The scent of blood teased Nate's nostrils, drawing his gaze to a crimson trail on the inside of the girl's thigh and reminding him that he hadn't fed recently.

"There were two feeding on her," he said, gesturing to the seeping punctures in her femoral artery. Some vampire had done a piss-poor job of sealing the wound.

John leaned in to examine the second bite. "Could have been just the one, tapping two places."

"Different size fangs. The one at her throat was female." Which, dammit, meant Marsden had another vamp to punish. "Alert me when you release the human."

Nate didn't wait for a response. He went straight to the bar, poured a double shot of O-neg, and took the edge off his hunger. His blood hunger, anyway. As he watched the grind of bodies on the floor, another need rose in him, one he hadn't sated in far too long.

Marsden came up behind him and clapped him on the shoulder. "That hot little piece of human ass at the end of the bar has been eyeing you."

Yeah, he'd already felt her lusty gaze on him. "I don't need your matchmaking skills."

"You need *something*. You're wound around the axel, man. Want me to send her to your office?"

The human woman tilted her head to expose her slim throat as she ran black-lacquered fingernails along her cleavage in blatant invitation. He wondered if she was a starfucker who knew who he was, a legend in the blood arena, or if she was a run-of-the-mill vampire chaser eager for any set of fangs to penetrate her. Either way, Nate wasn't game no matter how strung out he was. He'd always preferred to get his blood and sex from females he hadn't seen screwing other males that night.

"No." He started to walk away, but Marsden's hand on his arm stopped him.

"Trust me on this. You need to work off some juice."

A chill shot up Nate's spine, and his jaw clenched so hard he could barely ask the question he already knew the answer to. "Why?"

Marsden's nostrils flared, the diamond nose stud glinting in the smoky light. "He's coming."

The demon who owned both Thirst and Gladius was coming for a visit. Nate waited for the hatred to sear him from the inside, but instead, his chest cavity filled with ice, and his entire body went so cold he shivered. Fade was the reason Nate had infiltrated the club's organization in the first place. He'd waited for decades to destroy the bastard, had gained his trust while growing stronger and amassing a fortune at the demon's expense.

Nate's hatred had eaten him alive for decades, but now it seemed that the hatred had been replaced by apathy. Once upon a time, Fade had killed the love of Nate's life, and it was now becoming obvious that the demon had also killed Nate. He searched deep inside himself in an attempt to find a flicker of life, but there wasn't even a spark.

He. Was. Dead.

Chapter 2

Incoming emergencies got Vladlena Paskelkov's adrenaline surging and brought her to life like nothing else. As a nurse at the only hospital that catered to vampires, demons, and other various underworld creatures, she got to see things she'd never encounter at a human facility and, as with most medical people, the more bizarre or horrific the injury, the more excited she got.

It wasn't as if she *liked* seeing anyone hurt, especially not the young of any species. But she'd inherited the medical gene from her father, who had been a surgeon at this very hospital.

Until he was tortured and killed by The Aegis, a society of human demon slayers who called themselves Guardians and made it their mission to rid the planet of evil.

Lena had been bitter, but not for long. Her father, though he'd been good to her, had walked a sinister path, and she was surprised the slayers hadn't killed him sooner. She'd also learned to like a few Guardians, including one who used to work at Underworld General but now ran The Aegis, and one who was mated to the hospital's chief of staff.

And speak of the incubus, Eidolon, a dark-haired, impossibly hot Seminus demon, jogged into the bustling emergency department and snagged a pair of surgical gloves from the supply stand.

"What have we got?"

Lena gloved up as she spoke. "Male shifter, unknown breed. Found like the others, with multiple wounds, no vitals when the paramedics found him, but Shade got him jumpstarted."

Eidolon smirked. "What were Shade's exact words?"

Shade, Eidolon's brother in charge of the hospital's paramedics, rarely minced words. Yes, he'd given her all the technical jargon, but only after his more personal observations.

"Hell's fucking rings," she said, doing her best Shade imitation. *"Dude looks like he went through a wood chipper."*

One dark eyebrow arched. "That's more like it." The red rotating light at the ambulance bay doors lit up, signaling the ambulance's arrival in the underground lot. Before the doors opened, Eidolon turned to her, lowering his voice. "Did the serum work?"

All the adrenaline that had been surging through her veins turned to sludge, and she absently rubbed the spot on the back of her hand where she'd given herself the injection.

"No." She cleared her voice to rid it of the sudden hoarseness. "I didn't shift."

Pity dulled Eidolon's espresso eyes. "I'm sorry, Lena. I'll keep working on it."

He didn't say anything more. What was there to say? *Sorry you're a freak who can't shift into your animal form, even with a drug that works on everyone else? Sorry you're going to go insane and die?*

Over the years, she'd been through therapy and lessons, desperate to shift into her furry form before she turned twenty-four, when the inability to shift would kill her. Yesterday, on her twenty-fourth birthday, she'd injected a drug Eidolon had developed as a catalyst for those who couldn't shift any other way. It hadn't worked. She was a failure among failures, and it was probably a good thing her father wasn't alive to see how, very soon, she'd lose her grip on reality and grow violent before finally dying in agony. Shifters with her problem rarely survived more than six weeks after turning twenty-four, and she'd already started marking off days on the calendar. So much time wasted. So much more she'd wanted to do.

This really sucked.

The ER doors whooshed open, and Shade and his partner, a werewolf named Luc, wheeled in a bloody male on a stretcher. As they hurried the patient to a room, Shade rattled off vitals, the dismal numbers putting an immediate damper on hope. Lena had only been out of nursing school for a couple of years, but she knew a goner when she saw one.

The acrid stench of death clung to this male like a dire leech, and . . . she gasped, grinding to a halt as Shade and Luc lifted the patient onto a table.

"Vladlena?" Eidolon's right arm, which was encased in glyphs that ran from his fingertips to his shoulder, lit up as the healing ability inherent to his species channeled into the male. "You know this patient?"

"Vaughn." She stumbled to the side of the bed, her legs threatening to give out on her. "He's my brother."

Vaughn had been the only one of her three brothers who hadn't tried to kill her. As the runt of the litter, she'd been the target of their vicious games, and if not for her father, they'd have slaughtered her. Now that he was gone, Van and Vic had made several attempts on her life . . . which was one of the reasons she pulled a lot of double shifts at the hospital. Here, she was safe.

Eidolon motioned for another nurse to take over for Lena,

and she didn't argue. Vaughn needed care she couldn't give right now. Not with the way her hands were shaking and her mind was spinning.

Dear gods, he'd been torn to shreds. One arm looked like it had been chewed nearly off. Deep bite wounds left skin and muscle flayed in massive slabs that peeled back from exposed bone. His throat had been torn open, and blood seeped through the layers of pressure bandages.

One of Vaughn's eyes was swollen shut, but the other opened, and his bloodshot gaze latched onto hers. Recognition flared in the blue depths, along with unthinkable pain.

"Hey." She took his hand, tried not to cringe at the icy-cold, clammy skin. "You're at UG. You're going to be fine." She offered a trembly smile that faltered when she glanced up at Eidolon, whose expression made a liar out of her. "Vaughn, what happened? Who did this to you?"

"Th-thirst . . ." His voice was barely a rasp, his words gurgled through blood. "Club . . ."

He convulsed, and her co-workers became a flurry of action. Shade pulled her back with gentle hands as Eidolon tried to save her brother.

Time became fluid, elastic, stretching without giving Vladlena any sense of how much of it had passed before Eidolon finally looked up at the clock and spoke the words no one wanted to say—or hear.

"Time of death, 3:22." The doctor looked over at her, his powerful shoulders slumped in defeat. "Lena, I'm sorry."

She nodded, her throat too clogged with emotion to speak.

"Shade." Eidolon lifted a sheet to cover Vaughn's body. "Where did you find him?"

"Same place as the others." Shade gave Lena's shoulders a squeeze and stepped away from her, though he stayed close. "In the sewers beneath Fifth street."

Shade's words barely registered. She'd latched onto a rhythmic tapping noise that rose up even over the din of the bustling emergency department outside the cubicle. It took a moment to realize what it was; her brother's blood, dripping to the obsidian floor. Odd what the brain focused on when it didn't want to think about something horrible right in front of you.

"What is going on?" Lena whispered.

Shade's dark hair brushed the collar of his black paramedic uniform as he shook his head. "I don't know, but your brother is the only one to make it through the hospital doors alive."

"This is the third victim this week." Eidolon stripped off his gloves. "The human and demon realms have been in turmoil lately, but this is too specific to be related to the apocalyptic events."

Turmoil was a mild way to put what was happening, given that the Four Horsemen of the Apocalypse had recently appeared, and at least one apocalyptic Seal had broken. The hospital had been dealing with the violent fallout nonstop, and Eidolon had been forced to hire unschooled help and train them on the job just to keep up with the patient load.

Shade casually kicked a towel beneath the exam table to stop the sickening drip of Vaughn's blood. It was a small thing, but a thoughtful one, and Lena could have kissed the demon for it. "So what the hell are we dealing with?"

"Fight club." Wraith, Shade and Eidolon's blond, half-vampire brother, sauntered up, his leather duster flapping around his boots. "You're dealing with some sort of underground gladiator fights."

"And you know this, how?" Shade folded his arms over his broad chest in that universal big brother pose Vaughn used to give her while he waited for an answer he knew he wouldn't like.

Wraith blinked, all mock innocence. "I wasn't always a model citizen, you know."

Vladlena glanced over at her brother's lifeless body before quickly looking away. "He wouldn't have been involved with something like that."

"Maybe not willingly," Wraith said. "These places are run by the same kind of scum who run dog and cock fighting rings."

Her hands tingled, and she realized she'd been hanging onto the stethoscope around her neck like it was a lifeline. "What are you saying?"

"That your brother could have been bait. Used to train fighters. Or he could have been forced into fighting."

The strawberry milkshake she'd had for dinner soured in her stomach. Pinpricks of pain spread through her fingers as she pried them away from the ancient stethoscope, which used to be her father's. "Where do these things operate?"

Wraith jammed his hands into his jean's pockets. "The really skeevy ones are run in Sheoul, but the most profitable ones are here in the human realm."

"Hey, guys, look at this." Shade held up Vaughn's arm, and under the glow of the ultraviolet lamp on the wall, a stamp glimmered beneath blood on the back of his hand. "One of the other victims had a similar stamp."

"Thirst," Wraith murmured. "Nice place."

Vaughn's voice rang through her head. *Th-thirst.* She sucked in a harsh breath. "That's what Vaughn said when he came in. I thought he was asking for water. What is Thirst?"

"Vamp club." Wraith propped his hip against the counter and crossed his booted feet at the ankles. "Shifters and weres go too, and a few humans who are in the know about us."

Vaughn had been even more of a recluse than she was. So

why he'd go to this vampire club was a mystery. A mystery she was going to solve. If she had only a few weeks left to live, she'd make the most of them, and she'd get revenge for her brother.

A forbidden thrill shot through her at the thought, and yep, that had to be a symptom of the pending insanity, because the idea of violence had never excited her. And somehow, she couldn't even bring herself to be upset about it . . . which was probably another symptom.

Very gently, she tucked Vaughn's hand under the sheet. "Looks like I'm going to pay a visit to a vampire hangout."

"Lena, if Thirst is a cover for a fight club, it's too dangerous for you." Eidolon's tone softened to the one he used with children. "When your father asked me to give you a job, he also asked me to look after you if anything were to happen to him."

She stared at the handsome doctor, surprised by his admission, but it didn't change anything. "You can't stop me," she blurted out, and wasn't that mature? She might as well stomp her foot, too. Breathing deeply, she found her big girl voice. "I need to do something that matters in the time I have left."

The doctor closed his eyes for a moment, and when he opened them, they were resigned. "Give me an hour to do some research."

"I'll do recon," Wraith said, his blue eyes bright with mischief. She didn't even want to know what he had planned. With Wraith, it could be anything.

Shade popped a stick of gum in his mouth. "I need to clean the rig, but let me know if you need anything."

The brothers left her alone with Vaughn, and she sat with him, remembering all that they'd been through, from games of hide-and-seek as cubs, to mourning their father's death. An hour later, Lore, the fourth Seminus brother, arrived to take Vaughn to the morgue.

"I'm sorry, Lena." Lore placed his hand—gloved to prevent any accidents with the lethal power he wielded—over hers. "I'll treat him well."

As he wheeled Vaughn away, Eidolon arrived with a cup of coffee. He handed it to her, and she took it, hoping the hot liquid would ease the chill that had settled in.

"You can access Thirst either through a secret entrance behind a human Goth club called Velvet Chain," he said, "or from a hidden door in the sewer beneath it. Since it's mainly a vampire club, non-vamps are expected to donate blood."

"Not if they work there." Wraith swept in the way he always did, like a tornado. "The club employs six medics. And they're hiring."

Eidolon frowned. "How do you know?"

"Because they're now short two medics. I convinced one to quit."

"And the other?" Eidolon asked.

"I convinced him to die." Wraith flashed fangs. "It was that douche you fired last year for swapping out patients' pain meds for vitamins."

"Excellent." Eidolon nodded in approval. "But I still don't like the idea of Lena going into that den of violence."

"It's not your decision," she said quietly.

"You're right," E said. "And I wish I could send someone with you, but we can't afford to lose any more hands."

"It's okay. I have to do this."

Wraith clapped her on the shoulder. "We'll check in on you."

Before she had a chance to thank him, Eidolon rounded on her, danger rolling off him in a scorching wave she felt on her skin.

"If anything happens to you," he said, in a voice as deadly as she'd ever heard from him, "I promise we'll bring that club down so hard nothing will be left standing."

"Especially not the fucks who run it," Wraith added, his eyes glittering with anticipation.

Funny thing. People talked big, said stuff like that all the time but never followed through. Without a doubt, these guys meant every word.

Chapter 3

Vladlena was a nervous wreck as she entered Thirst for the second time that day. Earlier in the afternoon, she'd spoken with the assistant manager about the medic job. He'd been impressed with her credentials, and after the interview, he'd sent her on her way with high hopes for a callback. Four hours later, she'd gotten the call.

Marsden had spoken with Eidolon, and now all she had to do was impress the big boss, some vampire named Nathan.

She halted just inside the main entrance and eyed the crowd, which seemed heavy for only six o'clock in the evening. But then, the patrons who came here lived all over the globe, so really, time in an underworld club was meaningless.

The scent of lust, blood, and booze was thick in the air, and as she navigated her way toward the medic station, she caught whiffs of aggression, as well. No doubt a place like this saw its share of fights. But it wasn't the regular bar fights she was interested in. There was a sick, twisted sport going on here, and she'd make sure those responsible for her brother's death paid.

One of the bouncers pointed her to Marsden's office, which was far down a long hallway at the rear of the club.

"Thanks for coming, Vladlena." He dipped his head in greeting as she entered, and she wondered if the gelled spikes in his ash-brown hair were as sharp as they looked. With his funky hair, piercings, black-painted nails, and jeweled fangs, he was one odd-looking guy. "Like I said on the phone, everything looks great. Getting Nathan's okay is mainly a formality at this point, but he'll probably have some questions for you." He pointed to a door across the hall. "Good luck."

The "good luck" didn't sound promising, and she wondered what she was going to be dealing with. Inhaling deeply to steel herself, she tapped on the door. A gruffly spoken, "Enter" was the response, and she pushed open the door, unease curling inside her chest.

At first, she didn't see him. She was too busy admiring the giant oak desk scattered with some sort of tickets marked with GLADIUS, the exotic—and expensive—Persian rug, the artwork on the walls. Then she stepped fully inside and looked toward the wet bar to the right.

He was standing with his hip propped against the bar, long fingers caressing a glass of amber liquid, his crystalline azure eyes drilling into her. Shiny, black-blue hair fell in a straight curtain below his broad shoulders, and damn it, she hated when males had better hair than she did. Sharp angles defined his face, from high cheekbones to a strong jaw, and when one corner of his mouth lifted into a half-smile that revealed a gleaming fang, her pulse did an excited flutter.

Her roommate, Blaspheme, would say that from his expensive loafers to his well-fitting black slacks and gray silk shirt, this male exuded pure, hardcore sex.

Not that Lena would know anything about that.

"Um . . . hi, Mr. Sabine. I'm Vladlena—"

"Take off your clothes." His husky voice, tinged with a faint French accent, was so mesmerizing that his words didn't register for a few seconds.

Finally, she blinked. "Excuse me?"

"Marsden sent you, right?"

"Yes, but—"

"Then strip."

He moved toward her, and with every step, her heart hammered faster. He'd been carved from a stone slab of danger, power, and grace, and if he possessed even an ounce of softness, she'd eat the file she was holding. The room shrank as he closed in on her, erotic energy pulsing off him and making her skin tingle. Those wide shoulders rolled, reminding her of a lion on the prowl, and although at five-nine, she wasn't short, he was at least seven inches taller. He could crush her with his pinky finger, and here she was, in the place her brother had lost his life, alone in an office with the male who might be responsible.

"I didn't know that getting naked was part of the job requirement." She was proud of the way her voice didn't waver. Much.

His expression hardened even more, something she hadn't thought was possible. "Jesus. Where did Marsden find you?"

This was not going well at all, and she clutched the file in her hands tighter to keep them from shaking. "I applied for the job this morning."

"He's taking applications?"

"You'd rather your medical personnel pop in off the streets with no training?"

A deep frown pulled at his brow, and then he laughed, and good gods, he was impressive when he did that. "You're here for one of the medic positions."

So the guy was handsome, but not too bright. "Of course." Taking a swig of his drink, he dropped his eyes to her feet. Slowly, he dragged his gaze back up her body in a blatant, sensual appraisal before settling on her mouth.

"Well, then," he drawled. "How badly do you want the job?"

Nate waited for a reaction from the female—beyond the shocked-out expression that included a dropped jaw, wide eyes, and utter speechlessness, anyway. He'd figured out immediately that she wasn't a screw sent by Marsden . . . well, almost immediately, though he hadn't determined why Mars *had* sent her. In the first few seconds, he'd just been happy his lieutenant had sent an attractive but plain female who was actually wearing clothes, and not one of the fang-fuckers from the club decked out in an outfit more appropriate for the bedroom than a bar.

This female was different from anyone he'd ever seen at Thirst, from her scuffed black flats and well-fitting but conservative charcoal slacks to her long-sleeved sweater. Her minimal makeup emphasized high cheekbones and full lips, and he had the oddest urge to ask her to take her blond hair out of the tame, hip-length French braid so he could see if it was as silky as it looked.

Maybe the doe-eyed librarian act was her game. Maybe she drew in the males who wanted to tap a wallflower. Nate had never been that kind. He liked hardasses who knew what they were getting into when they bedded a vampire, but as he'd sized up Vladlena, he began to see the appeal.

But then he'd seen the nervousness in her eyes, heard the note of fear in her voice. Some deep, dark part of him had awakened, and the thrill of the hunt seized him. It was a small rush, barely a ripple in the pool of numbness he'd been drowning in, but Jesus, it was as if a thread of life had been thrown to him, and he was going to cling to it for as long as he could.

"Well?" His body buzzed as he studied her, the way it did when he inadvertently drank blood from a coked-up human, but this was better. Purer, without the fuzzy edges. "You just going to stare at me, or are you going to offer up some incentive for me to hire you?"

Her slender throat worked on a few swallows, and he followed the column of smooth ivory skin lower, to the V neckline of her forest-green angora sweater. Just as he dove south to the smooth swells of her breasts, she thrust a file at him.

"Here's your incentive." She waited until he took the file, and then she stepped back, as if wanting to get away. It made him want to cage her between his body and the wall just to show her that if he didn't want her to escape, she wouldn't. "Eidolon, the head doctor at Underworld General, prepared that for you. It lists my accomplishments and special skills."

He nearly chuckled at her attempt to divert him, but he was having too much fun watching her squirm. "*All* of your special skills?"

Again, her soft brown eyes flared. "Eidolon wouldn't know all of my special skills, since he has enough integrity to not require that his employees sleep with him."

"Is that so." He set his glass on the desk and flipped through the file, not focusing on particulars. "So tell me, why are you leaving this great place where the upstanding boss doesn't want his nurses on their backs?"

"My reason for leaving is my business. But as you can see, I come with the highest recommendation."

Fair enough. But something about this female was off, and Nate had learned a long time ago to trust his instincts. She was too fidgety, too . . . something.

Curvy. Curvy is something.

Putting the lid on his less-than-helpful inner voice, he ran his thumb over the loopy whirls of her writing. "The file says you're a shifter. What species?"

"Tiger."

Not bloody likely. He inhaled deeply, seeking her scent. Through the tantalizing aroma of vanilla was a wild undertone of feline . . . and canine. Mostly canine, in fact. He'd have pegged her for a wolf, so why was she saying she was a tiger? It wasn't any of his business, but again, something was off. He'd encountered every species of shifter alive, and he'd never come across one with this particular blend of scents.

His sixth sense was telling him to send her packing. The club had enough troubles, and it operated on a delicate balance. He didn't need this female messing up anything or causing problems. And yet, she intrigued him with the very qualities that were making him twitchy.

"Okay, Tiger Lady, why are you applying to work here?"

"I need a job, and I work well independently, but I don't want to work in a human hospital or clinic."

"Why not? It would be a hell of a lot safer, and you don't strike me as someone who likes to take risks."

There wasn't a tiger shifter on the planet who didn't like to cozy up with danger, but she didn't deny his accusation. "Humans provide fewer challenges, medically speaking."

Her chin lifted, and though she was shorter than he was, she somehow looked down her nose at him, all superior-like. Interesting. Usually females batted their eyelashes and gave him smoky take-me eyes. The superior thing sent another rush through him, piquing his interest even more. Hell, he was actually getting hard.

He picked up his glass again and studied her over the rim. "So you like challenges," he murmured.

"I love a good fight." An odd darkness infused her voice, setting off his internal alarms.

"What do you mean by that?"

"Just what I said. Challenges are what make life interesting, don't you think?"

He wondered what she'd do if he *challenged* her right up

against the wall. His cell buzzed with a text message, and what do you know . . . opportunity was knocking. Buzzing. Whatever.

He looked over at Vladlena, who was shifting her weight nervously. "Can you start work now?"

"Right this minute?"

"If I like how you perform, you get the job."

She glared at him for a heartbeat, as if trying to decide how he meant, "perform," and then she shrugged. "Why not."

He took her to the medic station, where Marsden met them with a big, bleeding male with a gaping laceration that had opened up his arm from shoulder to elbow. Blood streamed from his mashed nose and lips, and a piece of his ear had been torn off.

Vladlena leaped into action, snapping gloves out of the dispenser on the wall and then grabbing a towel to put pressure on the laceration as she guided the male toward the exam table. When he growled at her, Nate's first instinct was to deck the guy, but she handled that like a seasoned pro as well.

"You do not growl at your nurse." There was an underlying growl of her own in her words, but it was soft, almost gentle, bringing to mind the sound of a mother wolf chastising her young. "I have to help you, but I don't have to make it comfortable. Got it?"

The male settled down, surprising the hell out of Nate. Mars nodded in approval and then jerked his thumb toward the hall. "I'm going to check on the other participant in the dance floor brawl." He took off, and Nate turned back to Vladlena, who was reaching for the rolling med kit next to the bed.

"Now," she said, "let's get some vitals. What's your species?"

"Warg," the male grunted, and yeah, Nate figured. Were-wolves, or wargs, as they liked to be called, were growly by nature, and they tended to be larger than other animal-based underworlders and humans—probably because they grew an extra inch or two after being bitten and turned into a werewolf.

She inspected his mouth and airway for any of the teeth that had been knocked out. "Was it a fist or foot that did this?"

Before the warg could answer, there was a shout from outside, and a vampire burst into the room. The warg came off the table, and Nate leaped to intercept him.

"Not in my office," Vladlena snapped, and for a moment, the warg paused.

Unaffected by her command, the vampire lunged. A pure animal in his rage, he struck out at Vladlena, knocking her into the cabinets.

Fury ripped through Nate with the force of a summer storm, and then he was moving faster than his thoughts, ramming his fist into the male's nose and popping a double-tap into his throat. As the vamp's head rocked back, Nate seized him by the neck and slammed him into the wall. He felt the sting of a blade slash at his gut, but he was too lit to let it slow him down. If anything, the pain fed his need to draw blood, and he reached for the fucker's wrist, snapping it with a quick twist of his fingers. The vamp shouted in agony and dropped the blade. Now Nate was going to tear the bastard's head off.

Literally. One of the interesting things about being a day-walker was that he was stronger and faster than "normal" vampires, and he was going to make use of that right now—

Marsden's hands came down on Nate's shoulders to wrench him away from the nightcrawler as three of the club's security guys wrestled the warg and vampire to the ground, cuffing them roughly.

"Get 'em out of here," Mars snapped. "If they want to

fight, they'll do it outside. Then give them a fucking map to Underworld General. They aren't setting foot in here again."

Nate whirled around to Vladlena, and when he saw her on the floor, trapped by a shelf that had fallen on her, the pinprick of life he'd felt penetrate his veil of indifference earlier widened. Son of a bitch, if she was hurt . . .

He and Mars tag-teamed the shelf, lifting it off her.

"You okay?" Nate offered her a hand, and she took it, surging to her feet as if she hadn't just been wearing a two hundred pound wooden shelf.

"I'm fine." She started to brush herself off, but when she looked at him, she froze. "But you're not."

He looked down, surprised to see the gash that ran from his right side to his left hip. And that's when the pain hit. Oddly, the only thing he could think of was that now Vladlena had an excuse to touch him.

Chapter 4

Vladlena did not like her boss. At all. But she was a trained medical professional, and he was bleeding. Badly. Besides, he'd saved her from what might have been a vicious beating, and while she didn't doubt that his motivation was more about not wanting to lose another medic than about chivalry, she was grateful.

"Get on the table." She peeled off the gloves she'd used on the warg, washed, and snapped on new ones as Nate did as he was told.

Interesting. He definitely didn't seem like the type to follow instructions, but he hopped up on the table and laid back as if he were reclining to watch TV in bed.

And there was an image she needed to get out of her head, because she suddenly saw him on red silk sheets, his black hair spilling over a pillow, and she was right there, straddling his hips and running her hands up what was surely a magnificent chest.

She cleared her throat—and her mind. She was a professional, after all. "You're going to have to take off your shirt."

He worked the buttons, his long fingers seeming to take an unnecessarily long time. As he peeled the shirt away, he sucked air, and now that the wound was exposed, she could see why. The knife the vampire had cut him with had been serrated, leaving ragged edges on an already deep laceration. The slice had also gone through his leather belt and slacks.

"You'll have to undo your pants too." She swore she saw the faintest glimmer of amusement in his expression before it shuttered.

His hand hovered over his belt buckle. "Close the door. I don't need my employees seeing me like this."

The idea of shutting herself in a room with him sent flutters of both trepidation and excitement through her. The excitement was something that shouldn't happen, not until she knew more about his involvement in her brother's death, and she gave herself a mental scolding as she closed the door.

"There." She turned back to him. "Happy?"

"I've been opened up from ribs to crotch. I'm not jumping for joy."

"You're already starting to heal," she pointed out, and then she stopped talking, because he tore open his fly and her mouth no longer worked.

He didn't wear underwear.

So much for being a professional. Giving herself a much-needed kick in the butt, she fetched a tray of supplies and returned to him.

"I'm going to clean the area—"

"With your tongue?"

She jerked back. "What?"

"That's what my vampire medic would do."

"Eew. And no. I'm not a vampire, and even if I were, that's just not . . . protocol."

"Did your boss at Underworld General tell you that? The one who doesn't make you fuck him?" That glimmer of amusement was back.

"You know, I don't think you need medical assistance at all." His wound was closing up quickly, though there was a three-inch gash where the knife had entered that was deeper than the rest of the laceration, and it could definitely use stitches or glue.

"I think I do." Smiling, he tucked his hands behind his head. "So do me."

With a huff, she swabbed blood from his skin with plain water—vampires sometimes had allergic reactions to disinfectants. It was probably inappropriate to notice how hard his flesh was, how deeply cut the muscles were, and how firm his skin was, but then, *he* was being completely inappropriate, so she found it hard to chastise herself.

"So, Vladlena" he said, "why didn't your little voice trick work on me?"

"Call me Lena. And . . . voice trick?"

"I saw the way you were able to settle the warg down with only a few words."

"Ah, that." She shrugged. "It only works on canines."

"Odd for a tiger, don't you think?" He peered at her so intently through half-lidded eyes that she felt stripped bare. Vulnerable.

She pushed aside the whisper of panic that said he might not believe her cover story, but she hadn't wanted to draw any suspicion by revealing that she was a hyena. *A hyena who can't change into a hyena. A hyena who has never displayed a single hyena trait.* She was the worst shapeshifter ever.

"We all have unique gifts." Time for a subject change. She probed the worst of the damage. "You're very lucky the blade didn't enter an inch higher, or your stomach would have been punctured."

"And that's bad?"

She dabbed at the deep laceration, and though it must have hurt, Nate didn't even flinch. "For a vampire, yes. All your other organs heal quickly, but because the stomach pumps the blood you ingest through your body, it can bleed you out."

"Wouldn't kill me."

"No, but it'll make you weaker than a newborn baby for several days."

He watched her finish wiping down his skin. "How long have you been a nurse?"

"You'd know the answer to that if you'd read my file."

A lazy grin turned up the corners of his mouth. "Maybe I like the sound of your voice and want to hear it from you instead."

Insufferable vampire. "A little over two years. I went to college and nursing schools in the human world, and then I got a job at Underworld General."

And talk about a culture shock. Human medicine and demon medicine were two completely different animals. Every demon species was different, from their anatomies to their vital signs to the type of treatments they could tolerate—or not tolerate.

"What drew you to the medical field?"

"It's in my genes," she sighed. "My father was a surgeon at Underworld General." As a child, she'd bandaged her stuffed animals, moving on to nursing neighborhood pets, and as she got older, the sound of an ambulance's siren would fill her with excitement and longing.

"Was?"

"He's dead." She tossed the bloodied materials and dragged the rolling tray of supplies closer with her foot. "Killed by The Aegis."

"Bastards." He shifted, which made his fly gape open a little more. Nope, he definitely didn't wear underwear. "What about the rest of your family? Mother? Siblings?"

"My mother hasn't been in my life since my brothers and I were weaned." Mainly, that was because she'd wanted to kill both Vaughn and Lena to rid the world of two runts who hadn't thrived and who had needed extra care in their first few months to survive. Lena's father had run her mother off, and she hadn't seen her since.

"How many brothers?"

Lena's first impulse was to lie, to mention only the two living ones, but no, she wanted him to get a glimpse of the pain she'd felt when she saw Vaughn in shreds.

"I had three. One was killed recently."

His hand came down on her wrist, startling her. "The Aegis?" His voice was surprisingly mellow, his hold gentle, and for a moment, she was tongue-tied. But then she remembered that this vampire might very well have had something to do with Vaughn's death, and she casually dislodged his grip.

"I'm not sure who is responsible," she said. "But when I find out, I'm going to make them pay for what was done to him."

"I get that," he muttered. "Just don't take too long, or it'll get to the point where it won't matter anymore."

"Sounds like you have some experience with that?" she asked, as she reached for the tube of skin glue.

His jaw tightened so forcefully she heard the pop of bone. "Everyone thinks anger simmers, only growing hotter until you finally release it in some massive explosion."

"Doesn't it?"

"Absolutely. But if you wait too long, all that rage burns out. It'll flame hotter and hotter, until it consumes all the fuel, and then you're left with nothing. Fire is the ultimate sanitizer." His voice was bleak, scoured of the passion she'd seen in him up until this conversation.

Avoiding his gaze, she applied the Dermabond to the laceration. "Who did you lose?"

Silence stretched, and for a long time, she didn't think he'd answer. When he did, his voice was cold but even. "My mate." He cocked his head, his assessing gaze stripping her bare again. "Are you mated?"

"Me?" She suppressed a laugh. "I'm too busy for a social life."

"That's what people say when they don't *want* a social life."

She hated that he'd seen through her. She'd always found excuses for not going out with her friends, but what it came down to was that she was defective. Who would want a shifter who couldn't shift and who would someday go insane and die?

"And you?" She capped the glue and tossed it to the cart. "I suppose you aren't too busy for a social life?"

"I'm not too busy. I admit I don't want one. My work *is* my social life."

As if on cue, music from the club kicked up a notch, vibrating the very air with a deep bass beat that tugged at Lena's very insides. "So what do you do for fun?" she asked casually, when she suddenly felt anything but.

An extremely wicked grin exposed his fangs, and her senses flamed in response. "I have sex. Wanna have some fun?"

Man, Nate loved making Vladlena squirm. Mostly, he was being obnoxious, but he definitely wouldn't be averse to getting her naked.

Which was weird, considering that she wasn't his type, and he had never embraced the any-port-in-a-storm attitude Marsden had made into a lifestyle.

"You know," Lena said in a breathless rush, "in a human establishment, I could sue you for sexual harassment."

"Only if I was harassing you."

"You are."

Bullshit. The flush of her skin, the heat radiating from her, the pitch of her voice . . . it all made a liar of her. It also engaged the predator in him—it had been a long time since he'd had to give chase to make the kill.

Time to pounce.

"I can feel your desire." He propped himself up on his elbows, forcing his body closer to hers. "You want me. Therefore, it's not harassment. It's bringing the natural conclusion about sooner than later."

Her outraged gasp made him laugh. "You are so . . . so . . ."

"Sexy?"

"Arrogant."

He'd take that. "*And* sexy."

Huffing, she shoved the rolling supply tray away. "Don't you have a club to manage?"

He made a noncommittal noise as he swung his legs over the side of the exam table. "Technically, I'm off work."

"And technically, I'm not working, remember?"

He was up in a flash and had her backed against the wall before he even realized he'd moved. She looked up at him, as surprised as he was by his sudden movement, but he rolled with it, totally I-meant-to-do-that, even though he wasn't sure if his slightly impulsive behavior was a good thing or a bad one.

"If you're not working, you should be playing," he murmured, moving as close as he could without touching her. He wasn't going to give her an excuse to push him away.

"If, by play, you mean have sex—"

"I do." Now he leaned in a little, loving the way her breath hitched as his mouth lowered so close to hers that he could feel the warm rush of air between her parted lips. "But you know what's almost as good?"

Her heart rate leaped, the beat so loud it thrummed in his ears and made his mouth water. Her voice was barely a murmur over the sound of her pulse. "What?"

"This." He brushed his lips over hers, slowly, tentatively, giving her the chance to stop him.

She didn't. But fuck, she was in imminent danger of heart failure if it didn't slow down. Her nervousness was a tang in the air, and if he had any decency in him, he'd back off. Instead, that thread of life he'd been clinging to since she walked through his office door became a rope, strengthening his resolve.

He wanted to taste her. Wanted to sink his fangs into her throat and feel her pulse tapping against his teeth as her life force flowed into him.

He'd settle for tasting her lips.

For now.

Her lips were velvety, warm, and they parted more as he swept his mouth back and forth in invitation. Her response was hesitant, but curious. From the delicate scent of her desire that rose up all around him, to the spark in her eyes and the rapid pace of her breathing, it was clear she wanted this. But her body was stiff as a steel beam, screaming with awkwardness.

Maybe it's because you're her boss and she's afraid you'll fire her if she doesn't kiss you, you dolt.

Cursing himself, he whispered against her lips, "Your job isn't at risk. It never was, and I apologize for playing with you like that. You're hired no matter what." Huh. Maybe he still had an ounce of decency left in him.

"Okay," she whispered back, and those gorgeous eyes of hers locked onto his, heating him and making him feel like she was caressing him from the inside.

Groaning, he increased the pressure against her mouth. "Open for me," he murmured, and after the briefest hesitation, her lips parted just enough to allow him to stroke the tip of his tongue over the tip of hers.

This time, her reaction was immediate, intense, and shockingly abrupt, as if a dam had burst. She grabbed his biceps hard enough to send a small shock of blissful pain through him, and her back arched, putting her hips in contact with his, and she kissed him back with a hungry growl.

All of that set him off like nothing ever had. What had been mild arousal became a high-level blast of lust that clouded his thoughts and damn near had him taking her to the floor. He wanted her softness under him, her full hips and breasts buffering the hard planes of his body as he pounded into her. Only the faint vibration in his pocket kept him from stripping her down and diving between her legs.

"Dammit," he breathed, as he reached into his pocket for his cell phone. He was going to throw the damned thing away if it kept interrupting him.

Lena's wide eyes were glazed and unfocused, her face flushed, and yeah, she'd been his for the taking. He snarled viciously as he stepped back from her and looked down at the text message. GLADIUS. NOW.

"What . . ." She swallowed. "What's Gladius?"

"None of your business." Sexual frustration and annoyance at being sloppy enough to let her see the message put an edge on his voice. He jammed the phone back in his pocket and tried to ignore the hurt in her expression, because if she was so sensitive that a few harsh words bothered her, she wasn't going to last a week in this club.

The reality of that thought didn't stop him from wanting to draw her into his arms and apologize, though.

And what the fuck was up with the apologies and this touchy-feely crap? All his compassion had been beaten out of him in the arena, so why the sudden desire to protect this female as if she were nothing more than a lost young cub?

"Well," she said crisply, "you can go to hell."

He blinked. "For telling you to butt out of something that isn't your business?"

"No. For being a jerk about it."

Well, well. The tiger had claws, but as much as he'd like to see how far they extended, he had to go. "Go home,

Vladlena. Be here tomorrow night at seven. A uniform will be waiting for you."

She muttered a few mild obscenities under her breath, and he hid a smile as he stalked out of the office. Yep, she definitely had claws, and he couldn't wait for her to use them on him.

Chapter 5

Lena's heart had still been beating madly long after Nate left. Something about him both terrified and thrilled her, and crazily, she liked it. She'd spent so long being sheltered by her father and protected by those around her that getting out on her own was a hot rush. The fact that she'd succeeded in the first part of her goal—getting a job at Thirst—was even more of a rush.

It was the first job she'd ever gotten on her own. Granted, it wasn't a job she was keeping, but at least her father hadn't pulled strings to get her here.

She'd gone home and contacted Eidolon, letting him know she was safe. Then she'd gone to bed, for all the good that had done. She'd been restless, tossing and turning, and her mind kept going to Nate. She couldn't get his spicy, masculine scent out of her nose. Couldn't forget how his skin had felt under her fingers or how his lips had been so soft on hers. Couldn't wipe his great-looking face and body out of her brain.

She also couldn't rid herself of the nagging feeling that he was somehow involved in Vaughn's death, and something told her that those tickets on his desk and the message on his phone were the key.

Now, as she finished donning form-fitting black scrubs with the word THIRST, the T fashioned to resemble a medical cross embroidered in red on the left shirt pocket, she was determined to do a little snooping.

Thirst was hopping, but so far, there were no injuries, so Lena explored, eyes peeled for . . . well, she didn't know what, exactly, she was looking for. She chatted with the bouncers, wait staff, and bartenders, fishing carefully for information, but nothing they said raised any flags.

A broken wrist from a fall on the dance floor took her away from her investigation for an hour, and then she was back at it after spying Nate enter the club and make a beeline to the private section as if there was a fire. When he disappeared into his office, she followed, checking behind her to make sure no one saw her.

All clear. His door was closed, so she eased up to it and listened. Nothing. Not a sound came from inside. Taking in a deep, bracing breath, she tapped on the door and wondered what kind of excuse she'd come up with for disturbing him.

Fortunately, she didn't need an excuse, because he didn't answer. She took another calming breath, but it did nothing to still the nervous flutters in her belly as she tried the door handle.

Unlocked.

She slowly pushed it open. Inside, there was no sign of Nate, but where could he have gone? She'd seen him enter.

"Mr. Sabine?"

When no one answered, she closed the door and scrambled to search the office, starting with the file cabinets, which were locked. Same with the desk, dammit. She stood behind the desk, thinking. Her father had kept a similar office in his house, and it hadn't been until he'd been killed that she'd discovered the dark secret he'd withheld.

She and Vaughn had stumbled across an opening in a wall behind a full-length mirror. The hidden passageway had led to a torture chamber that had verified all the rumors she'd heard about her father. It had been a nasty shock, and she wondered if any such passage she might find in this office would lead to as great a surprise.

She checked the most obvious places first—behind pictures, mirrors, the bookshelves. Nothing. She managed to knock over a bookend and stub her toe on a chair leg, though. A superspy she was not, and she prayed no one heard her impression of a bull in a china shop.

Just as she was about to give up, she moved to the massive wine rack behind the bar. She manipulated the bottles, being extra careful not to drop one. They were, no doubt, expensive.

When she wiggled a black bottle near the top of the rack, she felt the slightest give. Excited, she pushed on it, and half of the rack cracked open . . . only an inch, but she didn't dare open it more until she knew what was behind it. She listened, prepared to nudge the door farther, but the sound of voices constricted her chest and cut off her breath.

Shit!

Heart pounding, she tugged the rack closed and scurried out of the office. Her muscles went watery and stopped working as she closed the door, and she allowed herself a moment to collapse against the wall and just breathe. Automatically, her fingers found her stethoscope. Touching it in times of stress was a strange habit, and one she needed to break. She just hadn't found the willpower to buy one of her own, one that wouldn't carry memories of her father.

Voices from behind the office door broke her out of her thoughts. Both male, one Nate's. Unfortunately, she couldn't hear specifics, but if the tones were any indication, he wasn't happy. The other male sounded . . . amused. And something about his voice sent shivers up her spine.

The door jerked open, and she jumped, whirled, and came face to . . . chest . . . with a man—no, definitely demon—who stood at least seven feet tall and was twice as wide as she was. His movie-star good looks were negated by the evil he radiated; She felt it beneath her skin, like a million worms wriggling in her muscles. He looked down, his black eyes targeting her as if she were a steak and he was a hungry lion.

"What have we here?" His voice was both seductive and frightening, and the sense of things writhing under her skin increased. *What species is he?*

Suddenly, Nate was there, taking her arm and pulling her away. "She's not for your pleasure, Fade." His hand tightened on her arm almost possessively. "She's an employee."

The demon raised a tawny eyebrow. "Employees are definitely for my pleasure."

"Not this one. We're short on medics, and we can't afford to lose another one."

Tension crackled in the air between the two males, thickening with every second.

"I, um . . ." She licked her dry lips. "I should go."

Nate turned to her, keeping his hand on her arm. "Why are you here?"

"I wanted to know how much authority I have to purchase supplies," she lied.

He studied her for so long that she started sweating—and regretting not putting on an extra layer of deodorant. The stethoscope around her neck began to feel like a noose. Finally, he nodded.

"Purchase whatever you need. See Marsden about setting up a personal payment account."

She offered a shaky smile, which fell when she saw Fade leering at her out of the corner of her eye. "Thank you. I'll just . . . go now."

"I'll walk with you," Fade purred, and her marrow froze. She'd encountered evil in her life—her father included. But this male . . . he made the others pale in comparison. And unlike inside Underworld General, Thirst had no spell preventing violence to protect her.

"Walk by yourself." Nate's voice was a portent for trouble. "I have business to discuss with her." His fingers dug into her arm, a silent signal to agree with him. As if that was even a question. "In my office."

Nate had no idea what had come over him, except that he knew what Fade was planning to do to Lena. The demon was on the prowl for dinner and sex, and for him, they were the same thing. No way was Nate going to lose a skilled medic on her first day on the job.

And as much as it pained him to think it, Nate also didn't want that bastard touching her the way Nate had. The way Nate wanted to. He could still remember how her lips had tasted of berry gloss, how her skin had felt like smooth satin. Fade would bruise that luscious skin and make those lips bleed.

A low growl vibrated through his chest at the thought, and he had to make an effort to tamp it down as he escorted Lena into his office and then sent a text to Marsden, warning him to keep an eye on Fade. They couldn't stop their boss from causing trouble in his own club, but they could do their best to redirect his focus. And right now, Nate's number one goal was to redirect the asshole away from Lena.

"What was that about?" she asked, when he was finished texting Mars.

"Nothing. Just stay away from Fade, got it?"

"You don't have to tell me twice," she muttered. "Who is he, anyway?"

Nate tossed the phone to the desk a little too forcefully,

and it slid to the floor. Fuck it. It could stay there. "He's the club owner."

Head cocked in a decidedly canine manner, Vladlena studied him as if he were some sort of puzzle to solve. "Clearly, you don't like him. So why do you work for him?"

And wasn't that the question of the century. Literally. He knew why he'd come here to work, but why he was still here . . . not so sure.

"Are you always so nosy?"

She graced him with a sunny smile that fit her so well. From her glowing, tan skin to her bright blonde hair, there wasn't an ounce of darkness in her. As great as she looked in the tailored black scrubs, he was tempted to order cheery yellow ones to suit her better.

"Must be the cat in me," she said breezily.

"Funny, but I'm not seeing a lot of cat in you."

Her smile faltered, but she recovered with an admirable deflection away from his observation. "Are you going to answer the question?"

"I didn't think I owed you any answers."

She shrugged one delicate shoulder. "I suppose you don't. But it would be nice."

Nice? *Nice?* Where had this female grown up? She was the least underworldly creature he'd ever met. He liked it. She reminded him of life before he'd been turned. Life before it had become a waking nightmare.

"Let's make a deal," he said. "You tell me why you're really here, and I'll tell you why I work for Fade."

The color drained out of her face so fast he nearly jumped to catch her if she passed out. "I don't know what you mean."

"Your reaction tells me otherwise."

She stiffened. "I should get back to the office—"

He blocked her path. "What's your hurry?"

"I have a job to do."

"I'm the boss, and I say your job can wait."

Angry red splotches colored her cheeks. "No wonder your other medics quit. Did you bully them, too?"

"Nope."

She folded her arms over her chest, pushing her breasts up and out. She should do that more. "So I'm special. How lovely."

"*They* didn't keep secrets from me." What color of bra was she wearing? She seemed like the type to wear practical beige or pure, sensible white.

"My secrets are my own, and you have no right to them." She snapped her fingers and pointed to her face. "My eyes are up here, Mr. Sabine."

Busted. Hard. He forced his attention away from his raging libido. "I have a right to them if they affect my business."

"They don't." She adjusted the well-worn stethoscope around her neck, even though it hadn't moved an inch. She'd done it out in the hall as well.

"Why do you do that?"

"Do what?" she asked, and his eyes flicked to her fingers, which hovered over the time-whitened black tubing, and she jerked her hands to her sides. "It was my father's."

"So it's a comfort."

Her cheeks pinked delicately, as if a painter's brush had swept rose stain across them. "I know it's stupid. I just haven't had time to get a new one."

"You're a terrible liar." He reached out to brush out of her eye a strand of hair that had escaped its braid, letting his fingers linger on her warm skin. Gods, there was such life in her, life that pulsed vibrantly under his fingertips and revved him like a motorcycle at full throttle. "Tell me, how do you survive in our world when you're so transparent? Who has taken care of you all this time?"

He hadn't meant his softly-spoken question as an insult, but she jerked away from him with a hiss.

"Shut up," she snapped. "Just . . ." She slapped her hand over her mouth, her expression stricken. "I . . . oh, geez, I'm sorry." He let her gather her wits, forcing himself to not reach for her again. "Look, I'm a little sensitive about this, okay? I'm trying to make it on my own. I'm out from under my father's thumb, and I'm tired of being protected and sheltered and treated like I'm made of glass. I can do things by myself. There are things I need to do before I die, you know?"

She made dying sound imminent. Yes, as a shifter, she was long-lived, but she wasn't immortal. Still, he sensed she was young, and she probably had a few hundred years left in her, so why the rush to do things?

"So, is this job part of your trying to make it on your own?"

Her brows pulled down into a deep frown. "Yes," she said, as if that thought had only now occurred to her, and maybe surprised her a little. "Your turn. Why are you working for a man you hate?" She stepped closer to him, and he doubted she even realized it. She was too busy regarding him with that you're-a-mystery-to-solve look again. "This has something to do with the fire you were talking about, doesn't it? The way it can burn so hot that it burns itself out."

Clearly, he'd said way too much to her, and even more clearly, she was too smart for her own good. Unable to think while she was staring at him with those too-knowledgeable eyes, he turned away from her and braced his hands on the bar. He sensed more than heard Lena move closer, and when her hand came down on his arm, it was as if he'd jammed his finger into an electrical socket. His body jerked, his muscles tensed, and intense, searing heat melted the marrow deep in his bones. Gods, when was the last time he'd reacted like that to a woman?

The answer to that was something he didn't want to think about, because he hadn't even had that response to his wife.

The thought turned into a growl that pumped out of his

chest as though it had been building steam for years. Too late, he realized he might have frightened Lena, but oddly, she didn't flinch. In fact, she began a gentle stroking action up and down his spine that both soothed him and put him into orbit.

"Don't," he rasped, even though he wasn't sure why he didn't want her touching him like that.

She ignored him, keeping up the light strokes. "Have you been with anyone since your mate died?"

His laugh was brittle to his own ears. "She didn't die. She was murdered. And I haven't been celibate, if that's what you're asking."

"No, it wasn't what I was asking."

Frowning, he stood straight and turned to her. Her hand fell to her side. "Then what were you asking?"

"If you've loved anyone since."

His head jerked back as if he'd been slapped, and he actually stepped backward to keep his balance. "Why?"

She matched his step, moving forward, and a freakish thread of panic wove through him. "Some species mate for life. I know vampires don't, but the blood bond can be strong. I've seen them waste away and die of broken hearts."

"I'm not burned out from a broken heart," he said tightly. "I'm ashed from hatred."

"So you think there's nothing left except the hate?"

"I know there's not." Hell, he even doubted the hate was still there most of the time.

"Then why do you continue to work? To feed? Why not just step into the sun and end it all?"

Because the sun doesn't fry me. But yeah, he understood what she was asking. He'd asked himself the same question on a regular basis.

He scrubbed his hand over his face, unable to believe he was having this conversation with someone who was as alive as he was dead. "Ending it would mean I cared enough to do it."

"So you care for nothing." She peered up at him through long golden lashes, her gaze a bold, hard challenge. "Nothing at all fires your blood?"

His cock stirred, as if it, too, was implying that he was a liar. "Oh, there's one thing that fires it."

Lena's expression was one of subtle triumph. "And what's that?"

"You." He raked his gaze over her, his blood racing faster with every second he lingered on her feminine curves. "For some reason, you engage my prey drive."

"So you see me as prey?"

"Touch me," he said in a low voice, "and find out."

Chapter 6

Lena had never been so tempted to obey a command. As a nurse with an innate instinct to nurture and heal, she itched to treat Nate's wounds. As an adult female whose libido was going berserk, she longed to run her hands over every inch of his hard body.

As a shifter with a clock counting down the days to her death and who had always been "different," she just wanted to be normal for a little while. She wanted to know what being with a male was like. Oh, she couldn't go all the way—shifters were incapable of having sex before their first shift. Males couldn't get erections, and a female's hymen broke during her shift, but was impenetrable before that. Eidolon had offered to attempt to surgically remove hers, but she'd turned him down, because seriously . . . how embarrassing.

Now she was regretting that decision. She didn't have long to live, and she was going to die a virgin.

And really, could she be more of a drama queen?

Nate's blue eyes blazed down at her. "So you aren't going to take me up on that challenge, I see."

Challenge? The very word made something rise up in her . . . something besides lust, anyway. It was a call to action, a desire to run him into the ground the way a wolf chased a deer. For the first time in her life, her animal instincts, which she'd begun to doubt she possessed, came alive, and it was one hell of a rush.

So yes, she was going to die a virgin, but she wasn't going to die untouched.

Boldly, she stepped into him, enjoying the tiny flare of surprise that flashed across his face. He hadn't expected her to act, had he? The knowledge that she'd surprised him filled her with even more power.

She palmed his chest, felt the ripple of firm muscle beneath her hand. "Challenge accepted."

A growl rattled through his chest, the masculine, needy sound spiking her temperature. "Do you know what you're accepting?"

Not. A. Clue. Well, maybe. She might be a virgin, but she wasn't innocent. She'd grown up in her father's house, and he had a . . . healthy . . . appetite. She couldn't count the nights she'd heard the noises from his bedroom or walked in on his exploits. And then there was college, and her roommate . . . but none of that could compare to what went on in the supply closets at Underworld General. When a hospital was run by sex demons, there tended to be a lot of . . . sex.

There was the slightest tremor in her hand as she took his and pressed it to her breast. "Show me."

No hesitation. In one massive surge, he was on her. Taking her mouth with his, he pushed her back against the wall. His tongue pushed deep, tangling with hers, penetrating and retreating in a carnal rhythm that coaxed a moan of acquiescence from her.

"You're so beautiful," he murmured against her lips. "Sweet. So . . . pure."

Pure. Yeah, okay, but not by choice. She'd wanted this for so long. She should probably feel guilty, given that she still hadn't ascertained the extent, if any, of his involvement in Vaughn's death, but if she was wrong and Nate wasn't involved, she couldn't pass this up. Besides, the closer she got to him, the more information she could get from him, right?

The justification for what she was doing was lame, and she knew it. But she also knew what her body was feeling. She'd been aroused before, had been attracted to males, but never like this. It was as if her body had been a dormant volcano, and now it was awakening after countless years of only minor quakes.

Her blood flowed like lava in her veins, liquid heat erupted between her thighs, and inside her chest, an aggressive growl shook her all the way to her bones. Closing her eyes and shutting off her mind, she let her body react. Nate's hands came up to cup her face, his fingers splayed to hold her for his kiss. His thumbs stroked her jaw as his tongue caressed her lips.

Desire swirled and coiled tight, fueled by Nate's sensual energy, and she found herself arching against him, rolling her hips to rub on the hard ridge of his erection. He made an erotic noise of approval and intensified the kiss, sweeping his tongue over her teeth, the roof of her mouth, and nipping at her lips.

Shivering despite the steamy heat building between them, she clung to his biceps, pulling him as close as possible, loving the way his size made her feel so feminine. She wished they were at her apartment, or at a hotel . . . anywhere but here. She wished . . . what? She couldn't remember where her thoughts had been headed, because Nate's hands slid down her throat and shoulders, then lower. One arm slipped behind her back while his hand drifted over her breast, and her knees nearly buckled.

He seemed to know, and pushed one thick thigh between her legs to brace her against the wall. The move also put the most delicious pressure against her core, and she gasped with pleasure.

"That's it." His voice was a husky, ragged drawl as he kissed a sizzling path along her jaw. "Let me hear you."

"No doubt," she said in a raspy, turned-on voice she didn't recognize as hers, "your ego likes that."

She felt him smile against her skin. "My ego doesn't need boosting, but yes, it likes it." One hand slid down the back of her pants while the other tugged at the drawstrings at the front. Her pulse thudded obnoxiously loud in her ears as he cupped her butt beneath her panties.

Was she really going to do this? He hissed, and she realized she'd dropped her own hands to his rear and was squeezing the firm globes through his slacks. She'd also lifted one leg to put her mound in contact with the bulge behind his fly, and her question about whether or not she was really going to do this was answered.

She wanted this. Desperately. So desperately that when he started to push her scrub pants down, she helped, hooking her thumbs under both her panties and the pants and shoving them to mid-thigh. Nate didn't waste time taking them off. His hand slipped between her legs, and when his fingers found her wetness, they both groaned.

Her head lolled back against the wall, and if there had been any nervousness before, it was gone, replaced by a mindless, primal desire to get this male on top of her, inside her, all over her. She nearly wept at the realization that he couldn't be inside her, but then sparks shot through her at the sweep of his thumb at the top of her cleft, and all that mattered was reaching that ultimate peak.

Panting, aching, she unzipped his slacks and released his massive erection. When she wrapped her hand around his shaft, his mouth fell open and before her eyes, his fangs lengthened and his lips blushed red. Oh, oh . . . my. Her head involuntarily tilted to the left, exposing her throat. The fact that she'd so easily offered herself should have bothered her . . . *would* bother her later . . . but for now all she wanted was to feel those gorgeous canines buried deep in her flesh.

"Please," she whispered.

Instantly, his head came down, the tips of his fangs striking her throat . . . but not penetrating. For a long, breathless moment, he did nothing, though his fingers continued to play in lingering, smooth strokes back and forth through her slit. A heartbeat passed. Two. Three. And then, with a sound similar to a purr, Nate closed his mouth over her throat but didn't bite.

"No," he said roughly, giving her the gentlest nip over her jugular. "No marks."

Before Lena could protest, because right now she'd willingly take his mark, he dipped one finger inside her entrance, using his fingertip to circle the ultra-sensitive tissue. His thumb brushed lightly over her clit, tiny, teasing flicks that became firmer as she rolled her hips into his hand, desperate to land his touch where she needed it. At the same time, she squeezed his shaft, her strokes clumsy and unpracticed, but if the little hitches in his breath were any indication, he didn't seem to mind.

He captured her mouth again, and between her legs, tension mounted. "You're amazing," he murmured. "I've never met anyone like you."

His words were a silken caress that made the world shrink so that only they existed. He changed the tempo of his strokes, and the slick friction had her writhing, panting, running right to the edge and leaping off it.

"Yes," she cried out, the orgasm tearing through her, a whirlwind of sensation that robbed Lena of all her senses and maybe even her consciousness for a moment. Her legs turned to gel, her vision went dark, and if not for Nate's big body, she'd have slid to the floor.

As she came down, she wondered how she was going to tell him she couldn't go any further than this.

Maybe she didn't need to. She pumped her fist slowly up and down his rigid length. Maybe she could pleasure him the way he'd pleasured her—

, A knock at the door froze that thought and brought a nasty snarl from deep in Nate's throat. His lips brushed her neck as he snapped, "What?"

"We have business." Fade's voice was an icy, crisp command that instantly dropped the temperature in the office.

Nate swore under his breath. "I'll be out in a minute." He stepped back from her and zipped up with a small wince. "Stay here," he told her in a low, hushed voice. "Give me three minutes to get the demon away from here, and then get out."

She tugged up her pants, feeling suddenly exposed and seriously embarrassed. "Why the caution?"

"Because he wants you, and if he knows I do too—" He cut himself off with a curse, and goosebumps shivered over her skin, but she wasn't sure if they were pleasant ones that came as a result of being wanted, or prickles of foreboding for the same reason.

With that, he left her, half-dressed, disheveled, and seriously conflicted.

Nate's temper balanced on a machete's edge as he slipped into the hallway, careful to make sure the door was locked behind him and that Fade didn't get a glimpse of Lena. Man, he'd been close to Heaven in there, could still taste Lena on his tongue, could smell her on his body. Her sweet sounds of passion were still ringing in his ears.

And his cock and fangs were both throbbing with hunger that wasn't going to be sated anytime soon. He was a ticking time bomb, and he really wanted to go off on Fade in a bloody, painful explosion.

The evil smirk on the demon's face said he knew exactly what had happened in the office. "You have a female in there."

"I always have females in there." Nate started down the hall toward the guarded door that led to the secondary entrance to Gladius from Thirst. "What's so important?"

Fade didn't follow immediately, but Nate kept walking, swearing under his breath and hoping the bastard would follow—and that he'd be distracted enough by the question to forget about Lena. Nate had never worried about Fade's interest in Nate's bedmates before, but then, the females had never been anything but one-night stands to him. Lena captured Nate's interest more than anyone else had since his mate died, and if Fade caught on, Lena could pay with her life for Nate's lack of control.

"I'm going to open a new fight club," Fade said, catching up with Nate. "The underworld turmoil is starting to affect the human population, and I foresee an opportunity to franchise."

"What, you want to be the McDonald's of death matches? In case you haven't noticed, in most countries even animal fights are illegal."

"The Apocalypse is coming, vampire. And in the aftermath, the world will be changed. Demons will walk the earth, and they love blood sport."

No shit. "Demons will arrange for death matches in their own backyards at that point. Why would anyone pay to see them?"

"People can grill burgers in their backyards too, and yet, fast food chains are making a fortune on them."

Nate wondered if Lena liked burgers. He'd love to watch her eat one. There was just something incredibly sensual about watching a female eat meat . . . especially if it was something he'd prepared himself.

And what the hell? Clearly, all his blood was still in his dick.

He thrust his hand through his hair and came to a halt, letting his fantasies run to ripping the demon's throat out instead of watching Lena eat hamburgers. "So you intend to provide cheap entertainment without the hassle of procuring fighters, setting up an arena, managing cleanup . . ."

"All while providing comfort, food, and drink." Fade grinned. "I'll make legends of some fighters, stars everyone will want to be with. For a price, of course."

"And, no doubt, you'll make sure any competition is squashed." The disgust that bubbled up when Fade grinned wider at that was startling. It had been decades since Nate experienced any kind of negative reaction to the demon's machinations. "So why are you telling me this? Does this have something to do with the 'business' you mentioned?"

"I want you to manage it."

Oh, hell, no. "I'm happy here."

Fade waved his hand in a dismissive gesture. "Your happiness is not my main priority. You will oversee all elements of the business, from groundbreaking to building and hiring."

This wasn't going anywhere good, and Nate started walking again, as if he could outrun the demon and his unholy plans. "Have you chosen the site already?"

"Yes." Fade fell into step with Nate. "With so many plagues mowing down humans, poisoned land is available on every continent. I'll open clubs everywhere, but this first one will be in a South American jungle. You'll leave tomorrow to assess and lay claim to the site. It should only take a couple of days."

"Send Marsden. Or Budag. I have business here."

Fade snarled, and Nate resisted the urge to snarl back. "This isn't up for debate. You will go, and next week, on the eve of the new moon, you'll return to the site to perform a sacrifice."

Instincts twitching, Nate halted in the middle of the hallway. "Something tells me you've already chosen the victim."

"I have. A lovely virgin I found in your own club."

Nate let out a bitter laugh. "There hasn't been a virgin in this club in . . . well, ever."

"Oh, you're so wrong." Fade clapped his hand on Nate's shoulder, his eyes little more than black, oily pools "Your new medic, Vladlena, is untouched."

Fuck. Very deliberately, Nate schooled his expression into neutrality. If Fade had even the slightest suspicion that Lena interested Nate at all, there would be no talking the demon out of this.

"I can't lose another medic. They're too hard to find. Get another virgin." And seriously? She was a virgin? No . . . way. Then again, it would explain a lot. Like the pesky purity and innocence he'd been sensing.

"A sacrifice means nothing if it isn't important. She's important to this club, and therefore, perfect." Fade lowered his voice to a dark, dangerous rumble. "There will be no more discussion on the matter, but to make sure you don't fuck me over, I'm sending Budag to keep an eye on you. After you secure the site, you will return there with her and torture her to death."

Since the demon wouldn't be swayed, Nate's only choice was to play along. For now. "As you wish."

If Fade got his way, Lena would be dead next week. But he wasn't going to get his way. Nate was. As soon as Nate returned from his trip, he'd make sure Lena couldn't be sacrificed.

Because she'd no longer be a virgin.

Chapter 7

Lena had been employed at Thirst for four days now, and her time here had turned out to be a bust. Nate had gone missing, the door to his office locked so she couldn't explore whatever lay behind the wine rack, and aside from that creepy Fade guy lurking around with a seemingly keen interest in her, she hadn't uncovered anything even remotely unusual. Nate and Marsden ran a tight ship, and anyone who broke rules, from employees to patrons, paid the price. They didn't even allow drugs in the place, which, according to Shade and Wraith, wasn't normal for a place like this.

Something else that she didn't think was normal was the way Marsden hovered, appearing out of nowhere to run interference when Fade got too close to her. Nate's assistant also made sure she had everything she needed, and once, he even asked if she liked hamburgers. If she hadn't been here in an undercover capacity, she'd actually enjoy working in the club.

Then there was the package Marsden had delivered a few minutes ago. She'd opened it, thinking it contained medical supplies. Her eyes had stung at the sight of the new stethoscope inside . . . an extremely expensive stethoscope with a gold-plated chestpiece and eartubes. There was no note, but she knew the gift was Nate's doing, and his act of generosity leveled her. He understood her silly attachment to the one that had belonged to her father, knew that if she bought one, it would almost feel like a betrayal.

Nate had saved her that pain, and she was having a hard time holding onto her belief that he could be the monster she'd initially believed him to be.

"Nice necklace you have there." Con, a blond vampire mated to Eidolon's sister, Sin, stood in the doorway to the medical office, one shoulder propped against the doorjamb. All of the Sem brothers, as well as Sin, had come to check on her, and Eidolon called her every day when she was at home. Today Con had drawn check-on-Lena duty.

Lena smiled down at her new stethoscope. "Standard issue around here."

"Uh-huh." Con let out a dubious snort. "Even E doesn't have one like that. You selling organs on the black market or something?"

"It's not that expensive." She looked up from disinfecting the exam table that had been bloodied by yet another drunk idiot who picked fights with bigger guys. "And I don't need a babysitter. I'm doing fine by myself."

Her father might have kept her completely secluded and sheltered, but in the nearly three years since his death, she'd gained some healthy independence. She'd forced herself to try new things and go to new places, and she hadn't regretted a minute of it. Activities that appeared scary were never as bad as she'd thought, and she'd even done the human club thing with her roommate once. She hadn't gotten brave enough to hit an underworld club yet, but after seeing how Thirst was run, she was ready to give it a try.

"I'm not babysitting," Con said. "Just checking on you. We all wish we had more time to devote to this, but with the way the underworld is churning . . ."

He didn't have to say anything else. The world was on the verge of Armageddon, and there were a lot more important things to deal with than a fight club that was only one of hundreds, maybe thousands.

"I get it," she said. "I appreciate all your help."

"Yeah, well, we might have something for you soon. Wraith is looking into whatever Gladius is. He sent a message just before I got here. Said he has a lead, asked for an hour to squeeze some dude for info, but he indicated that this is the break you need."

Con's news should have put her on the moon, but instead, all she felt was dread. As much as she wanted to find those responsible for killing her brother, she wanted Nate to not be one of them.

She pasted on a smile. "Great. Can't wait."

Con's keen ears must have picked up the sound of footsteps, because he said quickly, "We want you back at UG. Eidolon will give you a raise."

"I'll match it and add 20 percent," Nate said from behind Con, and her heart gave a little flutter. The stupid thing seemed to have missed him.

"We want her back," Con said, not missing a beat.

Nate stepped inside the medic office, his blue-black hair gleaming under the harsh lights. "She's mine."

Con cocked a tawny eyebrow. "Yours?"

"Thirst's," Nate ground out. "I've come to promote her, in fact."

"Is that so? Convenient timing."

Nate's ebony brows slammed down over eyes that darkened dangerously. "It's my club. My timing conveniences me, and me alone. When I want something, I get it." He shifted his gaze to her, and his eyes darkened more. "And I want her."

There was no mistaking the heat banked behind those

long lashes, and Lena's breath caught. No male had ever looked at her the way Nate did, and she liked it.

Con, however, did not. He went taut, as if preparing to defend her, his silver eyes flashing like razor blades, but quickly, she put herself between them with a casual smile and took Con's forearm.

"I'll walk you out," she said cheerily. "It was nice of you to stop by. Tell Eidolon I'll consider his offer."

A barely audible rumble sounded behind her, and a tingle of pleasure skittered over her skin at the possessive quality of Nate's growl. Even if he only wanted her for the club, it was nice to be valued. Oh, she knew that UG valued her, but here she had fewer supervisors and more autonomy. It was . . . cool.

Remember why you're here, idiot. Vaughn is dead. Right. Talk about a cold splash of water.

Con stopped at the doorway. "It's okay, Lena. I can find my own way out." His gaze shifted to Nate, and he bared his fangs before returning to her. "Just take care of yourself. If you need anything—" once again, he gave Nate the you're-dead-if-you-harm-her look "—anything at all, you know to call."

"I know." She went up on her toes to kiss him on the cheek. "And thank you."

Con strode away, and when she turned back to Nate, once again, her breath was stolen from her lungs. Dressed in faded jeans and a navy T-shirt that clung to every sculpted muscle like shrink-wrap, he stood next to the exam table, his black mane cascading down his back and around his shoulders in a shimmering waterfall, his big body vibrating with lethal power. He was . . . magnificent.

"Is he your lover?" Nate's voice was deep, husky, and she shivered with feminine appreciation.

"Hardly. He's mated to my boss's sister."

"*I'm* your boss."

Damn. Nice screw-up. "Of course you are. It's just that I worked there for a long time, and it's hard to get used to the fact that I'm not there anymore."

He didn't look convinced, but he said nothing. Instead, in brutal, heart-pounding silence, he strode to the door and closed it.

The click of the lock was the loudest sound she'd ever heard, and she actually jumped like a twitchy rabbit.

Riveted by curiosity and the mere sight of him, she watched as he wheeled around and closed the distance between them. As he looked down at her, his expression was a curious mix of hunger and regret that she didn't understand.

"Now," he said softly, "we finish what we started in my office."

Nate was fucking *lit*. The time he'd spent in the jungle at the site of the new fight club had worked him into a knot of nerves and need. He'd long ago determined that the more primitive the environment, the more his baser instincts surfaced.

It didn't get more primitive than the South American rain forest.

Thanks to the make-out session in his office with Vladlena before he left, he'd already been coming out of his skin, but then the trip to the steamy jungle jacked him up even more. Standing beneath ancient trees, on soil touched only by beasts as he inhaled the clean, unpolluted air that smelled of rain, plants, and a jaguar that had passed recently, had made him vibrate with pure, animal desire. He'd wanted to hunt, to feed, to mate.

He'd understood the moment he'd set foot on the site why Fade had chosen it. There was an elemental power at play there, and no underworld creature would be able to resist it.

A gladiatorial arena placed on the soil would become the demon equivalent of the Roman Colosseum, and with the blood sacrifice to bind evil to it . . . it was conceivable that the land could be claimed in the name of Sheoul—or hell, as humans called it.

The very idea was horrifying, but right now Nate was having trouble concentrating on anything but the female in front of him. He was so aroused, so on fire that he expected to see smoke from the friction of his clothes on his skin. Finding her with that asshole vampire, their relationship so familiar, hadn't helped. Nate had wanted to destroy the male, deliver his fangs to Vladlena on a necklace, and then rut with her on the very ground where he'd won the battle.

And wasn't *that* sexy. He nearly rolled his eyes. Damned jungle had turned him into a caveman.

Running with the caveman thing . . . he got all testosterone-buzzed at the sight of her wearing his gift. It might be a mere stethoscope, but she'd accepted his offering, and for some reason, it made him want to beat his chest and drag her into his lair. Instead, because a sliver of civility had pierced through the jungle haze, he gripped her shoulders and pushed her against the wall. She didn't protest. Not that he expected her to; the scent of her desire filled the room with her special perfume, ratcheting up his need even more.

But ultimately, this wasn't about his desperation to get between those toned thighs. This was about saving her from an excruciating death on an altar—a death he was tasked to be responsible for.

No, he couldn't profess that he didn't want this for himself—he'd been unnaturally obsessed with Lena since she walked into his office. Even her virginity should have been a turnoff. He'd avoided virgins like their veins ran with holy water instead of blood. But in Lena's case . . . *damn*. A purr vibrated his chest at the thought of being her first, of laying claim to her the way no other male had.

Of taking her for his own and keeping her.

Except that couldn't happen. This would be a one-time thing, because if Fade even *suspected* that Nate wanted her, she was dead.

Or worse, if Fade found out that Nate had been the one to take her virginity. And Nate was well aware that there could be worse.

Shoving that thought out of his mind, he cupped the back of her head and lowered his mouth to hers. Again, she didn't fight him. In fact, she opened for him, her hands coming down on his ass to pull him closer. He was already hard— hell, he'd been hard for days—and her soft belly cradled his aching erection with just enough pressure to be considered torture.

Man, he wished he could take his time with her, could ease her into her first time, but the clock was ticking, and when this particular hourglass ran out, so would her life.

Inhaling raggedly, he palmed her fine ass and lifted her so her legs were around his waist and his cock was in contact with her core. They both groaned at the sensation, and as he slid her up and down while rocking into her, her groan turned into a soft cry of pleasure. He spun toward the exam table, because while he couldn't seduce her properly in a soft bed, he could at least make sure her first time wasn't against a wall or on the floor.

"Need to be inside you," he murmured against her lips. "Need to make you scream my name."

"Yes," she breathed. Her back arched, and her hot center rubbed him so perfectly, so sweetly, he damn near came right then and there. "Wait . . ." In his arms, she stiffened. "No. I can't."

"You don't have any patience." He nipped her jaw, then licked the tender skin there. He couldn't wait to be at her throat, taking her inside him as he moved inside her.

Her palms flattened against his chest, and before he could put her on the table, she writhed hard enough to make him lose his grip, and her feet hit the floor. "I'm not having sex with you."

"Yes," he said roughly, "you are."

He seized her by the waist and hauled her against him, one hand going to her scrub bottoms' drawstring. The storm of lust gathering inside him intensified, a raging force of nature fueled by the residual stir of the jungle, unquenched thirst for Lena, and a carnal instinct to possess the female he'd had in his sights for days.

Lightning fast, she hauled off and slapped him. "Release me." She didn't wait for him to obey. With a surprisingly vicious stomp on his foot, she threw herself backwards, crashing into the supply tray and knocking metal instruments everywhere.

She didn't get far. "Dammit, woman!" He caught her around the torso and pinned her between his body and a cabinet.

Son of a bitch. This couldn't have gone worse, but it was too late to turn on the charm, and he knew it. He'd never forced a female in his life, and he wouldn't cross that line now. But he'd do what he had to in order to save her life. Steeling himself for her response to what was going to be the most dickheaded thing he'd ever said or done, he wrapped his fingers around her throat and bared his fangs.

"You'll sleep with me, or you're fired."

Her throat convulsed beneath his fingers and her eyes shot wide open. "Excuse me?"

"You heard me. Fuck or flee. Your choice."

She began to tremble, and gods, he felt like a bastard. "You . . . asshole."

"Guess that's your answer." He released her and stepped back. "Pack your shit, turn in your uniform, and never come back to this place. Do you understand me, Lena? Never, ever return." He wheeled around and yanked open the door, stopping when a miscellany of medical supplies pelted his back.

"Go to hell, Nathan." She beaned him with her stethoscope, which fell to the floor next to his feet, sprawled like a dead snake. "Go. To. Hell."

Not a problem, he thought, as he exited the office. He was already there.

Chapter 8

Vladlena stood in the medical office like a dolt, stunned to the core. Dangling from her fingers were the set of keys she'd lifted off Nate when she'd realized what he wanted from her and how serious he was about getting it.

What didn't sit well with her was the sickening knowledge that had she been able to have sex with him, she would have. He wouldn't even have had to threaten her. She'd have been his for the taking.

Gods, she was an idiot.

She looked around at the supplies scattered on the floor, some of them a result of her clumsiness, some from hurling them at Nate. How could he have turned into such a cold-hearted bastard like that? The answer smacked her upside the head with a big, fat, *duh*-stick. What else had she expected from someone who was most likely pitting fighters against each other in death matches?

The reality was a welcome cold fist to the solar plexus. Anger and hurt collided, but panic quickly overshadowed the mix. She was out of time. If she didn't find the fight club now, she never would.

Eschewing stealth, she crossed the dance floor, stalked

down the hall to Nate's office, and knocked loudly. No answer. She tried the door. Unlocked. So she didn't need his keys after all.

She placed them on the desk, but before she did anything stupid, she made a quick call to Underworld General and left a message with the triage nurse. After hanging up, she tripped the secret door. It swung open with no more sound than a whisper of air, revealing exactly what she'd both hoped and dreaded to find; a passageway.

She took one deep, bracing breath, and started down the stairs.

At the base, she became aware of her surroundings, that they were nothing but a cold, claustrophobic tunnel of cement and stone. As she walked, the sound of cheers rose up, growing louder, until she couldn't hear herself think, but she could definitely feel her stomach churning.

It was real. It was all real, and Nate, that . . . that . . . *dick* . . . was smack dab in the middle of it all.

Rounding a corner, she caught sight of an opening ahead. A mass of bodies blocked her view of whatever was beyond, but if the snarls, growls, and grotesque wet thumps were any indication, she'd found the fight club. Unwelcome visions of her brother being in the middle of all this assaulted her brain, and she squeezed her eyes closed and halted for just a moment.

Get it together . . .

She started moving again, pushing her leaden feet forward, and too late she noticed the two sentries standing just outside the entrance. Her heart tripped over itself, and so did her feet, but thankfully, even as she fell forward out of the tunnel, one of the big males merely grabbed her, smiled, and released her into the crowd. Apparently, they were there to prevent people from entering the tunnel, not leaving it.

The air was ripe with the scent of blood, lust, and fury. Quickly but carefully, she eased through the crowd, searching for the public entrance. Once she found that, she could get the hell out of here and back to Underworld General to report the location—

A hand came down on her shoulder, and she whirled, drew a harsh, startled breath when she came face to face with Fade, whose eyes were glowing crimson.

"You don't belong here, little girl," he grated.

Before she could say a word, he jerked her into him, squeezed her neck, and all went black.

Chapter 9

For decades, Nate had been dead, his heart little more than a desiccated knot of muscle sitting uselessly in his chest. But as Gladius's manager, Budag, rubbed his bald head and told Nate about Vladlena's foray into the fight club, Nate's heart began to stir.

No, not just *stir*. It went mad with fear, worry, and dread. That damned shifter nurse had performed CPR on him, resurrecting his cold, undead self.

"Release her," Nate ground out. He looked past Budag's hulking shoulder from where he stood at the tunnel threshold between Gladius and Thirst. The crowd was wound up about something, and bloodlust was in the air.

"No can do, vampire." Budag's deep voice rattled Nate's temper. "Fade already put her in the ring for a bait match."

Nate lost it. He slammed the demon into the wall and got right up in his face, fangs bared, ready to take a chunk of flesh out of him. "You fucking lie! He wouldn't have done that. She was going to be a sacrifice—"

"Since she stuck her nose where it didn't belong, she was no longer desirable as a sacrifice." Budag's almond eyes crinkled with amusement. "At least, not a sacrifice for the new fight club. The Neethul twins are enjoying her *plenty* as a sacrifice."

Nate didn't waste another second. Heaving Budag aside, he plowed through the crowd, shoving people out of the way as he hauled ass to the ring. His heart, if it beat, would have stopped at the sight of Lena, her uniform ripped and bloodied, trying to fend off the two elf-like demons who were toying with her. And there was no question that they were toying. He'd seen the brothers fight, and right now, they were like hellhounds with a cornered cat.

Nate didn't think. He acted. Acted himself right into the arena and caught the demons by surprise. Taking advantage of their temporary confusion, he punched his fist into one of the males' neck and ripped out his throat. Blood and strings of gore dripped from his hand, and the audience roared.

The remaining Neethul barely cast his dead brother a glance as he came at Nate with a *deflesher*, a thick chain with a razor stirrup at the end. Wielded properly, the weapon could fillet a six-inch wide strip of flesh off the entire length of an arm and leave it bare to the bone.

The demon was an expert with it.

Shit. All around, the crowd hushed, leaving only Lena's scream and the whistle of the chain as it cut the air. Nate dove to the blood-soaked sand and rolled, lashing out with his feet. The razor stirrup slammed into the ground next to Nate's head as his kick caught his opponent in the knees. The Neethul fell but was up again in an instant.

So was Nate. Before the demon could do a rewind with the chain, Nate slammed into him, knocking them both into the cement retaining wall. Sharp teeth sank into Nate's shoulder, and son of a bitch, that hurt.

Dimly, through the haze of pain, Nate heard the crowd go ballistic, their chants of, *"Kill! Kill! Kill!"* buzzing in his ears. His past came down on him in a shroud of memory, and just as it had been all those years ago, it would be that way again.

With a snarl, he gripped the demon's head and twisted. The snap of spine was swallowed by the audience's noise, which became deafening when Nate dropped the body and left it, twitching, on the ground.

Lena was standing a few feet away, her face bruised and pale, one eye blackened and blood trickling from the corner of her swollen mouth. She'd been battered to hell and back, but defiance burned in her eyes. Hate, too, and he didn't blame her.

Still, she didn't resist when he took her hand and led her to the gate used to transport both the dead and the living in and out of the arena. The giant iron rack rattled and clanged as it heaved upward, but Nate didn't have a chance to be grateful that they were being let out.

Fade stood there, flanked by three burly *rhino-fiends* who worked in the "zoo" one level below, the dark, dank area where fighters and bait creatures were kept. None of them looked happy, Fade least of all.

"Obviously," Fade rumbled, "you didn't learn the first time you took a female from me."

Nate tightened his grip on Lena. "I don't want to lose a good medic," he said, even though he knew his excuse was both tired and lame. If it hadn't worked before, it wouldn't work now.

Fade knew it too. And he wasn't going to let slide the fact that Nate had killed two of his most popular fighters. The Neethul twins had been fairly new to the fighting scene, but their good looks and penchant for cruelly toying with their victims had been big draws for the crowds.

"How stupid do you think I am?" Fade signaled to his goons. "Lock them up." His smile at Nate was pure evil.

"Congratulations, Sabine. Once again, you get to watch your female die."

For about thirty seconds after Fade shut his creepy mouth, Lena was sure Nate was going to explode into violence. After what she'd seen him do to the Neethuls, she knew he was very capable of it. In fact, the tension rose up in him so strongly that she could feel it in a tangible crackle in the inch of air between them and see it in his massively descended fangs and red-glowing eyes. But even as the demons tensed for battle, Nate calmed, almost as if the air had been let out of him.

He'd walked meekly alongside the demons, though he hadn't let go of Lena. It wasn't until they were thrown into a cell together that the depth of his anger became clear. As Fade's laughter and the guards' footsteps melted away, Nate rounded on her, fists clenched, the fire burning in his eyes again.

His voice was warped with rage. "I told you to leave."

"You fired me for not sleeping with you," she shot back, strangely grateful for his anger, because it kept her from falling apart. "I didn't think you really had any right to order me around after that. You don't even have any right to be angry with me, asshole."

"How did you find Gladius?" he snapped, as if she hadn't even spoken. "Did you follow me down here?"

"It doesn't matter how I found it. What matters is that you're a bastard. A sick, twisted, evil bastard who operates a business where death is *entertainment*." She could have sworn she saw hurt flash in his eyes before they became chips of ruby ice again, but that didn't stop her rant. "Why did you bother to save me? You should have bet on the outcome like everyone else."

"Shut up." His voice was as cold as his gaze.

"What's the matter? Did I strike a nerve? Feeling a little guilty? Or are you upset that you got yourself into trouble with your boss?"

He took a step forward. "I said, *shut up*."

"Or what? You'll kill me? Newsflash, buddy. It's going to happen anyway. But you can bet that if I disappear, my colleagues are going to tear this place down and feed it to you before they slaughter your ass."

Actually, she hoped they'd pull a cavalry and rescue her. She just had to pray Eidolon and his brothers got her message before she was fed to the lions. Or whatever creatures were screeching in the nearby cages.

One second Nate was standing near the door, and the next he was chest to chest with her, pinning her against the wall. It didn't escape her notice that they spent a lot of time in this position.

"Your colleagues," he ground out. "At Underworld General? It's time to stop with the games, little shifter, and tell me who the fuck you are and why you're really here."

"Bite me."

That was *so* the wrong thing to say to a vampire who was teetering on the edge. He struck like a viper, sinking his fangs deep in her throat, and despite the dire situation, despite her anger and hurt and confusion at how he'd treated her and his involvement in the fight club, she gasped with pleasure. The initial sting turned into a lovely burn that spread through her body in the form of liquid heat. Vampires could make feeding horrifically painful or orgasmically wonderful, and clearly, Nate had gone with the latter.

But she couldn't allow this. She hated him. Really. Weakly, she flattened her palms against his chest and shoved, but she didn't need to. His head snapped up and he stepped back all by himself, surprise glittering in his eyes.

"You're no tiger," he snarled. "Damn you, has everything about you been a lie?"

She slapped her hand over the punctures in her throat. "Me? You're the one who has a hidden door in his office. You're the one who's been hiding a club where people fight to the death."

His nostrils flared, and his gaze zeroed in on her neck. Before she could protest, he peeled away her palm and licked the fang punctures, sealing the wound.

"Gods," he murmured against her skin. "You taste like dark chocolate, and honey, and . . . canine." He tore away from her, leaving her swaying unsteadily and relying on the wall behind her to hold her up. He faced away from her, his hands running through his hair over and over, as if doing so was as important to his existence as blood. "Why? Why are you here?"

"Because you murdered my brother."

He wheeled around. "Who was your brother?"

"Given the number of people who probably pass through your arena, I doubt you'll remember him," she said bitterly.

"Who?"

"His name was Vaughn." She raised her chin, meeting his gaze so he could see her pain. "He was a hyena shifter who died last week."

"Hyena . . ." Nate's brow furrowed. "Blond. Mismatched green and blue eyes."

"So you do know who he was."

Nate's tongue flicked over one of the fangs he'd sunk into her flesh. "You're not a hyena any more than you're a tiger."

"I am," she ground out. "And you killed my brother."

He snorted. "Your brother killed himself."

With a pained cry, she launched herself at Nate. He caught her easily, well before she landed a single blow. "You son of a bitch," she screamed. "You evil, heartless son of a bitch!"

From the nearby cages, she heard catcalls and cheers, as well as a few curses. Nate tugged her against him, his arms wrapping tightly around her, caging her so she couldn't strike out.

"Shh." His soft voice didn't penetrate her anger. "Hey. Listen to me. Your brother came to us. He made a deal for a fight."

"No. *No!* He wouldn't—"

"He said he was dying."

Dying? She stilled completely, freezing solid against Nate's big body. "I don't . . . I don't understand. Why did he say that?"

"I don't know." He relaxed his hold, but still cradled her against his chest. "All I know is that he wanted to fight one of our champions, a hyena named Vic. And Vaughn made a provision that if he died in battle, Vic would leave Vaughn's sister alone. I guess that's you."

"Oh, gods," she whispered. "Vic. He's here?"

"Yeah. Nasty bastard. Why would Vaughn want Vic to leave you alone?"

"Because," she said, on a shaky inhale, "ever since my father died, Vic and my other brother, Van, have tried to kill me every few months."

Curses fell from Nate's mouth. "So Vaughn was here to guarantee your safety."

His hand cupped the back of her head with surprising tenderness, and his voice softened, which was something she couldn't afford to do. If Nate was telling the truth, he hadn't killed Vaughn, exactly, but he was still a scumbag who ran a vile operation.

And yet, she didn't pull away. She told herself she needed the support because her legs had gone all noodle. She told herself she was cold, and while he wasn't overly warm, he wasn't as icy as the air that smelled like raw sewage. She told herself all kinds of lies, because right now, she couldn't handle the truth, the mind-boggling realization that hate was not the only thing she felt for Nate Sabine.

"Poor Vaughn," she murmured. "He should have come to me. He didn't need to sacrifice himself for me."

"He loved you." Nate paused. "Is there a reason he wouldn't shift?"

"What do you mean?"

He made long, soothing passes over her braid. "He didn't shift when he was fighting Vic. It put him at a huge disadvantage. I thought it was strange, because even if his intention was to lose, he clearly hated Vic and wanted to hurt him. Vaughn could have done a lot more hurting in animal form."

A knot twisted her insides. *He said he was dying.* Those were Nate's words. Her brother was dying. He didn't shift. Oh . . . oh, gods. He didn't shift because he *couldn't.* He'd been dying for the same reason she was.

"Lena?" His hand stopped stroking her hair. "Lena, what's wrong?"

"I know why he didn't shift." She swallowed. "He couldn't. A shifter who has never turned into his animal dies shortly after they turn twenty-four. It's why I didn't leave when you fired me. There was no point."

"What do you mean, there was no point?" He pulled back to look her in the eye. "Wait . . . in the arena, you didn't shift. You can't, can you?"

"No," she said quietly. "And because of that, I'm dying too."

Chapter 10

A sick, bitter sadness shattered the anger Nate had felt over Lena's revelation of deception. He'd rescued her from the Neethul brothers because he couldn't bear the thought of losing her. Now, thanks to a fucked-up genetic glitch, he was going to lose her anyway.

"Can't someone at Underworld General do something?" His voice was humiliatingly hoarse.

"We've tried." Lena heaved a sigh and plopped down on the straw-coated floor. "There's nothing left to do."

"Why would you and Vaughn be unable to shift when your other brother can?" Nate went down on his heels in front of her.

"Both of my other brothers can. I've seen them. I never saw Vaughn do it, but I guess now I know why." She rubbed her arms as though cold. "I think it might be because we were born different. When shifters give birth in animal form, the babies are born that way too. But Vaughn and I weren't. My father had to protect us from our brothers for years. Even our mother wanted to kill us."

He stripped off the T-shirt he'd worn straight in from the

jungle and wrapped it around her shoulders like a shawl, and was surprised when she didn't argue. "What a way to come into the world."

Shivering, she tugged the ends of the shirt tight. "What about you? How did you come into the world?"

"The supernatural one?" At her nod, he made himself comfortable on the ground. "It was two hundred years ago. I was twenty-seven, stumbling home after a night out with the boys in Paris. It was dark, foggy. Right out of a Jack the Ripper movie. I heard what sounded like a brawl coming from an alley, and like an idiot, I investigated." He remembered being horrified when he saw what looked like a huge, armored man in a bloody battle with a hooved, red-skinned, horned thing. "Now I know that one of the males doing battle was a demon. The other . . . he was a vampire, but not one like I've ever known."

"What happened?"

Nate had stood there, shitfaced and blinking, as if it was all a drunken mirage. "The vampire killed the demon, but he was injured. Badly. He had a gushing wound in his neck, and when he saw me, his eyes lit like the fires of hell. I tried to run, but he was on me and feeding before I could stumble two steps."

"So he forced you to drink his blood to turn you?"

"That's the weird thing," he said. "There was no blood exchange."

She frowned. "You sure you just don't remember? Because to make a vampire—" Blushing, she cut herself off. "Sorry. Duh."

Gods, she was cute. How the hell could she be a hyena? She couldn't. He'd have tasted it in her blood. The same blood that had left a trail in the corner of her mouth. Without thinking, he reached out and wiped it away with his thumb. He wanted to linger, to frame her face in his hands and kiss away her pain, but the wariness in her doe eyes told him she still wasn't ready to take him for anything other than a miserable son of a bitch who profited off the blood of others.

Reluctantly, he dropped his arm. "I'm sure he didn't do the blood exchange. He wasn't normal. I can't explain it, but whatever he was, he turned me . . . and made me different."

"Different?"

He lowered his voice, because he'd learned a long time ago that this wasn't something to be said out loud. "I can walk in the sunlight."

Lena blinked. "That's . . . that's not possible."

"I know. And yet, I can hang out on a tropical beach at noon."

"Okay, so then what?" she asked, sounding very much like a medical professional digging to the bottom of a mysterious ailment.

"I went home to my wife. I don't remember much, but I remember waking up so fucking hungry." He hadn't understood what was going on, only that he was starving, and the sound of Eleanor's beating heart was driving him mad. "I attacked her. Nearly drained her." She'd screamed, pummeled him with her delicate fists, calling him a monster. Which he was. "Afterward, she lay there on the bed, pale and limp, and a weird instinct to feed her my blood came over me, and . . . I did. But I didn't know what I'd done. When she died a couple hours later, I went insane. That's the only way to describe it. I took off, and the next decade was a blur. My mind came back gradually, and I decided I needed answers. I traveled all over Europe, trying to find the asshole who turned me, looking for other vampires. It was a shock to learn that other vamps couldn't go out in the daylight."

"You're the only one?"

"There have always been rumors of others, but I've never found any. And I learned real fast not to announce my own sun-loving nature." Other vampires either tried to kill him out of jealousy, or they wanted to experiment on him in order to find a way to cure their own issues with severe sunburn. "So anyway, eventually I realized it was possible that Eleanor could be a vampire, given what I'd done to her." He closed his lids, but that didn't shut out the memory. "I found her, in London. She hated me for what I'd done to her, and she'd moved on, right into Fade's arms."

"Oh, damn," Lena breathed. She touched his knee, a soothing gesture he didn't think she realized she'd made. "That must have been hard for you."

He had to clear his throat of the lump of emotion before he continued, and it struck him that the memory wasn't what was affecting him, but Lena's concern.

"I was furious," he said, "but I still loved her. So I seduced her away from him." Nate looked down at Lena's hand, which looked so dainty on his leg. "That proved to be a fatal mistake. I didn't realize what he was. He chased us all over Europe, and when he caught us . . ." He trailed off, his mouth drying up and acid scouring his veins. Fade had tortured the fuck out of both of them, and then he'd dragged them both to one of his fight clubs, where he'd tortured them some more.

She took a deep breath and let it out slowly. "What happened, Nate?"

"He put Eleanor in a pit with two Cruentus demons. She put up a good fight, injuring one so badly that he had to be put down. But the other killed her. I had to watch the whole thing."

"I'm so sorry." Lena's nimble fingers stroked his leg. No one since Eleanor had offered him comfort like that. He'd missed so much in his life, and it had taken Lena to make him realize it. Now it was too late. "So did he let you go?"

"He made me fight. He was pissed that I didn't die the first time in the ring. Or the second, or the twentieth. Turns out that I'm more powerful than other vampires. Probably connected to the sunlight thing. Eventually, I grew numb to the death around me, and I started craving the fights. A way to release my hatred, you know?" No, she probably didn't. "All the while, I plotted escape, and when I thought the time was right, I pretended I was over what Fade had done to me and Eleanor, and I made a deal with him. I'd fight his biggest rival's champion, and if I won, he'd release me."

"So you won."

He snorted. "Nearly died, and I needed a week to recover, but I won." He listened to the screech of some creature, took a deep breath, and continued. "I was still full of hate, but I knew I couldn't kill Fade—I'd seen too many try. So I figured I'd do it from the inside."

Lena regarded him steadily, with no judgment in her gaze. "You started working for him."

"Yep. I claimed to be desperate for money, and since I'd once run a tavern, he thought I'd be useful in his social clubs. I had it all figured out. I was going to ruin him, sabotage his business so his customers would either kill him or bring Justice Dealers down on his head. Problem was, he was two steps ahead of me. He found my only living relative. My nephew."

Her fingers tightened on his leg. "What did he do?"

"Cagey bastard got a vampire to turn him so he'd live long enough to keep me under his thumb. Then he gave him a job here so I'd have to see every day what I'll lose if I don't keep the fight club from going under."

She sucked in a surprised breath. "Marsden. He's your nephew, isn't he?"

"Yeah. But he doesn't know it. I was turned when he was only two, and I didn't want to expose my sister and him to what I'd become, so I let them think I was dead." He rolled his eyes. "Guess I am." Okay, technically, he was. But for the first time since being turned, he didn't feel that way. Lena had made him very much alive. "You should have left when I told you to, Lena. You should have gone and never looked back."

"You know why I couldn't." She shot him a glare. "And you pissed me off."

Right. That. What the hell . . . he might as well tell her the truth. It wasn't as if any of it mattered now.

"I was trying to save your life," he said. "Fade needed a virgin sacrifice for a new fight club he's breaking ground on. If you wouldn't sleep with me, I had to get you the hell out of the club and keep you away."

She blinked. "How did you know I'm . . ."

"A virgin? I didn't. He did."

She cocked a blond eyebrow, clearly dubious about his intentions. "So you thought you'd be saving my life by having sex with me?"

Sounded so lame when she put it that way. "Ah . . . yeah. But I underestimated your willingness to hang onto your virginity."

"I think you overestimated your effect on the opposite sex," she said wryly.

"Me? Nah." He winked, enjoying the brief moment of levity. "You wanted me."

She made a low, needy sound that would have lit him on fire if they were anywhere but being held captive in a moldy dungeon. "I did want you."

"Then why did you refuse? We could have avoided this mess if you'd just slept with me."

"I can't have sex." She averted her gaze as though ashamed. "Another shifting issue. It's impossible for me."

Now he felt like an even bigger piece of shit for coming down on her when she didn't jump into bed with him. "I'm sorry," he said gruffly.

Footsteps pounded outside the cage, keeping him from

saying anything else. Not that he knew what to say. When Fade and two of his henchmen stopped at the door, he wasn't surprised.

"It's time." Fade tapped on the door's iron bars in an annoyingly cheery tempo. "With me, Sabine. Your female is going to the arena."

Nate exploded to his feet, putting himself between the demon and Lena. "You're not touching her." He hadn't been able to protect Eleanor, but by the gods, he'd die before he let Lena be killed.

The two *rhino-fiends* raised their weapons—lightning sticks, demon inventions that cast a bolt of something that was a cross between electricity and acid. As it stunned you into temporary paralyzation, it ate away the flesh around the area it had struck.

"Nate," Lena murmured, her palm coming down on his back. "Please. Go with them."

That wasn't going to happen. Time for plan B. He pegged Fade with a hard look. "I need to talk to you. Alone."

Fade nodded at one of the grayish demons with him, and the thing opened the door.

Lena clutched Nate's arm, holding desperately tight. "Whatever you're planning . . . don't." She lowered her voice as he turned to face her. "I'm dying anyway. Please, don't make this harder on yourself."

"Lena." He cupped the back of her head and put his lips to her ear. "I haven't had anything worth living for in a long time. Now I do. Trust me."

He felt guilty for lying, because although what he'd just said was the truth, there was more to it. He also hadn't had anything worth dying for in a long time. Now he did.

Without looking back, he exited the cell and walked with Fade to the staging area, an open room containing magical artifacts, painted symbols, and an altar. Fury built with every step, all the hatred that had burned out coming back with a vengeance, and Nate welcomed it like an old friend. Once inside, he rounded on the demon.

"Put me in the ring, motherfucker. Put me in there instead of her."

"That would hardly be fair," Fade growled. "We don't have a fighter who can beat you."

"*You* can."

Fade's eyebrows shot up. "You're challenging me?"

"Challenging? I plan to kill you. But if I lose, Vladlena goes free." The demon would take the deal, because the source of his power didn't come from combatants who won—it came from those who lost. It was why the fight club was so popular . . . people from all over came to fight and lose, knowing they could get whatever they wanted upon their deaths . . . wealth for their children, revenge on an enemy, protection for a loved one. The catch was that if you lost, Fade collected your soul, and most challengers didn't realize just what "losing your soul" meant.

In this case, it meant that Fade traded the souls he gathered to the highest bidder, and there were people you did *not* want to own your soul.

"And if I lose?" Fade asked.

"The club is mine."

Fade hesitated.

"Come on," Nate cajoled. "You know you won't lose. And even if you do, you can resurrect."

Fade hissed. "How do you know?"

"You think I didn't learn everything there was to learn about your sorry ass?" Nate had just signed his own death warrant. Fade couldn't risk anyone knowing the truth about him. An enemy who knew how to kill him permanently . . . yeah, not good for someone who had so many enemies.

"What else do you know?"

"You mean, do I know that Budag is your *vivacant?*" Nate smiled. "That he, and he alone, can bring you back to life? Yeah, I know that. The only reason I haven't killed him is that I couldn't risk you finding out I did it and taking it out on Marsden."

Fade's skin rippled, the texture alternating between wrinkled and smooth, the color doing a chameleon between tan, red, and the surrounding gray walls. The dude was both excited and angry, something Nate had seen only a handful of times. In his research, he'd learned that the skin thing was a reaction to stress, a natural process that increased the demon's strength and stamina. Not good.

Fade snatched a parchment from the stack on the altar and slapped it down hard on the stone. "Let's write this up, vampire. And then I'm grinding you into hellhound food."

Chapter 11

It had taken everything Lena had not to break down as Nate walked away. She might not know his world like he did, but she had keen senses, and she'd smelled trouble.

Which came in the form of three ugly, horned demons bearing those funky knotted sticks. She'd started to fight them, but after they'd explained what the sticks did, she decided to save her strength for when it would do her more good. Now, blindfolded and shackled, Lena tripped and stumbled her way down the passage, the two demons on either side of her dragging and pushing if she slowed down.

The sound of an anxious crowd, and of blood, bowels, and excrement grew stronger, and she knew she was once again entering the vile arena. One of the demons removed her shackles while the other stripped off her blindfold, and then she was shoved through the gate into the blinding light of the pit.

The first thing she saw was Nate, barefoot, bare-chested, wearing only jeans. His hands were fisted around an ax handle as he faced Fade, who held a wicked curved blade and a wooden stake. Every drop of color drained from Nate's face when he saw her.

"Hey, sis."

She wheeled around. "Vic," she gasped. "What . . . what are you doing?"

Vic pegged her with those black marbles he called eyes. "I'm finally going to rid the world of your weakness."

"But Vaughn—"

"I told Vaughn I'd leave you alone on your turf. This is mine." His body began to morph, the sound of bones cracking and reshaping so unbelievably loud in the noisy club.

Lena backed away, knowing full well that when the ten-second process was over, she'd be facing a 250-pound hyena that was far more powerful than its full-animal counterpart.

"This wasn't part of the deal!" Nate snarled.

Fade's laughter rang out, echoing endlessly. "You die, she lives. That was the deal," Fade said. "But if she dies before you do . . ." He shrugged. "Well, that can't be helped, can it?"

A low-pitched, jagged growl brought her attention back to Vic, who was now all animal. All monster. Drool dripped from his open mouth, which exposed sharp teeth meant to rip flesh from victims while he ate them alive. Terror welled as she eased backward, scanning the area for a weapon. Unfortunately, there was nothing, and though both her father and Wraith had spent time with her in Underworld General's gym, teaching her self-defense, she knew damned good and well that her meager hand-to-hand skills weren't going to help her against the beast in front of her.

Nate moved so fast she didn't see him until he was at her side, swinging the ax. Vic yelped as the blade grazed him in the shoulder, but then Fade was there, his weapon coming down in a vicious arc.

Nate whirled, narrowly avoiding being beheaded, but his own swing at the demon went wild, leaving an opening for Vic. Her brother lunged, catching her forearm between his jaws. A firestorm of agony accompanied the crunch of bone.

Screaming, she punched him in the head, but she was no match for the brother who had beaten her in every battle since they were cubs. He shook her like a rag doll, and her world became a blur.

A warm spray splattered her face—her own blood, she realized, as Vic sent her flying into the wall. Pain shattered her ribs, spine, and arm as she crumpled to the ground. Though she could hear the battle between Nate and Fade clearly, she could barely see through the veil of red dripping into her eyes. In a split second, though, her vision filled with fur and teeth. She twisted, barely avoiding having her face ripped off, and at the same time, she jammed her good arm back, nailing the hyena in the throat.

Vic gagged and fell back, but murder burned like coals in his eyes. When he came at her again, she knew she was dead. Hot, fetid breath scoured her face and claws tore into her shoulders. In a frenzy fueled by fear and adrenaline, she kicked, hit, lifted her knee to nail the beast in the gut.

Once again, blood sprayed her. Arterial blood, and a lot of it. Vic had killed her. He'd finally . . . dropped to the ground? She blinked, scrambling backward in the sand like a crab. Vic's body, split open through his rib cage, lay sprawled against the wall, twitching as it shifted back into human form.

Nate had killed her brother. Maybe it was wrong of Lena to not feel bad about it, but right now she didn't care. Ax blade dripping with streaks of shiny crimson, Nate tried to swing back around to Fade, but saving her life had already cost him. Fade's blade flashed, and Nate went down, hamstrung all the way to his thigh bone.

"Nate!" Hauling herself to her feet, she staggered toward him.

The crowd cheered, their bloodthirsty chants ringing in her ears. Fade leaped into the air, his spin-kick landing hard on Nate's jaw. Before Nate could recover, the demon seized

Nate's wrist and flung him like a Frisbee across the arena. Nate's body hit the far wall with a thump.

He didn't move.

"No!" Horror and pain squeezed Lena's heart, and as Fade sauntered toward Nate, stake poised to strike a death blow, her legs gave out. Confusion and helplessness collided, spinning her emotions out of control. She wanted to scream, but nothing would come. She wanted to help Nate, but she couldn't get her limbs to work.

Her entire body stung, stretched, felt like it was coming apart at the seams. Was she . . . *yes*. She was shifting. Massive gray paws hit the ground, the wrong color for a hyena, but screw it, she didn't care. Power ripped through her . . . power and strength and clarity. Without hesitation, she tore across the arena, a sense of elation, of freedom, singing through her veins with every leap and bound.

She hit Fade in the back and closed her jaws around his head. Even as she crunched down on his skull, she heard a commotion, a ripple in the crowd.

She scented them before she saw them—Eidolon and his brothers. His sister. Con. And several others from the hospital and Eidolon's extended family. Even some members of The Aegis.

She didn't think, just . . . shifted back before any of their weapons tore through her like Nate's ax had done to Vic. Her saviors were like locusts, sweeping through the place and fighting the guards. Eidolon and Shade rushed to her, but she shook her head.

"I'm okay. But Nate needs help."

Help was putting it mildly. He was unconscious, a stake sitting dead center in his chest and multiple, deep gashes all over his body, some gaping so wide that shredded muscle spilled out like raw meat. One leg was nearly severed, and his handsome face was all but unrecognizable.

"We need to get him back to UG, stat." E's tone was grim

as he kneeled next to Nate. "The stake in his chest is a frag spike."

Fear was an icy spear in Lena's gut. Frag spikes were designed to kill vampires the same as a regular stake, but they fragmented like a bullet when they entered flesh, allowing for more chances to strike a lethal blow. Even if they didn't kill right away, the slivers took on lives of their own, traveling around the body until they found the heart.

"Lena," Shade said, even as he signaled to one of the medics for a portable stretcher, "do you want this?"

She knew what he was asking. Inside the hospital, the brothers performed their duties on even the most vile creatures. Outside was another story. If she gave the word, Shade and Eidolon would put Nate out of his misery right then and there. But Nate wasn't the monster she'd thought he was, and she nodded.

"I want this more than anything," she said softly. "Save him."

Chapter 12

Nate hadn't felt this crappy since . . . well, he couldn't remember when. Consciousness was elusive, and when he did manage to grasp it and hold on for more than a few moments, pain wracked him and made him wish for slumber again.

Except that he needed to be awake, because he kept hearing Vladlena's voice, and he was desperate to know that he wasn't dreaming her softly-spoken words.

Slowly, he pried open his eyes. A grayish fog swirled all around him, but through it he could make out hospital equipment and walls scrawled with red symbols. On the ceiling, thick chains hung in neat loops, and when he turned his head to look out the open doorway, he saw people in scrubs moving past. Beyond them . . .

He blinked. Blinked again. The fog didn't clear, but a person came into focus, a person he hadn't seen since the day he became a vampire.

It was the male who had turned him.

The massive guy hadn't changed; he was still wearing some sort of plate bone armor, and his pale hair still hung to his shoulders, with two thin braids at each temple. Tattoos on his throat writhed as he spoke with a Seminus demon in a black paramedic uniform.

Nate waited for the hot, searing hatred to wash over him, the way it always had when he thought of the male who had taken Nate's mortal life from him. But nothing happened. Nate had fantasized about finding the bastard and dismembering him slowly, making him pay for what he'd done.

Now . . . now Nate was oddly calm about seeing the guy. The person Nate really wanted to see was Lena, and so far, she was a no-show.

Nate.

She might be a no-show, but her sweet voice was a soothing whisper in his head. Closing his eyes, he let the male who'd made him a vampire disappear, and he concentrated on Lena, wishing he'd had a chance to make love to her.

Nate.

He inhaled, caught a whiff of the fresh scent unique to Lena's silky skin. Rolling his head to the side, he opened his eyes again. She was standing next to him, dressed in purple scrubs, fiddling with an IV bag of blood. And she was wearing his stethoscope.

"Hey." Her smile wrapped around his heart, and he smiled back like a besotted fool. "It's about time you woke up. As soon as this bag empties, you should be back almost to 100 percent."

"Are you . . ." He had to clear his throat of what seemed to be a year of disuse. "Are you okay?"

"Eidolon healed me when we first came in. Two days ago, in case you're wondering." She took his hand, her warm palm heating him. "For a while there, I thought I was going to lose you."

He'd thought that too. But then she'd come out of nowhere, all fur and fangs, and . . . "You shifted," he whispered. "I saw you." What she'd shifted into was another question. He'd never seen anything like the huge, beautiful canine.

"I'm free, Nate." Her voice was full of charming, childlike excitement. "I'm going to live."

Nate pushed himself up on one elbow. "How did it happen?"

The sound of a cleared throat brought Nate's head around. A dark-haired male in scrubs and a white lab coat stood in the doorway.

"Seems our Vladlena is a rare crossbreed. I'm pissed that I didn't think of that sooner."

"Why would you have?" she asked. "My father said I was his."

"He also said you were born in human form. I didn't put that together with your inability to shift."

"Crossbreed?" Nate asked.

She nodded. "Apparently, my dam mated with a wolf the same day she mated with the hyena I thought was my father. Who *is* my father." There was a heartbeat of silence before she added, "He might have been an evil sonofabitch, but he was good to me."

"You'll have to tell me about him someday," Nate said, and she gave him that smile that knocked him off his axis again. "So how could two different species produce offspring? And how come your other brothers are hyenas?"

Eidolon spoke up. "Littermates can have multiple fathers. As far as interspecies shifter breeding . . . in most cases, it can't happen. But hyenas are the one shifter species that can sometimes breed with both felines and canines, though the cubs are usually stillborn. Those who survive birth rarely live beyond infancy. I've never heard of any making it to adulthood." He scrubbed his hand over his face. "I'll bet the fact that your father was a doctor saved your life. He said you and Vaughn were sick a lot as babies. Even if he didn't know *why* you were sick, he was able to treat you."

Lena's fingers stroked the back of Nate's hand absently. "What made me finally be able to shift?"

"Adrenaline," Eidolon said. "Probably combined with strong emotion. Whatever it was, you powered through the block you had." A commotion started up outside the room. "That's my cue. Nate, you should feed as soon as possible, and take it easy for a couple of days. Other than that, you two can both take off. Lena, call me later."

The second the doctor was gone, Nate jackknifed up, hauled Lena into his arms, and yanked her down on top of him. The pinch of pain in his chest was worth having her body against his. "I'm sorry, Vladlena." He stared into her eyes, praying she could see the intense regret in his. "I'm so sorry I got you into that mess."

She shook her head, making her braid tap against his neck. "I'm not. I mean, I could have done without nearly being killed, but because of it, I was able to shift. Really, being in that arena saved my life."

"I killed your brother."

Her hand came up to cup his cheek. "He'd have killed me if you hadn't."

Thank gods she was cool with what he'd done, because he wouldn't take it back even if he could. That bastard had deserved to die. A sudden flare of panic shot through him as the events in the arena came back to him.

"What happened to Fade? And the club. Shit . . . Marsden—"

"Marsden's fine," she assured him. "In fact, he was here a little while ago to check on you. Gladius has been shut down, and Fade's dead."

If only that were true, and the reality was like water on flame. The demon would hunt Nate and Lena to the ends of the earth. "He can be resurrected."

A wicked smile touched her lips, stirring the embers of the fire that had just been doused. "Sin recognized his demon species. His remains are being stored in the morgue until we can identify and kill his *vivacant*."

Damn, Lena and her colleagues were awesome. "I can help with that." He kissed her, a fleeting brush of his mouth over hers. "Oh, hey, I want to find that vampire I saw earlier."

"You'll have to be more specific," she said wryly. "This place is crawling with the fangy sort."

"Tall. Blond. Wearing armor. He's the guy who turned me." He kissed her again, this time just long enough to get a taste of her peach lip gloss. "I want to thank him. Never thought I'd say that."

She frowned. "The only male who fits that description I've seen isn't a vampire. He's one of the Four Horsemen of the Apocalypse."

Nate snorted. "Yeah, right."

"Seriously." Her head bobbed and her dewy skin took on an excited flush that might have unearthed some jealousy if Nate wasn't so . . . reeling. "His name's Thanatos. He was here a little while ago."

Yeah, that was enough to make him dizzy. "Those guys are real?"

"Very."

Nate blew out a stunned breath. "Maybe I didn't see my sire, then. Must have been hallucinating."

Closing his eyes, he buried his face in Lena's neck, taking in the soft floral notes of her shampoo and soap. She smelled clean, like a shower, and all of a sudden, all he could think about was getting her under a spray of hot water, naked, with his hands lathering every inch of her skin.

"So do you want to comb the hospital for your sire?" she asked, her voice a husky murmur. "Or would you rather go home? Because I know which I'd rather do."

So did he. For two hundred years he'd searched for his

sire, and now, he realized, it didn't matter. The past was no longer important. Only the future mattered, and he was going to make sure that future included Lena.

Vladlena was going to have sex. And it was about freaking time.

Before leaving the hospital, Nate had showered and dressed in scrubs for the trip home. Then they'd taken a Harrogate bus to his place—a charming manor in the French countryside. At first she'd been surprised by his home, expecting him to be more of a city-dweller with a modern apartment. But within minutes, the cozy but utilitarian furnishings and masculine decor made as much sense as a mane on a lion. It was as if stepping over the threshold transformed him from an intense, alert vampire into a male at ease inside his own territory.

She also noticed that even as he relaxed, building a fire and pouring glasses of wine, he never stopped watching her, his gaze growing hotter by the second, until they both combusted and ended up naked on the rug before the hearth.

Lena didn't even remember how their clothes came off. Didn't matter. All that mattered was that they were tangled together in such a tight knot that they might never unravel. Nate's muscular thigh was between her legs, pressing against her core with the most amazing pressure that both soothed the throbbing ache and made her squirm for more.

Vladlena might have been sheltered, might have been a little naive. But she'd had orgasms, by both herself and at Nate's skilled hand. And now that she knew how much better it was to climax with a male who oozed sex with every fiber of his being? *Her* prey drive had been engaged.

And Nate was the prey.

"Now," she moaned, sliding his hand from her breast to her belly and pushing it lower.

He smiled against the skin of her other breast, taking a break from the maddening flick of his tongue on her nipple. "How I ever thought you were innocent is beyond me."

She arched, rolling her hips in blatant invitation. "Let's get rid of all doubt."

Chuckling, he put his lips over her sternum in an open-mouthed kiss that included a lot of silky tongue. It was awesome, but not what she wanted, and she fisted his penis to show him what it was she *did* want. His hiss of pleasure accompanied a hot sting of fang tips scraping on her skin, and gods, she nearly came. A climax had built like steam without warning, and she had to resist the temptation to ride his leg to completion like a horny . . . well . . . wolf.

That had been shocking news, but it had made sense, had quieted the nagging voice that had always told her she was different. Now she knew why, and she didn't care how it had happened or who her biological father was. She'd always lived in the present, and presently, a hard-bodied, sexy vampire was kissing his way down her belly.

Her breath caught as he went lower, pressing a lingering kiss in the crease between her leg and her sex. Okay, she thought she'd been ready for this, but suddenly, her heart was battering her ribs, her lungs had turned to cement, and—

He licked her. The flat of his tongue went right up her center, and she melted into a liquid puddle of need. She squirmed, unsure how to handle this, but his hands shot out to still her, one arm lying heavily across her pelvis and the other spreading her for the onslaught of his mouth on her swollen flesh.

Obviously, Lena hadn't experienced oral sex, so she had no frame of reference when it came to skill. But when Nate plunged a finger inside her core and latched his lips onto her pleasure center, she'd have to go with really, fantastically, *majorly* skilled. She thrashed and writhed in his grip, and the orgasm that had been boiling erupted. He worked her through it with long, sweeping passes of his tongue and pressure-intense sucks on her clit. She was pretty sure she shouted his name, and then he was on top of her, his glorious fall of hair tickling her skin, the tip of his penis poised at her entrance.

His gaze caught and held hers, brimming with concern and molten heat.

"Don't be afraid," he whispered.

"I'm not." She framed his face with both hands and looked deeply into his eyes. "I want this more than anything."

Slowly, he lowered his mouth to hers. Her entire body quivered with anticipation as his mouth touched her lips. Even though she'd just had a world-class climax, she raised her hips, seeking his possession.

"Shh," he murmured. "Almost." Outwardly, he was calm, in control, but the slight tremor in his voice gave him away. He was as affected by this as she was.

She opened up to him . . . her mouth, her legs, her entire being. Tenderly, carefully, his tongue breached her lips, stroking, penetrating and retreating. She became lost in the rhythm, so lost that she barely noticed the head of his penis pushing past her entrance.

"So . . . tight . . ." His voice was gravelly, strained, and she knew he was struggling for control. "Am I hurting you?"

"Not even close." Grabbing onto his powerful shoulders, she dug her nails in, loving the way it made him hiss with approval and push deeper inside her.

"The shift . . ." He buried his face in her neck and shuddered, his big body heaving, as though the effort to remain motionless was killing him.

"It broke my hymen." His penis twitched inside her, hitting something sensitive that made her pant. "Please, Nate. *Now.*"

His hips punched forward, seating him all the way inside her. She gasped at the sensation of being so full and stretched, but it definitely wasn't an unpleasant feeling. Just the opposite, and as he began to move, slowly at first, and then with more urgency, erotic energy lapped at her, the waves growing larger, building with every thrust.

She arched into him, wrapping her legs tightly around his waist to ride his rhythm. He lifted his head to watch her through slitted lids, the blue of his eyes glowing behind them. In the dancing light from the fire, his hard-cut muscles bunched and flexed, the taut layers rolling beneath perfect skin.

This was so beautiful, more so than she'd ever imagined. Even his weight was wonderful, a counter to her femininity that made her feel so protected.

The speed of his thrusts increased, and his body trembled. *Ah . . . yes. Right . . . there.* Throwing her head back, she gasped at the sudden, hot ecstasy that coiled in her core. He made a desperate sound deep in his chest, sending a surge of passion roaring through her. She ground against him with an untamed urgency he seemed to call forth from her with sinful ease.

Her orgasm hovered close, searingly hot, and when he lowered his mouth to her throat, the tips of his fangs resting on her skin, she practically begged him to bite her. Eidolon had ordered him to feed, after all.

"Thank you," he rasped, but instead of a bite, he swirled his tongue over her vein. "Oh, gods, Lena . . . we were . . . made for each other."

She believed it with all her heart. They fit together perfectly, and she wanted to do a lot more fitting together. Often.

Finally, he sank his teeth into her flesh. Heat swamped her, a fever of pleasure that blistered her skin and set fire to her insides. The climax swept her up and away, so she could feel only Nate. His release was as powerful as hers, if the way he pounded into her with hard, uncontrolled bursts was any indication. It went on long enough for her to come again, her hips coming off the rug and his name coming off her lips.

Abruptly, he sagged on top of her, though he shifted his weight to prevent her from taking it all. She would have, gladly. But this was good, too. He was still inside her, and she got to stroke his muscular back and thank him without saying a word.

After a moment, he rolled onto his side and adjusted her so they were facing each other, bathed in the warm glow of the fire. He touched her face, his thumb brushing over her cheekbone in lazy, soothing strokes. "Did I hurt you?"

"Not even close."

Possessive eyes focused on her. "Work for me."

Whoa. Okay. Not words she'd expected to hear. "What? You mean like, at Thirst?"

"It's mine now. That was the deal with Fade. Thirst, Gladius, it's all mine."

An anvil dropped onto her chest. "Gladius."

He smiled. "Dismantling it will be the first thing I do. But I've put a lot of work into the club. It's a decent place, and I want you there. I want you in charge of the medic station."

She couldn't deny that the offer was tempting. To have autonomy . . . something for herself . . . it was what she'd always wanted. But she owed Underworld General so much, and with the way the underworld was spinning out of control, they couldn't afford to lose her.

"I have a job already," she sighed.

"You don't have to choose. Work at UG, but oversee the medic station and personnel at Thirst. You can hire your colleagues at the hospital to fill in or moonlight. You can use Thirst for training. I don't care. It would be yours to do what you want with it."

Closing her eyes, she thanked whoever was listening that she'd found this male. The canine instincts she hadn't even known she possessed had somehow sensed that behind his hard outer shell there'd been a caring, loving vampire in there even when he was being a jerk. And now she understood the reason he'd been such a bastard at times.

But that didn't mean she was going to let him walk all over her.

"Well?" He swept his lips tenderly over hers. "What do you say?"

She opened her eyes. "I'll do it, but on one condition."

He cocked a black eyebrow. "And that would be?"

"I don't work *for* you. I work *with* you. The medic stuff will be entirely mine."

"Woman," he said, pressing a series of kisses along her jaw, "you can have anything you want. I owe you."

"For what?" She tilted her head to give him better access, because that felt so . . . damned . . . good.

"For saving my life." His voice lowered to a husky, mesmerizing purr, and against her hip, she felt his shaft stir. "For giving me life. I was dead before. You brought me back, Nurse Lena."

She shifted so she could nuzzle his ear. "You did the same for me. So where do we go from here?"

"If you'll have me, all the way."

"To the end?"

He pushed up on his elbows and rolled to mount her. As she accepted him into her body, he locked gazes with her, his eyes glittering with passion and promise. "To the end."

Dear Reader,

I can't tell you how awesome it has been to be included in a project with some of my favorite authors. I hope you enjoyed my story, and if so, you can find more books set in Nate and Lena's world in my Demonica and Lords of Deliverance series. In the Lords of Deliverance series, which focuses on the Four Horsemen of the Apocalypse, you'll learn more about Nate's daywalker status and his sire.

The books are, in reading order:

Demonica series:

Pleasure Unbound
Desire Unchained
Passion Unleashed
Ecstasy Unveiled
Sin Undone

Lords of Deliverance series:

Eternal Rider
Immortal Rider (coming Winter, 2011)

Happy reading!

Larissa Ione

Darkness Eternal

ALEXANDRA IVY

Chapter 1

London, England

Uriel had very specific plans for the upcoming evening.

First up, dinner in bed with a luscious, golden-haired fairy who tasted like champagne and boasted skills that could make a vampire howl like a damned werewolf. Even without a full moon.

Next on the agenda, a round of sparring with the latest batch of foundlings that had arrived in London. In the past few years Victor, the clan chief of Great Britain, had instituted a law that demanded all recently created vampires must spend at least the first decade of life being trained at his lair. And since Uriel was second in command, as well as Victor's best warrior, it meant it was his duty to oversee their fighting lessons.

And if there was time left before dawn, he intended to meet with the soldiers who had recently returned from their hunt in northern England.

Since rumors of the return of the Sylvermyst had spread through the demon world, Victor had sent out nightly patrols to search for the evil cousins of the fey. It aggravated the hell out of Uriel that he wasn't allowed to take his place in the chase.

Unfortunately when he'd accepted his position as Victor's right hand man, he had given up his place in the field. Now he was stuck plotting strategy, drawing up scout rotations, and researching the history of the Sylvermyst in the massive library beneath Victor's lair on the outskirts of London.

He was also on call 24/7 to his chief.

Which was why he was headed through the vast labyrinth of hallways, dressed in a pair of faded jeans and a sweatshirt, instead of lying naked on his bed with a beautiful fairy doing bad, bad things to his eager, eager body.

Climbing the marble staircase and strolling down the crimson carpeted hallway, Uriel ignored the priceless Greek statues and pictures that lined the walls and the explosion of gilt that framed the arched windows.

He understood Victor's need for a gaudy display of wealth and power, but damn. A man could get a brain cramp from such an overexposure of frou-frou.

Especially those idiotic frescos that were painted on the lofted ceiling.

Uriel grimaced. The images of angels with fiery swords defending a gaggle of humans against a horde of demons might be some sort of priceless work of art, but to Uriel it was a never ending source of annoyance.

He was a brutal killer and a ruthless enemy to those who would threaten his clan. But for all his grim reputation, he was cursed with finely carved features and a halo of curls that perfectly matched his light brown eyes.

As beautiful as a fallen angel . . .

He'd heard those words a thousand times over the past four centuries.

Sometimes they were a sigh on a woman's lips. And sometimes a mocking taunt from his brothers.

They always managed to make him want to hit something.

Really, really hard.

Stepping into the vast library, Uriel halted in the middle of the fancy-ass carpet and watched as Victor lifted himself from behind the heavy walnut desk and crossed toward a matching sideboard.

He wasn't the hulking brute that most people expected of a clan chief. Actually, dressed in a silk shirt and black slacks he looked every inch the English aristocrat with his elegantly carved features and glossy black hair pulled into a neat braid. But a closer inspection revealed the hard muscles beneath the designer clothing and the promise of death that lurked in the pale silver eyes rimmed with black.

Victor was a predator.

Pure and simple.

"Uriel, join me," the ancient vampire commanded, turning from the sideboard to press a small glass of amber spirits in his hand. *"Salud."*

The aged cognac slid down Uriel's throat as smooth as honey. Liquid fire.

"Martell," Uriel breathed with a lift of his brow, easily recognizing the expensive liquor. "I'm afraid to ask."

Victor leaned against the sideboard, his arms folded over his chest.

"Excuse me?"

"You only break out the good stuff when you want something. Usually something that includes blood, death, and/or mayhem."

"Is that any way to speak to your beloved clan chief?"

Uriel snorted. "I will agree that you're my clan chief."

Victor sipped his cognac, a somber expression settling on his lean face.

"We have been through interesting times, haven't we, old friend?"

Uriel's vague unease became downright apprehension. Despite his vast age, Victor wasn't prone to maudlin musings.

So, what the hell was going on?

"Some more interesting than others," he slowly admitted, setting aside the Waterford crystal glass.

He suspected that he didn't want something so easily breakable in his hands when Victor finally got to the point of this little *tete a tete*.

Victor nodded. "True."

"What's on your mind, Victor?"

"I sense we're approaching momentous days."

Uriel might have laughed if he didn't sense the same damned thing.

It had started small.

The growing unrest among the demon world. The recent flurry of sacrifices by the Dark Lord's disciples to return him from his exile to this world. The rumors of the Weres regaining their ancient powers and the discovery of a new Oracle who would sit on the Commission (the powerful council who ruled the demon world).

But more disturbing than all of those combined were the nasties that were crawling out of the shadows at an alarming rate.

Demons that everyone had assumed were extinct or banished along with the Dark Lord.

Including the Sylvermyst.

"Is that a polite way of saying that things are about to go to hell?" he demanded of his chief.

Victor grimaced. "In a hand basket."

"What can I do to avert the looming apocalypse?"

"For now I need you to track down the missing gypsy."

Uriel muttered a sharp curse.

He should have been expecting this. Despite his fierce protests, Victor had invited their fellow vampire, Tane, to remain in the lair four nights ago, along with his companion, a female Jinn half-breed called Laylah. During their brief stay they'd discovered that the Jinn mongrel had a human mother being held captive by a female vampire and her pet mage.

Not that Uriel gave a shit, but Tane had managed to convince Victor that his beautiful Jinn was somehow important to the future of the world, and that her captive mother must be protected.

"The female from the vision that the mage conjured?" he gritted, even knowing it was a stupid question.

What other gypsy could it be?

Victor's lips twitched, as if he agreed with the stupid part.

"If it's true that she is Laylah's mother then we have to rescue her from Marika and her nasty wizard," he said, his tone nonnegotiable. "Tane's afraid they'll use the female to force Laylah to hand over the child."

Uriel snorted. The only thing he knew about the mysterious baby that Laylah was hiding was that it was somehow connected to the return of the Dark Lord and that the female vampire, Marika, was desperate to get her greedy hands on it.

"You know as well as I do that the entire thing stinks of a trap," he growled.

Victor shrugged. "There's only one way to find out."

"Why doesn't the Jinn go after the female?" he demanded. "It's supposed to be her mother, not mine."

"Jinn *half-breed*," Victor unnecessarily corrected him, his eyes narrowing at Uriel's odd behavior. Understandable. Uriel had never been a "yes-man." Victor didn't have the patience for kiss asses. But he didn't usually pitch a fit over such a small request. The problem was, Uriel didn't want to share the reason for his reluctance to get involved. "Tane and Laylah must return to Chicago and protect the baby." There was a deliberate pause. "Besides, I offered your services, which is my right as your chief."

"There are others more suited to play the role of Knight in Shining Armor."

Victor didn't move. He didn't have to. His power swirled through the air, slamming into Uriel with enough strength to make him grunt in pain.

"Are you questioning my decision making skills, Uriel?" he asked, oh so softly.

Uriel grimaced. "I'm not suicidal."

"I'm beginning to wonder."

"I just don't know why you would choose me for this chore."

"When did searching for an exquisitely beautiful woman become a chore?"

"When she . . ." Uriel bit off his revealing words.

Too late.

"What?" Victor demanded.

"Nothing."

Victor pushed away from the sideboard, moving to stand directly in front of Uriel.

"Uriel, is this because she is the supposed mother of a Jinn mongrel?"

Uriel clenched his hands. Had Victor become a mind reader?

Damn. Talk about disturbing.

"I logically understand that she was more than likely a victim," he said stiffly. "A Jinn wouldn't hesitate to rape and impregnate a helpless female." His hand instinctively lifted to rub the scar that was directly over his unbeating heart. "Bastards."

"But?" Victor prompted.

With a restless motion, Uriel turned on his heel and paced toward the window that overlooked the manicured parkland. He could easily sense the dozen vampires who patrolled the grounds, as well as the vast series of tunnels that ran beneath the estate. Closer at hand he could detect Juliet, Victor's mate, and in the private quarters the fairies who happily provided dinner (and whatever else might be desired) for many of the warriors.

Including the exquisite fairy that was supposed to be on his menu.

"But I would rather return to our hunt for the Sylvermyst," he said between gritted teeth.

Victor remained silent a long moment, then he moved to stand at Uriel's side, his gaze boring into Uriel's profile with a tangible force.

"I have never pressed you to share what happened in your battle with the Jinn, even when I eventually realized that you had been . . . altered by the encounter," he said, politely referring to Uriel's sharp surge in power. A vampire gained his full strength within the first few decades of his transformation. It was unheard of for one to acquire a master level after centuries of life. "I think it's time you shared."

"And if I choose not to?"

"I won't force you."

Uriel unclenched his jaw, accepting the inevitable.

He'd known from the minute Tane had arrived in London with his half-breed Jinn that the truth would have to come out.

Fate was too much a pain in the ass not to interfere . . . again.

"It's not much of a story," he said, reluctant to start. Not only because he had done his best to block out the painful memories, but because Victor was not going to be pleased.

His lips quirked.

Hell, that was the understatement of the year.

"Then it shouldn't be difficult to tell," Victor pointed out. "You can start from when we went to the docks to battle the Jinn."

Uriel kept his gaze trained out the window, tracing the moonlit gardens, but in his mind he returned to two centuries ago, when Victor had led his clan (along with his stubborn mate) into the tunnels beneath the London docks, determined to drive away the full-blooded Jinn who'd set up residence there.

He hadn't known what to expect. None of them had. Jinn were forbidden by the Oracles to settle in this dimension. They were too powerful, too violent, and too talented at ensnaring other demons into becoming their mindless slaves. Not to mention they were immoral bastards.

Uriel, however, had been stupidly confident that an entire clan of vampires would be able to convince the forbidden demon to move on to a less dangerous location.

"After we split off in the tunnels, Johan and I headed toward the Thames in the hope of cornering the beast," he said, his tone brittle.

"A solid strategy."

"We hadn't gone far when we entered a cavern." He could still recall the damp, musty smell of the barren cave that had been edged by the unexpected scent of an approaching thunderstorm. "Johan circled left while I circled to the right. I sensed something was near, but it was . . ." He shrugged, turning his head to meet Victor's searching gaze. "Elusive. Like a bad cell phone connection flickering in and out of service."

Victor nodded, his expression grim. Uriel knew the older vampire's memories of the battle with the Jinn weren't exactly shiny happy thoughts, although his mate did manage to kill the bastard in the end.

"A full-blooded Jinn is not of this world. It's why they're so difficult to hunt and even more difficult to kill."

"So Johan found out," Uriel agreed dryly. "One minute he was standing near the entrance to the cavern and the next he was being skewered by a bolt of lightning." Uriel shuddered. Johan had been his brother for two centuries. He'd deserved a better end. "He had no warning. No chance."

Victor reached over to lay a hand on Uriel's shoulder. "Johan was a warrior. He understood the dangers of his position, just as you do. You aren't to blame for his death."

"You think I blame myself?"

"Don't you?"

Uriel gave a sharp shake of his head. "No."

Victor wasn't convinced. "Uriel."

"I don't blame myself for his death," Uriel assured his companion, unable to hide the bitterness in his voice. "I blame the Jinn for keeping me alive."

Chapter 2

Victor was predictably baffled by the blunt confession. "What the hell does that mean?"

"After Johan was destroyed the Jinn appeared in front of me." Uriel had a vivid memory of the demon who had taken human shape, although there was nothing human in the lethally beautiful face and the slanted lavender eyes that held an unearthly fury. "I tried to fight, but I was no match for him."

Victor's fingers gave his shoulder a comforting squeeze. "The only way to hurt a Jinn is to destroy his *tiglia*."

Uriel nodded. Victor had discovered during his battle with the Jinn that the demon's actual essence was kept in a wooden box. At the time, however, Uriel had only known that his fierce blows had done nothing but amuse the bastard.

"He could have killed me. Instead . . ." The words became lodged in his throat.

"What?"

Stepping back, Uriel yanked his sweatshirt over his head to expose his chest.

"Instead he grabbed me by the throat and used his other hand to do this."

The *this* was the thick scar in the shape of a fist that was seared into his flesh.

Victor made a sound of shock as he caught sight of the disfigurement for the first time. Uriel had always been careful never to be seen without a shirt. Even when he was with his lovers. He didn't want nosy questions.

And there would most certainly be questions.

A vampire's ability to heal even the most grievous injuries made certain that their bodies remained flawless no matter how many centuries they might survive. It was only when they were being simultaneously starved and tortured that they scarred.

Or when they were in the hands of a demented Jinn.

"Bloody hell," Victor breathed. "I've never seen anything like it."

Uriel squashed the urge to snatch up his sweatshirt and cover the revealing wound. What was he? A warrior or a squeamish wuss?

Still, even in the company of the only person in the world he trusted, he felt vulnerable, exposed.

"Don't ask if it hurt," he awkwardly muttered.

"No need." Victor lifted his gaze with a puzzled frown. "You don't get marked like this without it hurting like a bitch. Does it still bother you?"

"Not physically."

Victor lifted his hand, holding it over the scar without actually touching it.

"I sense . . ."

"Power," Uriel finished the sentence.

The silver eyes widened as Victor abruptly realized where Uriel's sudden increase of power had come from.

"Ah."

"Exactly."

"I have to admit I wasn't expecting that." Victor slowly

shook his head. "Of course, I wondered what had happened to increase your strength, but . . ."

"But you didn't suspect that the Jinn had juiced me up?"

"I can safely swear that was at the very bottom of my list," Victor dryly admitted. "I've never heard of a Jinn sharing his power with anyone, let alone a vampire."

Uriel flinched at the memory of the white-hot pain that had drilled into his chest, spreading through his body like an infection.

"At the time I didn't know what the hell he was doing. I assumed I was about to meet my well deserved end." His lips twisted with a bitter smile. "Imagine my surprise when the bastard simply disappeared, leaving me with a pretty new tattoo."

"Did he say anything?"

"He said . . ." Uriel hesitated, bracing himself for Victor's response. There was the potential that his chief would consider the secrets he'd kept hidden worthy of a death sentence. Not the most comforting thought. "He said that I was to be *'the instrument of his revenge'*."

Victor's brows snapped together, his power slamming through the room with frigid force. Uriel hissed, struggling to keep his own powers leashed. The potential for violence quivered in the air, just waiting for the smallest provocation to erupt.

Uriel didn't intend to be that provocation.

"Why didn't you tell me what happened?" Victor growled.

"You had just rescued your new mate from the gaping jaws of death," he reminded his chief. "You didn't leave your private lair for over a month."

Victor's aristocratic features briefly softened. Like Pavlov's dog, Uriel wryly acknowledged. Victor might be a fierce clan chief who enforced his laws with a brutal strength, but he melted at the mention of his mate.

"Ah yes," the ancient vampire murmured. "Now that was a month to remember."

Uriel refused to acknowledge his stab of envy.

What was the point?

Many of his fellow vampires joked that becoming mated was a fate worse than death (at least until they became mated themselves) but Uriel had secretly longed for the day when he would meet the female destined to stand at his side for all eternity.

Until he'd been cursed by the Jinn.

Now he accepted that he could never put his potential mate in danger.

Not if there was the slightest risk he could be forced to lose control.

"Besides, I thought the beast was amusing himself," he continued with a shrug. "Like a cat with a trapped mouse. It wasn't until days later that I realized he'd given my powers a dose of steroids."

The silver eyes shimmered with anger. "And it didn't occur to you that the Jinn's mark might compel you to carry out his mysterious revenge?"

"Of course." Uriel reached into the pocket of his jeans to pull out a wooden box no larger than his thumbnail. "That's why I carry this."

Victor hissed at the unmistakable symbol branded into the wood.

"A *thana* hex."

Uriel nodded. It was a rare hex that could only be performed by imps with royal blood running through their veins.

The damned thing had taken him years to track down and cost over half his fortune to purchase, but it had been well worth the trouble.

One flip of the lid and he would be dead.

Quick, easy, and supposedly painless.

"Death in a box," he said, returning the hex to his pocket. "If I ever feel myself being forced against my will I can end it before any damage can be done."

There was the sound of approaching footsteps from the hallway and with a scowl Victor crossed to meet the young vampire at the door who handed him a cell phone. The conversation was brief, but the clan chief's temper didn't seem to be improved as he shoved the phone back into the servant's hand and turned to glare at Uriel.

"I don't have time to finish this conversation, but believe me, my brother, it's not over."

"Brilliant," Uriel muttered.

Crossing back to his desk, Victor grabbed a sheet of paper and shoved it toward Uriel.

"Here."

Uriel paused before reluctantly taking the proffered paper, his brows lifting as he realized it was a map of England.

"What's this for?"

"I negotiated with the local coven. They cast a searching spell." Victor stabbed a finger at the odd markings that were drawn at three spots on the map. "These are the locations that blocked their magic."

"What does that mean?"

"It means someone with magical abilities is trying to hide something." Victor moved his finger to the mark placed over the plain of Salisbury. "I would suggest you start here. The witches claimed they could sense black magic in the area."

Stonehenge?

Bloody hell. Could the mage be any more cliché?

Belatedly realizing his chief was headed back to the door, Uriel abruptly lifted his head, a flare of panic twisting his gut.

"Victor."

The older vampire halted, glancing over his shoulder. "Yes?"

There was an unmistakable warning in the silver eyes. Victor had given his orders. Now he expected them to be obeyed.

No matter Uriel's reluctance.

Uriel gave a resigned shake of his head. "Nothing."

Victor continued out of the room, his power still thick in the air.

"Don't disappoint me."

Chapter 3

Kata had lost track of how many years she'd been trapped in the dark, iron-lined cell that was buried six feet beneath Stonehenge. She knew it had to be close to two hundred, but the days had become a continuous blur as she lay on the narrow cot, held motionless in the mage's spell.

At the moment, it didn't really matter. Once she managed to free herself, she would tally the time she'd been held hostage and ensure Marika and Sergei suffered for every damned minute they'd stolen from her.

Marika . . .

A dark revulsion spread through her at the mere thought of the vampire bitch.

Amazing considering that four centuries ago she and Marika had been twin sisters and deeply devoted to one another.

The daughters of a powerful Romani elder they were openly prized for their dark, sultry beauty. Their hair was long, and as glossy as the finest ebony. Their eyes were dark and framed by long lashes and their pale features were delicately carved. Their sensuous lips had prompted epic poems and the sight of their lush curves attired in simple peasant blouses and skirts had inspired countless fights among the males of the tribe.

But Kata and Marika had never taken an interest in their beauty. From the time they were old enough to walk they had realized that their true power lay in their magic.

Although not witches, they both possessed the traditional magic of the gypsies. They could heal even the most grievous wounds, they could read the signs of nature to predict the weather, and of course, they could conjure curses that made grown men tremble in fear.

They could also speak to one another mind to mind, no matter how far the distance between them.

They had been destined for greatness until that fateful night that Marika had been called to heal an elder from a nearby tribe. Kata had stayed behind to tend to a child who had fallen and broken his arm earlier that day. If only . . .

No.

Nothing could have altered the fact that Marika had been attacked and drained by a vampire.

At first Kata had thought her sister dead. What else could it be? Not only was Marika missing, but the sense of her that was always nestled in the back of Kata's mind had abruptly disappeared.

Unfortunately, she hadn't been able to leave well enough alone. One of her more persistent faults. She had continued to send out mental calls for her sister, unable to accept the inevitable.

And eventually Marika did return.

Only it wasn't Marika.

The demon might have her sister's face and they might still be psychically connected, but the demon who had murdered her sister was an arrogant, brutal predator who had hunted Kata down and caged her like an animal.

For two centuries Kata had been held as her sister's prisoner, kept on a leash in her lair. Then two centuries ago the power-hungry Marika had joined forces with a Russian mage, Sergei. Together the two had plotted to use a child to resurrect the Dark Lord to this dimension.

The only problem was that the only child that they could use for the creepy resurrection was hidden in the mists between worlds.

A deal breaker for anyone with a claim to sanity, since the Jinn were the only known demons who could enter the mists, and no one wanted to negotiate with a Jinn. The powerful demons were cunning, heartless creatures who were as untrustworthy as they were beautiful. But, Marika's profound lust for power outweighed something so tediously human as commonsense and with Sergei's assistance they'd lured a Jinn into their trap using Kata as bait.

Kata's mind instantly veered from the memory of being locked in the tiny cell with the Jinn. There were some things best left buried. But nine months later she gave birth to a beautiful baby girl, Laylah.

Well aware that Marika intended to use her half-Jinn daughter to enter the mists and retrieve the child, Kata had managed to smuggle the baby to a witch who had used her magic to keep Laylah hidden.

Infuriated, Marika had demanded that Sergei put Kata into her current prison. In retaliation, Kata had sought to curse the vindictive bitch. Unfortunately that had inspired the mage to wrap her in thick layers of spells that were even more imprisoning than the lead-lined cell that held her.

She couldn't move, couldn't speak, couldn't even open her eyes.

If not for the fact that she maintained her connection to Marika to watch the world from a distance, she would have gone completely mad.

Not that being mentally linked with a psychotic vampire was a joy ride. Marika had a nasty temper under the best of circumstances. Once Kata had snatched away her means for ruling the world, she'd become downright surly, indulging her love for pain at every opportunity. Still, Kata had managed to stay aware of the changing world, and best of all she'd known that Laylah remained safely hidden.

Then fifty years ago, the damned mage had found Laylah and forced her to enter the mists to retrieve the child of the Dark Lord.

Laylah had swiftly managed to escape with the baby, but Kata had known it was only a matter of time before she was once again hunted down.

Which was precisely what had happened just a few days before. She'd sensed Laylah in England, and tried to warn her. She shared the same mind connection with her daughter as she did with her sister, but she'd been too late.

Marika and Sergei had discovered her presence and while Laylah had swiftly fled, they'd been hot on her trail.

Even worse, her psychic link to her sister and daughter had become oddly erratic, as if there was something blocking her powers.

While she was currently struggling with all she was worth against the spells that held her captive.

Laylah was in trouble, and she had to reach her.

Lost in her dark thoughts, she was distantly aware of the Sylvermyst who guarded the tomb where she was held prisoner. They never bothered her, but she didn't doubt that even if she did manage to free herself from Sergei's bonds, they would prove a difficult barrier to her escape.

A worry for later.

Then she stiffened as her senses picked up an intruder closer at hand.

Yannah.

She didn't know who, or even *what*, Yannah was.

She had to be a demon, of course. No human, or even

witch, could possibly pop in and out of the buried cell. But since Kata had been near comatose from Sergei's spell she had no more than a vague image of a small creature with a low, musical voice who had fluttered about her unconscious form and soothed her when she was troubled.

Over the years she'd become accustomed to the female's unpredictable visits, assuming that if she wanted to hurt her she'd have already done the deed. Not even the most patient demon spent two centuries fussing over a person before striking a death blow.

In fact, she'd begun to think of her as her guardian angel.

Caught in her frantic battle to free herself, Kata was unprepared when the spells that were holding her prisoner abruptly shattered.

With a strangled gasp she fell off the narrow cot. Still entangled with the shroud that had been thrown over her, Kata was incapable of stopping herself from smacking face first onto the hard floor.

Typical.

"Oof."

"Are you hurt?" A small, heart-shaped face with the almond shaped eyes that were entirely filled with black suddenly appeared in front of her.

"Yannah?" she breathed.

"That's me."

Kata managed to roll onto her back, her gaze sliding over the female's tiny body that was covered by a plain white robe and the fair hair that was pulled into a braid that fell past her waist.

She might have been mistaken for a child if not for the piercing wisdom that shimmered in the dark eyes.

And, oh yeah, the mouth full of razor sharp teeth.

Blessed mother.

Fighting her way out of the shroud, Kata rose to her feet,

her hands absently smoothing down the thin white night-gown that fell past her knees.

"What happened?" she demanded.

The tiny demon wrinkled her nose. "The spell is broken. The mage is traveling through distant lands." Her head tilted to the side, as if she were mentally searching for the missing Sergei. "Very distant."

Kata shivered. There was nowhere distant enough.

Bastard.

But for the moment she was more interested in the stark void in the back of her mind.

"Marika?" she whispered.

Yannah smiled, revealing her pointed teeth. "Ding dong the witch is dead."

Kata sucked in a shocked breath, feeling nothing but a savage flare of satisfaction. It had taken years to accept that the creature who walked around with her sister's face wasn't Marika, but instead the coldblooded bitch who'd killed her. Now she had no trouble rejoicing in the thought of the world without the evil vampire.

She did, however, have difficulty in believing she was really and truly rid of her.

"You're certain she's dead?"

"Quite, quite dead." Yannah wrinkled her tiny nose. "A shame really."

"Shame?" Kata's fury (that had had four long, hideous centuries to stew) abruptly boiled over. "I hope the bitch burns in the pits of hell for all eternity."

"Oh, I'm certain justice will be served."

"Good."

"But you aren't silly enough to think your sister . . ."

"That creature was not my sister," Kata hissed. "She killed my beloved Marika and stole her body."

"Yes, yes." Yannah waved an impatient hand. "Cue the violins."

Kata frowned. "What?"

Without warning the small demon moved forward and poked her finger in the middle of Kata's stomach.

"Shut up and listen."

"Ow."

Yannah was supremely unrepentant. "Do I have your attention?"

Kata rubbed her stomach. The poke hadn't truly hurt, but it did smash her image of Yannah as a sweet, harmless creature who was only there to offer comfort. There was a power that pulsed in the air around her and a ruthless purpose that shimmered in the depths of her black eyes.

"Do I have a choice?"

"Didn't I say it was a shame Marika was dead?"

Kata remained wary, wondering if this was some sort of trap.

"You did."

"Well, it isn't because anyone will mourn her passing."

"Then why?"

"Because she made a nasty provision in the event of her untimely demise."

"Provision? I don't believe it." Kata's lips curled at the thought of Marika's flagrant conceit. "The cold-blooded creature was too arrogant to believe anything could kill her."

"It wasn't arrogance, it was strategy." Yannah wagged a finger. "Tricky, tricky vampire."

Kata sank onto the edge of the cot, her head aching and her stomach queasy.

Not surprising.

In the span of five minutes she'd been jolted out of a spell that had kept her imprisoned for centuries, she'd been violently stripped of her connection to her sister, and every muscle in her body was cramping as they came back to painful life.

"I feel like I am going to throw up," she husked, "could you please speak clearly?"

Kata wasn't looking for a plethora of sympathy, but she sure as hell didn't expect Yannah to smack her on the back of the head.

"Use that brain in your pretty head. Marika was betrayed by Sergei. He was supposed to tell her the very second he discovered the location of your daughter and managed to kidnap her."

"Yeah, I got that. She wasn't a bit pleased when the bastard forced Laylah to steal the child of the Dark Lord and tried to keep the baby hidden from her. Do you think I was any happier? He tortured my poor girl."

"What you felt is meaningless."

Kata scowled at the tiny demon. Dammit. If Yannah was her guardian angel then she'd gotten ripped off.

Big time.

"What's your point?"

"Marika realized her pet was a bad, bad boy," Yannah said, as if Kata hadn't been intensely aware of Marika's fury when she'd discovered the mage had not only betrayed her, but had allowed Laylah and the baby to slip from her grasp.

"Yeah, her insane fury gave me a migraine for months."

"It also made her realize that while she needed his magic for her evil plans, she had to make sure he didn't decide that she was expendable. If he could get his hands on the child again, he might very well decide to keep the glory for himself."

Kata snorted. "What's that saying? 'No honor among thieves'?"

"Precisely. And you were her . . ." Yannah narrowed her gaze, searching for the perfect words. "Ace in the hole."

Kata shoved an unsteady hand through her tangle of dark curls. She didn't have to be a psychic to know she wasn't going to like what Yannah had to say.

"How?"

"When your daughter disappeared Marika forced the mage to cast a spell linking the two of you together."

Well that seemed . . . redundant.

"Why?" She gave an impatient lift of her shoulder. "We've been linked together since our birth."

Yannah nodded. "Yes, your minds, but not your souls."

"Our souls?"

Yannah grimaced. "For lack of a better word."

Kata froze, a sick dread forming in the pit of her stomach. "What exactly does that mean?"

"Marika wanted to make sure that Sergei couldn't kill her without risking you as well."

"So if she dies . . ." Kata couldn't finish the sentence. It was too horrible.

Yannah, on the other hand, didn't have a damned bit of trouble.

"You get sucked into the underworld with her."

Kata surged to her feet, panic screaming through her body as she headed across the small cell.

"Blessed goddess."

"Where are you going?"

"I have to get out of here," she muttered, tugging at the handle of the lead-lined door.

"You can't outrun the spell."

"If I can find a witch she can break the spell."

"There's no time." Yannah made a sound of impatience. "Where is that vampire?"

Swearing at the lock that refused to budge, Kata turned to glare at the tiny demon standing in the center of the sparse cell.

"Vampire?"

"He's late. Really, I cannot be expected to take care of everything," Yannah muttered, making Kata wonder at the woman's sanity. That was all she needed. Yet another crazy demon interfering in her life. Then abruptly Yannah's expression cleared. "Ah."

Kata frowned, her non-demon hearing belatedly picking up the sound of shouts from the Sylvermyst guards and the unmistakable clank of swords slamming off one another.

"Fighting?" she whispered in confusion. Who the hell would know where she was? Let alone try and battle past the layers of protection Sergei had placed throughout her prison. "Someone is coming."

"I would move away from the door," Yannah warned.

"Why?"

The question had barely tumbled from her lips when there was the god-awful screech of twisting metal as the massive door was forced off its hinges. With a gasp, Kata managed to leap to the side, avoiding being squashed beneath the wreckage. She couldn't, however, avoid the large man who charged into the cell directly behind the door.

With the force of a cement truck he slammed into her, sending them both crashing onto the hard floor.

"Oof." The air was painfully knocked from her lungs and her head smacked against the floor.

It took a moment before the fog in her brain cleared enough to take stock of the heavy beast crushing her against the lead floor.

And even longer to convince herself that she wasn't imagining the breathtakingly beautiful face that hovered a mere inch above her.

An angel . . .

What other creature possessed such pale, exquisite features? Or dark eyes as soft as velvet? Or a halo of burnished brown curls?

Her heart forgot to beat as she became lost in those beautiful eyes, her breath once again squeezed from her lungs.

He was just so . . . beautiful.

Straight out of a fantasy, how-do-I-get-him-in-my-bed-this-second gorgeous.

Desire, raw and demanding, pulsed through her. Dear goddess. His hard body fit against her with tantalizing perfection. And his scent. A rich musk that made her blood heat with a potent hunger that was as shocking as it was unfamiliar.

Kata knew that she had only to close her eyes to become lost in his dark enchantment.

Then the cold blast of his power filled the room and her insane thoughts were shattered.

A vampire.

A damned vampire.

It was no wonder he could melt a heart at a hundred paces. The evil creatures used their beauty as a lethal weapon.

She pressed her hands against his hard chest, too late realizing her danger. But oddly he didn't strike, despite the terrifying flash of his huge fangs. Instead he regarded her with a horror that matched her own.

"You," he breathed, looking as if he'd seen a ghost. "Bloody hell."

"Who did you expect to land on top of?" she snapped, her terror of vampires overwhelmed by a bizarre annoyance that her first reaction had been "oh-my-God-please-take-me-now" while his had been pure male disappointment. "Lady GaGa?"

He blinked, clearly startled by her grip on the modern world and pop culture.

"I was told you were caught in a mage's spell."

"Who told you?"

"Your supposed daughter."

"Laylah." An instant warmth curled through the center of her heart. She had known that Laylah was in the company of a vampire before she'd lost contact with her, but she hadn't expected her daughter to send a bloodsucker to rescue her. It was . . . touching. "I should have known that she would . . ." Her brows abruptly snapped together as his words truly sunk in. "What do you mean *supposed?*"

He stared down at her with a predictable arrogance. Vampires had *I'm superior to you* stamped into their DNA.

"We have no proof beyond the word of a treacherous vampire, a psychopathic mage, and a female who magically appeared in a vision at a suspiciously opportune moment to reveal she is Laylah's mother and being held hostage by her evil twin sister." His lips twisted to a sneer. "It's like a bad fairy tale."

Kata slammed her hands against his chest. She loved her daughter, but Laylah obviously had piss poor taste in choosing a Knight in Shining Armor.

"Get off me, you oaf."

"Not until I'm certain this isn't a trap."

She shifted beneath his heavy body, futilely trying to wiggle away from him. If the brute thought he could knock her to the ground and then insult her, then he was in for an unpleasant surprise. She might not possess the strength of a demon, but she wasn't entirely helpless.

"Do you know what I am?" she hissed.

Concentrating on her efforts to escape, Kata missed the sudden stiffening of the vampire's body and his muffled groan.

"Is that an invitation for further exploration?" he demanded, his low voice suddenly thick with awareness. "A little blatant for my taste, but I'm willing to play."

She told herself that it was shock that made her stomach

clench and her heart race. And as for the sizzle of excitement that shot through her . . . well, that had to be anger.

Anything else would be sheer insanity.

"It's a warning that unless you get off of me this instant I will curse your most prized possession," she said between gritted teeth. "And I'm not talking about your sword."

Chapter 4

Uriel glared at the woman pinned beneath him.

Nothing had gone right from the minute he'd left Victor's lair.

He'd journeyed directly to Stonehenge only to run headlong into a brick wall.

Literally.

The damned mage had left a dozen different snares to trap the unwary. Twice Uriel had been dropped into hidden pits. The first one had been lined with bricks embedded with silver spikes that had seared away the flesh of his palms and feet before he'd managed to climb his way out. The second pit had been filled with rabid hellhounds he'd been forced to fight through to get to the door that led to the cell he could sense deep below ground.

It had taken days to heal his wounds and gather enough strength to continue his trek downward. It had taken even more days to dodge the Sylvermyst who patrolled the tunnels and then, at last, barrel his way through the heavy door.

Was it any wonder he wasn't in the mood for surprises?

And Kata was a surprise, he grudgingly admitted.

He'd expected her beauty. She was a twin to Marika, after

all, and as much as he might detest the cold-blooded bitch, no one could deny she was stunning.

But while Kata shared Marika's glossy curls and midnight eyes set in a pale, perfect face, they had nothing in common.

Marika was cold arrogance edged with the promise of pain.

Kata was . . .

Heat and passion and the promise of endless pleasure.

He bit back another groan as she wiggled her lush, sexy body beneath him.

Dammit.

This was supposed to be a simple snag and bag.

Kata should have been playing Sleeping Beauty so he could toss her over his shoulder and get the hell out of the cramped prison. From there it was a straight shot back to Victor's lair and wham-bam-thank-you-ma'am he was washing his hands of the unpleasant duty.

Instead she was very much awake and wiggling beneath him in a way that had him painfully aroused and a breath from ripping off her too-thin nightgown and easing the sharp hunger that had slammed into him without warning.

What was wrong with him?

Debating that pertinent question, Uriel belatedly caught the odd scent of brimstone. Jerking his head to the side he watched as a tiny female demon in a white robe crossed the cell to regard him with a mysterious smile.

"I just knew the two of you would hit it off," she murmured, her voice a low sing-song. "But you might want to brace yourselves. We're about to be sucked into hell."

His brows snapped together. "What the . . ."

"Hell?" The woman smiled to reveal an impressive set of razor sharp teeth. "Yes, I just said that."

"Who are you?" he growled, instinctively shifting so his body was shielding Kata. And how crazy was that? "Actually, let's start off with *what* are you?"

"I'm Yannah. And as for what I am . . . hmmm." She tapped a finger to her chin. "Do you believe in fairy god-mothers?"

"No," he snapped.

She sighed. "A pity."

Beneath him, Kata used the sudden distraction to scramble free from the weight of his body, her gaze pinned on the far wall of the cell.

"Yannah," she breathed, "something's happening."

"The gateway is opening," the tiny demon announced.

With a liquid motion Uriel was on his feet, yanking the large sword from the scabbard angled across his back.

He'd packed light when he'd left Victor's lair. A pair of jeans, a black T-shirt, combat boots, and his weapons.

What else did a vampire need?

"Gateway?" he growled.

Yannah nodded. "To the underworld."

Uriel glanced toward the swirling mist that was forming near the lead-lined wall.

"Christ. I told Victor this was a trap," he muttered, whirling to point the tip of his sword in the center of Kata's chest. "Close the gateway, witch, or I'll carve out your heart."

She didn't so much as flinch, her eyes flashing with a proud fury.

"I'm a gypsy, not a witch, you dolt."

Uriel ground his teeth, refusing to admit his fascination with the woman's passionate courage. Dammit. The gates of hell were parting. Now wasn't the time for distractions.

"You can call yourself the queen of England if you want, just close the damned gateway."

"I didn't open it."

"Gateways to the underworld don't just open on their own." He pointed the sword toward the tiny Yannah. "You."

"Not me." Yannah wrinkled her nose. "Sergei."

Uriel's hand tightened on his sword, his gaze searching the small cell.

"The mage?"

"He cast a spell binding Kata to her twin," the demon explained.

"And your point?" he prompted.

"Marika has been destroyed."

"Good," he said. "Someone should have chopped off the bitch's head centuries ago."

Kata slapped her hands on her hips. "Did you miss the part where I'm bound to my sister?"

He shrugged. "Can't you . . . unbind yourself?"

"No."

His gaze shifted toward Yannah who gave a sharp shake of her head.

"Don't look at me."

"Brilliant," he growled, grabbing Kata's upper arm and hauling her toward the broken door. A timely evac was obviously in order. "Let's go."

"Too late," Yannah said, then with a small smile she simply disappeared.

Shit.

Uriel yanked Kata off her feet, holding her against his chest as he darted through the door, but even as he entered the tunnel leading out of the prison he knew Yannah had been right.

It was too late.

There was an unnerving sensation of electricity dancing over his skin and then the world abruptly melted around him.

Yep, there was no other way to describe it.

From one step to another the hard rock beneath his feet disappeared, along with the dirt walls of the tunnel, sending him tumbling through a choking darkness.

Uriel swore, wrapping his arms protectively around Kata as he twisted to fall backward. He didn't know where they were going to land, but he was fairly certain it was going to hurt.

Two seconds later his worst fears were confirmed.

Not only did they hit the ground with enough force to crack several bones, but the rocks that were scattered across the stone floor were sharp enough to slice through his flesh.

Momentarily stunned, Uriel couldn't stop Kata from scrambling out of his arms. She had a small smear of blood on her cheek, but otherwise she appeared unhurt. Thanks to him. Not that he was expecting a profusion of gratitude. Christ, she didn't even make a token show of concern at the sight of his broken and bleeding body, instead she was rising to her feet and studying their surroundings with a barely restrained terror.

He understood her terror.

Hell lived up to its nasty reputation.

Tentatively rising to his feet, Uriel clutched his sword as his gaze scanned the vast cavern that took "bleak" to a whole new level.

Pools of red-hot lava flowed between the black, jagged rocks, the glow shimmering off the towering stalactites and stalagmites giving them the image of the teeth of some gruesome monster.

Worse, the superior senses he depended on were muted by the strange atmosphere.

He couldn't smell a damned thing beyond the acrid stench of brimstone, his sight was limited to the cavern spread before him, and he couldn't detect if they were alone or if there were a thousand demonic souls preparing to attack.

He had spent the last four hundred years being the predator, not the prey.

He didn't like feeling vulnerable.

In fact, it made him downright pissy.

Just like Kata's supreme indifference to him made him pissy.

What was wrong with the female?

He was the one forced to come rushing to her rescue despite her intimate past with a Jinn. And yet she was treating him as if he were an unwelcomed intruder, while he . . .

He what?

Uriel grimaced.

Why deny it? He was plagued with a brutal urge to protect the luscious gypsy. An urge that was nearly as powerful as his unwanted desire. Such instincts were dangerous in a vampire. It indicated a bond with the female he wasn't prepared to accept.

He wanted to believe it was a spell. Or maybe an insidious Jinn trick.

A pity it felt so painfully real.

Frustration spilled through him. Wasn't it bad enough he'd waltzed right into a trap that had sucked him straight into hell? Now he had to be obsessed with the woman entirely responsible for his current troubles?

Indifferent to his annoyance, Kata wound her way through the lava that could so easily destroy her fragile flesh.

"Yannah," she called, her tone frantic. "Yannah."

"Dammit." Shoving his sword back into its sheath, he moved to stand at her side, barely resisting the need to snatch her into his arms. "Are you trying to attract the attention of every nasty beast in the underworld?"

"Is that where we are?" She shot him a glare, as if this was entirely his fault.

"How would I know?" Uriel cast a disgusted gaze around their noxious surroundings. "Despite popular opinion I didn't crawl out of the pits of hell."

She wrapped her arms around her waist, her chin stuck to a defensive angle.

"Hard to believe."

"Since you're entirely to blame for our presence here, I wouldn't be tossing around insults, luv."

"I didn't ask you to come barging into my private cell."

"No," he swiftly countered, "your daughter did."

Without warning her features softened. "Laylah," she breathed.

"Yes."

"I'm sorry," she lowered her head, hiding her beautiful face behind the thick curtain of her dark hair. "I only wanted to warn her. I didn't intend for her to endanger herself or anyone else to find me."

He lifted his hand to brush back the glossy curls, only to yank it back.

"It no longer matters," he gritted. "We need to find a way out."

"Out?"

"Unless you want to stay?" he drawled. "Maybe see if they have a bus tour?"

She abruptly tilted back her head to meet his chiding gaze, appearing unbearably young. Whatever spell the mage had used to keep her alive had ensured she hadn't aged beyond her early twenties in human years.

"Do you have to be an ass?"

"I . . ." His words choked in his throat as he noted the damp shimmer in her magnificent eyes. "Are you crying?"

"No," she ridiculously denied, spinning toward the swirling lava. "Leave me alone."

He should.

Victor had requested that he go in search of the captured gypsy, he hadn't said a damned thing about protecting the female from the hordes of beasts rumored to fill the underworld.

No one would blame him if he abandoned her to her fate.

Unfortunately, he hadn't become Victor's right hand man by tossing aside his duty when things got tough. When he started a job, he finished it.

And that's the reason he reached out to tug her gently into

his arms, his thumbs brushing away the tears that stained her cheeks.

"Kata. Shush," he murmured. "I will find us a way out of here." He glanced toward the distant opening across the cavern. "Or die trying."

Her dark gaze held an unmistakable fear. "Are you sure we aren't already dead?"

"What?"

"How can we be in the underworld if we didn't die?"

A faint smile touched his lips as he allowed his hands to skim down the slender length of her throat.

"Warm skin, a steady pulse . . ." Barely aware he was moving, Uriel lowered his head to touch his lips to the hollow behind her ear, nuzzling the satin softness of her skin. "The scent of tiger lilies," he husked. "I can assure you that you're very much alive."

"Oh." She shuddered, the scent of her arousal perfuming the air while Uriel planted a trail of kisses to the revealing pulse at the base of her neck. "What are you doing?"

"I think I should double check," he said, the driving pleasure in touching her overcoming his small claim to intelligence. "We can't be too careful."

"I warned you, vamp . . ." Kata breathed, her hands lifting to his chest. She no doubt intended to push him away, or maybe something even worse, but instead her fingers splayed over his rigid muscles, the heat of her touch searing through the thin material.

"Uriel," he rasped.

"What?"

"My name is Uriel."

She shivered. "Uriel."

Chapter 5

During the long years of her imprisonment, Kata more than once skirted the edge of madness. Not only from the endless days of being trapped on the narrow cot, but from sheer loneliness.

Even with her ability to view the world through Marika and Laylah, as well as Yannah's occasional visits, she'd been tortured by her isolation. She was a human who'd been raised by loving parents who'd been openly affectionate. To be suddenly denied the comfort of her family and loving tribe was worse than death.

She craved companionship with an aching need.

Which was the only reason she was tilting back her head to encourage his seeking lips, and why her hands were lifting to tangle in his thick curls. It was why she arched closer to the growing promise of his erection . . .

Blessed mother. Ruthless desire blazed through her, belatedly jerking her out of her self-delusion.

Mere comfort didn't make a woman's heart race with a wild excitement or her stomach clench in anticipation.

This was lust.

Raw, desperate, savage lust.

"Stop." Her hands returned to his chest, but this time she didn't allow herself to become distracted by the chiseled muscles and icy power. "Uriel, are you out of your mind?"

With a low groan, he lifted his head, his eyes dark with a hunger that echoed deep inside her.

"I must be," he muttered thickly, dropping his hands with insulting promptness. "There can be no other excuse."

Refusing to acknowledge the pang of loss, Kata stepped backward, wincing at the sting of heat on the back of her legs. Damned lava.

"You said something about getting us out of here," she said stiffly.

"I did."

She lifted her brows. "And?"

He grimaced. "And it is something a man says to comfort a hysterical female."

"I was not hysterical."

"You were crying."

She hunched a shoulder, refusing to admit her brief moment of vulnerability. If Marika had taught her nothing else, it was that the least hint of weakness could be exploited.

"So what you're saying is that you don't have any clue of how to get us out of here?"

His jaw tightened, as if he was offended by her accusation. "Maybe if you'd warned your daughter that anyone who was sent to rescue you was going to be sucked into hell I might have been properly prepared."

"More likely you wouldn't have come at all."

"It wasn't as if I had a choice."

Kata flinched at the stark words.

Well wasn't that just the freaking cherry on top of the god awful day?

She'd already sensed that Uriel hadn't been first in line to play the role of her Knight in Shining Armor, but she hadn't realized that he had been actually unwilling.

"You were forced?"

He ignored her question, pulling out the massive sword.

"We can't stand here hoping a gateway will open." He began weaving his way through the puddles of lava and razor sharp rocks. "Let's go."

She hesitated only a moment before following him along the narrow path.

"You didn't answer my question. Were you forced to rescue me or not?" she gritted.

He kept walking. "Does it matter?"

Did it?

Hell yeah.

Why?

She didn't have a clue.

All she knew for certain was that it hurt to know she was nothing more than an unwanted duty for the aggravating vampire.

"I . . ."

"What?" he prompted.

"I didn't know my soul was bound to Marika's until just before we met," she said, for whatever reason needing him to know she hadn't deliberately led him into a trap.

He muttered something too low for her to catch, leading them through the gap at the back. He was forced to bend nearly double as they squeezed through the opening and entered . . .

A cavern that exactly matched the cavern they had just left.

Kata grimaced, not bothering to point out that there was every possibility that there was no escape from the ghastly place. Why bother?

The same thought had to be going through Uriel's mind.

Not that he bothered to share what he was thinking. She might as well have been a stray dog for all the attention he was giving her.

Annoying ass.

In silence they crossed the cavern, nearly reaching the opening in the back when Uriel abruptly whirled around, his eyes searching the shadows.

"Damn."

She frowned. "What now?"

"Something's following us." He tilted back his head, as if testing the air. "Several somethings."

"Demons?"

"Phantoms," he corrected her.

"Perfect," she muttered, instinctively ducking as he darted past her and swung his oversized sword at the translucent creature that formed out of the steam rising from the lava pits.

There was a shriek of fury and Kata bit her lip as the phantom struck out, knocking Uriel into one of the stalagmites with shocking force. Grimly the vampire shrugged off his injuries, charging back at the enemy that had turned its attention to Kata.

She saw the gleam of malevolent red eyes among the black mist that made up the phantom before Uriel was leaping in front of her, his sword dropped to his side as he instead held out his hand and released a burst of power.

The phantom tried to halt its forward charge, but it was too late. Uriel's icy power wrapped around the creature, crushing it before it could dissipate back into the lava.

Watching the battle, Kata very nearly missed the second phantom that rose from the lava behind her. It wasn't until she felt the stinging pain in the center of her back that she belatedly turned to face the danger.

Without Uriel's brute strength or his vampire powers, Kata was severely limited in her defensive skills. And why shouldn't she be? Until Marika had become a vampire, the only defense she'd needed was the sharp edge of her tongue. She was a healer, not a fighter.

A damned shame she wouldn't be able to convince the hovering creature to settle matters with a smile and a handshake.

Hell, she didn't even know if it had hands in all that swirling mist.

Taking a step backward, Kata held up a clenched fist and chanted soft words beneath her breath. They burnt across her brain as if they were being etched in fire, then, as she finished the spell she released the curse and let it fly toward her attacker.

She didn't have a clue if it would hurt a phantom.

The thing didn't have a corporeal body, but it did have an essence that could take physical form.

All she could do was hope for the best.

For a minute nothing happened.

Well, that wasn't exactly true. The creature continued to float forward, while from behind she could hear the dying shrieks of Uriel's opponent. But her curse seemed to be a complete bust.

Desperately searching her mind for something, *anything*, that might hurt the phantom, Kata sucked in a startled breath as the air suddenly began to thicken with the force of her words. Her curse was not only working, but it was growing with an intensity she'd never been able to conjure before.

Obviously a perk of being in hell, she wryly accepted, taking a hasty step backwards as the phantom began to pulse, almost as if it were being inflated from the inside. Then, with a scream that nearly deafened Kata, the creature exploded.

There was just no other way to describe it.

One minute it was a hovering mass of black mist, and the next, tiny shreds of an oily substance were dripping off the nearby stalagmites.

She barely had time to admire the stunning results of her

curse when Uriel was scooping her off her feet and tossing her over his shoulder.

"Hey . . ." Her head bounced against the hard muscles of his back as he leaped over pools of boiling lava and hurried toward the side of the cavern. "Stop. Put me down."

He ignored her protests, ducking through a hidden opening into another cavern. This one similar to the previous one, but with enough differences to comfort her with the thought they weren't going in endless circles.

Not that she had much of a chance to admire the passing scenery.

Uriel charged from one cavern to the next, not halting until she began to pummel his back with small fists. Swaying upside down was making her queasy.

"Dammit, I told you to put me down," she rasped.

Muttering his opinion of women who didn't have the sense of a Flandra demon, Uriel set her onto a path that ran between two sheer cliffs. Kata refused to peer over the edge. She didn't want to know if there was a bottom far below. Or what might be lurking down there.

Things were bad enough.

Uriel seemed to agree.

"Satisfied?" he demanded, his gaze never straying from her pale face.

She licked her dry lips. "Maybe we should split up."

He blinked, studying her as if she'd grown a second head. "Split up?"

"You know, you go one way and I go another." She waved her hand. "It's a fairly simple concept."

"I understand the concept," he growled, "I just don't understand why you would be so idiotic as to suggest it. You wouldn't last five minutes without my protection."

It was true.

Although her curse had worked against the phantom, she wouldn't be able to conjure another one until she'd had a chance to rest. And she very much doubted that phantoms were the only nasties that were waiting to crawl out of the shadows.

But she'd been stripped of her pride and dignity by Marika. She wasn't going to let it happen again.

She wasn't this vampire's charity case.

"What does it matter to you?"

"I think the better question is why you're trying to get rid of me?" He narrowed his eyes in suspicion, his face bathed in the reddish glow that filled the cavern. He should have appeared . . . frightening, even sinister, standing there with his big sword and flashing fangs. Instead his male beauty was so ethereal it made her heart ache. "Do you and Yannah have a gateway hidden to escape through once you've managed to get rid of me?"

She clenched her hands. Beautiful or not, she wanted to punch him in the nose.

She was trying to do this for him, the jerk.

"Yes, this is all some elaborate trap that I invented with Yannah just on the off chance an annoying vampire was forced to come to my rescue," she mocked. "Ingenious, is it not?"

"The trap wasn't meant for me, it was meant for Laylah."

Kata sucked in a shocked breath, raw fury racing through her at the unjust accusation.

She'd endured endless years of being held captive and unbearable torture to protect her daughter. And she would endure centuries more if necessary.

"You bastard." Without thought she launched herself toward the aggravating vampire, wildly pounding her fists on his solid chest. "I have sacrificed everything to keep my daughter safe. Everything."

Uriel hastily sheathed his sword, wrapping his arms around her trembling body and pulling her close.

"Easy, Kata."

She tilted back her head to stab him with a warning glare. "Don't ever say I would try to harm her again."

"Fine." He lifted a hand to gently smooth her hair from her face, his expression guarded. "If this isn't a trap, then why are you trying to get rid of me?"

"Maybe I don't like you," she muttered.

His eyes flared with a heat that could rival the lava that spilled over the cliff just a few feet away.

"I could change that if I wanted to," he husked.

And he could.

She might not want to acknowledge the poignant awareness that swirled between them. Or the peculiar sense that she'd been waiting for this particular man to crash into her life since she'd been a simple gypsy maiden. But ignoring the dangerous sensations didn't make them go away.

"Please, Uriel . . ." she whispered, acutely aware of the soft stroke of his thumb over her cheek.

"Tell me why you're trying to get rid of me."

She heaved a resigned sigh. Stubborn demon.

"It was my demented sister who is responsible for sending us here and there's no reason for both of us to suffer."

His lips twisted. "And you think splitting up will end my suffering?"

"We both know you're much more likely to escape without me slowing you down." She shivered as his thumb shifted to stroke her lower lip. "So go."

"No."

"Why not?"

He frowned, as if annoyed he might be forced to actually consider his motives.

"I always finish what I start," he at last said.

Always finish what he started?

Lame. Truly lame.

He better hope that he didn't need a reference if he intended to make a career out of rescuing maidens in distress, because as far as she was concerned, he sucked at it.

"I'm not your obligation," she snapped.

"You are for now."

"Because my daughter sent you?"

"Because my clan chief sent me."

Kata rolled her eyes. She loved Laylah, but why on earth would the girl get involved with vampires?

"Fine, you came, you saw, you conquered. Now go away."

"I'm not leaving without you." He folded his arms over his chest. "Get over it."

Okay, that was it.

She'd tried to be nice. To put his welfare above her own.

Now she just wanted to kick him in the nuts.

"Look here, you arrogant ass, I've . . ."

"There's no use in arguing with a vampire, my dear," a soft, melodic voice interrupted her tirade.

Whirling around in shock, Kata pressed a hand to her heart as she caught sight of the tiny demon she'd thought lost forever.

"Yannah, thank goodness," she breathed, barely noticing that the demon's white robe was perfectly pristine and her hair smoothed into a tidy braid. Unlike Kata who looked like she'd been to hell and back. Literally. "I feared . . ."

"I was dead?" Yannah helpfully supplied.

"Yes."

"Silly girl." Yannah waved a hand toward the far side of the cavern. "My house is just on the other side of the lava pit."

Kata shook her head in confusion. Over the years she'd accepted Yannah's habit of popping in and out of her cell without giving any actual thought to where she came from.

But even if she had, her first thought wouldn't have been the underworld.

"You live here?"

Yannah sniffed, unexpectedly offended by Kata's blatant disbelief.

"I'm not sure I like your tone. My neighborhood happens to be quite nice, and for your information I have a very lovely flat in Mayfair for when I'm on the other side."

Kata parted her lips to apologize, only to be cut off as Uriel stepped directly between her and the female demon.

"You can travel between worlds?" he growled.

"No time for questions." Yannah said as she turned to the side.

Waving her hands over the edge of the cliff in intricate motions, Yannah ignored Uriel's impatient demand for explanations.

Kata frowned. Was the demon pretending to conduct an orchestra? Calling for reinforcements? Totally losing her mind?

The answer was far more unexpected.

The darkness in front of her began to shift, as if it were alive. Then, without warning, Yannah chopped her hand downward and there was a strange sound, as if the very air was tearing in half.

Blessed mother.

Kata shook her head, stunned by the outrageous display of power.

"Come on." Yannah impatiently waved for them to approach. "Through here."

Tentatively Kata edged toward the opening. She didn't want to offend Yannah, but she wasn't sure she entirely trusted the strange creature.

Uriel, on the other hand, had no trouble being blatantly offensive.

Stepping to her side, he pointed a finger at the opening.

"Where does this go?"

"Didn't I just say there's no time for questions?" Yannah turned to Kata with a baffled expression. "Was he hit on the head?"

"Yannah . . ." she started to soothe, no more anxious than Uriel to step through a hole in space.

A pity she wasn't given a choice.

Studying the gaping hole in what might be the very fabric of the space/time continuum, Kata missed Yannah creeping behind her. It wasn't until she felt the demon's tiny hands on her ass that she belatedly realized her danger.

She gave a choked shout of alarm at the same time that Yannah shoved her forward.

Chapter 6

Uriel was rarely caught off guard.

A complacent vampire was a dead vampire.

But distracted by the lurking promise of an escape route, he hadn't realized the tiny demon's intention until too late.

Swearing as he watched Kata being pushed into the portal, Uriel didn't hesitate. Knocking aside Yannah, Uriel charged forward, managing to wrap his arms around Kata's waist as they both plunged through the shimmering mist.

There was the sense of freefalling through a tunnel of black nothingness and Uriel instinctively tugged Kata closer to his body. At the moment, she was the only real thing in the whirling darkness.

Wrapped in her sweet scent of tiger lilies and the tantalizing warmth of her lush body, Uriel was struck by a piercing desire to keep falling. Anything just so he could keep this woman in his arms.

Insanity, of course.

He was a vampire.

They didn't do "happily ever afters." Or even "I'll call you tomorrow."

At least not until they found their mate.

And this woman couldn't be his mate.

Could she?

Before he could actually consider the disturbing question, their freefall came to an abrupt end.

Tumbling through the other side of the portal, Uriel hurriedly turned to keep Kata protected as they emerged into a heavily-wooded forest.

His back smacked painfully onto the moss covered ground as his feet tangled in the undergrowth. Not that he noticed the rock poking into his shoulder or the overhead cry of angry birds disturbed from their nests.

Instead he hissed in fear as a light breeze stirred the thick canopy of leaves and the dappled sunlight brushed over his skin.

It had been centuries since his last glimpse of the sun. With good cause.

Vampires plus daylight equaled instant death.

Something he'd tried to avoid over the years.

Now he braced himself for the searing pain.

A pain that never came.

Astonishment slowly gave way to the recognition that this place was nothing more than an illusion. There could be no other explanation.

Yannah had somehow created this bubble of paradise in the midst of the underworld.

But how? And more importantly, why?

Distracted by the possibility of spontaneous combustion, Uriel nearly forgot the bundle of lush woman he held in his arms. At least until she squirmed out of his grasp and darted away.

"Kata."

Forcing himself to ignore the unnerving sunlight, Uriel hurriedly followed behind her, nearly running her down when she came to an abrupt halt at the edge of a large glade.

Sensing her tension, he studied the meadow dotted with

wildflowers and the shallow stream that wound a lazy path through the grass. So far as he could tell they were alone in the strange vision, but that didn't mean there weren't dangers lurking among the surrounding trees or the distant hills that were silhouetted against the horizon.

Even paradise had its serpent.

At his side, Kata gave a slow shake of her head, her beautiful eyes wide with disbelief.

"No . . ." she breathed, "it can't be."

"Do you sense something?"

She shook her head, cautiously taking a step forward. "I know this place."

Even knowing it was an illusion, Uriel had to battle his instinctive reluctance to step from the shade of the trees into the sundrenched glade.

"Careful, Kata."

She tilted her head to meet his worried gaze, her skin brushed with golden sunlight and her dark curls spilling down her back in a glorious tangle.

"What is it?"

For a moment he was speechless. She was so . . . exquisite. But it wasn't her beauty that held him captivated. Or at least, not entirely.

He'd known some of the most stunning women in the world over the years. Imps, fairies, humans, and vampires. But none of them stirred his hunger as this woman did.

Was it her earthy curves on full display beneath the nearly transparent nightgown? Or the passionate life that smoldered in the dark eyes? Or the fierce spirit that Marika and the damned mage hadn't been able to crush despite their best efforts?

Whatever the cause, it was all he could do not to yank her against him and take her in a storm of raw need.

He clenched his hands. Bloody hell, this place was obviously screwing with his head.

And his body, he ruefully acknowledged, his erection pressing painfully against his jeans.

"We haven't left the underworld," he said, grimly battling back his attack of lust. "This is all an illusion."

"How can you know . . ." Her confused expression abruptly cleared as she glanced up at the sun that was blazing from a clear blue sky. "Oh."

"Exactly."

She frowned, her gaze returning to the picturesque view. "It seems so real. It even smells as I remember."

"This place has some special meaning to you?"

Her expression softened. "As a child my family traveled with our tribe through the lands that are now called Hungary. My father was an elder and my mother was a healer."

"They had positions of power," Uriel murmured, not surprised. Kata had been trapped in a nightmare for centuries, but she'd not only survived, she'd managed to protect her beloved daughter.

It took incredible strength that she'd obviously inherited from her parents.

"Yes, which meant they shouldered heavy duties," she said, a wistful smile curving her lips. "When they felt the need to escape their responsibilities they would bring my sister and I here. I cherished those days. It was the only time we could be alone as a family."

There was no mistaking her emotional connection to the image spread before them.

"I don't like this," he rasped.

"You don't like what?"

"Was Yannah a part of your childhood?"

"Of course not." She blinked in puzzlement at his abrupt question. "We knew nothing of demons before Marika came to us as a vampire."

"Then how did she know to create this particular illusion?"

He watched Kata's pleasure in her surroundings briefly falter at his question.

"Perhaps she can read my mind," she at last suggested.

"Perhaps." Uriel shrugged. It was a rare talent, but not unheard of. "Then the next question is why," he persisted. "She must have some purpose in bringing us here."

"You think she's responsible for opening the gateway to hell?"

Did he?

The tiny demon certainly had the power.

And God knew she was erratic enough to offer help one minute and then trap them both in hell the next.

But he wasn't going to leap to conclusions.

"I think we would be fools not to suspect she has her own agenda," he compromised.

Her lips twisted into a bitter smile. "Who doesn't?"

He bristled at her accusation. "I'm at least honest about my purpose in following you," he said, even knowing the words were a lie.

Oh, his purpose had been clear enough in the beginning.

Victor commanded him to locate and retrieve the gypsy.

Simple and straightforward.

It was only after he'd crashed into Kata's prison that his unwanted duty had become something else.

Something dangerous.

Thankfully unaware of his tangled thoughts, Kata gave a restless lift of her shoulder.

"Maybe Yannah created a place to keep us safe until she could get us out of here," she suggested, clearly wanting to assume the best.

He snorted. "Do you believe that?"

Her dark eyes flashed with annoyance. "I don't know what I believe, and right now I don't care. For the moment there's no scalding lava, no bottomless pits, and no creepy ghouls trying to suck my soul. I intend to enjoy a few minutes of peace."

With a flounce (yes, it was an unmistakable flounce) Kata crossed to the meandering stream and settled on the sloping bank. Then, with a sigh of pleasure she allowed her bare feet to dangle in the crystal clear water.

Uriel swore as he leashed his instinctive urge to snatch her back into his arms until he could be certain there weren't any lurking dangers.

Maybe she was right.

They would know soon enough if this was a trap. Why not take a few moments to appreciate the peace?

Not that it was the peace he was appreciating as he moved to settle on the mossy ground next to her. Stretching out his legs, Uriel leaned back on his hands and allowed himself the rare luxury of savoring the sight of Kata drenched in sunlight.

His fangs lengthened, his ready hunger returning with a vengeance as the bright light revealed the dusky temptation of her nipples and the feminine shadow at the apex of her thighs. Bloody hell. A low growl trickled from his throat as a cool breeze stirred the satin strands of her hair, teasing at the tender curve of her neck.

Abruptly she turned her head to meet his heated gaze.

"You're staring at me," she murmured.

Unable to resist temptation, he reached out to run his fingers through the thick satin of her hair.

"You look too young and innocent to have a child."

Her brows lifted. "Was that a compliment?"

"A statement of fact."

"Ah." She wrinkled her nose. "I suppose that's the upside of playing Sleeping Beauty." She blinked, as if hit by a sudden thought. "Of course, with Marika dead and Sergei missing, I suppose the spell to keep me from aging is gone."

A strange pang of unease clutched his heart at the mere thought of Kata growing old . . . dying.

"There are means for humans to stay young."

She shrugged. "That's actually at the very bottom of my Worry List."

"What's at the top?"

"Laylah." She said it without hesitation, her first thought for her daughter despite the fact that she was currently trapped in hell with no certain means of escape. "I've always been able to sense her, but now there's some sort of interference between us." She bit her full bottom lip, her expression troubled. "She could be hurt and I wouldn't even know it."

His hand cupped the back of her head, his chest tightening with the oddest urge to . . . what?

Offer her comfort?

Impossible. That's what humans did, not demons.

But there was no halting the need to lower his head and brush his lips softly over her mouth.

"Marika's dead," he found himself saying softly. "That has to be a good sign."

She gave a hesitant nod, her heart picking up speed at his light caress.

"Yes."

His gaze drifted downward, lingering on the swell of her breasts that spilled over the neckline of her nightgown. He swallowed a groan as he hardened with astonishing speed.

"Not to mention that Laylah's in the protection of one of the most powerful and ruthless vampires in the world," he continued, his voice thickening. "There are few things that could hurt her."

"That isn't entirely comforting," she said dryly.

He jerked his head up, a frown marring his brow. "You have a prejudice against vampires?"

Her magnificent eyes narrowed, her expression revealing just what she thought of his hint of outrage.

"Can you blame me?" she demanded. "I was tortured for the past four centuries by a vampire. It didn't inspire a lot of warm fuzzies for your people."

Uriel considered being annoyed.

He was the one who was supposed to be heroically overcoming his aversion to a woman with intimate ties to a Jinn while she was supposed to be melting in gratitude at his daring bravery.

Instead, he threaded his fingers through her hair, his other hand lifting to cup her cheek.

"She hurt you."

Her eyes darkened with unwelcomed memories. "She enjoyed causing pain."

"Not all vampires are like her."

She shivered, but Uriel sensed it was not entirely due to her thoughts of Marika.

"I hope not, for Laylah's sake," she said, her breath catching as Uriel skimmed his hand down the curve of her cheek.

"And for your own?"

Her lips parted in unconscious invitation, a tiny pulse fluttering at the base of her throat.

"I don't know what you mean," she husked.

He leaned forward, absorbing her sweet scent as he allowed his lips to explore the tender slope of her shoulder.

"I can sense your . . . need."

Kata stiffened at his blunt words, even as she knew the scent of her stirring arousal was no doubt blatantly obvious to Uriel. If she'd learned nothing else during her captivity, it was there was no hiding anything from a damn vampire.

Just one of the countless reasons they were so annoying.

"What you sense is a woman forced to be alone in a cramped cell for the past two centuries," she futilely tried to bluff.

He lifted his head to flash an arrogant smile. "No, you desire me."

"After two centuries of celibacy I would desire a filthy, rotting zombie . . ."

"Me," he growled, moving with a liquid speed to pin her against the mossy ground. She made a sound of surprise, but before she could react he was blatantly rubbing his fully erect cock against her lower stomach. Oh . . . yes. Sheer pleasure jolted through her. His smile widened at her soft moan of approval. "You want me deep inside you."

Blessed mother, she did.

Could anything be more insane?

He was a vampire. They were trapped in hell. And he was precisely the sort of arrogant bastard that set her teeth on edge.

She should be punching him in the nose, not smoothing her hands over the sculpted perfection of his chest. But damn . . .

Even with her hatred of vampires she couldn't ignore the impact of his astonishing beauty, or the knowledge that he'd risked his life more than once to protect her.

And then there was that burning, aching, ruthless need.

It wasn't just the loneliness that plagued her, no matter what she claimed. Or the random lust of a woman who'd been without sex for a very, very long time.

No, this gnawing desire had started the moment she'd first laid eyes on Uriel. And as much as it pissed her off to admit it, he was the only one who could ease her torment.

Dismissing the countless reasons this was "the worst idea ever," Kata skimmed her hands upward to frame his beautiful face, drowning in the velvet heat of his gaze.

"Uriel," she breathed.

Stark hunger flared through his eyes. He lowered his head and nuzzled a path of destruction down the curve of her throat. Kata quivered, squeezing her eyes shut at the erotic feel of his fangs scraping against her tender flesh.

Oh . . . goddess.

She should be terrified by the threat of those enormous weapons so close to her veins, but instead she lifted her hips to rub against the hard thrust of his cock.

Uriel groaned, his fingers easily tugging down the straps of her gown and stripping it from her willing body. Then with the same swift efficiency he shed his own clothes, tossing them aside before cupping her breasts in his hands, his thumbs teasing her nipples to tight beads.

Kata kept her eyes tightly closed, basking in the sensation of the warm sunlight that spilled over their entwined bodies and the soft moss beneath her back. Illusion or not, she'd been trapped in that dark, spartan cell for centuries. The sense of being free and returned to her beloved homeland was nearly as heady as the feel of Uriel's gentle touch.

She sucked in a sharp breath as his lips traced the line of her collarbone and then over the curve of her breasts, swiftly revising her thoughts.

The sun and illusion of freedom were delightful, but Uriel's touch . . .

It was magic.

The cool, clever fingers that skimmed down her body with a heart-melting skill. The seeking lips that closed over the tip of her aching breast. The press of his erection against the precise point of her pleasure.

She threaded her fingers through thick curls, her back arching in silent encouragement.

Uriel growled in appreciation, his tongue flicking over the sensitive tip of her breast as his hand explored the generous curve of her hip. Slowly his hand skimmed downward until he could tug her legs further apart, his fingers running a lazy path up and down her inner thigh. Kata forgot to breathe as she restlessly stirred beneath him, her body trembling with need.

"Please," she moaned.

He nibbled a path to her other breast. "Say it," he husked.

"Say what?"

"That you want me."

She didn't even hesitate. What would be the point? Even if he weren't a vampire he would know that she was desperate to ease her burning lust.

"I want you."

A smug smile curved his lips. "Mine."

Kata stilled. She wasn't disturbed by his claim of possession. It sounded unnervingly right, even if she wasn't ready to admit it. But, she'd be damned if he thought he could make her go up in flames without feeling a few sparks himself.

Lifting her heavy lids her stomach clenched in anticipation at the need blazing in his dark eyes. Deliberately she shifted her hands to trace the smooth planes of his back. Beneath her fingers she could feel his muscles flex at her touch, his fangs flashing in the sunlight as his lips parted in pleasure.

"Kata."

"Do you like?" she teased.

He growled low in his throat. "I like."

She chuckled, her fingers skimming over the curve of his ribs and then discovered the hard ridges of his stomach. She savored the feel of his muscles clenching beneath her exploration before lowering her hand to the thick jut of his erection. Just for a moment she hesitated, a strange voice in the back of her mind warning that making love with Uriel was one of those life changing decisions.

"Please . . ." Uriel muttered, his voice a harsh rasp.

Shrugging off the premonition, Kata allowed her fingers to curl around the straining cock, amazed by the cool perfection of his skin that sheathed the rigid length. Heat pooled in the pit of her stomach as she stroked downward, reaching the soft sack before exploring back to the blunt tip.

Uriel's groans filled the air as she pushed downward again, his lips capturing her mouth in a kiss of raw desperation. Pleasure jolted through her. So much for his smug conceit.

Now he trembled with a need that matched hers.

Lost in her heady sense of power, Kata continued her daring caresses, only halting when Uriel abruptly grasped her wrist, a low growl rumbling in his throat.

"Enough."

"And I thought vampires were famous for their stamina," she teased.

"Don't worry your pretty head about my stamina."

"Are you certain?"

"I'll be happy to demonstrate it as long and as often as you want. But first . . . you had your fun, now it's my turn," he warned, smiling down at her with a predatory expression. "And payback is a bitch."

Kata shivered, her eyes sliding shut as he lowered his head and nibbled his way down the curve of her neck. Her body bowed in pleasure as he paused to tease the aching tips of her breasts, his tongue sending a blaze of passion through her veins. Gently he captured one nipple between his teeth, chuckling softly as she cried out in delight.

"Damn, that feels good," she whispered, lifting her hands to grasp his shoulders.

"We can do better than good." With slow, savoring kisses, Uriel journeyed down the shallow curve of her stomach, smiling against her flesh as she wriggled beneath his teasing caresses. "I want you to scream for me, Kata."

Kata's hips lifted off the soft ground as he stroked his mouth over her hip bone and down the tender skin of her inner thigh.

"Scream? You're not that . . . oh. Oh." Her chest was so tight she could not breathe. "Do something, Uriel, I can't take much more."

"Tyrant." Uriel relentlessly tugged her legs apart, slipping down the bank to kneel between her thighs. "I need to taste you."

"But . . ." Her protest died in her throat as he shifted and stroked his tongue through her damp curls.

She cried out at the pure bliss that trembled through her body. Oh, this was decadent. Decadent and wicked. And if anything or anyone tried to interrupt, she'd rip out their hearts with her bare hands.

Quivering, she allowed herself to drown in the exquisite sensations. Over and over his tongue dipped into her gathering dampness, stroking with a steady rhythm that was custom designed for maximum pleasure.

Oh, he was fantastic.

A top of the line, first-class lover that made all the years of waiting worthwhile.

Then, gently he sucked the hidden nub into his mouth and Kata screamed as the entire world shattered in a burst of shimmering stars.

Caught off guard by the sheer force of her release, Kata was barely aware of Uriel sliding up her body and entering her in one smooth thrust. But as he captured her lips in a demanding kiss, she instinctively wrapped her arms about his shoulders and arched her back to meet the plundering strokes of his erection.

"Perfect," he husked against her lips, his entire body trembling as he jerkily surged in and out of her body. "You're perfect."

Kata barely registered his soft words, lost in the mind-numbing pleasure that was once again building in her lower body. With every thrust he pressed deeper into her body, his fullness creating a delectable friction.

"Yes, Uriel . . . yes . . ." She urged him to a faster pace, raking her nails down his back as he drove into her with a single minded purpose.

"Mine," he rasped as he scraped his fangs down the line of her throat. "My sweet Kata."

With one last surge he tumbled them both over the edge of reason, remaining buried deep inside her as her scream of fulfillment echoed through the glade.

Chapter 7

Uriel smiled as Kata's cries became soft moans of completion, his body still trembling from the pleasure of her wild passion.

Bloody hell.

He expected the explosion of bliss. He'd never experienced a woman with such a savage desire. And with Kata's eager response to his touch, the resulting earth-rocking, mind-blowing, the-best-orgasm-ever had been inevitable.

But what he hadn't expected was the primitive surge of possession that had settled in the center of his heart.

Mine.

The word had whispered over and over in his mind, settling deep in his soul.

Feeling Kata stir beneath him, he reluctantly rolled to the side, tightly tucking her against him. He growled at the satin slide of her naked skin and the beat of her heart that echoed in his own.

He hadn't shared her blood, but already she was an intimate part of him.

A smile curved his lips as Kata tilted back her head, a shell-shocked expression on her beautiful face.

"That was . . ."

"Only the beginning," he promised, his hand cupping her full breast.

The dark eyes flashed with ready fire. "Hey, don't be making plans that include me, vampire."

He chuckled, his finger circling the dusky nipple into a hard peak.

"Then don't be making promises you don't intend to keep."

She moaned, her back arching and her hands running up the bare planes of his chest. But even as he shivered with a raw jolt of anticipation, she gave a startled gasp pulling back to study his chest with a frown.

"Oh, Uriel," she breathed.

"What?"

Her fingers tenderly stroked the scar that marred his skin.

"You've been injured."

With a hiss Uriel was on his feet, his hand instinctively covering the wound.

Christ, he'd forgotten.

Lost in the stunning power of his awareness of Kata, his mind had refused to remember that this was an impossible dream.

No.

It was worse than impossible, he fiercely reminded himself.

It was dangerous.

She studied his tight expression with a frown, slowly sitting upright.

"Uriel?"

"It was a long time ago," he muttered.

Her eyes narrowed. "Then why are you still angry?"

Angry?

He wanted to fall to his knees and howl at the bleak desolation that filled his heart.

It was one thing to know he was denied the promise of a

mate when she was a mythical creature that might or might not make an appearance in his life. It was another to be given a glimpse of paradise only to have it snatched away.

"Because it's a reminder that my future is no longer my own," he said in stark tones.

Cautiously she rose to her feet, her hand reaching toward his chest.

"You sound like Yannah."

"Don't," he growled, jerking away.

"Tell me what happened."

He hesitated, before giving a faint shrug. He admired her courage too much to lie.

"I had a rather nasty encounter with a Jinn beneath the docks of London," he grimly confessed.

She paled, her hand trembling as she pushed back the heavy tumble of her dark curls.

"A Jinn?"

"Yes."

"When?"

"Two centuries ago, give or take."

Her expression was impossible to read, although she was too intelligent not to realize the significance of the date.

"You battled?"

He made a sound of disgust. Even after two centuries it still rankled he'd made such a pansy-ass showing against the Jinn.

Hell, a dew fairy could have done more damage.

"You could call it that," he groused. "As much as I hate to admit it, there wasn't much of a fight. I barely sensed the Jinn's approach before he'd killed my brother and captured me."

"And he did this to you when you tried to escape?" she husked.

Uriel's bitter laugh echoed through the nearby trees. "No, he allowed me to leave. This was his curse."

"A curse?" She looked genuinely confused. No big surprise. Uriel was still trying to puzzle out what the hell had happened. "Are you certain?"

He rubbed the scar that had throbbed with a low intensity ache since his escape from the London docks, belatedly realizing that the throb had become more pronounced since his unexpected journey into the underworld.

A coincidence?

It had to be.

He couldn't allow himself to consider anything else.

If he went postal and hurt Kata . . .

Yeah, he so wasn't going to go there.

Not even in his darkest 'what ifs'.

"Painfully certain," he said, his voice clipped.

"What did he do?"

"The bastard made me his slave."

Dropping his bomb of shame, Uriel abruptly turned to dive into the water of the stream. The cool, crystal clear water washed over his skin, although it couldn't wash away the helpless fury that pulsed through him.

Surfacing, he shook the hair out of his eyes and turned to find Kata standing at the edge of the stream, her dark eyes troubled.

She was so beautiful that she made his heart ache.

The dark curls wildly tumbled around her lovely face. The ivory satin skin. The lush curves.

An intoxicating, earthy woman that called to a man's most primitive desires.

"What did he do to you?" she softly asked.

He clenched his teeth against the savage longing that clutched at him.

He had to keep her safe.

Nothing else mattered.

"He said that I was to be *the instrument of his revenge*,"

Uriel repeated the words he'd shared with Victor almost two weeks ago.

She averted her face, wading into the water until it lapped over the full curve of her breasts.

"You think this Jinn is the father of Laylah?"

He couldn't deny her accusation. "Since there's only been one Jinn sighting in London for the past millennium it seems like a safe assumption."

"And that's why you treated me like I carried the plague."

He flinched at her harsh accusation, not wanting to remember his arrogant disdain.

"I've done everything in my power to rescue you."

She refused to look at him. "You think I'm a Jinn whore."

Even knowing it was a truly stupid idea, Uriel couldn't stop himself from moving through the water to stand directly before her. Gently he grabbed her shoulders, battling back his surge of lust.

"I know that Marika held you against your will."

She turned her head, her eyes snapping with her ready temper.

Kata would never be a soothing female. She was passionate, turbulent, and unpredictable.

She was also intensely loyal, courageous, and the very essence of female temptation, he acknowledged with a bleak sense of loss.

"And yet you suspect I might actually have enjoyed being trapped with the handsome demon?" she accused him.

He wouldn't lie. Not to this woman.

"At first."

"And now?"

"Now it doesn't matter," he said with simple honesty.

She once again turned away, studying the trees that lined the far bank as if she had a sudden fascination with the tiny violets that were hidden among the moss.

"Right."

"Kata. Look at me," he said softly.

"No."

"Please."

Grudgingly she snapped her gaze back to glare at him. "Satisfied?"

"No. I'm . . ." Words failed him.

"What?"

"Furious," he at last managed to rasp.

She jerked as if she'd been slapped. "I didn't ask you to soil your vampire hands with my tainted . . ."

"Shut up and listen to me," he interrupted her.

The very air vibrated the force of her anger. "You're an idiot if you think I won't hurt you just because we had sex."

"We didn't have sex, we made love." He cupped her face in his hands, shuddering at the erotic sensation of the water stroking over their nude bodies. He moved close enough that the tips of her breasts brushed his chest. "Or do I need to remind you?"

Her breath caught, the scent of her swift arousal perfuming the air.

"Uriel," she growled in warning. "Don't."

His lips twisted, but he refused to release his grasp on her face. He wouldn't let her believe he thought she was anything but glorious.

"Kata, what happened between you and the Jinn . . ."

She poked a finger into the center of his chest, her expression stubborn.

"I won't discuss it."

"Fair enough," he swiftly agreed. "Someday you will trust me enough to share your past, but for now you can keep your secrets."

"Big of you."

He ignored her sarcasm. "All I care about is the Jinn's curse. And what he might force me to do."

Her anger faltered at his blunt confession. With a frown, she lowered her gaze to his scar.

"The demon is dead." Impossible to know what she felt about the creature's violent demise. "How do you know that his curse didn't die with him?"

"Because I can still feel his power."

"That doesn't mean the spell remains active."

"It's not a risk I'm willing to take." He held her gaze, his expression somber. "Not with you."

"I don't understand."

"You're mine."

Something flared to life deep in her eyes.

Something hot and wild and shockingly primal.

Then, with an obvious surge of panic, she was swiftly trying to disguise her instinctive response.

"So you've said, but then you remembered I'm the mother of a Jinn half-breed," she accused him, her voice brittle.

He shook his head. "No, then I remembered that I couldn't risk my mate just because I desire you beyond all reason."

Chapter 8

As show-stoppers went, this one was a doozie.

She was supposed to be angry with him.

Who the hell did he think he was judging her for what had happened two centuries ago?

Did he think that she'd asked to be kidnapped and held captive by her nutcracker of a sister? Or that she'd wanted to be involved in the evil scheme to create a Jinn half-breed for the sole purpose of returning the Dark Lord to the world?

It was bad enough that a part of her would always feel guilty that the Jinn had made certain their time together hadn't been rape. Did Uriel have to dredge up the memories she wanted to keep buried far in the back of her mind?

Now, however, she was . . .

Hell, she didn't know what she was.

Flabbergasted? Gobsmacked?

Full on monty, had-to-be-losing-her-mind excited?

With a shiver, she studied the unearthly beauty of his face, wondering if this was some sort of painful joke.

"Mate?" she croaked.

His lips twisted in a humorless smile. "Does the thought horrify you because I'm a vampire?"

"I'm not horrified," she swiftly denied. "I'm shocked."

"Why?"

"Why?" She snorted. "Do you want a list?"

His velvet gaze skimmed down to the thrust of her breasts, lingering on the nipples that hardened beneath the feral heat of his inspection.

"The top three should be sufficient," he said, his voice thick.

She yanked away from his lingering touch.

How was she supposed to think of anything besides wrapping herself around him and doing lovely, wicked things when he was so close?

"We barely know each other," she finally managed to choke out.

He shrugged. "A vampire often recognizes his mate within the first hours of their meeting."

Her pulse stuttered, a perilous warmth exploding in the center of her heart.

Mate.

Oh . . . shit.

It was madness. Complete and utter madness.

So why wasn't she shrieking in outrage instead of feeling like she'd just drunk an entire keg of her father's ale?

She gave a dismissive toss of her head, even knowing she wasn't fooling Uriel.

"Well gypsies prefer a long courtship that includes a lot of bling."

"Some perhaps." He reached to brazenly cup one breast in his hand, a smile curving his lips as she gasped in pleasure. "Others enjoy being swept off their feet."

She shivered, heat blazing through her. "Arrogant."

His eyes smoldered with a ready passion. "Lie to yourself if you want, but you can't hide the truth from a vampire."

She couldn't lie to herself either as it turned out. Not when sensual anticipation flowed through her veins like warm honey. Or when she was instinctively moving back toward him to press against the welcomed strength of his male form.

Not that she was ready to accept his shocking claim that she was his mate.

Was she?

"Fine, we're sexually compatible," she conceded.

"More than compatible," he growled, his erection pressed against her lower stomach. "Combustible."

Combustible. Yeah. That just about summed it up, Kata acknowledged, vividly aware of the silken slide of the cool water across her highly sensitized skin and the golden spill of sunlight that only intensified the heat blazing through her.

She craved this man with an insatiable hunger that she sensed would plague her for the rest of her life.

Regardless of how long or short that life might be.

"What about the fact that you hate anything and everyone connected with Jinns and I hate vampires?"

His arm circled her waist, squeezing her so tight not even the water could come between their entwined bodies.

"They say love conquers all," he growled.

Kata wrinkled her nose, not nearly so confident.

She loved her sister only to discover that she'd become the enemy.

She loved her daughter, only to have to sacrifice everything to keep her safe.

Love was . . . dangerous and painful and messy.

Now, however, didn't seem the time to argue the point.

"I'm human again," she instead pointed out. "Within a few years I'll be old and gray."

The dark eyes flashed with an intimidating ferocity. "Never."

She frowned. "I won't be turned."

He shrugged, undeterred by her refusal to be made into a vampire. Understandable. Once a vampire was created they lost all memory of their previous life. She would no longer be Kata, but a new creature that was as likely to try and rip out his throat as to be his mate.

"The fey can brew potions to keep you young."

She shifted her gaze to the delicate wildflowers that lined the bank of the stream.

His soft words were reminding her of when she'd been young and the world had been filled with possibilities. Including the hopes of a loving husband and a small tribe of children.

Blessed mother. She'd gone through the misery of having those dreams crushed once.

Was she willing to put herself in the position of having them destroyed again?

"This is a ridiculous conversation," she muttered, more in an effort to convince herself than him.

Uriel stiffened, then with a low groan he lowered his head, pressing his lips to the pulse beating at the base of her throat.

"More than that," he rasped, "it's futile."

"Futile?"

Slowly he pulled back, his expression somber. "If the Jinn's curse is still active then I'm a walking time bomb. I won't put you at risk."

Contrarily, she was offended by his attempt at self-sacrifice.

Did he think he could claim she was his mate in one breath and then toss her aside in the next?

"Shouldn't that be my decision?"

"No."

"That's it? Just no?"

"That's it."

She scowled, glimpsing the ruthless warrior who first came searching for her.

"Look, you stubborn vampire, if I decide you're going to be my . . ." She struggled to form the word. "Mate, then that's what you'll be." She leaned forward to nip his chin. "Got it?"

He shuddered, his fangs erupting as his hands skimmed down her back to cup her ass.

"And you call me stubborn?" he muttered.

Her mind fogged with a craving to wrap her legs around his waist and forget everything but the fierce need to ravish this beautiful vampire.

But first she had to get something straight.

"It's been almost four hundred years since I've been able to make my own decisions," she reminded him. "You're not going to take that away from me."

He was wise enough not to laugh at her empty words. Okay, she was trapped in the underworld with no plan of how to escape, but still she needed to feel some control over her life.

Stupid?

Of course.

But weirdly necessary.

"No, I would never take away your freedom," he softly agreed, "but neither will I allow you to be hurt." He suddenly scooped her off her feet and headed toward the shallow waters. "Not if I can protect you."

Uriel intended to protest against his arrogant assumption that she needed his protection, but all thought evaporated as Uriel sank onto the mossy bank, settling Kata on his lap so her back was pressed against his chest and her legs fell on each side of his powerful thighs.

"Uriel," she breathed, feeling oddly vulnerable as he buried his face in the curve of her neck and his hands began a slow, delectable exploration of her exposed body. "What are you doing?"

He cupped a full breast with one hand while allowing the other to blaze a sizzling path down the damp skin of her stomach. "Seizing the moment."

A groan was wrenched from her throat, her head dropping back to his shoulder as his fingers stroked boldly through her eager clit.

"It feels like you're seizing more than the moment," she husked in approval.

He teased at the hard peak of her nipple even as he slid one finger into the damp channel between her legs. She hissed in pleasure, her arms lifting over her head to wrap around his neck.

"Who knows how long this illusion will last?" he said against her shoulder, his fangs lightly scraping the tender skin, although he was careful not to draw blood. "We should enjoy the solitude while we have it."

Kata didn't intend to argue. Her eyes slid closed as she concentrated on the sensation of his finger penetrating her with a slow thrust. It felt so good. So . . . she groaned, already sensing the looming climax.

"I suppose you have a point," she moaned, turning her head to press her face into his thick curls.

She breathed deeply of his cool, masculine scent, her body bowing with a coiled tension as he caught the tip of her breast between his finger and thumb.

"You will soon discover I'm always right," he assured her.

"Oh yeah?"

"Oh yeah."

As if to emphasize the truth of his words, Uriel grasped her by the waist and with one smooth motion he had her poised above his erection. Kata made a small sound of pleading as he lowered her onto his hardness, her entire body shuddering with satisfaction as he filled her.

"Christ, you're exquisite," he breathed, lifting his hips

until he was buried so deep inside her that Kata would swear they were now one.

"I bet you say that to all the women," she muttered, shaken by the intensity of the sensations charging through her.

She could deal with lust. Even if it was titanic, oh-God-nothing-will-ever-be-as-good-again, lust.

But the tender rush of emotion that flooded through her was far more potent than mere lust.

It was the sort of feeling that made females sacrifice everything to hold onto.

"There are no other women, Kata," he groaned, pumping into her with a slow, magical pace. "Just you."

"Uriel . . ."

"Ssh," he halted her protest, kissing a path of destruction up the side of her neck. "Just let me love you."

Kata shoved aside the warning voice in the back of her mind.

What did it matter?

More than likely they would never get out of the underworld alive.

Why not do as Uriel suggested and simply seize the moment?

"Yes," she breathed, forgetting everything but the explosive pleasure.

Chapter 9

Kata wasn't sure how much time passed.

Actually, trapped in the illusion it was almost as if time had stopped completely.

The sun remained firmly fixed in its current position in the sky. There were no drifting clouds, no changing shadow. And even the wildlife scampered from one tree to the other in a pattern that was growingly predictable.

She did know that she and Uriel had made love three more times. That was deliciously easy to keep track of. But it could have been a few hours or an entire day since Yannah had trapped them in the strange world.

No doubt she should be bothered by the thought.

It seemed like it should be important.

At the moment, however, she was floating on a wave of bliss as she sprawled in a bed of wildflowers, held tightly in Uriel's arms.

A smile curved her lips.

As a lover Uriel was spectacular.

He could be raw, and fiercely driven in his passion. Or he could be slow, and gentle, and so breathtakingly patient that she had begged, pleaded, and at last, threatened until he gave her release.

As a man . . .

Her smile twisted.

She was beginning to accept he was equally spectacular.

Shifting at his side, she tilted back her head to study the vampire next to her.

Her heart lurched at his sheer beauty.

The elegant sweep of his brow and proud curve of his nose. The high cheekbones and sensuously carved lips. The dark, soulful eyes that held a wary pain that spoke of the years he'd been forced to remain isolated, even when he was surrounded by his clan.

He didn't need to tell her that he was as protective of his brothers as he was of her. He would always keep those he cared about at a distance, always fearful he might be compelled to harm them.

In many ways he'd suffered as much as she had over the past two centuries.

Perhaps that's why they felt so intensely drawn together.

Well, that and the brilliant, mind-blowing sex, she wryly added.

"I think I truly must have gone to heaven," she murmured, her hand lifting to drift over his exquisite face. "Complete with my own beautiful angel."

He summoned a pretend scowl at her soft words. "Bloody hell, not you too."

"Excuse me?"

"There's nothing angelic about me."

She slowly smiled, remembering a few of his more inventive moves.

"That's true." She ran her hand over the smooth skin of his stomach, relishing the ripple of muscles beneath her fingers. Mmmm, pure male perfection. "I can testify that you're wicked through and through."

A smug glint entered his eyes. "Thank you."

"I assume your resemblance to an angel is a touchy subject with you?"

"I'm a warrior."

"And warriors can't be pretty?"

His hand lifted to tangle in her curls, his smile revealing his massive fangs.

"Careful, Kata, you tease me at your peril."

Her heart forgot to beat as she became lost in the velvet darkness of his eyes.

"Tell me about your life."

His brows lifted at her abrupt question. "Do you want to hear of my heroic feats or my astonishing skill with the females?"

She rolled her eyes. Like she didn't know firsthand that he was a lethal predator and an even more lethal lover.

"I want to hear about you. The real you."

He stilled, as if no one had ever been interested in anything beyond his more obvious skills.

"I am second in command to Victor, the clan chief of Great Britain," he said.

She smiled at the hint of pride he couldn't hide. And why shouldn't he be proud? Before her captivity, Kata had taken pleasure in the fact she and Marika were considered the finest healers in all of Europe.

"A big shot, eh? No wonder you're so arrogant."

"Authoritative," he corrected her.

"Bossy."

"Only when necessary."

"Which is always," she wryly pointed out. "What else?"

He shrugged. "There is nothing else."

"I don't believe you." She reached to stroke her fingers

down the chiseled line of his jaw. "You can't spend all your time killing things."

"No. I teach the younger vampires how to kill things."

She heaved a sigh. "You don't have any hobbies? No secret dreams?"

His expression became guarded, his years of keeping others at a distance painfully obvious.

"What about you?" he said as he smoothly deflected her probing. "What are your secret dreams?"

"To be a mother to Laylah," she confessed without hesitation. "Although I suppose it's two centuries too late to claim such a role. I'm not sure she'll ever understand why I had to leave her."

"You had no choice."

"That doesn't mean she'll be prepared to forgive me."

"She'll forgive you."

She met his steady gaze, desperately needing to believe him.

When she'd handed her baby over to the witch who had promised to keep her hidden, Kata had felt as if someone was ripping out her heart.

Only the absolute belief that it was the only way to keep Laylah safe had given her the courage.

Still, the fear that Laylah would never understand why she'd made the choice to give away her baby had gnawed at her for endless years.

"How can you be so certain?"

His hand cupped her cheek, his thumb brushing her lower lip. "Because when she traveled to London she risked everything to come in search of you."

A tentative hope warmed Kata's heart. "Did she?"

"Nothing could stop her." Uriel smiled wryly. "And, of course, she refused to leave London until Victor had sworn he would stop at nothing to rescue you."

She smiled, shifting to brush her lips across his mouth as she savored his words of comfort, allowing them to heal a portion of her heavy guilt.

"Thank you," she murmured softly.

A peaceful silence settled between them before Uriel lifted himself on his elbow to study her with a brooding gaze.

"Music," he said abruptly.

She blinked. Okay. That seemed a little random.

"What?"

"I love music and when I have the opportunity to travel to my private lair in Wales I spend my time learning to play a new instrument." He shrugged, obviously uncomfortable. "I have nearly mastered them all."

Kata hid a smile, oddly charmed by the embarrassment that he couldn't entirely disguise.

"Why was that so difficult to share?"

"Because my brothers would be merciless," he muttered. "Victor would no doubt insist I walk around strumming a damned harp."

Her laughter filled the glade at the image of Uriel with a harp in his hands. His resemblance to a celestial being would be unmistakable.

"Hmmm. I see your point," she admitted.

"Of course, if you were to join me in my lair I would be happy to . . ."

He bit off his words as an unmistakable chill pierced the air.

"Uriel," Kata breathed, scrambling to her feet to tug on her forgotten gown.

"I sense it." He was swiftly at her side, pulling on his jeans and T-shirt before snatching up the long, extremely sharp sword. "Vampire."

There was another burst of cold, and Kata hissed in horrified disbelief.

No, it couldn't be.

Not even her shitty luck could be this bad.

But even as she tried to convince herself it had to be some ghastly mistake, the familiar sense of doom settled in her heart.

"Marika."

"Impossible."

She clenched her hands, a combination of hatred and fear blasting through her.

"It's not a stench I would forget," she hissed. "Not ever."

Uriel muttered beneath his breath, his gaze surveying their surroundings with the intensity of a trained warrior.

"Then she must be part of the illusion."

Kata shivered with disgust. "No, not an illusion. A nightmare."

"Kata." The sound of her sister's taunting voice drifted through the air.

Uriel leaned down to steal a brief kiss, his face a tight mask of determination.

"Keep her distracted."

"What?" Without answering, he was flowing toward the trees. In less than the beat of her heart he'd disappeared among the shadows. "Damn."

Alone and feeling like the mouse about to be cornered by a cat with vicious fangs and a nasty attitude, Kata forced herself not to bolt as Marika stepped from behind a large rock.

Uriel told her to distract the bitch, and by God, that's what she would do.

"Ah, there you are, sister dearest," Marika purred, a taunting smile curving her lips. "Did you miss me?"

Kata swallowed the bile that rose in her throat.

Not surprisingly seeing Marika was like looking in a mirror.

Same dark hair and eyes, same pale skin and curvaceous body that was currently covered in one of the satin designer gowns that Marika adored.

What was surprising, however, was that she looked as well-groomed and sophisticated as if she'd just stepped off the pages of *Vogue*.

Dammit.

She was supposed to be dead and even now suffering some grim torture in the bowels of the underworld.

Was there no justice in the universe?

"You really should learn how to stay in your grave, Marika," she gritted.

Marika gave a toss of her dark curls, prowling forward with an expression of blatant anticipation.

It was a look that always came before the pain.

Hours and hours and hours of pain.

"What's the fun in that?" she demanded.

"The fun is that I would be rid of your miserable existence forever. The mere thought makes me giddy with joy."

Marika halted mere inches from her, her frigid power wrapping around Kata like chains of ice.

"What happened to my sweet Kata who prayed every night that her sister would be returned to her?"

Kata clenched her teeth. She wouldn't flinch, she wouldn't flinch, she wouldn't flinch . . .

Her chin tilted, her expression defiant. "She realized that her sister had become a monster."

"A monster?" The dark eyes narrowed in suspicion as Marika leaned forward, sniffing the air around Kata. "So says the woman who reeks of her vampire lover. Where is he?"

Kata swore. So much for being a distraction.

"You know, Marika," she said, desperate to keep the demented woman's attention locked on her. "It took me awhile, but I realize now that becoming a vampire wasn't what made you evil."

"No?"

"No, it's your lack of anything resembling a heart."

Marika's shrill laughter sent a chill down Kata's spine. Dear goddess, it was bad enough that the woman walked around with her sister's face without adding a creepy cackle.

"Kata, if I didn't have a heart would I have made sure that we would be kept together even after death?" Marika pressed a hand to her unbeating heart. "What could be more sentimental?"

"That was selfishness, not sentimentality. You were only trying to protect your own skin by forcing Sergei to bind us together."

"True. Now, however, I have a much more basic reason for appreciating the spell."

"And what's that?"

With a pout, Marika stretched out a hand to run a crimson nail down Kata's cheek, leaving a trail of blood in its wake.

"I'm feeling a little peevish at my unfortunate death. I was, after all, destined to rule the world," she complained. "Let's hope a few centuries of punishing you will help ease my disappointment."

Her churning fear was briefly forgotten as a flare of pure relief raced through her. She didn't know what the hell was going on, but at least Marika believed she had died.

It gave her hope.

"Tell me, Marika, was it Laylah who struck the killing blow?" she asked sweetly.

The dark eyes flashed with fury. "The bitch got lucky."

Kata smiled. "Do you believe in karma?"

"I believe that the sins of the daughter must be paid by the mother." Marika lifted her hand, her fingers curled to slice her claws through Kata's tender flesh. "Starting now."

Braced for the blow, Kata was unprepared for the flash of movement from directly behind Marika. Thankfully, her crazy-ass sister was equally oblivious and, even as she swung her hand toward Kata's face, Uriel was slamming into her with bone-breaking force.

Kata stumbled to the side, struggling to keep her balance as the two predators hit the ground with enough force to split the earth. Uriel managed to land on top, his fist slamming into the back of his opponent's head with a sickening crunch.

It wasn't a fatal blow, but it should have been enough to put the female vamp out of commission for a few minutes. Instead Marika turned with a fluid motion and sank her fang's into Uriel's throat.

Kata's heart faltered as Uriel grabbed Marika's hair and ripped her from his flesh, his blood gushing from the wound. His roar of pain echoed through the glade, sending animals fleeing in terror.

Barely aware she was moving, Kata had snatched up a large branch that was nearly hidden in the grass and was charging forward. At the same time, Uriel was lifting his sword and with one sharp motion he was plunging it into Marika's heart.

Kata halted, shuddering at the sight of her sister sprawled on the ground with a massive blade sticking out of her chest.

She hated the miserable, sadistic creature with every fiber of her being, but it was still disturbing to see the image of her sister pinned to the ground like something from a horror film.

Waiting for Uriel to finish the kill by cutting out the vampire's heart, Kata sucked in a shocked breath as Marika grasped the blade with both hands and yanked it from her flesh.

It shouldn't have been possible. Such a wound should have paralyzed her at the very least. Not even the most powerful demon could shrug off a huge, gaping hole in the center of their chest.

Caught off guard, Uriel was barely able to yank his sword from her grasp and hastily rise to his feet before she was launching her attack.

He swung the sword, cursing as Marika dodged the blow and struck him across the face. She wasn't as strong as Uriel, but she still packed a hell of a punch. And worse, it seemed as if nothing could hurt her.

Uriel's head snapped back, and Marika was once again at his throat, almost as if she intended to gnaw through his neck.

And maybe she did.

Evil bitch.

Tightening her grip on the branch, Kata grimly marched forward. She wasn't stupid enough to believe she could hurt a vampire with a stick, not unless she managed to stab it through the cold-blooded leech's heart, and with her luck she was more likely to stick it through her own. But she was feeling like the last gazelle at the watering hole and the weight of the branch in her hand gave the impression she wasn't completely helpless.

Stupid, but necessary if she was going to be able to concentrate enough to conjure a curse.

Fiercely she blocked out Uriel's terrible wounds and his losing effort to hold off Marika, who was not only weirdly immune to her injuries, but clearly in the throes of a crazed bout of bloodlust.

Instead she turned her mind inward, focusing on the small spark of power that smoldered in her soul.

It was the same power that she used to heal, but instead of allowing the energy to flow from her in a soothing, fixed stream, she instead twisted it with the dark impulses that lurked in every creature, and held it in a tight knot until she unleashed it with a savage burst.

Muttering the words her grandmother had taught her as they had sat beside the campfire, Kata pointed her hand in Marika's direction, releasing her power in a torrential blast.

The air sizzled with the force of her curse and for a moment Marika faltered, her crazed gaze shifting toward Kata with an expression of blatant panic.

"That's right, you vicious whore, die," Kata hissed.

There was a gurgling sound as a disgusting foam began to spew from Marika's mouth. The curse was a particularly nasty one that Kata had never used before. Then, obviously the sort of vampire who was swift to take advantage, Uriel rushed forward to swing his sword directly at her exposed neck.

That should have been the end of it.

Shut-the-door-turn-out-the-lights-fat-lady-singing end.

Marika, however, was already shrugging off the potent curse and with a shocking display of power she was springing in the air and vaulting over the swinging blade.

Holy . . . shit.

Kata gripped her stick, her mouth dry and her heart lodged somewhere near her tonsils.

Trapped in a sense of nightmarish disbelief, Kata watched Uriel deliberately place himself between her and the gruesome freak that had once been her sister.

"Kata, find a way out of here," he growled.

"No." She shook her head. "I won't leave you."

With a low growl, Uriel turned to stab her with a savage glare, his T-shirt drenched in blood and throat still mangled from Marika's attacks.

"Then we both die."

She bit her bottom lip. She wasn't stupid. She knew their only hope of survival was to somehow find the means to escape from the bubble of illusion.

But every fiber of her being rebelled at the thought of abandoning Uriel.

"What the hell is she?" she muttered.

"Invincible," Marika taunted, her spooky laugh once again filling the glade. "Don't be wandering too far, sister dearest. Once I've disposed of your lover we can start enjoying our special time together."

Uriel stroked a hand down her cheek, his expression pleading.

"Go."

Briefly pressing his fingers to her cheek, Kata abruptly turned and charged across the glade.

She heard her sister's screech of fury and the answering roar of Uriel, but she kept her gaze grimly trained on the low hills that swelled before her. Without her curses she had nothing that could help Uriel defeat Marika.

All she could do now was pray for a miracle . . .

No, that wasn't all she could do, she belatedly realized.

Kata slowed as she reached the foot of one low hill.

Why was she running as if she could find some magical doorway?

There was only one way out of the illusion.

Stepping behind a large rock, Kata shoved her hair out of her face with a shaking hand and sucked in a ragged breath.

"Yannah," she called, her voice echoing eerily through the still air. "Yannah?"

Distantly she could hear the sounds of Uriel's battle with Marika and closer at hand the rustle of a squirrel scurrying through the undergrowth, but from the demon who'd trapped them here . . . nothing. Nada. Jack squat.

"Yannah, dammit, where are you?"

There was no warning.

One minute she was alone, frustration boiling through her like acid, and the next Yannah was standing before her.

"No need to screech, Kata," the tiny demon complained, smoothing her hands down her pristine white gown. "There's nothing wrong with my hearing."

Kata clenched her hands together. It was that or wringing Yannah's slender neck.

"Really?" she said between gritted teeth. "Then you knew we were being attacked by Marika and you just decided to leave us trapped here?"

"Don't be silly, I was busy."

Kata stabbed a finger toward the battle that continued on the far side of the glade. "Well, I've been a little busy myself."

"Yes, you have." A sly smile curved Yannah's lips. "No need to thank me for giving you some privacy with your pretty leech."

"You expect me to thank you?" Kata's eyes widened with furious disbelief. Oh yes, she was going to throttle the little demon. But not until she'd gotten them out of this mess. "You locked us in here with my demented sister who has become a vampire zombie."

Yannah's brows pleated, as if she were giving serious thought to Kata's accusation.

"Oh, I don't think she's technically a zombie."

Kata blinked. "Are you kidding me?"

"I never kid about zombies."

Sucking in a deep breath, Kata counted to ten. "Then *technically* what is she?"

Yannah lifted her hands in a vague motion. "I'm not really sure."

Great. Just freaking perfect.

"Is she a part of the illusion?"

"No."

"But she's dead?" Kata pressed. "I mean . . . dead dead?"

"Yes."

Kata frowned, sensing that Yannah was hiding something from her.

"You don't sound particularly confident."

"She shouldn't be here."

"No shit," Kata snapped. "She's supposed to be frying in the pits of hell, but obviously she's not." Turning her head, Kata's heart stopped as she watched Uriel fending off the feral vampire, his powerful body covered in blood and his elegant movements becoming sluggish. "Yannah, you have to get us out of here before she kills us all."

Chapter 10

Unlike many of his brothers, Uriel had never been arrogant enough to assume he was invincible.

Not after his painful encounter with the Jinn.

He understood that vampires might be at the top of the food chain, but there was always the danger of meeting a bigger, badder opponent who could kick his ass.

So even with his secret boost of power from the Jinn, he devoted hours to perfecting his fighting skills.

Which was the only reason he wasn't already a pile of ash.

Still, it was taking every trick he'd learned over the centuries just to keep Marika from ripping out his throat. And while his strength was rapidly draining from his numerous wounds, his adversary was as fresh as a fucking daisy.

He could only hope that Kata had managed to find a means to escape.

Almost as if the mere thought of her had created her from thin air, he heard the sound of her voice calling from across the glade.

"Uriel." She waved her arms over her head to gain his attention. "This way."

He swallowed a sigh of frustration.

Dammit.

Couldn't one thing go right?

He turned, accepting that even if Kata had found a way out of the illusion she wouldn't leave without him.

"Oh no, you don't." Perhaps sensing that her prey might slip from her grasp, Marika flowed to stand between him and the beckoning Kata. "We're not done playing."

Uriel deliberately allowed his sword to dip in a weariness he didn't have to pretend, his other hand slipping into the pocket of his jeans. He had one shot at disabling the female long enough to reach Kata. It all depended on catching her off guard.

Marika's dark eyes flared with smug triumph.

She was confident of her impending victory.

Hell, why not?

If Uriel was a betting man he'd put his money on the insane vampire who couldn't die.

A humorless smile twisted his lips as he deliberately stumbled over a patch of grass, seeming to lose his balance.

That was all the encouragement Marika needed.

With a cry of anticipation she launched herself forward, her hands curled into lethal claws and her fangs fully exposed.

Uriel forced himself to wait until the last possible second, then yanking his hand out of his pocket he tossed the wooden box directly at her face. The death spell activated with a tiny pop, the magic halting her in her tracks.

He didn't hesitate. With a fierce roar, he lifted his sword and swung it in a tremendous arch.

The blade whistled through air, offering a belated warning, but Marika was too lost in her bloodlust to notice. With lips pulled into a snarl and her icy power pulsing through the glade she launched herself at Uriel, managing to rake her claws down the side of his face even as his sword connected with her neck.

"Wrong, bitch," he hissed. "Game over."

Her dark eyes widened in shock as she at last realized the danger, trying to move to the side as the sword slid smoothly through her neck. It was all too little, too late and despite her frantic efforts she was helpless to halt the inevitable.

Uriel put his entire body behind the blow, slicing the sword cleanly through the vampire's neck. He watched as Marika's head flew through the air, landing on a patch of wildflowers, her eyes still wide with shock and her body dropping with a lifeless thud at his feet.

Not that he was deceived.

Not this time.

He grimaced at the lack of blood flowing from her lethal wound and the twitch of her limbs. She should be turning to dust, not laying there flopping like a fish out of water.

He didn't know what the hell Marika had been transformed into, but he was fairly certain that she wasn't going to allow a little thing like the lack of a head to stop her.

Almost as if to prove his point, a slender hand jerked outward, the fingers barely missing his foot as they dug into the ground and began to tug the body toward the missing head.

For a second, he was transfixed, unable to accept what he was seeing. Then, shaking off the paralyzing horror, Uriel turned to race toward the waiting Kata.

Flowing with a speed only a vampire could match, he was swiftly at Kata's side, his senses on full alert at the familiar scent of demon.

"Yannah was here," he said in flat tones.

Kata nodded, her face pale with weariness and her lovely eyes dark with fear. Still, there was a gritty courage in her expression and a determination in the angle of her shoulders that filled Uriel's heart with pride.

This woman was a survivor.

"Yes." She pointed toward the shimmering mist that swirled in midair. "She created a gateway."

Uriel narrowed his gaze. "Where is she?"

"She disappeared."

"Again?"

Kata shrugged. "Are you surprised?"

Uriel muttered a curse.

He'd spent the past two centuries making sure he was in command of every situation. After his encounter with the Jinn he'd been obsessive in his need for control.

Now he was blundering from one miserable, insane situation to another. And in the center of the mess was Yannah, popping in and out like a damned cuckoo bird.

"I'm tired of her jerking us around," he muttered. "What does she want?"

"I don't know and I don't care." Kata glanced over his shoulder, shuddering at the sight of the headless monster that had once been her sister. "I would rather burn in the pits of hell than give Marika the satisfaction of killing me."

"Damn." Reaching out, he grasped her hand, sourly confident they were fleeing the frying pan directly into the fire. "Don't let go."

Together they stepped through the mist, the sensation of electricity dancing over his skin making Uriel shiver. Dammit, he hated magic. Then, they were shrouded in blackness, falling forward to tumble through a sense of emptiness.

Uriel struggled vainly to pull Kata into his arms, already knowing they were going to have a hard landing. The sudden entrance into the gateway on the other side, however, ripped her away from him and before he could react, they were being slammed onto a hard floor with enough force to rattle his fangs.

With a groan, he lifted his head to discover the latest disaster awaiting them, not at all surprised by the seemingly endless expanse of black, volcanic rock that ran between rivers of fire or the poisonous clouds that floated in the distance. Overhead the sky was a sickly shade of crimson with bolts of lightning that streaked toward the ground without warning.

The only surprise would be if they weren't back in the underworld.

Shifting his gaze, he swore at the sight of Kata lying sprawled a few feet away, her tiny body perilously near the liquid fire.

"Kata."

He surged to his feet, keeping his sword in one hand while he moved to her side.

"I'm okay." With an obvious effort, Kata slowly stood, grimacing at the hellish vista spread before her. "Or at least as okay as I'm going to get."

Uriel desperately wanted to pull her into his arms and offer her comfort, but a swift glance over his shoulder revealed that the gateway was still open.

As soon as Marika healed she was going to be on their trail.

"We need to move."

Despite her obvious weariness, she gave a swift nod. "Do you sense Yannah?"

"That way." He grudgingly tilted his head toward a path leading through the black rock.

Kata didn't hesitate. With that impulsiveness he was beginning to learn was a part of her passionate nature, she was headed through the red-tinted shadows. Uriel hastily reached out to grasp her arm and spin her back to face him.

"Wait," he commanded.

She met his frown with a heavy sigh. "I know you don't trust her."

Trust her?

Not even if she grew wings and put on a halo.

"Do you?" he growled.

Kata bit her bottom lip, visibly considering her words. "She makes me nuts," she said slowly, "but I think she's our only hope of getting out of here."

"And that says it all, doesn't it?" Uriel gave a shake of his head, conceding defeat. Kata was right. What were the odds of running into another demon who not only had the ability to open gateways, but was willing to help them? "Let's go."

In silence they moved along the pathway, the air growing progressively more oppressive and the lightning increasing in intensity.

Uriel tested the air. He could vaguely sense Yannah in the distance, but closer at hand there was . . .

Danger.

He didn't recognize the strange scent, but it was making his instincts bristle.

Reaching behind his back, he slid his dagger from the sheath attached to his jeans.

"Here," he said, pressing the finely crafted weapon into Kata's hand.

She frowned, awkwardly clutching the leather-bound hilt. "I don't know how to use it."

"Stick the pointy end into something."

Her eyes narrowed. "Don't tempt me."

They both froze as the sound of Marika's maniacal laugh abruptly echoed through the stagnant air.

"Bloody hell," Uriel breathed.

"For god's sake, you cut off her head," Kata rasped. "What else can we do?"

"Run," he said without apology.

Any good warrior understood the importance of a strategic retreat.

Grabbing her arm, he urged her down the path, his sword held at the ready. He knew what was coming from behind, but there was no guarantee there wasn't something worse waiting for them ahead.

Hell, it was almost a given.

It didn't take long to fulfill his pessimistic theory.

They had just reached a crossroad in the path when the ground beneath their feet split and a nightmarish creature surged out of the opening.

Kata screamed, stumbling backward. Uriel didn't blame her. He wanted to do a little screaming of his own.

Even by demon standards the thing was gruesome.

Shaped like a worm, it rose up to nearly eight feet in height. He couldn't see any eyes, but its mouth gaped open to reveal several rows of razor sharp teeth. There were large barbs on top of its head and its skin was a pasty white and covered with a thick slime that dripped onto the stone with an audible hiss. Acid.

Like the nasty thing needed added ammunition.

Gripping his sword in both hands, he stepped between the beast and Kata.

"I'll keep it distracted. Follow the other path . . ."

"No," she sharply cut off his words.

He growled in frustration. "If you don't go now we'll be fighting Marika along with this . . ." He had no idea what the thing was. "Oversized worm."

She grabbed his arm. "I'm not leaving you again."

"Dammit, Kata."

"Look, you may not want me as a mate, but as far as I'm concerned you're stuck with me." The words rang through the air with the clarity of a bell. "Forever."

Uriel yanked his head around, unnerved by the serene expression on her beautiful face. As if she hadn't just proclaimed herself as his mate.

Meeting her steady gaze, his heart squeezed with a painful need he could no longer deny.

Oh . . . Christ.

What did it matter how many times he had warned himself it was too dangerous to have Kata as his mate? That he had to keep her at a distance?

The simple truth was that he was irrevocably bound to this woman whether they ever completed the mating ceremony or not.

"You're mine," he softly declared.

"Yes."

His hand lifted to cup her cheek. "Which is why I couldn't bear it if anything happened to you."

"Then don't send me away," she said, her pleading gaze a weapon of mass destruction on his heart. "Who will protect me if you're not beside me?"

"Kata . . ." he groaned.

Sensing that victory was in her grasp, Kata turned her head to press her lips to the center of his palm.

"We've both been alone too long. Together we can face anything."

He was whipped, he wryly acknowledged.

A pleading glance, a soft word and he was a lost cause.

But, he didn't care.

If a miracle occurred and they managed to get out of the underworld, he would happily devote himself to Kata's pleasure.

It was surely the reason he was created?

"I can't say no to you, even when I know I should," he admitted.

She flashed a smile. "That's promising."

"Only if we get out of here alive."

"Good point."

They turned to the worm-like creature who continued to snake its way out of the rock. Uriel grimaced. No doubt the moment it was free all hell was going to break loose, but how did he kill the damned thing?

In the end, the monster took the decision out of his hands.

With a high-pitched cry, the worm swooped downward, aiming his massive teeth directly at Uriel's head. Uriel held his ground, stabbing the sword upward to pierce the tender skin of the worm's mouth.

The thing screamed and jerked backward, nearly snatching the sword out of Uriel's grip. At the same time a shower of acid sprayed over his skin, burning deep into his flesh.

Bastard.

Gritting his teeth against the pain, Uriel shifted to make certain he stood between the creature and Kata, swinging his sword before the beast could repeat his attack.

The blade slid through glutinous hide with sickening ease. Like a knife through pudding. Worse, a disgusting flood of acid belched from the wound, forcing Uriel to back away.

Dammit. He needed to be rid of the thing before Marika could catch up with them.

He was busy debating whether he could lure the creature toward the nearby river of fire when Kata moved to stand at his side, her brow furrowed with concentration and her arm lifted to point the dagger at the worm's head.

Uriel swore. Did she think that tiny dagger was going to cause any damage?

About to tug her back behind him, Uriel was halted as she muttered a harsh word and her curse blasted through the air, hitting the worm with shocking force.

There was a spine chilling cry from the worm, then it suddenly froze, as if it had been incased in ice.

"You might want to step back," Kata warned, easing away from the towering beast.

Uriel was swift to obey her warning.

He didn't understand magic, but he was smart enough to stay out of its path.

For long minutes nothing happened. Shifting uneasily, he was beginning to assume that the show was over when there was an odd sound of a crack echoing through the air. Was the surrounding rock being shattered?

But it wasn't the rock.

No. Even as Uriel took another step backward the towering worm began to crumble, the once spongy flesh now as brittle as chalk.

Flakes of the creature floated through the air as the heavy body crashed onto the path, causing a mini earthquake. Uriel's attention, however, had shifted to Kata who was clearly on the brink of collapse.

Angling his sword so the blade was pointed backward, Uriel scooped her into his arms and with one mighty shove was leaping over the decaying body of the worm.

"Damn," he muttered, his heart clenching with fear that she'd perilously drained herself as he gazed down at her too-pale face. "You're a dangerous woman."

A weary smile touched her lips. "Don't you forget it."

"Never," he swore, tucking her tightly against his chest as he followed Yannah's fading scent down the pathway.

Bloody hell, he had to get her out of here.

So far shit-ass luck had kept them alive.

It was bound to run out eventually.

On perfect cue a wave of Marika's frigid power stirred the toxic air.

"Oh Kata, I smell you," she cooed.

Crazy bitch.

In his arms Kata giggled, her eyes half-closed as if she weren't entirely with the program.

"Fee, fie, fo, fum," she sang.

"Stay with me, Kata," he muttered, charging down the center of the pathway with reckless speed.

On each side of him the rivers of fire offered liquid death and behind him was a psychotic vampire he couldn't destroy. If there was another danger looming in front of them then they were screwed.

"I'm never going to leave you," she softly murmured.

"No." He bent his head to press his lips to the top of her head, accepting that whatever the future held, Kata would always be in his heart. "You're never going to leave me."

Running through the crimson shadows, Uriel could feel his strength waning. Since leaving Victor's lair he'd spent a large chunk of time in one battle after another. He needed to rest.

And more importantly he needed to feed.

A damned shame he wasn't going to get either of those things any time soon.

He kept up his punishing pace until it became obvious that he wasn't going to outrun Marika and that a magical door wasn't going to open to lead them to safety.

Soon he would be too weak to offer Kata any protection.

It was obviously now or never.

Bending downward, he gently settled Kata on the ground, arranging her so as to lean her back against a rock that jutted from the pathway.

She frowned, clutching at his arm in confusion. "Uriel?"

"I love you," he husked, brushing a tender kiss over her lips.

"Such a smart vampire."

"It might take me awhile, but you'll discover I'm trainable."

Her wicked smile pierced his heart. "Which is why I adore you."

With a groan, he forced himself to straighten. Then turning, he moved down the path to block the approaching vampire.

Unable to pass, Marika was forced to come to a halt directly before him, a mocking smile curving her lips.

"Get out of my way and I might let you live long enough to pleasure me," she drawled.

Uriel didn't bother to hide his shudder as his gaze skimmed her from head to toe.

Christ, she was once again perfect.

Even her gown was spotless.

As if she'd never had her head chopped off her body.

It was creepy as hell.

"I'd rather die, you nasty freak," he rasped with an unmistakable sincerity.

Marika hissed, exposing her fangs in female fury. "That can be arranged."

With one fluid motion, Uriel had his sword pointed toward the bitch and was braced for yet another skirmish.

One he couldn't win.

He grimly dismissed the voice of doom.

If he was going out, he was going out fighting.

Dammit.

Preparing to attack, Marika stroked her tongue down the length of her fang.

"So pretty, it's a shame you won't be a good boy for me," she drawled. "Still, there's always Kata to keep me entertained."

Uriel didn't have the opportunity to answer her taunt.

Even as he lifted his sword there was an odd sensation in the small space between them. As if the air pressure had suddenly changed.

Then, with a dramatic motion, the very fabric of the world was ripped open and a man stepped onto the path.

No, not a man, Uriel silently corrected himself, an icy dread forming in the pit of his stomach at the sight of the delicately carved features, the thick mane of golden blond hair, and the luminous lavender eyes.

The Jinn might pass as human, but the cruelty that was etched on the pretty face proved he was very much a monster.

Ignoring Uriel, the demon reached to grab Marika by the throat and lifted her off the ground.

"You need not worry about entertainment, leech," his voice filled the air with a power that nearly drove Uriel to his knees. "I intend to keep you fully occupied."

"You." Marika's eyes widened in horror. The Jinn laughed and Marika tilted back her head with a scream. "No!"

Chapter 11

Uriel's hand lifted to press against the scar on his chest, the dull throb becoming a jagged pain that radiated through his entire body.

He recognized the bastard, of course.

The memory of their encounter under the docks of London was seared into the very fiber of his being.

But of all the strange, bizarre, or downright dangerous creatures that Uriel might have expected to make a magical appearance, the Jinn was at the very bottom of his list.

Instinctively his hand reached into the pocket of his jeans, only to curse when he recalled he'd wasted the death spell on his futile attempt to escape from Marika.

Shit.

He wasn't going to play puppet for the damned Jinn.

He'd throw himself into the nearby fires first.

Prepared for battle, Uriel frowned as the Jinn ignored his presence and instead concentrated on the female vamp who struggled in his grasp.

"Did you truly believe you could abuse my offspring and not pay the consequences?" he roared.

Marika futilely clawed at the Jinn's arm, her nails unable

to penetrate the shimmering silver coat he wore that matched his trousers.

"You're dead," she wailed, the stench of her desperate fear filling the air.

A malicious smile curved the Jinn's lips. "My physical connection to your world was severed, which is the only reason I did not destroy you the moment you threatened Laylah. But now . . ." The lavender eyes glowed with anticipation. "Now you are in a domain where I can easily travel."

"No, please." Marika went limp in his ruthless grasp. "This is a mistake. It was Sergei who wanted to hurt Laylah. All I've done is try to protect her."

"You are correct, it was a mistake," the Jinn readily agreed. "One you shall learn to regret for the rest of eternity."

"Kata. Help me," Marika pleaded. "Tell him that I'm innocent."

Uriel muttered his opinion of females who had more courage than sense as Kata was suddenly standing at his side, her hand clutching his arm in an effort to keep herself upright.

"Innocent?" she hissed in disbelief.

"I'm your sister."

"You're an abomination and I hope you spend the rest of your very long life screaming in endless agony," Kata hissed.

The Jinn glanced toward Kata, an oddly wistful expression softening the venomous beauty of his face.

"Your wish is my command, my lady," he murmured.

With disgusting ease the Jinn tossed Marika upward, a wave of his slender hand freezing her in midair. The bitch appeared more startled than alarmed at first. Then, murmuring a soft word, the Jinn released his power and the distant lightning was suddenly altering its course to strike her slender body with sickening force.

Over and over the lightning bolts slammed into her and

Marika's shrieks filled the air, along with the horrifying scent of burning flesh.

Scooping Kata off her feet, Uriel turned her away from the hideous sight and darted down the pathway. He didn't think for a minute they could escape the Jinn, but Kata had endured enough without witnessing Marika's brutal torture.

Whatever she'd done to Kata, she had once been her sister.

He'd managed to go far enough to mute the vampire's screams when the pathway before him abruptly crumbled into nothingness. Skidding to a halt, Uriel carefully set Kata on her feet before turning to confront the approaching Jinn.

"That's close enough," he warned, his sword eager to draw some Jinn blood.

Perhaps sensing his suicidal thoughts, Kata placed a restraining hand on his arm.

"Uriel," she pleaded softly.

The Jinn's attentions shifted in her direction, his expression once again softening.

"Kata." His voice was low, hypnotizing as his hand stretched out to lightly touch her cheek. "As beautiful as ever."

Grabbing Kata by the waist, Uriel pulled her away from the beautiful demon, his primal mating instincts overcoming any hope of sanity.

He would kill anything that tried to take away his mate.

"Don't. Touch. Her."

Big surprise, the Jinn simply laughed.

"Did you not learn your lesson on the last occasion our paths crossed?"

Without warning Kata stepped between the bristling males. "Please."

The Jinn gave an obedient nod of his head, obviously devoted to the beautiful gypsy.

"Regretfully, I don't intend him harm." He flicked a disdainful glance in Uriel's direction. "He has served his purpose."

Uriel frowned. "My purpose?"

"The most powerful of Jinns are given the talent for premonition. I knew that Kata would need a protector and that it could not be me." His lips curled into a sneer. "You were chosen."

"That's why you bound me?"

"It was the only means to give you the power you needed to keep Kata safe."

"And?" Uriel prompted, unwilling to believe that the Jinn could be so selfless. Not when he vividly recalled the creatures words of warning during their last encounter.

You shall be *'the instrument of his revenge . . .'*

The lavender eyes warmed with an evil amusement. "And I needed you to live long enough to lure Marika into my lair."

Uriel shook his head in disgust.

He'd been so determined never to become the Jinn's puppet, and yet, he'd been dancing to his tune all along.

Far less conflicted by the Jinn's machinations, Kata stepped forward to lightly touch his cheek.

"Thank you," she said softly.

Uriel growled deep in his throat, but Kata was swiftly moving back to his side, leaning against him as he placed a possessive arm around her shoulders.

"Now what happens?" he demanded.

"Now you return Kata to the world where she belongs." The Jinn lifted his hand and Uriel felt a wrenching pain as his connection to the demon was severed. "Treat her well."

All the fury and frustration and ruthless dread that had plagued him for the past two hundred years was forgotten as Uriel gathered Kata in his arms.

He didn't care why he'd been chosen to be Kata's savior. Or what had happened between the two of them in the past.

The future was all that mattered.

"I intend to devote my life to her happiness."

"If you fail . . ." The lavender eyes glowed with an unmistakable warning. "I will be waiting."

Seemingly convinced that his commands would be obeyed, the Jinn waved his hand and the air next to Uriel was split open.

Uriel didn't allow himself to question whether this was yet another trap. What did it matter? It couldn't be any worse than where they were.

As they stepped through the gateway, the sound of Marika's screams were still ringing in his ears.

It took nearly a week before Kata was fully recovered from her adventures through the underworld.

After falling through the gateway, they'd discovered themselves face first in the center of Stonehenge.

Thankfully there hadn't been any pits of fire or monstrous worms or demented zombie vampires lurking nearby, and with a mutual breath of relief, Uriel had taken them directly to Victor's lair near London.

Since then she'd been cosseted and fussed over as if she were a princess rather than a common gypsy.

Victor had arrived with news that her daughter Laylah was safely in the hands of her vampire mate. Victor's beautiful fey mate, Juliet, had visited with the rare herbs to keep her from aging.

And even Yannah had made an unexpected visit, smugly expecting Kata's gratitude for having led her straight into the Jinn's lair, claiming it was the only means to break the bond between her and Marika. Once satisfied that Kata was sufficiently impressed, she'd claimed she was off to America to offer her assistance to the Child of Chaos.

Whatever that meant.

And then there was Uriel . . .

No man could have been more attentive, more devoted to making certain she was fully recovered.

With a smile, Kata snuggled closer to the delicious vampire as he led her back to his private lair, deep beneath the elegant estate.

Tonight he had surprised her with all the trappings of a traditional gypsy wedding.

There had been a magnificent feast followed by festive dancing. He'd offered a bride price to be given to a human charity that assisted with abandoned children, and given her a necklace made of golden coins. Then they'd stood together before a dozen guests and proclaimed they were man and wife.

It had been everything she'd dreamed of as a young, dewy-eyed girl, but now she was ready to be alone with her man.

More than ready, she acknowledged as a sensual heat swirled through the pit of her stomach.

Impatiently waiting for Uriel to open the heavy steel door that was protected by a dozen different locks, alarms, spells, and hexes, Kata at last stepped into the large bedroom, only to give a startled gasp.

Despite the elegance of the mansion, Uriel's own lair was surprisingly modest with more attention paid to comfort than fashion.

This evening, however, the quilt covering the heavy oak bed was decorated with hundreds of rose petals and the matching furniture draped with the vibrant silk scarves that Kata adored.

"Dear goddess," she breathed.

Uriel wrapped her in his arms. "Do you approve?"

She tilted back her head to meet his velvet brown gaze. "Very much, husband."

"Mate," he whispered softly.

"Not yet."

He groaned, his fangs flashing in the firelight. "You're ready?"

With a wicked smile, Kata shrugged off the spaghetti straps of her blue gown, allowing the satin fabric to slither down her body and pool at her feet. Her smile widened as he ran a hungry gaze down her naked curves.

"Completely and utterly."

"Kata."

With a speed that made her head spin, Kata found herself lying flat on the bed, surrounded by the earthy scent of roses and covered by Uriel's hard, naked body. She hadn't even noticed him removing his formal satin robe.

Laughing in delight, she looped her arms around his neck.

"I love a man of action."

"And I love you."

Holding her gaze, Uriel raised his arm and scored the inner skin of his wrist with his fangs. Then, with a solemn motion he pressed his bleeding wound to her mouth.

Kata closed her lips over the wound, greedily drinking the gift of his blood.

Her reaction was instant.

And wondrous.

Heat, pleasure, and overall an astonishing awareness of Uriel surged through her with giddy intensity.

Oh . . . goddess.

Moaning she allowed the golden warmth to fill her, his love for her a tangible force that healed the wounds of the past four hundred years.

"Now, Uriel," she breathed.

Uriel gently removed his wrist, covering her mouth with a kiss of raw urgency.

Kata was quick to respond, wrapping her legs around his waist as he entered her with one slow thrust. At the same time, he sank his fangs into the tender curve of her neck, the momentary pain quickly replaced by an erotic bliss that made her nails dig into the broad width of his back and her hips lift to meet his frantic pace.

She cried out as pleasure exploded through her, followed swiftly by the sensation of Uriel's own shuddering climax that echoed deep inside her.

Uriel pulled back to regard her with a startled glance, obviously as stunned as she'd been by the sheer intimacy of their bond.

"My mate," he murmured, the guarded wariness that was so much a part of him at last shattered as their hearts and souls were melded together.

They were one.

Two parts of a whole.

Skimming her hands down his back, Kata basked in the knowledge that she was at long last home.

"For all eternity."

Kane

JACQUELYN FRANK

Prologue

Kane burned. His mind, his every sense, but most of all his body burned with need and lust unlike anything he had ever felt before. The Samhain moon was growing heavy and full, it would be at its apex in a matter of days, but it may as well have been scorching its full influence into him in that very instant, that was how ravaged he was feeling.

Or maybe it was just because of her.

He'd followed her for three days now, either in person or with the power of his mind, stalking her every step since the moment he'd first laid eyes on her. He was Demon, a creature born to the night, born with powers beyond human understanding. Every Demon favored a specific element: Air, Fire, Water, Earth, Body, or, as in his case, Mind. He was powerful, capable of great feats . . . and yet always weaker than other Demons around him. They called him fledgling. A child. A nearly hundred year old child. He was a mere two years from earning a little more respect. Then he would be an adult. Not quite the deeply respected Elder that his brother was, nowhere near the astounding Ancient that Gideon was, but it would be better than that accursed title of fledgling.

But however much or little his contemporary Demons

thought of him, this young female, this human, had lived for barely a quarter of his lifetime. She was ignorant of so much, ignorant of his kind and the other Nightwalkers that lived on the borders of her world. Maybe that was why she was so carefree in the way she lived her life. Granted, she was marred with emotional scars that others had so thoughtlessly burdened her with, but in spite of that she still managed to be vivacious and earthy, as vibrant as her brilliant red hair and sparkling green eyes. As clean and clear as her pristine pale skin.

Someone else had taken notice of her brilliance. He was unworthy. Even she thought so. The inept creature had bored her almost from the outset, and yet she carried on their date, trying to find comfort in his plainness and his constancy. Kane had been tracking this absurdity from a distance, pacing furiously as the ridiculousness of it all burned at his patience. But there was little he could do about it. She was human and to him she was forbidden. By all rights he should have turned his back on her days ago. He should have written her off completely. Keeping track of her, whether from near or from far, would only lead to trouble.

That trouble had come. It had come in the form of this overwhelming burning, this savage sense of lust and ownership that could not be denied. He couldn't bear her being on that useless creature's arm another second. Now he was flying to her side in a series of uncontrolled bursts of teleportation, each jump taking him closer to her and each jump leaving behind an ever more violent burst of smoke and sulfur in his wake. His emotions were out of his control and therefore his powers were also out of his control. But none of that mattered. He was close. Closer. Soon he would put this fiasco to an end. He would rip her from the side of this clown she was trying to make worthy of her.

He materialized on the seedy New York street in a violent flash, only his power to influence the minds of others camouflaging the frightening display from those nearby. His beauteous redhead and her so-called date walked on, completely oblivious to his presence.

He stalked after them quickly, his eyes tracking all the shadowy corners and alleys nearby. His distaste for her escort trebled. What male worth anything would bring a woman to a place such as this? Didn't the fool realize the dangers all around them? Did that weak excuse for a human male honestly think himself capable of protecting her should danger present itself?

In truth, the thought wasn't even in his mind, Kane realized as he scanned them both. The shocking fact was, he was barely even focused on the treasure walking by his side! All of this fool's thoughts were eagerly focused on the film they were going to see. Apparently its special effects and coveted director warranted more attention than the one-of-a-kind sultry creature on his arm.

Disgusted, Kane seized control of both their minds at once. They stopped still for a moment and then Kane shaded out any awareness and recollection of her from the human male's mind and sent him on his way to the moving picture that seemed to mean so much to him.

And now he was alone with her. Mere steps away. It would be child's play for him to beckon her, to bring her to him as a willing, compliant thing. Oh, but that was not what he wanted. He wouldn't take her as a mind-numbed slave. It was her spirit that so enthralled him.

He would only alter her perceptions a little bit, just so she would forget what she had been doing, thus opening an opportunity for him to enter her life. But first . . . first he needed to touch her. Just one blessed moment of contact. Something to soothe this burn within him. Something to calm it a little so he could think straight and function properly.

Kane reached for her, his hand trembling as he did so, the vibration indicative of the power of his feelings, of his weakening restraint. His palm burned with anticipation, prickles dancing the length of his long fingers so that they twitched. Her unknowing smile was soft and serene. It could be anything he wanted it to be. It could be beatific, it could be wildly ecstatic. For now it remained that lovely neutral as he touched the tips of his fingers to the curve of her high cheekbone.

Oh, Sweet Destiny. It practically hurt, the overwhelming sensation of rightness and relief that rushed through him. He cradled that gorgeous face against his palm and fought off an emotional wash of tears that pricked behind his lids. His. She was *his*. At last he had her in his grasp, he had crossed the line and, contrary to all the warnings pounded into him his entire life, lightning had not come to strike him down. What was so bloody wrong about this, he wanted to know. Yes, she was human and he was Demon, but weren't they more alike than unalike? Were they not both made of flesh? Did they not both crave the touch and presence of that special someone . . . of a passion that blinded the soul? The world was not coming to an end! It was just beginning!

And then lightning struck.

Like the snap of a magician's cape being pulled away to reveal a tiger in a cage, Jacob the Enforcer appeared before him. Dread and horror rushed into Kane from all vectors, the shock of suddenly standing toe to toe with his Elder brother slamming into him like a sucker punch. This was Jacob at his most frightening. His most terrible. Yes, he was still the same brother who had raised him and loved him all of his life, but this was the side of Jacob no Demon saw until he had crossed Demon law. This was the Enforcer. And he had come to punish Kane.

Kane's throat went suddenly and brutally dry, his heart seizing in what he had to confess was fear. The punishment for what he had just done was the most severe a Demon could face, next to being put to death. His hand jerked away from the redhead's cheek as if she'd burned him and his concentration broke from her. She blinked, suddenly becoming aware that she was sandwiched between two strange men and had no idea how she had gotten there.

"Take hold of her mind, Kane. Do not make this worse by frightening her."

Kane obeyed instantaneously and she relaxed. The resulting peaceful beauty that washed over her was enough to distract him even from the knell of Jacob's presence. He marveled at how soft and sweet she looked. He knew her mind and nature matched her looks. It was only the cold warning look from his sibling that kept him from touching her again.

"Jacob, what brings you out on a night like this?" he blurted out, unable to think of anything else to say. After all, they were blood brothers. If Jacob was going to give anyone a pass, wouldn't it be him?

"You know why I am here," the Enforcer said, nipping that thought right in the bud with a chill, disciplined tone that warned Kane not to test his mettle.

"So maybe I do," Kane admitted. And still, the immediate danger didn't seem to be getting through to the rest of him. It was taking everything in his power to keep from reaching for her again. Even though it made him look quite a bit guiltier than he really was, he lowered his gaze to the spotted, dirty sidewalk and shoved his hands deep into his pockets. He gripped hold of the fabric on the inside of those pockets and forced himself to hold on. "I wasn't going to do anything. I was just . . . restless."

"I see. So you thought to seduce this woman to appease your restlessness?" Jacob asked bluntly as he folded his arms across his chest. His manner was that of a parent scolding a wayward child. It could have been an amusing thought, considering Kane was just about to enter his second century of life, but the matter was too serious by far.

"I wasn't going to hurt her," Kane protested. He would

never hurt her. She was precious. She was everything. He would love her as deeply and as thoroughly as he could.

"No?" Jacob asked, his sarcasm very obvious. "Just what were you going to do? Ask politely if you could visit the savageness of your present nature on her? How does one word that exactly?"

Kane fell stubbornly silent. He knew that the Enforcer had read his intentions from the moment he'd decided to stalk his prey. Arguments and denials would just worsen the situation. Besides, the incriminating evidence of his transgression was standing between them.

For a brief, passionate moment, Kane's thoughts filled with vivid mental imaginings of what could have been more incriminating. He suppressed a shudder of sinful response, his eyes falling covetously on the woman standing so beautifully serene before him. Had Jacob been even slightly off his irritatingly perfect game and come into the picture a half hour later . . .

"Kane, this is a difficult time for our people. You are as susceptible to these base cravings as any other Demon," the Enforcer said with implacable resolve. It was as though Jacob were the one who could read Kane's mind, rather than the other way around. "Still, you are a mere two years from becoming an adult. I cannot believe you have me chasing you down like a green fledgling." There it was. That word again. That . . . *term.* "Think of what I could be accomplishing if I were not standing here saving you from yourself."

The remark was like a kick in the pants, and it smarted. Sweet Destiny, it was true. Near Samhain his brother Jacob was weighted down by his responsibilities even more than usual. The last thing he had needed was to be chasing after his own baby brother. Jacob had never asked for his mantle of responsibility. He had inherited it suddenly and unexpectedly when their eldest brother Adam had suddenly gone missing, presumed dead at the hands of some necromancer and a nefarious summoning spell many centuries ago. Jacob had lost a beloved brother and inherited a ponderous duty in one fell swoop. Now he was the pariah of his people. A necessary evil, as it were. Sort of like the internal affairs division of the human police. They were necessary, they were members of the same brotherhood, but oh, how they were held in contempt.

"I'm sorry, Jacob, I really am," he said at last. Kane felt utter shame washing over him as he appreciated the position he had put his beloved sibling in. It actually surprised him that he hadn't thought of the consequences of his actions and how they would affect Jacob. He glared up at the Samhain moon and knew that was where the blame belonged. Kane's throat closed with a sharp sense of remorse that knifed through him.

It was as overpowering as the dread that was welling up within him. He'd betrayed the sanctity of their laws, and there was a punishment for that. A punishment that made an entire species catch their breath and back away whenever the Enforcer entered the vicinity. Kane could suddenly feel the weight of Jacob's position, and it sharpened his regret to a point of pain in his chest.

"You will send this woman home safely by reuniting her with her escort and making sure she remembers nothing of your misbehavior," Jacob instructed softly. "Then you will go home. Your punishment will come later."

"But I didn't do anything," Kane protested, a swift rise of inescapable fear fueling his objection.

"You would have, Kane. Do not make this worse by lying to yourself about that. Do not try to convince yourself that I am the villain others like to make me out to be. That will only cause us both pain."

Kane recognized that truth with another upsurge of guilt.

Sighing resolutely, he closed his eyes and concentrated for all of a second. Moments later, the redhead's escort loped back across the street with a smile and a call to her.

"Hey! Where'd ya go? I turned the corner and suddenly you weren't there!"

"I'm sorry. I was distracted by something and didn't realize you'd gone, Charlie."

Charlie linked his arm with his date's and, completely oblivious of the two Demons barely a breath away, drew her off, chattering incessantly about that ridiculous movie he was so damn excited to see. It grated on Kane's nerves to hear it, set off a screaming sensation in his blood to allow her to walk away from him. But what else could he do? She was forbidden and Jacob would fight him if he tried to do otherwise. Sweet Destiny, fight with the Enforcer? Even Gideon the Ancient had not been able to come out a winner against Kane's powerful brother.

"Good," Jacob commended Kane, unaware of how the fledgling had to struggle to stay where he was, to let her go into the dangerous night and a ridiculous date where she wouldn't be even slightly appreciated for the wonder that she was.

Kane sighed. Nothing about this felt good. Not the position he was currently in, and certainly not turning her back over to that inept buffoon who knew nothing of how precious she was . . . of how exquisitely, painfully she was capable of making a male feel just by her very presence in a room.

"She's so beautiful. Did you see that smile? All I could think about was how much I wanted her to smile when . . ." Kane flushed as he looked at the Enforcer. He had not intended to speak aloud. He had not wanted to confess so much to his brother. Oh, nothing would change the inevitability of the consequences to come, but there was a sanctity to what he felt for his redheaded human torturer. It was private. Nothing to be shared with others. "I never thought this would happen to me, Jacob. You have to believe that."

When it came down to it, Kane didn't want Jacob to think he had purposely brought them to this pass. He loved his brother.

"I do." Jacob hesitated for a moment, for the first time making it obvious to Kane that this had been a terrible struggle for him, no matter how well he projected otherwise. "Do not worry, Kane. I know who you really are. I know that this curse is hard for us to fight. Now," he said, his tone back to business, "please return home. You will find Abram there awaiting you."

This time, Kane brushed away the welling trepidation within himself. He did it for Jacob's sake, knowing how deeply the situation cut the Elder Demon, even though the Enforcer's thoughts were too carefully guarded for Kane to read. "You must do your duty as you would with anyone. I understand that, Jacob."

Kane then gave the Enforcer a short nod of kinship. After glancing around to make sure they were unobserved, he exploded into a burst of sulfur and smoke as he teleported away.

It took everything . . . every fiber of control he could muster, not to stray from the course Jacob had demanded of him.

Chapter 1

Agony.

Sweet and bitter all at once, it raced through his blood, stretching every muscle and stripping down his control to the very thinnest of threads. Swallowing down a groan lest the others hear him, he bent forward in his chair and braced his elbows on his denim-clad knees.

This was intolerable. It was a recipe for disaster and devastation. His rushing and pounding heart would not bear the strain of this pace for all the hours that stretched out before him.

Peace, he whispered into his own mind, *find peace. Think on it a moment. Here you are, by her side, where you never thought to be again. You thought you would never be allowed within miles of her again, and yet now you can reach out and touch her . . .*

But he didn't dare reach out to the unconscious form of the woman in the nearby bed. He was terrified that if he began to touch her he would not be able to force himself to stop. The fever in his blood was what made that fear boil so hot and so true. It was a caution he must heed. No matter what. No matter how tempting a figure she was to him.

It wasn't her beauty or shapeliness that captivated him, or even the fiery brilliance of her coiled and curling hair. The former had been starved and drained away from her in by a terrible illness and the latter had been dulled as well by the same culprit. Still, whenever he looked at her, all he saw was the vibrant green-eyed beauty who had stood mere inches away from him, stood within his reach, a sensual, vital, and beautiful creature without compare. He had touched her then. For an instant, a single charged moment that had struck down through him like a killing spear, and he had known the feel of refined pale skin and forbidden human warmth. She had scorched against his fingertips like ignited butane, burning so sweet and clear and clean.

That single touch had nearly written a warrant of death for her.

Kane swallowed in pain that had little to do with the fire of a full Samhain moon crackling in his blood. Oh, yes, the curse of moon madness had flared through him in agonizing ways before, a struggle of morals and conscience every Demon, male or female, young or old, had to wrestle through each time the moons of Samhain and Beltane came around full, but never before had he crossed boundaries and broken laws to reach out and touch a human woman.

This human woman.

"Corrine."

Kane whispered her name in a raspy voice, trying out his newfound right to speak it . . . just as he was shockingly now permitted to be at her side. The very idea of it was baffling. A week ago he'd stalked her and been duly set back from the forbidden line he had crossed. But now . . . now a new truth was known. A new understanding. Maybe it had been madness that had fueled his hunt for her, maybe it had been a curse that had compelled him to break Demon law . . . or maybe it had been fate and Destiny. Maybe he had not stalked random prey at all, but instead had been driven by a single, sharp truth.

She was meant to be his.

The truth of it was known now. A single touch of his hand had awakened a change within this human woman who wasn't entirely human. Dormant Druid DNA, the perfect complement to his own Demon genetics, had woken inside her with a vengeance. The reaction was volatile and demanding, needing power and energy to complete the conversion.

Power she simply didn't have living in the simple ways of humanity. It was *his* power the change needed to feed off of. His and his alone. No other Demon would do. No other man would do. It was his abundant and complementary power she would need to fuel her existence from now until the day one or the other of them died.

And because he had been slapped back by the Enforcer, Kane had not been there to provide that desperately needed energy resource. The result had been the starvation of what had once been a vibrant and sensually stunning beauty, leaving behind a pale-grey and fragile girl who now tottered on the precipice of life and death. If he stepped too far away from her for even a moment, he might just as well shove her over that cliff.

So here he stayed, sitting in reach of her, staring at how she had been ravaged because of their ignorance of what she was. But *he* had known. Some instinct had called from his depths, demanding he take what was meant to be his. He had been so sure of it, so determined she was his even though it was against everything his brother had raised him to believe.

Kane had known she was meant to be his. He only wished it hadn't taken such brutal damage to her to make that clear to everyone else. Almost as much as he wished to control the fire of need burning in his every last cell.

It was called the Imprinting, this thing between them. Though it was a very rare connection between two Demons, he was quite familiar with the lore of the symbiotic bond. Every Demon was. It was something every Demon longed for just as all young men and women longed for soul mates and true love.

Kane ran a hand back through damp, ebony hair, the already mussed curls licking around his passing fingers in clingy determination that matched the guilt riding deep and sore within him. The Imprinting was a sacred event, the ultimate connection between complementary souls. The couple involved began to exchange the essences of themselves from the very instant they touched. Between Demons it was the emotional and spiritual bond that threaded the two together, but with Kane and Corrine it was the physical one that had been crucial. He was supposed to provide for her and protect her, keep her safe, strong, and treasured. It was his right . . . his duty. Destiny had gifted him with her, his mate, and he had . . .

He had almost destroyed her. He had driven her almost to the point of death. Kane couldn't stand the thought and it chilled him even as his stomach turned. The sensation of powerful guilt was bracing and welcome. It was the only thing that cooled the fiery call of Samhain in his blood.

Because nothing stood between an Imprinted pair on the night of Samhain. On this night, above all others, they would be driven into each others' arms. The demand to mate would be imperative; there was no ignoring it.

But his mate lay unconscious and inaccessible. He could not touch her . . . and he could not leave her side. Only his essential energy could revive her from this state of deathly limbo, and he must stay near for that to aid her. But with Hallowed moon madness screaming in his head, it was taking all of his significant discipline to keep from clasping her to himself, to keep from doing the unimaginable to a help-less, weakened girl.

Kane was literally in hell.

Jacob watched his brother tensely from the outer hallway, hanging as far back as he could so his telepathic sibling would remain unaware of his presence and, more impor-tantly, his overriding concern. Newly Imprinted himself on Corrine's blood sister Isabella, he could easily feel the strug-gle his brother was wrestling with. It was a credit to the fledgling's mental control that he was sitting there so deter-minedly. As a Demon of the Earth, Jacob had no access to the thoughts or emotions of others; those were the skills of Mind Demons like Kane. However, he knew the scent of a warm-blooded creature infused with lustful need very well. The mystical force of the Samhain moon would eventually wrest control away from his brother . . . just as it would wrest away his own control and force him to make haste to his Bella's waiting arms.

"He will not make it," he said softly to his companion.

"No," the Demon King, Noah, agreed grimly as he glanced into the bedroom. "He is too young by far."

"I am an Elder of great power and control and I do not think even I could keep away from Isabella tonight even if she were lying near death before me," Jacob growled in sharp defense of his brother. It was a grim truth and it galled the Enforcer to admit it. It would horrify any respectable male to no end even to think of using his mate sexually when she was injured or ill, but inside every Demon lay a beast that could devolve into something uncontrollable on the rare occasion. Those occasions always seemed to center around the volatile emotional conditions of lust, rage, possessiveness, and protectiveness. And it was always worse on Samhain and Beltane.

"Sweet Destiny," the King swore softly. "It infuriates me to think we have evolved so little that we would be compelled to something that amounts to rape in order to satisfy a biological urge!"

"Agreed. But this is an urge that ought to be mutual. It ought to be between immortals so powerful and dynamic that things like illness never become a part of the equation. This imperative does not take into consideration that a mate might not be fit for mating and it does not give us conscious control over ourselves in that instance."

Noah already knew this and it was apparent in his hard sigh. The Demon King was the offspring of one of the oh-so-rare Demon to Demon Imprintings that had taken place in their history. He had seen how his parents were driven to one another on a daily basis, connected beyond his scope of understanding, and he had always known that Samhain and Beltane meant he would have no access to his parents as they locked themselves away from the world in order to indulge in each other. No matter what. If they had been arguing for days or angry with one another, they were forced to put their differences aside and left only with the choice of satisfying nature's demand to mate.

It was a nearly foolproof plan meant to forever keep the Demon population thriving on this earth.

Tonight was an example of the horrible hitch in that plan.

Noah lowered his voice to the barest whisper of breath. "We will have to bind him."

"We will have to do more than that or he will simply teleport free of the bindings," Jacob pointed out grimly, feeling a sickly response to the realization that he was plotting to trap his brother in a literal hell on earth. "And we will have to bolt him down right beside her. Too much distance and she will die. By all rights she should already be dead. Only his presence spares her now."

"It will not be so sharp a danger for her with a little time."

"I wish I could say the same for my brother," Jacob replied, reaching up to rub at the wrenching tension in his neck. He could barely think; his psyche was torn with the needs of others. There was his would-be bride, with whom he was sharing an exclusive telepathic connection, inundating him with fear for her sister's life as she waited in the parlor downstairs. On the flip side of that coin was the Imprinting that demanded they come together soon. Very soon. There was his worry for Kane and the stress of knowing other Druids like Corrine had already died horrible deaths because he had unwittingly done his job as Enforcer and kept humans away from Demons, not realizing there were some with Druid DNA that were calling a particular Demon to them. And once they touched . . .

And he always made sure to wait until they touched. Once the Demon transgressor touched the human victim, it was irrefutable evidence he or she had crossed the line.

"Better this than the alternative," Noah remarked knowingly as he turned serious jade and grey eyes on him. "We had best get on with it. We shall use Legna to tamp down his ability to teleport for the moment. She is strong enough to master him, I think. But I believe, in the end, it ought to be his *Siddah* who binds him for the long haul. He will be better able to forgive those of us he loves much easier than those who are less intimate with him."

"I suppose we will see about that," Jacob replied.

In truth, Jacob could not see how his brother was ever going to be able to forgive him for putting Kane's destined mate in such horrible danger. Ignorance was no excuse, in Jacob's mind. In all these centuries as Enforcer, why had it never once occurred to him to question his duties? Why had he never thought to look deeper than the responsibilities thrust upon him?

And why was he the first to be rewarded with the incredible beauty and breathlessness of a Demon and human/Druid hybrid Imprinting? After destroying countless others' opportunities to know the same blessing, however unwittingly, why was he now to be the one to find joy?

Ironically, it was the soothing comfort of his mate's voice in his head that helped ease his guilt and put it to rest.

Chapter 2

Corrine awoke very slowly.

She never woke quickly. She had always despised mornings. As necessary as they were, right along with the whole job thing and the responsibility-to-pay-the-rent thing, she just hated motivating herself out of warm and cozy sheets and into wet and bracing showers. Give her Saturday and super lazy Sundays and she was a happy girl. She was as opposite her obnoxiously energetic and efficiently motivated sister as you could get. Especially when it came to Corrine's weekends. But since Isabella wasn't there prodding her awake and waving coffee under her nose, Corrine had to assume it was the weekend.

Yay.

She cracked an eyelid open and immediately shut it when the blare of colored sunlight struck her pupil. Groaning in complaint and refusal, Corrine burrowed her face back into her pillow's super soft belly. Then she turned and tried to curl up into a morning-resistant ball.

It wasn't until she knocked a knee into a distinctively warm body that she realized she wasn't alone in her bed.

That woke Corrine up like nothing else could have.

She jolted upright like a shot, a rush of cold washing over her and making her realize she was bare-assed naked even as she squinted against the harsh light all around her. All it took was a moment to focus, but as soon as she did, her jaw dropped so far open she heard the hinge pop. She was now staring in utter disbelief at the man . . . yes, it was definitely a man and not a freaking doubt about it . . . in her bed.

Okay, wait. Not her bed. His bed? Her bed was low and simply lacquered, this was a four-postered monstrosity made of what was probably a long extinct type of oak tree and had had dozens of slaves carving pictures onto it or something. Corrine dismissed that thought immediately though because she could only focus on the absolutely astounding body laid out beside her.

Oh. No. Inaccurate.

Tied down to the bed beside her! This forced Corrine's mind to race madly for some kind of explanation that would make sense.

I got drunk, picked up a hottie who was into kink, passed out before untying him.

That would account for everything, she thought with a kind of hysterical satisfaction. Except she didn't overindulge anymore. Not since college and the time she'd . . . well, she'd learned her lesson and had never again wanted to know what it felt like to wake up lost and confused in the wake of bad choices.

Rather like she was feeling at that very moment.

Corrine bit her lip anxiously as she took in the sexy beast beside her. Naked from the waist up, he certainly fit the description. Lean and athletic though he was, he was thick with nicely contoured muscles. Muscles pulled into taut relief by the shackles around each of his wrists and drawn up so tight his knuckles brushed the headboard. Thick cuffs circled each strong lower forearm and linked into dense steel chains that disappeared seamlessly into the wall. A wall made of pure concrete and stone! It was as if the cement had been poured over the chains while the building had been created.

Well, that was just much too kinky for her.

Corrine backed away from her chained stud, even as her darting eyes took in the raw, torn wood of the thick headboard and the whitish-yellow coloring of the wood's wounds. The shavings all around both head and footboards and scattered across the bedding attested to his having violently struggled against his bondage.

What the hell is going on here? Corrine wanted to know this even as she took in his wide shoulders, their breadth obvious even in spite of his awkward position of captivity. His handsome face was so classically beautiful, in a very dark and Romanesque fashion, that it absolutely fascinated her. Thick dark brows, distinct from each other and shaped with an elegant curve, seemed to point down toward the blade of his nose. Sculpted lips were tightly pressed together, as if he was hurting even in his . . . sleep? God, was he asleep? Or was he unconscious? Corrine's eyes darted down across the dusting of dark hair that created a light pelt that eventually narrowed to a single line bisecting him to his navel and beyond. It wasn't until she could see his bared belly that she realized his dark skin was painted with perspiration. She reappraised him to check the data, from hip points to the ebony hair curling back from his forehead. When she had determined he had some kind of fever or was in some sort of pain, she continued to let her eyes drift down the denim encasing his thighs and calves, the faded, snug material leaving very little to the imagination.

Corrine purposely drew her gaze away from his fly and glanced at his ankles. She inspected the shackles locked around them, the length of metal climbing almost halfway up his calves, which she could see when she dared to pick up the hem of his jeans with a single delicate finger. The footboard was just as chewed up as the head, with shreds of wood everywhere there as well. When she moved carefully to peek over the bed, she found those chains sinking directly into the stone floor just as they did the wall at the head of the bed. Only this time there were two chains per leg, as if someone had thought one chain wouldn't be enough to hold him.

No. She would never have agreed to something like this. And judging by the amount of blood staining the manacles and his jeans, he hadn't wanted any part of it either. He was tied down like some kind of dangerous animal.

Corrine fought her compassionate impulse to reach out and touch his face, which was vibrating with nervous twitches and spasms as if he was fighting his bonds even in his sleep.

What if he was dangerous?

What if she'd been kidnapped or something and thrown into . . . into . . . into a lion's den? Was he some kind of deadly killer? Some kind of Hannibal Lecter in need of a redheaded appetizer?

When bold blue eyes suddenly appeared in the face she was staring at, Corrine yelped in fearful surprise. She reacted, yanking sheeting around her body even as she scrambled for the edge of a bed that was just too damned big. It wasn't until she stumbled in the effort to make a hasty exit from the bed that she really began to feel the weakness in her limbs and the slowness of her reactions.

Corrine! Stop!

Corrine yelped as the deep, rich, vibrant voice reverberated around the inside of her head. Sheer panic and disbelief made her freeze where she was, on her knees in that bed. She had been watching him every second and knew for a fact he hadn't opened his mouth to speak. Her frightened eyes scanned the room, looking for another source for the voice. It had to be something . . . something other than what it had felt and sounded like. She looked for a loudspeaker, some kind of communications device, but there was nothing she could see. Nothing anywhere.

Drawn to those vividly blue eyes, she began to shake as his big body clenched, jerking his bonds all the tighter.

Don't be afraid of me, Corrine.

Corrine's jaw dropped open again. Those sexy lips had not moved a smidge, but it was all too clear from what she could see in his deep, imploring eyes that he was the one making the plea. She sat poised there for almost a minute, ready for flight and riddled with confusion. She had to be out of her mind. Maybe it was an effect from a roofie some bastard had slipped in her drink?

"What in hell is going on here?" she demanded to know, the pitch of her voice little more than a growl.

Then the son of a bitch had the temerity to smile at her. And somehow, maybe because of years of experience with this kind of reaction, she just knew it was loaded with condescension. The old "Aww, how cute, the redheaded temper thing!"

With quick angry eyes, she ran a contemptuous gaze over him. That lasted for about a second because once she made it past his belt line she realized he was . . .

Holy shit! She gasped when she realized he was fully— *fully*—aroused. *God, please tell me that is a full-on hard-on because if that's only a partial I might just have to stay and think about this for a moment.*

Corrine's captive stud suddenly erupted in laughter, resting his head back so the rich, rolling sound could bolt out of him and echo around the room. Since the entire place seemed made of stone and rock, the echo was rather significant. But that didn't bother Corrine nearly as much as the realization that he had heard her thoughts.

He heard my thoughts!

He really was inside her head!

Oh no, she thought with horror. No one knew what went on in her head, not even her sister Isabella. She had made an art out of snarky internal dialogues and editing them before they passed her lips. Well, at least since college she'd internalized and edited them. Her blithe tongue had gotten her in trouble more often than not before then, so she had learned to temper it. And if this guy really could read her thoughts and talk inside her head, he was about to prove to her all the reasons why.

Yes, Corrine, I can read your mind . . . and one day you will be able to read mine.

"The hell I will!" she blurted out. "Where are my clothes? I'm getting out of this freak show right now!"

"No, don't!"

Too late. She had reached the edge of the bed and put her feet down. First, the bed was much further from the floor than she had judged it to be and second, despite a good start, her legs simply refused to hold her. She hit the painfully hard floor in a pile of awkward, uncoordinated limbs, hurting herself in numerous places.

"Ow," she complained aloud.

"Corrine?" The demand was hard and full of restrained anger, but it was also laced with very obvious fear. Fear for her safety, perhaps. Or maybe he was just afraid she would leave him trapped and alone?

Corrine curled up against her thighs for a moment, closing her eyes and nursing her pain and heart-racing anxiety for just a moment. Jumbled thoughts and questions tripped over one another in her head. She didn't know what to focus on first. She didn't know which direction held safety and comfort and, just as importantly, peace of mind.

Moving slowly onto her knees, steadying herself with her hands, she tried to get her feet back under her. She made it only as far as her knees, and, panting softly for breath with her head hanging, Corrine tried not to give in to the sting of frustrated tears filling her vision. She was confused and was abruptly being forced to realize that she was weak and helpless on top of everything else.

"Corrine . . ."

His voice, spoken aloud in a softly coaxing tone, was as deep and compelling as it had been when it was ringing inside her head. Something about it helped her find focus, helped her draw herself out of her momentary emotional panic. She focused on him and his voice, even though she couldn't even see him over the high edge of the bed. Just the feel of his presence was enough to steady her.

"How do you know my name?" she asked, her own voice sounding rough and disused. She recalled having been ill. Yes. She'd called in sick to work several days in a row because the flu or something had been kicking her ass. She'd been weak and exhausted . . . something like the way she felt now, only it had been getting much worse.

"Is that important?" he asked. She could hear the sound of him shifting, the noisy clank of steel chains making a chill skip down her spine.

"No, I suppose not," she responded in a breathy whisper. She also realized the answer was obvious. If the guy really was a telepath, obtaining her name was no doubt a piece of mental cake. "God, I can't believe I am actually considering this is real."

Slowly, balancing carefully on her rubbery knees, she grabbed for the edge of the mattress and drew herself up until her eyes and nose could peek over it. There he was, laid out and trussed up like a Christmas goose. He was watching her every move, of course, those deep blue eyes steady and unreadable at the moment. His entire frame was locked tight with tension and where his skin was bare he was gleaming with perspiration. He looked like he was in pain. She recalled the blood around the cuffs that bound him and suddenly felt really stupid. She hadn't even stopped to consider that he was probably in just as much trouble as she was. She'd just acted like such a girl and freaked out.

"Corrine, listen to me very carefully," the captured male said, his tone both coaxing and compelling. "You have to get back up on the bed."

Corrine sat down sharply on her heels, a tired sigh jolting out of her as she rolled her eyes. *Well, that's easy for you to say. You don't have to scale a wall of mattresses with spaghetti arms.*

No, I don't, came the amused response deep inside her head. *But if you don't find a way to get back in this bed you will only get weaker and sicker as time goes on.*

It was bad enough that she was listening to a man's voice in her head where there ought not to be one, but listening to implied threats just topped the cake.

She turned her back hard against the mattresses and frame, sitting down stubbornly on the cold stone of the floor. Crossing her arms under her breasts she gave in to the urge to pout out her bottom lip.

"I'm just supposed to believe everything you say because you can . . . can . . ."

"Read your mind?"

"Yes! And it isn't fair that you know my name and everything I think. I don't know a damn thing about who you are and if you think I am getting back up into that bed with you—!"

"My name is Kane." He cut her off with the simple announcement. Then he switched to the more resounding impact of his mind within hers. *And if you do not get into this bed with me, you are going to die, Corrine.*

Corrine couldn't help the laugh that snorted out of her nose. It instantly mutated into a fit of giggles as the outrageous threat tickled the more perverse side of her sense of humor.

"Listen, buddy," she called up to him between chuckles,

"I've met plenty of men who thought they were God's gift to women, but no one has ever told me before that getting into bed with them was a matter of life or death." She giggled at that absurdity again. "I gotta give you points for originality though."

"Damn it, Corrine, get up here!"

"Or what?" she demanded. "What are you gonna do to me, bondage boy? Rattle your chains?"

"I could take control of your mind, turn you into a simple-minded puppet and have you climb into this bed like a well behaved puppy, Corrine. That is what I can do."

Cold dread sliced down through her chest and belly as she realized he was speaking the truth. Oh, she knew nothing at all about this weird telepathy stuff, but it was a dead-on fact that he had the power to speak into her mind. It wasn't much of a stretch to believe he could do what he said. Her heart began to race again at the idea of someone being able to take control of her in such an absolute way. Looking around in a frantic renewal of panic, she searched for the door to the room.

It was really, really far away. A good eighteen yards— okay, so maybe it was just feet—away. Christ the room was big! Or maybe it just felt that way because even the idea of crawling across all that harsh stone was exhausting. Corrine leaned forward, her hands touching the stone in the beginnings of a crawl, and suddenly there was an explosion of crashing steel and groaning wood from the bed.

"Corrine, don't! Don't leave! Damn you, you stubborn little—!"

"Stubborn?" Corrine sat back on her heels once more, turning her head to glare at the bed, if not the man within it. "You are chained to a bed, you idiot! My coming up there to keep you company isn't going to help either of us! Maybe if I can get out of here, I can find some help and we can both go back to our lives. Unless, of course, you enjoy being lashed down? If that's the case I won't interfere with your fun. But I happen to like my life out there in the free world!"

"Fine. Have it your way."

Corrine ought to have realized then and there that there wasn't even a hint of capitulation in his words.

Chapter 3

Corrine felt herself resolving into an awareness. It took only a heartbeat for her to realize that, not only was she back in bed with her blue-eyed boy in bonds, but she was curled up like a contented kitten across his chest. She tried to push away from him in her shock, but her body did not respond to her demands. She felt exhausted and her hair was drenched in sweat as though she'd just run some kind of a marathon. Worse yet, she was bare butt naked again, her breasts mashed between their bodies.

She realized then what he had done. He had made good on his threat to take control of her actions. Somehow he had seized her mind and forced her to climb back into bed with him. In a sudden and dreadful panic, Corrine wondered just what, exactly, he had done to make her break the awful sweat drenching her body.

"I didn't do anything," he snapped out with a scowl. "You're critically ill, Corrine. Just getting your stubborn little butt back in this bed was an Olympic event." He dropped his head back and stared up at the ceiling, his jaw set with angry tension. "I didn't want to make you come back like that, but you left me no choice."

"No choice?" She could barely hear herself. Corrine realized she was short of breath and so damn tired she couldn't even get a good mad on. "How about the choice where you leave me alone and let me do what I decide to do! You had no right—!"

"I had every right!" he bellowed suddenly into her nearby face. "If you'd just sit still and listen for five minutes you'd understand that!"

"Oh, really?" she hissed out snidely, sliding up against him just enough to put them nose to nose. "Go ahead. Make me understand why you're chained to a bed like some rabid dog and why you think it's life or death that I stay with you! I'm listening!"

Kane drew a breath, impatience and temper fueling his desire to hit her with the truth and use it against her. His mind was blind with emotion and need she couldn't understand. He shouldn't have had her curl up into contact with him, but he had not been able to help himself. He'd needed her nearness so much . . . oh, so much. The feel of her, just the smell of her gave him a measure of comfort, even as it created brand new tortures. It sickened Kane that she had thought the worst of him, that Corrine had thought he'd used his power over her mind to make her obey his need for sex, but maybe that was because the idea had, in fact, crossed his mind several times.

Corrine watched Kane turn his head aside, hiding his face against his biceps for a long, long minute. Her skin almost felt alive with the strange sense of energy she felt radiating from him into herself. It left an odd tasting tang on her tongue. Even in a sea of exhaustion, there was something wildly rejuvenating about the sensation. Slowly the sense of numbing weariness began to fade and a keen sense of perception replaced it. Once again she became acutely aware that he was in a great deal of pain. She felt it was focused physically at the biting raw places where the cuffs held him fast, and yet there was something else, something like a symphony of agony that radiated through him from head to toe.

She sat up as best she could manage, pressing flat palms against his chest as she slowly let her eyes walk over him. His dark hair was damp and curling in a messy collection of rings. His dark skin was as slick as hers; every vein and vessel beneath it was distended to the utmost.

Corrine cleared her throat, her anger fading when she acknowledged that, whatever else he was, Kane was suffering.

"Tell me what's going on," she asked him more gently this time. "Why are you trapped like this? Why don't you want me to find someone to free you? God, I can tell you're suffering from some kind of pain. Why won't you let me help?"

Kane looked at her, his crisp blue eyes hot with unspoken emotions she had no access to. Not unless he deigned to share them with her.

"I am being held here like this"—he jerked on the chains—"because right now I can't be trusted. The pain I am in is transient. It will pass." She saw his jaw clench briefly. "I just need you to understand one thing, okay?" He waited until she nodded. "There is a special sort of . . . of chemistry, between you and me. The moment you and I came into contact with each other, it made something happen to both of us. It made us change into symbiotic beings. That means—"

"I know what symbiotic means," she broke in tartly.

"I know you do," he sighed. "I meant to say, what that means for us is that we are each dependent now on the other. You became sick, Corrine, because I wasn't there to support you. You almost died because of it. Now you are weak and can barely function. You were in a coma until just a little while ago. And you'll go back into it if you don't keep close to me."

"Wait a minute . . ."

"No. You can't think about this now. You just need to go to sleep and rest. In a little while you'll start to feel better and then we can talk some more. Please, Corrine, just rest."

Corrine wanted to complain. She wanted to question him about things like: How did he know all of this? Was this real or just some kind of delusion that he truly believed with that unnerving conviction of his? And if this had all started the moment they'd met, how was it that she'd been sick since before meeting him?

But none of those questions made it past the point of thought flashing through her mind. Her exhaustion had rapidly caught up with her and before she could think to fight it, she slipped into a deep, natural sleep.

Or so she thought.

"Hmm."

"What?" Noah looked up from his reading when Abram made the speculative sound.

"Nothing really. Only, I find it fascinating to watch the mistakes that the young tend to make."

"If you mean Kane, he is hardly what I would call young. And mistakes are not exclusive to youth." Noah frowned at that, thinking of all he had learned recently about Demon history. A thousand years ago the Demon race had actually been comprised of two races. Demon and Druid. They had lived a symbiotic existence. Demons could not know the depth of true and meaningful love with a soul mate, without a genetically perfect Druid counterpart; Druids could never know their own power without that perfect Demon's touch to give birth to it. And, as Kane and Corrine were discovering, once that connection was made, they could not survive apart from one another. The Druid would whither away and die within a couple of weeks for want of the energy of the Demon it fed from, and the Demon would pine for its love, suffer untold depression, and usually seek an end at its own hand or simply waste itself away into death.

Yet, even knowing this, a millennia ago the Demons had taken an active hand in the destruction of the Druid race. Just because of a slight by one King to another King, whether real or imagined in the distant dust of history, the Demon King had declared war on the Druids. And what had been his first, most vicious attack against his enemy? To lock up his own people. All Demons that had been mated at the time had been locked away from their Druid mates.

The deaths had been in the thousands. The Demon King had wiped out nearly half the Druid population in one cruel act. Druids suffered and starved with their energy sources torn from them. Their loves torn from them. And the backlash of all those Druid deaths had made the Demon King's victory short lived, because Demons had killed themselves in untold numbers once they were set free. And those that did not take their own lives died of broken hearts and spirits in under a year.

No. Demons could not survive the death of their Imprinted mates any better than Druids could survive theirs.

In the end the Druid population suffered a complete genocidal eradication. Thus, there had not been a Druid born in a thousand years. They were gone and gone for good. In one fell swoop the Demons had exiled themselves to empty, loveless immortality. Imprinting between Demon and Demon was all but unheard of, though in rare instances it did happen. Instances like Noah's own parents. And yes, Demons did wed, joining with each other, producing offspring.

But those relationships never lasted very long. Maybe a half century. Maybe more if they were lucky. Never as long as they would have if they had been Imprinted. Imprinting was forever. It was exquisite and beyond compare, soul deep and heart bound. And it was gone.

Or so it had seemed for a thousand years. The truth appeared to be complex and yet simple at the same time. Druids, seeing the writing on the wall, had done the unthinkable. They had escaped Demon persecution and hidden themselves deeply amongst the infantile human race. They had given up any hope of ever knowing the power that hid in their blood, opting for survival instead. They had muddied their proud blood with that of the more savage humans around them. They had had no other choice at the time.

So all these long centuries later, after who knew how many genetic dilutions, they had been found once more by the Demons who needed them so badly. Demons who suffered near insanity twice a year and were quickly losing all control of who and what they were. Granted, the curse of Samhain and Beltane Hallowed moons had been a just dessert. They had deserved this horrible fallout.

But perhaps it was their maturity, their turn toward peaceful and benevolent ways that had brought them to this time and place. At long last, a Druid had resurfaced and Imprinted on their Enforcer, of all people. And lo and behold all that dilution, all that muddying . . . had only made them stronger. More powerful. Breathtaking. Corrine's sister Isabella was now an Enforcer too. She could read the ancient Demon and Druid languages as if she had been born to it. She fought like a dervish, with deadly skill and strength although she had never been trained to it. Before she and Jacob had crossed paths, before they had touched, she had been a quiet, simple librarian.

Well, perhaps that was an exaggeration. There was nothing about Bella that could be classified as simple or quiet.

Noah smiled at that, enjoying the newfound influence of Bella in his life. In all of their lives. Bella was beautiful and, for all of her short stature, she was a giant in her heart and her compassion toward others. She had taken to her new life like a duck to water, had taken all of Demon society into her heart. She had embraced her new life as a Druid.

Noah was not certain it would be so easy with Corrine. Jacob had had the advantage of time on his side, the luck of a few precious days when he was able to teach Bella about himself, his race, and their culture, and she had been given precious time to adjust to all the changes happening to her.

Corrine, however, had been starved to the brink of death. Coming back from that would not be easy. Nor would it be easy for her to understand why she was forever connected to the man bound beside her. Worse, Kane would not be at his best. The fever in his blood and in his soul would make him savage, make him reckless.

"Make certain he remains bound," Noah stressed to Abram, although the Mind Demon wouldn't have thought to do otherwise. "And don't worry about the flaws in his actions. I have faith that the mistakes of youth can be overcome and tempered into miraculous things."

It was so strange how she suddenly knew things to be the absolute truth and yet had no shred of proof to support her belief. Yet she knew. When she opened her eyes, she just knew that he had manipulated her into sleeping, exactly the same way he had manipulated her into getting back into bed with him. This time when she awoke, however, she didn't move even the smallest fraction of a millimeter. She just opened her eyes and lay quietly as she absorbed everything around her.

She was lying cozily across his chest still, her cheek pillowed on an impressive pectoral muscle. She could feel wiry little hairs under her cheek and tickling her nose as well, and each time she took a breath she was inundated with that smell . . . the smell of a strong, sexy male lying warm and within her reach. God, it had been such a long time since she'd lain intimately naked with a man, just quietly absorbing his presence. And even then, she couldn't recall any man having as much power in his presence as Kane seemed to have.

He was perplexing and confusing, everything about the entire situation seeming surreal and crazy, but in that moment it was as if she'd settled into the perfect niche. It was as if she belonged exactly where she was, even if she wasn't quite sure what that meant. The realization gave her an uncontrollable chill, gooseflesh running over her skin until she shivered, giving herself away.

"I already knew you were awake," he said, his voice hoarse as it whispered above her head.

It was fully dark now, and she wondered just how long she'd been asleep.

"Only an hour or two. It was sunset when you woke before."

"Okay, has anyone ever told you just how creepy that is?" she asked him sharply, lifting her chin to try to see him in the darkness. "How do you do that?"

She felt him shrug in spite of his awkward positioning. "I was born this way."

"People aren't just born that way. Not real people. Imaginary people maybe, comic book people or sci-fi movie people, but not real people."

"*My* people are born this way," he corrected her, the soft emphasis on the way he said "my people" making her take note of his distinction. "Not all, but many."

Still, she didn't ask. She wasn't sure she was ready to know.

Corrine sat up, pushing off against him to do so, grateful

to find she could move with comparative ease. She paused a moment, trying to recall the layout of the room. She slid up along his side carefully, and then reached across him, the shortest distance to the nearest lamp. She braced herself as she fumbled for the switch.

Kane had to bite back a groan of pure craving as the tip of her breast brushed just beneath his nose. As she leaned further forward he could smell the delightful musk of her sleep-warmed skin. Better still, he could smell himself on her, impressed into her from the hours spent lying close together. Oh, every minute of it had been utter torture, but it had been worth it to have this sweet result. Even now, as her sleek, bare body brushed in haunting teases all against his, he swallowed down the agony of his need and reveled in the minute pleasures of her warmth and softness being so close to him.

She finally found and figured out the key to the lamp. Since it wasn't electric, the gas flame surprised her and made her draw back with a little gasp. The reaction brought that same luscious breast back across his lips and this time Kane couldn't resist the temptation. He opened his mouth and snaked out his tongue, catching the soft flesh of her nipple quickly against his taste buds. Corrine yelped in surprise and jolted away from him, forcing Kane to curse his bound hands. Had they been free he could have caught her and held her to himself. He could have sucked on her until she completely discarded the impulse to escape and began, instead, to give in to the virulent chemistry he knew she was already starting to feel.

Corrine pushed away from him awkwardly, her shock at his boldness doubling when she felt the fiercely stunning flood of sensation that burst over her entire breast and embedded itself deep into the heart lying beneath it. That devastation of feeling compounded itself yet again when she got a good look at him. With his arms stretched taut over his head and his chest and belly on tight display, he looked every inch the restrained beast. He was shifting restlessly, his hips moving in an attempt to angle away from her, but it was a futile maneuver. Once again she could see that he was blatantly aroused. The massive bulge behind the denim was unrepentant, even if the owner was a little bit more so. Corrine couldn't help the knee-jerk flush of heat that rushed down the center of her body and up her neck to her cheeks.

"Stop," he rasped suddenly, the plea drowning in aching need. "Stop looking at me. Stop thinking . . ."

Kane groaned and Corrine realized abruptly where her thoughts had begun to drift and that he could read her mind. Blushing in earnest now, she tore her eyes from him, covering her hot face with cold hands and trying not to mentally acknowledge the damp traces of arousal left between her legs.

"Oh my God, what's wrong with me?" she gasped, a flustered tinge of red spreading all over her fair skin. Kane couldn't bring himself to look away, his gaze fixed as the lamplight flickered over her, illuminating the paths of pink that tinted her pale skin. She turned, searching, he sensed, for the top sheet that had been left on the floor earlier. She wanted to cover up the evidence of her reaction to their Imprinted chemistry. He was immensely satisfied when she couldn't find it. Knowing she would be stupid to waste her energy climbing down off the bed again, she crossed her arms from shoulder to shoulder, hiding little more than the stiffened points of her nipples.

"Nothing," Kane answered with a gruff croak of his voice. "Nothing is wrong with you. You're perfect."

She laughed at that, a hard sound full of bitter denial. "If that were true . . ." She stopped, a moment of panic lighting her eyes. She was remembering he had access to her mind, but it was too late already.

"If that were true," he finished for her, "then you wouldn't be alone."

"I . . . I'm not alone," she denied quietly, her face turning from him. "I have my sister."

"Corrine, there is nothing wrong with wanting a companion in your life," he told her.

Perhaps it was the infinite compassion in his voice that made her look back at him, but the sight of her brimming eyes stabbed into Kane like a huge, butcher knife.

"I've done everything I was supposed to do," she said softly, a hard sniffle trying to force back her feelings. "I went to school. I've got a good career. I live a strong and independent lifestyle. I'm good to other people as much as I can be. I take care of my family. I try so hard to do everything right . . ."

"Corrine, your lack of a partner has nothing to do with some kind of cosmic scorecard. Not in the way you think," he countered. "Destiny isn't punishing you by forcing you to be alone. Very much the contrary, sweetheart. She was simply making sure you were ready and open when your true mate came along."

She pushed back at the thick coiling curls of her cinnamon-fire hair and gave him a dirty look. "And let me guess. That special guy just happens to be you, right? How friggin' convenient for me that I just happened to get so lucky as to be held prisoner by your side, eh? Oh, wait. That's not luck, that's you insisting I'm going to croak if I budge so much as an inch off this bed! And can someone tell me again why I believe that ridiculous claim?"

Kane watched her pull back behind this caustic display with a sense of fascination. It was almost enough to make him forget the insistent desire punching through his body repeatedly. She was so beautiful. Even when she tried to be as prickly as a cactus, he found her utterly gorgeous.

"Because," he replied absently as his eyes dropped of

their own accord over her bare curves, "you've seen the proof of it. You left me and it hurt you. Drained you. Now, after only a couple of hours near me, you're able to sit up again."

"It's called rest," she argued. "You had nothing to do with it!"

"Oh really?"

"Yeah, really!"

"Then prove me wrong. Come here and kiss me."

Corrine gaped at him. "And just what the hell is that going to prove, besides the fact that I'm a gullible idiot?" she demanded.

"Come and kiss me and see."

He watched with amusement as she debated the wisdom of falling for what she thought was a prank, a way of conning her into cheap thrills. He forgave her for thinking so little of him. After all, she hardly knew him. He, on the other hand, knew everything about her. He'd staked her out, observed her, read her mind, and hunted her down. There wasn't a single thing about her, not even the deepest secret she had, that he wasn't privy to. He knew exactly who she was, and Kane knew she was everything he could ever have wanted. He also knew he was everything she had ever wanted. It would just take a little time to make her see that.

She chewed on her bottom lip for a long minute, forcing herself to keep her eyes on his face, studying him very closely to try to read what kind of game he was running on her. After a minute she made a little sound of disgust.

"Fine. Whatever floats your boat, sport. I'm going to love to see how you fast talk your way out of this one." With that, Corrine scooted up onto her knees, grasped hold of him with hands on either side of his face, and leaned forward until she was just about to lay her mouth against his. Kane didn't even realize it, but as she hesitated he began to pant heavily for breath. The closer she was, the more difficult it became for him to control the vicious hunger Samhain was beating into his body. His hands curled down into tight fists, the chains pulling taut with a chink of sound that made her glance up at his bound wrists. The small smile that touched her lips at the corners told him that she was enjoying her position of power over him. But he didn't begrudge her that. The tables were about to turn.

Corrine was super cautious as she touched the barest surface of her lips to Kane's. When he didn't move or make a single sound, when he didn't even so much as blink, she dared to move an increment closer. His mouth was nice, lax, and soft, completely lacking any aggression. Somehow she had expected him to try to press himself onto her, take instant command . . . to try to prove something to her. She certainly hadn't expected him to lie utterly passive and quiet as she tentatively kissed him. She drew back and cocked a brow at him. He chuckled, the sound short and clearly derisive.

"What are you? Two?" he mocked her. "I've seen twelve year olds kiss with more passion than that."

Kane's redheaded mate gasped with a hot flash of indignant fury. "Why you lousy son of a—!"

That was when Kane surged up at her and captured her scowling mouth. He caught the passion of that temper between them, letting the power of it loop them together like the surest of knots. It was true that all the information he and his brethren knew about the Imprinting had come from rare live examples and potentially embellished fairy tales, but one thing had always seemed to be consistent in the tales he'd heard. Nothing kick-started the Imprinting faster than fierce emotion, and some of the most ferocious was anger and outrage. Oh, he would have preferred love or even just blatant passion, but he was limited by the situation and could only work within certain bounds.

The kiss seared them together at their mouths, the crush of lips awkward and harsh at first because of his lurching, graceless attack on her. But he cheated for just a moment or two, his mind taking over her motor control so she couldn't rush away from him, the resulting paralysis dropping her against his chest and mouth.

The result was instantaneous ignition. Like a rocket roiling out burning fuel at liftoff, the sensation exploded over them both. Kane's libido screamed into overdrive, demanding all he had been denied when his brother and his King had bolted him down next to Corrine, forcing him to bear up under all her warm sighs and subconscious snuggling against his raw body. Her mind did not recognize him; the mores and hang-ups of her species interfering noisily, but when she'd been asleep, her body had had no doubt as to whom it craved. Now she was getting a crash course in what it had felt like for him as he had struggled through this sacred full moon. She would be untouched by it no longer. Never again, in fact. Kane growled inside in frustration as his shackles kept him from wrapping her into his embrace, kept him from dominating the moment anymore than he already had. But he knew Abram, his *Siddah*, who was keeping him from teleporting out of the bindings, would not free him until Noah gave him leave to do so.

So he dismissed the limitation and let it work in his favor. He slowly relaxed back into the pillows behind him and Corrine hastily moved forward to close any distance that might be created by the action. Ensnared by the shocking heat of Imprinted passion, she was stunned into reacting purely on instinct. Kane knew she had never felt anything like this in all of her human existence, but he liked the feel of her wicked delight and surprise as it burst through her in sprays of hot cinder and liquid lava. She reached to wrap her hands tightly around his head, seizing him firmly and fiercely as her lush mouth worked heatedly against his. Kane pulled for breath as his body strained with hardest heat for her. She opened her mouth and licked his lips with an achingly gorgeous invitation.

She sealed their mouths together and swiped her artful tongue against his. The pure flavor of her mouth burst against Kane's tongue and he ground out a deep sound of pleasure. But it was nothing compared to the shout that escaped him when she unthinkingly threw her leg astride his hips and settled her weight down against his fly.

Corrine did it to catch his kisses at a better, deeper angle. When she settled over him, though, she felt his entire being clench in response and need whiplashed back into her like a raging brushfire. She went liquid against him, pressing her rapidly overheating skin to his and rocking herself against his aroused body in thoughtless want. She never once broke their kiss, her slender, sensual body writhing with kinetic energy over his until he was shaking with the intensity of his desire for her.

"Touch me!" he gasped in command against her devouring lips. "Sweet Destiny, have mercy on me, Corrine, and touch me!"

Kane was straining so hard at his shackles that they were biting viciously into his flesh, the scent of fresh blood rising up sharply to compete with the pungent delight of Corrine's aroused body. Musk, sweet and sultry, shimmered against his senses as she drew her hands free of his hair and finally brought them down the expanse of his chest.

Corrine didn't understand what she was doing! A kiss, a simple kiss! That was all it was supposed to be. An obnoxious little peck to disprove the claims of her obnoxious bed-partner. Except suddenly there was a conflagration of positive proof that all his claims might have more than a little value. Every second she remained connected to him she felt revitalizing energy infusing her every cell. The weakness that had dogged her was fading fast and she suddenly felt starved. Starved for food, starved for energy, starved for a passion long due her.

This is it! This was what she had been looking for! This amazing, incredible feeling! It was like flying. It was all about dissolving into the ultimate and perfect passion. How? How could she possibly be finding this passion with a total stranger? Why now, of all the moments and of all the situations, why now? Why him?

And why, when he asked her to touch him, was she unable to resist doing exactly that? Suddenly she needed to feel him. All of him, everywhere she could possibly reach, just as quickly as she could. She kissed him until she could scarcely draw a breath, her hands running down the bare contours of his fine chest and tensed abdominals. Her skin was burning with the need to feel his hands and she tried to satisfy it by rubbing her body sinuously against his.

"Oh my God! Oh God, you feel so good," she cried out blindly, splitting her focus between the feel of him against her wriggling body and the sensation of his hot skin under her palms. Then the feel of his skin was replaced by the coarse thickness of denim and the burning heat of hardened flesh beneath it. The next thing either of them knew, her deft fingers were unbuttoning and unzipping his pants. She reached into his briefs and wrapped an eager hand around the incredibly thick circumference of his erection.

Kane broke from her mouth and shouted a vivid curse. His hips surged up into her grasp, forcing himself through her fingers. "Corrine!" he gasped, choking on his next demands when she slid her fist straight down his jutting length.

"Oh yes, yes, yes, yes, yes . . ." she hummed as she looked down the landscape of his body to see the prize she'd taken hold of. She couldn't get her hand completely around him and the realization made her body go wet with anticipation. It was as if she were possessed by something within herself that she had never encountered before. For a moment she tried to focus on the remnants of suspicion and confusion that had hounded her before she had touched him. Before she had tasted him.

Tasted him.

The craving for his taste seared through her mind an instant before it seared through his. Realizing what she was going to do almost unmanned him. The fever in his blood reached a boiling point as her fiery hair trailed down his torso. Tensed tight in anticipation, Kane threw out a desperate plea to his mentor, the man he called *Siddah*.

Let me be free! he begged Abram.

You know I cannot. Not without Noah's leave, was the reply.

I was seized in order to protect her from unwanted advances! You see she is willing!

She is possessed by the Samhain moon, Kane. You've used it against her to have your way. She is young, unskilled, weakened, and uninformed. The fact that she is being the aggressor at the moment is a mere technicality. Jacob and I raised you better than this.

Kane threw back his head and roared with the agonizing pain of his needful body and his stabbed conscience. It was the feel of her breath coasting hotly over the wet head of his erection that jolted him back to the issue at hand.

"Corrine, stop! Don't do this. Sweet Destiny, you have to—"

Her tongue touched against him and he felt it like a match burning a fuse into life. It was nothing tentative or shy; it was the bold stroke of a woman starved for the flavor of her lover. Kane jolted and his entire being seemed to gather energy up all at once. He had been suffering in need for so long beside her that this single contact had the power to drive him out of control. He was going to lose it all. Like an overeager boy fumbling clumsily with the precious gift of a young girl's innocence, he was going to create damage that could never be undone.

"Jason Deaver!"

Chapter 4

Kane blurted out the accursed name, a last ditch effort to rescue himself from the disaster he had created. He dragged the offensive moniker out of the deepest, darkest place in her mind and slapped her with it. She drew back so sharply and so suddenly that Kane had to fight not to sob with relief; to sob with devastation and loss. But now her suspicion was back, and pain and hurt were welling up fast and fierce in her eyes. She backed away from him as if he'd suddenly sprouted plague symptoms and curled her back into a cringe.

"What did you just say?" she asked him hoarsely, even though they both knew what he had said.

Kane needed precious moments to catch his breath, to calm the rage within his body. Abram was right. He could claim no satisfaction from Corrine while she was lost in the blind fever of the Samhain moon. When that haze cleared she would feel used and betrayed . . . and she would be right to feel that way. And even though it made him suffer vicious jabs of pain from unrealized release, he confronted her with the name again.

"Jason Deaver. You were fourteen to his eighteen. Infatuated and innocent, you thought you could trust him."

"Shut up," she hissed darkly at him.

"But he just wanted to get off, and he didn't give a damn about how you felt. He blundered around on top of you for what? Ten seconds? And then it was over and you—"

"Shut *up!*"

"—never saw him again." Kane drew a deep, unsteady breath. "I won't let this be like that, Corrine. I lost it for a minute there, I know, but I am not going to let you get all caught up . . . only to come down from it calling me the names you called him for years."

The Demon watched with no little suffering as she withdrew even further and curled up into her own body. She took Yoga, he knew, and so was in the habit of flexing her limber arms and legs around herself, but this was strictly protective. She was trying to erect an armor of limbs around her hurting heart and spirit.

The wound he spoke of was deep in her past, and it was true that she rarely even thought about it or took it out for examination. Corrine had considered it a hard lesson learned and had never forgotten since then to take everything a sexually invested male said with a very large grain of salt.

But she didn't know how to apply that lesson to this situation. She looked at him from the side of her eyes, seeing the way he struggled for control of himself, his breath coming so hard and his skin bright with perspiration. He was nearly stripped to his thighs, her eagerness and haste to hold him in her hands having been so sharp that she had . . .

Corrine's face flushed with new heat as she recalled exactly how she had felt and how driving that need had been. She felt a heavy thread of mortification for her unexpectedly wanton behavior. She closed her eyes, hiding her face against her updrawn knee and trying like hell to hide from her own embarrassment. What had gotten into her? It was to have been a simple kiss! How had that so rapidly evolved into her having his musky flavor on her tongue? What had . . . what had he done to her?

"It wasn't like that," Kane said, interrupting her thoughts.

"You've already proven you can take control of my mind and manipulate me like a marionette!"

"Do I look like I want a marionette?" he demanded in a sharp temper. "If I wanted a brainless sex toy, Corrine, I have the power to make you forget everything you'd do! You wouldn't be sitting there questioning me because you'd never even realize you'd missed a step in your daily life. And frankly, babe, if you and I are going to burn up the sheets together, I want you to remember every damn minute of it!"

"Why? Why me?" she yelled at him sharply and suddenly. "Why are you here like this"—she indicated his lashed down state—"and why am I here with you? You won't explain any of this to me and yet you expect me to simply accept and believe whatever choice bits of information you feel like doling out! Just tell me what is happening to me!"

"Don't you think I want to tell you all of that? I want nothing more than to clear the air and make you realize just how important all of this is!"

"Then do it, Kane! Stop pussyfooting around my delicate sensibilities and just explain this to me!"

"You're mine!" Kane blurted it out in a growl of frustration and need. The demanding conditions of the sharp moon that rose higher and higher with every second forced the claim out of him. "Mine! Not just for now but forever, Corrine! The person you've been searching for? That other half you've always known was missing from your soul? It's me. *Me*." Kane closed his eyes then and laughed with strained control. He couldn't bear to see that caustic, disbelieving expression on her face. She was looking at him as if he were some kind of horrible insect crawling up out of her drain. Unwanted. Undesired. Potentially dangerous and harmful.

Well, so be it. If she was going to think the worst of him, then what more harm could it do to throw a few choice logs on the fire?

"I'm not human, you know," he told her, a sudden grin striking his mouth. "And if you need more proof of that than what you've already seen, I'm momentarily going to have to disappoint you. My best parlor trick has been snuffed for the time being in order to keep me here." Kane jerked on the wrist shackles above his head. "And for that matter, you aren't entirely human either. I mean, you were, but then I touched you and apparently that set off this whole chain reaction that altered the hell out of your DNA . . . to the point that it almost killed you . . . and shot my sex drive into oblivion. See, I wasn't supposed to touch you, and I wasn't supposed to want you and I broke the law by doing both. I just couldn't stay away. You're just so remarkable . . . so strong and vital . . . so damn beautiful and independent. Yet you're covering up this chasm of loneliness inside. You called me to you. You were craving exactly what I can offer." Kane stole a glance at her. "Except the reality is that you think I am a lunatic. You think you've been kidnapped and thrown into some kind of weird human experiment or a practical joke. So I guess the odds of really getting to learn the things I want to learn . . . like what you feel like under my hands . . . like what you'll sound like when you laugh genuinely for me . . . I guess that's completely screwed up now."

Kane looked away from her, his long lashes lowering over suddenly hollow eyes. That he was utterly devastated by his situation was clear to Corrine. She could do little more than gape at him for the longest moment as she tried to process everything he had said to her. Of course, she ought to be telling herself he was insane because he thought he wasn't human, but all she could seem to focus on was the shivering thrill that raced beneath her skin when he spoke of touching her. She couldn't escape the way it made her feel when he spoke of craving something as simple as her laugh. She knew in her soul that it wasn't just a line, and she had never believed the words of any man with such conviction. Not since she'd learned that boys sometimes lied to get their way.

What was it about him that compelled her to believe in him so utterly? "If you aren't human, then what are you?" she asked.

Kane looked over at her briefly. His short laugh was a nearly soundless burst of air through his nose. "Well, pretty lady, my people are known as Demons. No wings, no fangs . . . not usually, anyway." There was a brief flash of a toothy grin and she could feel the mischief that swirled into his personality for that fleeting instant. It was an odd sensation, almost as if she were intruding directly into his mind. She wished for a moment that *she* could read *his* mind. Then she could figure out what he was up to. It wasn't the first time she'd had the desire to be able to read a man's mind so she would know if she could trust him. "We're people almost exactly like you. Except . . ."

"Except you can read the thoughts of others," she injected into the pause. "And we're not in some kind of hell, I take it?" Corrine looked up to indicate the stone room around her with its beautiful stained glass cathedral windows and rich castle-like appointments. It looked like a high end tourists' castle hotel, other than the gas lighting perhaps and the set of chains holding him securely in place.

"Oh, I'm in some kind of hell," Kane countered bitterly. But the sarcasm spoke as an affirmative answer to her question.

"So it's just a name. Demon."

"No. It's a culture, Corrine. A deeply complex culture with all the same sorts of mores, rules, and monsters as yours has. But it's a little more dangerous and it revolves around the night instead of the day. We live our lives, have jobs, find mates . . ." There was a distinct breech in his sentence as he slowly slid his gaze from the top of her head, all the way to the knees she was resting on beside him. The look was fast and fierce, beyond hot as it burned over her, and very, very clear in its intention. "Sometimes we have perfect mates. Soul mates. We call that connection an Imprinting. It's oh so very rare, Corrine, but when it happens . . ." He closed his eyes and drew in a slow, deep breath, his expression turning peaceful and passionate at the same time. "When it happens, we treasure it with all that we are. Just like you would."

"But"—she laughed nervously—"we don't usually just look at a total stranger and think 'There he is! That right there is my soul mate!' It's a long process, getting to know someone that well. It takes time to figure that sort of thing out."

"Not for us. Not for you and me. At least not physically speaking," he amended when she startled at his intensity. "This is a chemical connection, sweetheart. It's science. DNA and biological imperative. That much is written in our blood and cannot be changed. You and I are connected in this symbiosis of energy—" he indicated himself with his eyes, then looked at her—"and need for energy." He rushed onward when she seemed to be quietly listening, needing for her to hear him. "Some creatures in this world are driven by certain biochemical compulsions and some are driven by the turn of the seasons and time. My people are driven by both. And tonight . . . tonight is one of the most intense nights on our calendar. Tonight is Samhain, when the moon rises to its fullest in October. The weeks before and after are hard enough to deal with, but tonight is the worst. There's only one drive that seems to matter to us. And if we don't have our true mates, we'll try to satisfy it as best we can wherever we can. But if we find that one . . . that ever so precious one . . . then only that mate will do from that moment on. Civilization and logic and mores stop meaning anything to us; all we want is our mate. No matter what. Even if she doesn't know who we are. Even if she is sick and unconscious. It's a drive, Corrine, and I want to fight it with everything I have so I can approach you the right way . . . the way you deserve. The way I know you crave." *With sweetness and romance. Tenderness and caring. You want to be wooed and swept away and you think it's a fantasy that will never be fulfilled, but it will. It will. I just need to get through tonight. Then I can give you the romance as well as the passion. I can give you everything!*

But this is all just words and empty promises to her, he thought to himself, looking away from Corrine's very stunned expression. *She doesn't believe a word of it. Why should she when all she has known are liars who'll speak sweetness to her in order to coax their way into those amazing arms and that incredible body?*

Kane's eyes closed and the pain on his features etched into deeper lines. "Oh, honey," he sighed, "I know you don't believe me. To you I must seem like just one more in a long line of con artists. I've just got a better line right? More creative?"

Corrine didn't acknowledge him. Her brain was churning out other information. *I heard his thoughts!* she realized with no little sense of awe. She realized by his spoken words that he had not meant for her to hear what had rung like a conversation in her head. It had been loud and then soft, fading in and out of clarity, different from when he spoke directly into her thoughts in a clear and distinct manner. What was most telling was the sheer emotion behind his thoughts. When he'd spoken into her mind before, it had only been his voice she'd experienced. But this time she felt everything. She felt his frustration and his desperation. She felt, once again, that ring of utter truthfulness. He wasn't lying to her. She could tell. She could read his thoughts!

As well as his starkest emotions. His rawest needs.

They came barreling forward, rushing into her inexperienced, awakening mind like a defensive line of burly ball players. Crashing into her hard and fast, screaming his agonizing physical need.

"Oh my God!" she gasped, suddenly doubling over and reaching to clutch at the bed sheets. It flooded over her whole body, a tension of constant readiness and endless craving. Her heart began to race as fast as his was, her breasts filled heavily with a rushing heat of blood and awareness until her body shivered and her nipples came to painfully erect attention. Liquid fire melted through her every bone, hunger raged and clenched through every muscle.

This, she realized, was what he had been struggling with all this time. Corrine looked up at Kane with shock and dismay flashing briefly in her eyes just before savage appetite and need overran it.

"Corrine?" Kane was almost afraid of the look she was running over him, but it didn't keep his aching body from reacting eagerly to it. The fresh rush of blood into his already swollen penis hurt incredibly, but it was quickly forgotten as she slowly sat back on her heels, her hands releasing the bedclothes to run up her body. Thighs to hips, her palms slowly turning and fingers spreading as they coasted into the bend of her waist and over her belly. She rushed abruptly upward to cup her breasts, each hand kneading fiercely for a moment as she made a soft noise of frustration mixed with pleasure. Her eyes had long since slid closed, but now they opened so she could stare steadily into him.

"You didn't tell me how much this hurts," she whispered, a soulful groan coming out of her as she curved her spine against the rush of heated feedback coming from his reaction to watching her touch her own bare body. "You didn't make me understand the way it hurts! The way I make you hurt." She exhaled sharply and then reached out for him, her hair falling all around him in a curling auburn curtain as she leaned far enough forward to grasp his forearms just before that spot where the shackles bound him. "You didn't explain that you let them do this to you to protect me from you."

In truth he had shown very little to her. All he had given her so far was words and an underhanded trick to trigger her moon-fed libido. That realization reminded him that there was much more to him and his powers than telepathy and his currently thwarted ability to teleport. He needed to do something to distract her from what she was feeling. He didn't think he could man up twice in such a short period of time and pull away from the fire he saw burning in her liquid green eyes.

"I am not human," Kane reminded her, knowing she wasn't quite absorbing the truth of it. "I am not without power. Right now my *Siddah,* my mentor, keeps me from teleporting, which is my most significant power, but there is much more to the power of Mind than that. I may be young by my people's standards, but I have mastered much in my time."

Suddenly he seemed to be pulling free of the chains binding him, and Kane reached for her hand, interlacing his fingers with hers, and drawing her into a swirl of nonexistence. For a moment she could not breathe, felt as if she had no substance and no focus, and yet her mind had never felt so sharp. The next thing Corrine knew, she was standing on her own two feet, her fingers still locked within his grasp, and the crisp cold of an autumn breeze was rushing over her. She was out of doors, sunset streaking the horizon all around her, a lush lawn prickling softly beneath her bare feet. She was now clothed, her body wrapped warmly in a fiery red velveteen fabric, a dress with a high waist and ripples of feminine material flowing away from that high center point of her body. She tended to wear jeans and T-shirts, so she was not used to the feel of plush fabric billowing around her in the breeze. But, if she could choose . . . she had always been drawn to beautiful, classic fashions like this. Dresses that were soft and feminine and flowing. Of course, they were not very practical for day-to-day living in the bustling world of New York City. She was a counselor for endangered teens in the Bronx. What would they make of her if she came to work every day dressed like this?

And in red no less. She would never have chosen red. Didn't many of the fashion experts say redheads shouldn't wear red? The truth was, red washed her out terribly. She looked wan and sickly. The only thing possibly worse would be orange. But here it was, on her body, and even without being able to see herself, she knew it was beautiful. Beautiful on her, beautiful with her. He had chosen for her far more bravely than she would have chosen for herself and had done an amazing job of it. The narrowed sleeves warmed her wrists, making her seem so thin and fragile. Yet there was vigor in her body for the first time in days. She felt strong and healthy, felt full of energy and life.

She looked back at him and saw he was dressed as well. He had on the same faded denims as before and a shirt made of that same rich fabric as her dress, only in a dark teal he wore very well. Actually, he wore everything well. Would wear anything well, she realized as her gaze ran over him quickly. He was taller than she had realized, longer in the waist, stronger in his stance. Once again she appreciated just how beautiful he was. Breathtakingly beautiful as only a perfectly fashioned male could be. He was almost too handsome.

Then a strong breeze rushed over her again and she realized she was out of doors for the first time in what had to be ages. Days. Too many days. She closed her eyes and turned her face into the wind, taking in the deepest, cleanest breath she could manage. The air smelled so fresh and different, the touch of it carrying the crispness of late autumn in a way that chilled the tip of her nose.

"You're doing this?" she asked, even though she already knew. "We're really back in that place, lying next to one another, but you're doing this with your mind?" She didn't need to see his nod to know it was the truth. She held her free hand up to her eyes, shielding them against the brilliant light and colors of the waning sun.

"I would not be able to be out in this much daylight if it were real. I would still be sleeping, or very weak. Darkness is my daylight." Kane squinted his eyes against the fading brightness around him. His eyes, like all Demon eyes, were made for darkness. He could not see nearly as well in sunlight. But he knew the same was not true for her. Not yet, in any event. Humans, he knew, found much beauty in sunrises. And yes, they were lovely, but they had always meant borders to him. Restrictions. Time to rest. Quickly to rest, or he might find himself exposed to the deadly light of day that could kill a Demon as young as he was. He must spend the sunlit hours locked in rest, forced to sleep whether he wanted it or not, forced to wait for the day to hide itself.

But this had always been her world. And just as day was turning to night, now she would have to say farewell to blue skies. If she were to be his mate, she must change her ways to match his. It was a lot, he realized, for her to sacrifice. The truth was, she was sacrificing far more than he was. What was he saying farewell to, besides perhaps the torture of lonely Samhain and Beltane nights?

Corrine looked all around herself, knowing as she breathed it in that there was something foreign in the air around her. Not exotic, just different. But that was easily seen just by looking at the vast green landscape that surrounded her. She was encompassed by a great ocean of manicured green, rolling hills of it sprawling away from her in all directions. In the distance before her was a great stone building, what she could only call a castle. It was wider in body than it was tall, reaching high and then tumbling low, clearly made of a grand central mass that had been added to over time. There had been an attempt at balance, and the engineering of it was remarkable compared to castles that she had seen in pictures. But it was a fortress of stone no matter how you looked at it. Flags flew from its highest points, but there was nothing in the design of those flags that she found familiar. Nothing that hinted at state or country or an affiliation she recognized. There was writing in the crests, but she couldn't see what it was from this distance and she had a suspicion she wouldn't be able to read it even if she were closer. There were hedgerows and fountains, great sweeping drives of white stone that reminded her of a great manor from an Austen novel. The oaks that lined the drives waved at her with pale-colored leaves barely hanging on.

"Is this where we are?" she asked him. "Inside of that place?" She recalled the stone room she'd woken up in and how it had reminded her of an old castle room.

"This is the home of the Demon King, Noah. And yes, this is where we are. Somewhere on the third floor, beyond those colored windows. I wanted to show you some of my world from another perspective. Some of who and what we are."

That was when a cloud of smoke suddenly swirled into her view, several feet before her. It rushed around like a tornado, but it was no bigger than a man. Black and grey and silver streams curled around one another, and then suddenly resolved into the shape of a man made of smoke, and then a man made solid. Corrine's eyes had seen many special effects on movie screens, but nothing like the reality of what she'd just experienced. Even so, she wanted to reach out and touch him, to prove to herself that he was as real as he looked. How was any of this possible? A man appearing out of thin air? Another man who could read thoughts? It was all fantasy, pure and simple. And yet not. Here it was reality.

"Corrine, I'd like you to meet our King, Noah."

Corrine drew in a breath as the sunset sped up around her, drawing down dark violet skies and then a cloak of night around the handsome Demon King. He was larger than Kane by far, in height and in musculature, and everything in his bearing screamed of his great position in life. He was powerful, he was responsible for the well-being of an entire people, and he knew it.

But as darkness descended around them, Corrine quickly learned there was far more to him. Noah showed her his palms briefly, and then with a whoosh of sound they were engulfed in flame. Brilliant balls of fire swallowed up his hands to the wrists, and slowly he began to move them, creating bright arcs of light in the darkness as he sketched circles and swirls and arches. Then with a sharp snap of his wrists, fire raced up his arms and quickly engulfed all of his body. Everything inside Corrine that had been trained to respond in the human dimension screamed to see a man on fire. She was breathing so hard, the air cold and warmed all at once in her lungs as she stood there forcing her mind to accept the impossible.

And then, in a rush, the flames burst apart, flying around her in a great circle and touching a ring of torches amidst them that she had not noticed before. After he had lit their way, the Demon King disappeared.

She turned to look at Kane, but only had a moment to open her mouth before he put his finger then to his lips and then pointed forward. Her heart seized in her chest as she eagerly looked in the indicated direction. Another cloud was coalescing in front of her, only this time it seemed to have more weight to it than smoke. After a moment she realized it was dust she was seeing.

Kane grabbed her by her shoulders from behind, pulling Corrine into his warm body as he pressed his lips to the sweet spot just behind her ear.

"Corrine Russ, I'd like you to meet my brother. His name is Jacob, and he is the most powerful Earth Demon ever to walk the world."

And as he spoke, the man himself appeared. There was so much of Kane's features in him that she might have known they shared the same blood even if he had not told her so. Jacob's hair and eyes were as dark as Kane's, but it was those proud Romanesque features that linked them, from the long nose and strong chin to the sculpture of the full, knowing lips. Yet there was something in Jacob's eyes that Kane's lacked. The man behind her, for all the pain and hardship he'd experienced as he laid bound beside her, had an almost carefree quality to his aura.

Jacob did not. Here was a man who carried a great weight on his soul. Corrine had seen it before, in the eyes of young boys who were faced with the lures of gangsters every day, and the painful or deadly alternatives if they resisted. In their world there was no such thing as saying "no." Not without dreadful consequences. In Jacob's weighted aura, there was a tremendous responsibility.

Jacob spread his hands wide, his palms turned toward the ground, and suddenly everything around them began to rock and tremble. The earth beneath her feet quaked; then a wall of soil and stone lurched up between her and Jacob. It was so massive and raw that she could smell the loam, see the burrowing creatures that suddenly dangled from roots and such as their protective homes were unearthed. Dirt rained down like a soft summer shower, even as the wave rising before her shifted first to the right and then to the left. And in the next moment the entire monstrosity fell in on itself, rumbling and shaking until it had repacked itself into place. By the time Jacob took a deep, cleansing breath and looked up at her, there wasn't so much as a speck of dust out of place to bear witness to what had just happened.

"All right," she breathed. "You're Demons. Not human. I totally get it."

"But it is not all about parlor tricks," Jacob responded. "It is about long-held traditions, a long history of mistakes, and a painful responsibility to ourselves and those we coexist with. We cannot make mistakes. Mistakes cost us too dearly."

"Wow." Under her breath she whispered into Kane's ear. "Is he always so tightly wound?"

"Always," Kane assured her. "But he's getting better." A woman resolved out of thin air at Jacob's side and Kane's brother immediately reached to wrap an arm around her curvy hips and draw her flush to his body. It only took an instant for Corrine to recognize who she was.

"That's my sister! Isabella!" She lurched forward, suddenly needing to feel the steady and familiar irreverence of her sibling, but Kane held her tight.

"Remember, this is all a production of my powers. I don't know anything about your sister other than what she looks like. She would feel, smell, and act very flat to you, with no dimension. I've only met her once in person. I could draw from your memories of her, but the result would not catch all those special nuances that make her the person you love and are familiar with. Not unless I put all of my energy and focus into it and I am not old enough or strong enough to maintain our surroundings and do that as well."

"So there are limits to what you can do," Corrine murmured.

"Yes, of course. We are not all powerful. And besides, there's a bit of an ethical limit too, Corrine. I won't do things that will end up making you feel like you've been manipulated. Having your sister tell you how wonderful everything is for her, how wonderful we are, would be an outright manipulation of your trust and a misuse of your relationship with her. I am doing all of this to orient you to my world, to show you who and what we are, not to run some kind of propaganda gambit."

"I appreciate that."

"But even what you are seeing isn't really right," he said with no little frustration. "This is just a demonstration of power. It isn't showing you how truly good we are. How incredibly moral Demons like my brother are." He sighed. "I'm just not powerful enough or skilled enough."

Corrine turned around against his body, not taking the opportunity of his loosened grip and lax attention to move away from him.

"On the contrary," she said softly, reaching up to touch the edge of the wild dark curls lining his temple. "You've shown me that and more. If there is one thing I have learned at my job, it's that those with power like to use it against those without. The fact that this is the first time I've even heard of a Demon, in spite of those extraordinary things I just saw them do, proves that you all wield your power with incredible regard for those around you. Your morals are shown in just the way you have restrained yourself from trying to win me over with methods even we humans wouldn't hesitate to use against one another."

He looked at her then with such a combination of fascination and true adoration that she bent her head, hiding her face against his breast bone.

"When I first saw you," he whispered against the top of her head, "I admit it was your outer beauty that fascinated me. All of this glorious, fiery hair and your amazingly pale and perfect complexion. The way your eyes lit when you laughed, the way your curves filled out your clothing. But that was just the lure. As I watched you, as time went by and I saw the way you dealt with those around you . . . that was the hook. Oh, Corrine, that was when I realized you were going to mean more to me than just a passing fancy. It was such a deep, visceral reaction. I knew you were meant for me. Even though every logical part of me understood it was forbidden for a Demon to touch a human being with the intentions that I had formed toward you . . . I couldn't let go. I couldn't walk away."

Corrine went still as his words sank into her brain.

"What do you mean, when you first saw me?" she asked, even though she was already feeling the truth rushing to the front of her mind. Things he had been saying, things that had been happening to her. If his explanation of how a Druid and Demon connection worked was to be understood, then . . . "You've met me before all of this. You . . . you touched me before. If what you are saying makes any sense at all, then you touched me long before I actually got sick." She squirmed in his hold, trying to shrug him off. "Only, I don't remember ever meeting you before. Ever being touched by you before."

"Because when I met you, when I touched you, it was wrong of me to do so. It was illegal according to my people's laws. Jacob stopped me from . . . he made me erase your memory of any contact we had."

"So you all have been messing with my mind? You *stalked* me, felt me up or something and then messed with my head so I wouldn't remember? And now you're trying to tell me what an up and up and moral society you have?" She pushed him off herself completely, stumbling as she backed away. "And for all I know you've got my sister locked up someplace where I'll never see her. Or . . ." Kane could see the panic welling in her eyes, brimming in her voice. "God, how do I know what's real anymore? What can I trust anymore?"

He reached out to her, grabbing her by both of her upper arms and giving her a shake to stop the progression of her racing, panicked mind. It forced her wide green gaze up to his, forced her to look into his eyes and into him.

"Nothing I say or do is going to make up for the underhanded ways I have dealt with you in the past, and for that I am incredibly sorry. I know it was wrong. I beg your forgiveness for it. But the truth is I would do it all again. I don't think I would even have an ounce of free will that could compel me otherwise. Corrine, I am now, and will always be, tied to your side. Destiny laid out a plan for you and me.

She predestined that we should walk a powerful path together, that I should, in all things, be devoted to you. If that is shameful in your eyes, if that is something you perceive as nefarious and wrong . . . then I am so sorry. I am . . . heartbroken. I am at a loss as to how to be anything better for you than what I am. And to have failed my one true mate in this life shames me."

There was no denying the weight of the shame she saw in his eyes. It simply took her breath away. Whatever was truth and whatever was made up by the power of his mind, there was nothing as clear to her as his sincerity in that moment. She should have doubted him. She should have remembered all the games men had played with her all these years as they strove to take one thing or another from her. She should have held him just as accountable for his lies as she did the other males who'd lied to her.

But she didn't. For all of that history, for all of that mistrust and those painful lessons in deception, they had never touched the true heart of her. She had never stopped wanting forever after and a soul mate. She continued to crave a real partner in life who would support her when she needed it and who would look to her for support when he needed it.

When she looked at Kane, when she collated all he had been telling her and all she had seen and experienced so far, she saw exactly what she had been looking for. However, it would take a huge leap of faith on her part. There was a very fine line between what she craved and the attentions of a psychotic stalker. How would she tell the difference? How did anyone tell the difference?

"They can't tell the difference, to be honest," Kane said, reminding her how easily he could read her thoughts. "They go purely on faith. They have to trust themselves and what they are feeling. You need to trust yourself. You will make a wise, solid choice based on your intelligence and your instincts."

"I would," she breathed, pulling closer to him so she could gaze up into his clean, honest eyes. "But you have to admit, your power is enough to make anyone doubt the workings of their own mind."

"What can I do to make it better for you? To make it easier? Tell me. Anything. I'll do it."

"A promise. A promise that you'll never manipulate my mind again without asking me first. Even something like this." She looked up and around at the crisp dark sky filled with the stars. They were sharp, bright, and beautiful. Breathtaking.

"What you're asking . . . it will be hard for me. Let me explain," he said hastily when she frowned. "All of my life I've been trained to use the powers of my mind in all ways and in all things. Demons use their powers as reflexively as humans draw breath. I will never mean you any harm and I do not intend to lord my power over you, but my need to use power is unthinking. Just as you would thrust your hands out in front of you to break a fall, if I were in danger . . . if you were in danger, I would not be able to help my reaction."

She had to give him credit for his honesty. He had the power to make a promise and then do as he wished, wiping her memory of any transgressions or trespasses.

"That I *can* promise you," he said, interrupting her thoughts. "I can swear to you never to erase your memory of anything again . . . without your express permission. It is my philosophy that our experiences, both good and bad, shape our character. It does us little good to constantly remove what is ill from our memory. Yes, it gives us peace from trauma, but it is hard to know if that serves us or harms us in the long run. There may even come a time, in the future, when you will beg me for my skill and I will need to deny you. Understand I will do so only because it is morally right and hopefully best for you in the long run. My heart, however, will wish only to spare you any and all pain."

Kane reached up to touch her face, his pinky coming to trace over the high sculpture of her exquisite cheekbone. He took that peaceful moment, his first in so many days, to marvel over the contrast of his dark skin in comparison to hers. Oh, yes, in that part of himself which he had left behind in that room in Noah's castle, his blood still raged for her. His body ached for her. But for that single sweet moment he could treasure this one gorgeous difference between them, and the spectacular way his darkness enhanced her crisp, clean beauty.

Her lashes were a brilliant red, as were her brows, perfect complements to her spiraling hair. Her skin was rich like peaches and cream, the way he remembered it from before she had become so ill and come so close to death.

"I think," she whispered softly, close to his lips, "I read your mind before."

The confession took him aback, almost completely shattering his control over the illusion they were dwelling in. It was things like this, easy distractions like this that marked him as a youth amongst Demons. But to be fair, he'd had no clue she'd walked in his thoughts, and the fact that she had was proof positive that they were becoming more and more bound together.

"It's . . . it's a mark of the Imprinting," he told her, "though I confess I had not expected it with you being so weakened."

"They were . . . very vehement thoughts. It wasn't like when you speak into my mind. That's much clearer. These were weaker, with almost an echo, and yet there was strong emotion attached. Yes—" she searched his eyes hard. "It was more like reading your emotions than your thoughts, although I heard the words. You said, 'I just need to get through tonight . . . I can give you the romance as well as the passion. I can give you everything!'"

"It's true," he swore to her on a soft breath. "I know I'm

behaving like a beast, taking advantage of the chemistry the Imprinting has created between us, but I don't want it to be all about chemistry, Corrine. I don't want you to think that predestination is all this is; that I'll take our connection or you for granted; that I'll treat this as something easy or a foregone conclusion."

If anything, Corrine thought, he had proven just the opposite. Every time she had been overwhelmed by the ferocious heat of the Hallowed moon, he had done something to negate her desire, to distract her from it or break it off. Even this very illusion had been a way of veering off and away from the need that had overwhelmed her. And she was new to it all. From what she was understanding, it was even worse for him, and he had been suffering it for ages.

"Kane," she said, "take us back."

"Back?" he questioned, his voice full of breath. He was a telepath. There was no need for him to doubt her intentions or what she said. It was just his way of dodging the onrush of emotion and excitement that was flooding him. "Don't you . . . wouldn't you rather be here? Free from . . . from the way I am back there?"

And the real point of the illusion he'd created became clear to her. If he was here, orchestrating this scenario with all his will and concentration, then he could not subject her to the beast lashed by her side. He was protecting her from him. Trying to buy himself some time from what she understood was inevitable torture. Even now, as she glanced upward into the night sky, she could see the stars vibrating, making white, unstable streaks in their bed of darkness. His focus was unraveling.

She reached up to cradle his face in both of her hands, brushing her fingers over clean shaven contours that were much handsomer when they were real and covered in a brusque sheet of whiskers.

"Take me back," she breathed softly, her lips barely brushing his.

"Corrine . . . I can't control . . ." He began to breathe hard, his hands coming to grip her by the back of her shoulders. The stars began to drop out of the sky, streaking down like burning cinders, the grass beneath her bare feet lost the texture of the individual blades, sliding like sand under her heels.

"Then don't."

"I don't want to hurt you," he swore harshly. "I don't want to be what I am back there."

"I'm going to take care of it. This time, I will provide the escape we need."

And like a sudden deluge of water, the sky dropped in a sudden cloak of blackness all around her.

Chapter 5

Light resolved around her, the softness of the bed and the dampness of his skin jumped to life beneath her. In the span of a breath she was back in bed with him, back in that gaslit room. The moment she felt him for real beneath her, her body lit up as if it was on fire. The first difference she noticed between his illusion of himself and the reality was the rich, musky scent of his skin. It was like a personal sin, something created just for her, just to tempt her and fill her with heat. This time she welcomed the Samhain-driven need that filled her. Yes, she was throwing herself all in, having faith that everything she had learned was truth. Sometimes in order to reap the reward you wanted most, you had to take a risk. And somehow it didn't feel like so much of a risk. The burn sliding throughout her body was no illusion, no lie. It was as natural as anything could be.

Kane took in a slow breath, trying to order his thoughts and maintain control when he could barely hear over the noisy thumping of his heart. When she threw her leg over him and settled herself astride him, her sex brushed soft and wet across the center of his belly, the heat burning and beautiful. His sharp senses fed her sweetly aroused aroma to him and he strangled out a groan that marked his tortured conscience and his having reached his physical limits.

"Corrine, you can't . . . make choices . . ." He broke off when she laid herself flush with his chest, her hands braced beside his shoulders as she tempted him with the hovering nearness of her ripe mouth.

"You can't make choices either. You said it yourself. There is no choice here. We are chemical. A reaction meant to be. It's true, isn't it?"

"You're supposed to be—"

"Resting? Healing? You know this will revive me more than anything else."

Corrine kissed him with a warmly teasing stroke of her mouth. She liked his mouth, with its too-pretty fullness and the distinctive carving of his upper lip set in relief by a few days' worth of beard shadow. She remembered his taste from earlier and she began to seek it in slow, delighted brushes against his mouth. She was going to take the time to discover the perks of this hunger they shared.

Kane felt the brush of her breasts on his chest, her nipples drawing across pectoral muscles amped with sensitivity to the feel of her. There was nothing like it. Never had been, never would be. It was the sensation created by a complementary chemistry unique only to them. Kane exhaled into her mouth as she nibbled temptingly at him in brief, tasty little kisses.

That was when what she had said finally sank into his hormone-befuddled brain. With a jolt he drew back from her and stared up into her clear green eyes. She was clever and smart, but this was beyond all of that.

"You read my thoughts," he whispered in stunned delight. "You read my thoughts!"

"Yes," she agreed simply, as if it weren't a profound sign of her mind and body awakening to her Druid genetics, as well as their special connection to each other. She shrugged as if she read minds all the time. "That's how I knew you were telling me the truth about all of this. That's how I knew why you were bound, Kane. And it's how I know that you're suffering terribly without me."

She kissed him softly, but Kane abruptly jerked free of her again. "So that's what this is? Some kind of pity fuck, Corrine? If that's the case, then you can just take your ass off of me right now. I'll wait until you actually feel something for me, thank you very much."

Corrine reached to touch his face and he jolted away, but there was only so far he could go, trapped tightly as he was. She caught him between her hands and stared deeply into his eyes.

"I feel the same thing you do. Heat. Need. Craving that's driving you all but mad. I feel the biological imperative, just like you do. God, if you could feel inside me, Kane!" She was shifting against him, rubbing herself onto him until his belly was wetted by her and her sensual smell was driving into his spinning mind. Sweet Destiny, there was nothing he craved more than knowing what she felt like from the inside. And yet . . .

"I know," he croaked roughly, "I know all of this, Corrine. But you don't want a man for your body. You want one for your soul. That is what I want to be. Not just this!"

"See now, that's where you're wrong," she corrected him softly as she began to slide herself sinuously down the length of his body. "What I need is both, Kane. A lot of both." She sighed against his skin as she moved further along, her fingers toying with the already opened denim of his jeans. Next he knew she was stripping the fabric of his pants and briefs away, pushing it past his knees where it wouldn't interfere with her plans. "I guess you can read my mind and figure out just how long it's been since I last had sex," she noted.

"I could," he rasped. "But I'm a little distracted right

now." He swallowed noisily when she touched the lightest stroke of fingertips up his bared thighs. "And I'm trying to figure out why you're suddenly willing to be with me like this."

She laughed, looking at him as if he were simpleminded. "Because I read your mind, Kane. For one little minute I saw everything you were thinking and feeling." Corrine reached out and touched a fingertip to the bottom of his up-thrust shaft. Slowly, as she spoke, she drew her finger up his hot length. He was scorching the pad of her finger as she tested the texture of his soft skin and hard excitement. That burning level of heat was almost as fascinating to her as the scent of him, rich and male and ready, as it drifted around her. "I saw hours and hours of resistance against something impossible to bear up under. I saw how afraid you were that you'd hurt me. I felt how guilty you feel because of what has happened to me. It was all tumbled together at the very front of your mind, fresh and deeply affecting you." She reached the tip of his erection and took the time to tease the ragingly sensitive nerves there with brushes of that mischievous fingertip. "Don't you see? That's all I've ever wanted, Kane. Someone who cares about me more than he does himself." She looked up at him, a sly smile tilting one corner of her pretty mouth, making his already tight gut clench with fiery response. "Well, electrifying sex would be good too. So let's see if you can hit two for two."

"Ah, hell! Tied up?" he ejected in frustration.

"Hmm. Good point. Guess I'll do all the work this time. You can make it up to me later."

With an upward glide of warm skin stroking fully against him, she slid herself back into her position astride his hips, and this time she caught him directly between her thighs, the wet heat of her sex stroking suggestively over his pulsing erection.

Kane could hardly bear the sensation after holding himself in check for so very long. It was like a toxic dream materializing into full-bodied reality. He knew she was too weak and damaged to be playing the seductress the way she was, but the truth was that the more they satisfied the demands of nature, the faster she would heal. He couldn't possibly get any closer than inside of her, and the energy exchanged in a sexual encounter would be phenomenal.

Just having her at last would be phenomenal.

But . . .

"And in the dawn, sweetheart?" he asked as she began to rain soft, seeking kisses over his face and neck. "Are you going to wake to your world of light and realize you don't want to live in the night with me? Will you want to run from me then? Loathe me?"

The question gave her pause and she tilted her head to look at him in curiosity. Kane could have easily read her thoughts in that moment, no waiting necessary, but fear gripped him and he couldn't bear the idea that she would want to shed him like a bad dream if only given half a chance.

"Kane," she said, soft admonishment lilting out of her as she kissed his mouth with heavenly sweetness. "I've always known that in order to enjoy a mate who thinks of me before himself, I would have to do exactly the same in return. No one can earn such devotion without expecting to be required to return it."

Kane surged up into her kiss suddenly, catching her mouth as deeply as he could, kissing her so hard that he knew she felt the impact her sweetly optimistic vision of their future together had had on him. It was why he'd fallen for her in the first place. Pain and betrayal littered her history, yet she always hoped for the best . . . searched for the dream she had longed for, the one she'd had imbedded in her soul when she'd been born for him.

Corrine swallowed down his intensity and, using the lash

of her tongue, she stirred up even more within him. His bold taste burned all the way down into her belly and she devoured him in utter starvation. She was needy and stripped clean of energy, and only he could fill her up again. She kissed him until neither could catch their breath. She slid herself over him again and again, absently stroking his hard flesh over her sensitive clit until her entire body was humming with sensitive preparedness.

Kane broke away from her for the breath he needed to shout out in fury. "Damn you, Abram, let me out of these cursed chains and give me my hands!"

The Elder Demon who was preventing his ability to teleport ignored the demand once again. No matter what happened, only Noah's command would sway Kane's *Siddah*. And, of course, Abram had no idea where the Demon King was and no inclination to disturb him.

"Hush," his mate scolded him as she let her moist lips trail hot kisses down his body. "I always wanted a man completely at my mercy. Don't spoil my fun."

The Mind Demon ejected an unintelligible sound she took as capitulation as she ran her tongue along the arches of his lower ribs, and then moved slowly down his belly, breathing hotly over every wet place she made or discovered. Skirting his navel, she licked down the furred line of hair leading to his groin. Her free hand wrapped around him to keep him out of her path until she was good and ready to pay attention to him. His penis was drenched with her juices, transferred as she'd ridden against him. She used this to her advantage and stroked him heavily until she deemed herself ready to take a taste of him.

The touch of her tongue burned a wildfire reaction up his shaft and Kane's entire body seized with the sensation. He gasped, dizzy and agonized by her teasing, frankly shocked he didn't burst right then and there. He was watching as she slowly swiped her tongue across the head of his erection, licking away the copious pearly liquid weeping freely from it. The vision of her was such a magnificent sight to him, the stuff of his most forbidden fantasies. The savage sound and emotion roiling out of him as she drew him deeper into her mouth abruptly reminded him that she was still mostly human, while as a Demon suffering from the need to rut, he was a very savage and different beast. Her deprivation of energy had stunted her change, a change that was supposed to have made her able to bear the fierce brunt of Demon lovemaking.

Suddenly he was glad he was lashed down good and tight. The way she was making him feel right then, he'd probably have thrown her down and torn her apart with his intensity. Even so he couldn't help the blind need to thrust against her devilish little tongue. But she clearly didn't want him getting any ideas of his own, so she released him from her mouth and went back to her position astride him. Settling herself hot and wet against him, but not taking him inside yet, she leaned forward to dance the tip of one breast against his lips. He caught her suddenly and sharply with his teeth, making her gasp.

Tease me, will you? he thought fiercely into her mind.

Again and again, she promised him, her voice in his head breathless and aroused. He could see the flush of excitement all over her skin and the depth of her need shining in her eyes. Samhain was just as hard on her heels as it was on his, but she wanted him well beyond that. He could feel it. He could hear the chant going desperately through her thoughts. *I need you, Kane. I need you!*

"Corrine, I can't do this anymore!" He knew he was begging for her as he bucked up against her, seeking the entrance that eluded him. Sweet Destiny, she didn't understand! She didn't know how long he had craved the moment she was withholding from him. She couldn't know what this was doing to him! Kane gnashed his teeth and jerked savagely at his shackles. Wood cracked as the steel of his chains ground against it.

"Easy," she soothed with a slender hand stroking down his chest and belly. "I'm doing the work of two people here." Corrine narrowed liquid green eyes on him as her fingertips reached to touch the soft russet curls framing her sex which were thoroughly combined with his own. She reached two delicate fingertips to seek out her clitoris, coincidentally stroking over the burrowing head of his penis where she held him trapped between their bodies. For a long, torturous moment she teased them both like that, the flicker and stroke of her fingertips unraveling the focus of their minds in a strange disembodied concert. She was too untried to hold their mental link on her own, so Kane chained them together with clarity and strength, the cycles of their pleasure wrapping thoroughly around one another.

He was so amazed by the easy way she appeared to accept pleasure, the way she so willingly let it roll over her body, that he didn't expect the abrupt shift she made that started to bring him inside her. Kane's hands reached up to curl tightly around the steel links that held him imprisoned, suddenly needing the vicious grip as she slowly worked to impale herself on him.

At ninety-eight years of age, Kane was two years from being an adult in the eyes of his peers, but right then he had never felt more like a novice at life. The sensation of his perfect mate welcoming him with such exquisite perfection brought him to his proverbial knees. He shook his head, trying to stave off the dampness in his eyes, but with little success. He hated that he couldn't touch her, and yet there was something about her proud domination over him that made it all worthwhile.

Corrine closed her eyes, dropping her head back with a lusty groan that echoed high in the stone room. Kane was so hot that she felt as if she was impaling herself on pure burning steel. She worked herself down onto him, gasping at the ferocity of his heat and feeling wave after wave of his profound emotional response. Oh, how compelling it was to know he was feeling this way because of her! When he finally sank home inside her, she had to lean with flat palms against his chest, drawing hard for breath because of how intense the sensation was. Her entire body shimmered with delight and the ready edge of pleasure. She lifted herself and shifted back onto her heels, crying out as he met her with a defiant thrust of his hips. Her whole frame shivered with the impact and she almost fell over him. Instead she ended up braced against him and staring down into his brilliant blue eyes and their undeniable devotion.

She raised herself again, taking advantage of the moment to kiss his mouth as she drew forward over him. After a moment of swimming in the gaze of his eyes, she whispered to him. "You love me," she said softly.

"Yes." He punctuated the confession with another powerful thrust to meet her descending stroke. She lifted again almost instantly, breathing a moan of pleasure against his lips.

"Kane . . . Kane, you know I don't—"

He cut her off with a deep return into her slight body, rocking her forward so that their mouths met in a wild, soul-searching kiss. He let her settle back on her own this time, breathing hard against her damp, well-used lips. "You will."

Corrine felt the utter conviction pouring from him and a chill of delight shivered down her spine. He was once again telling her the absolute truth. His truth. A truth, she realized, she wouldn't at all mind living.

Sitting up straight and proud on her very personal stallion, Corrine took charge of her ride. Kane continued to match her tit for tat, sweat gleaming on his dark skin as he worked her body as fiercely as he could under the circumstances. He loved the way her entire body jounced, her breasts with their dark coral tips shimmering with impact every time she met with him. It was all so far beyond his expectations that his body reacted uncontrollably to her. At first he used the increasing bite of the wrist cuffs to help draw him away from the rampant urge to rush into orgasm, the warm wetness of his own blood a small price to pay if he could just keep control long enough for what she needed. But soon even that couldn't help him.

"Sweet, blessed Destiny, Corrine! You're perfect! You're—"

Kane gasped in a hard, sucking breath as sudden fire broiled through the bottom of his gut, sinking with an acidic burn into the seat of his pelvis. His whole body crashed against a tempest of pleasure he couldn't contain or control. His back arced off the bed, the power of his muscular body lifting her up with him.

Corrine felt the impulse of pleasure rushing through his body and mind, and once it slammed into him, it slammed into her as well. Chained together as they were by the power of Kane's mind, she was snared in the vortex of his explosive release, convulsive and bordering on painful. They both curled toward one another, their heads touching at their temples as they cried out against each other's ears. Kane's jolting release felt as if it would never end, and the greedy clutch of her body only perpetuated the situation. Then, gasping madly, they suddenly dropped onto the bed, their bodies nothing more than an exhausted pile of arms and legs.

Even before he finished catching his breath, Kane let out an irritated growl. Corrine looked at him in surprise when he uttered quite savagely, "Perfect bloody timing, Noah."

Then there was a sharp jolt seconds before Corrine hit the mattress face first, Kane having completely disappeared from beneath her. The startled redhead pushed up into a thick cloud of smoke and the heavy odor of sulfur. Then there was another snap in the air and suddenly Kane was on her back, his now-free hands sliding hungrily beneath her to seek out the delicious softness of her breasts.

"Kane!" she gasped, trying to turn under him so she could look into his face. His remarkable disappearing act had stunned her, but it was quickly overshadowed by the more remarkable feel of his hands on her body at long last.

"At long last?" He echoed her thoughts fiercely against her ear. "Let's see you suffer over a week of getting fully aroused every single time the slightest memory of your mate drifts into your mind. Then you can complain about the length of your denied hunger."

"Oh, I see," she breathed, "it's a contest, is it?"

"No contest," he argued hotly. "You'll never know what I went through."

"So you say," she shot back.

"No. So I know. You will never know the kind of denial I went through, Corrine. You'll never know it because I will never let you know it." As he made the promise, his hands went in different directions, traveling intimately over her slender body. "I can promise you this with all of my heart, sweetness."

Corrine sighed and smiled into the bed sheets. It was a promise she knew she could believe.

Epilogue

Kane rubbed at his nearly healed wrists, tugging his shirt-sleeves down over faint bruises. True, he could have had a Body Demon heal them for him, but there was something poignant about the sight, about touching them, about remembering what he had gone through that Samhain night. He wished he hadn't healed so fast. He wanted the reminders to last just a little while longer.

He looked up when he heard a door close softly. She appeared like a vision in a dream, wearing something that flowed like soft, shimmering silk around her. The color was a pale aqua, as though clean tropical water clung to her. The dress was unlike anything he'd ever seen her wear before, other than the gown he had chosen for her in an alternate reality. But he had known it was within her, the desire to wear such lush, beautiful things. And she wore it as though she had been born to it. As she walked down the stairs it was like watching an elegant queen.

"Hey, Sis!"

The moment was broken as a raven-haired speedball bolted between Kane and Corrine, throwing herself into her sister's arms. The sisters hugged fiercely, their opposite colored hair mixing together in an astounding clash of red on black.

"You'd think they hadn't seen each other in years," Jacob remarked wryly as he came to Kane's side and stood there in his usual stoic pose, his arms folded over his chest. But there was softness in his eyes and a slight smile on his lips as he watched his mate. To outsiders the change in him might seem small, but to Kane the alteration in his older brother was profound. It made Kane smile and put off his irritation at being thwarted from having his mate in his arms. Over these past two days he had come to know Bella much better, had learned how dynamic she was. There was much of her sister in her, but there was a wisdom and reserve in Corrine that made her somehow more special to Kane.

"She looks well," Jacob remarked.

"She's better," Kane agreed. "But we don't have what you and Bella have. I mean, her ability to read my thoughts is limited to times when we are very close and speaking of highly emotional things. And I cannot speak with her from any distance. I don't like it. I feel that I am missing a key piece of armor when it comes to protecting her. Knowing there are magic users out there and others who might try to harm her to get to me . . ."

"The odds of that are very low," Jacob said as he tried to reassure him. "Has she shown any signs of special ability?"

"No. Not yet."

"It may take time," Jacob mused. "We are grateful she is even alive. *I* am grateful." Jacob looked at his brother. "It would have crushed me to know I was the instrument that robbed you of the woman who would love you best."

Kane felt the power of his brother's guilt as well as his love for him, all in that single statement. It didn't even matter to him that Corrine had yet to declare her love for him.

She would.

In time, with his love and care coaxing her heart to his, she would.

Corrine looked up at him, over her diminutive sister's shoulder, and smiled at him.

He read her thoughts and his smile grew.

Dragon On Top

G. A. AIKEN

Chapter 1

Ghleanna the Decimator took another gulp from her battered ale cup and wallowed, quite magnificently, if she did say so herself, in her misery. It was ridiculous, she knew, to still be as devastated by all this as she had been. It would be going on six months and yet she could not move past it. Instead, she sat and she drank and she wallowed and she tried to forget. And this had been the way of things for a long time now. Too long, her kin would say.

This was all her own fault, though. She'd trusted where she shouldn't have, believed lies when she damn well knew better, and most importantly, forgot the one thing that no one else *ever* forgot—that her father was Ailean the Wicked. Also known as Ailean the Slag, well-known whore of the dragon *and* human world.

And, with a single stroke of idiocy, Ghleanna the Decimator had become Ghleanna the Idiot.

Ghleanna the Fool.

Ghleanna the Failure.

Yet perhaps "failure" was too harsh a word. She'd never thought of herself as a failure before. After years on the battlefield, she'd proved herself again and again. But a failure was how she felt now. Like a failure and a fool with no one to blame, but herself. So, in morbid shame and self-pity and with no wars or battles interesting enough to occupy her mind or sword arm, Ghleanna had returned to the safety of her cave home's ancient walls to be miserable and—if she were to be honest—hide. Venturing out only for food and ale.

Although these last few days she'd mostly just gone out for more ale.

She had no idea what her long-term plans were, but then again, should failures have long-term plans? Since Ghleanna wasn't sure, she drank more ale until sweet blackness took her and she didn't have to think about her inherent stupidity and the misery it had caused her anymore.

Ghleanna had no idea how long she'd been passed out, but as much as she might want to, she couldn't ignore the beating her head was currently taking. She forced her eyes open and watched the blunt end of a steel spear come down to crack her forehead again. She rolled away but the end of another spear hit her on the side of the jaw.

"Wake up, ya lazy sow. Wake up!"

"Leave me be, you mad bitches!"

"Is that any way to talk to your dear, sweet aunts?"

"You're not my aunts," she lashed back.

"Close enough. It's better than Great Cousins, isn't it? Makes us sound old, don't it, Kennis?"

"That it does, Kyna. Now get up before we strip the scales from ya bones."

Pissed that her kin didn't have the decency to leave her alone to wallow in her ale and drool, Ghleanna sat up and snarled, "What is it, you old hags? What is it you want from me?"

"Well, first, you can stop feeling sorry for yourself. Isn't that right, Kyna?"

"That's right, Kennis. Nothing worse than a mighty drag-oness sittin' around in a dark, dank cave, boo-hooing over some bloody mistake of a dragon."

"I am doing no such thing," she lied.

"Look at her lying to us, Kennis!"

"I see it, Kyna. Lying to us and thinking we won't know. It's a shame." Kennis shrugged. "I say we hit her again. On principle."

"I agree."

Ghleanna quickly raised her claws to protect her head. "Go away! Leave me be!"

"So you can sit here and continue to feel sorry for your-self? Over *him?* I'd rather put you down here and now, ain't that right, Kyna?"

"Aye. Like a poor, wounded horse."

"I hate all of you." Ghleanna let out a big sigh, dragging her claws through her too-long black hair. She hadn't cut it in months and it showed. She knew she must look like cold shit, but she'd not give her kin the satisfaction of acknowl-edging it.

"Hate us? Even though we're all worried about your worthless hide?" Kyna asked.

"All them brothers and sisters of yours *whinin'* about you. Och! The sound of it makes us mad. We had to do some-thing, didn't we, Kyna?"

"Aye, Kennis. That we did. Or kill them all just to make them stop. But that didn't seem right, did it, Kennis?"

"No. Not at all."

"So you come here to do . . . what? Exactly?" Ghleanna demanded. "Besides annoy the bloody fuck out of me?"

"You're lucky it was us come to fetch you, brat. Not sure your wake up would have been so kind if it had been your mother who'd come here instead. Isn't that right, Kyna?"

"Och! Beaten your scales to a different color, she would

have. She's been sick to death with worry over you, only to find out you're sitting in this cave, drinking your sorrows away on some cheap ale."

"Well, if I'd really wanted to end it all, I would have just used *your* ale," Ghleanna sniped.

The spear butt came at her again but this time Ghleanna caught and held it. "Stop hitting me with that bloody thing."

"At least her reflexes are still good. Now we just need to sober her up—"

"And bathe her. She reeks!"

"—and we can get her to our queen's court while it's still morning."

"Queen's court? Why do I need to go to Rhiannon's court?"

"Ohhh. Hear that, Kennis?"

"Aye, Kyna. *Rhiannon* she calls her. Like they're old friends."

"Best of chums!"

The twin She-dragons cackled and Ghleanna felt the need to start destroying things.

"She's gettin' pissy, Kyna."

"That she is, Kennis."

"So we better get her up and ready so we can get a move on."

Fed up, Ghleanna nearly roared, "I don't *want* to see Rhiannon! *So get the fuck out of my cave!*"

Kyna crouched down low so she could look Ghleanna in the eyes, one side of her snout pulling back to show row after row of deadly fangs, many having shown up as she'd aged.

"Now listen up, little girl. You can talk to your father and brothers like that if you want—but you'll not talk to us that way. And when the queen gives you an order—"

"—you get off your ass and you follow it. Or by the gods—"

"—we'll make you wish you had."

Ghleanna understood now why the Cadwaladr Twins had been sent to fetch her. Although many of her siblings would put up a good fight, only her brothers Bercelak and Addolgar really had a chance at taking her, but neither would because she was their sister. The same with her father. And her mother was a peacekeeper, not a fighter. So her kin had sent the most feared Dragonwarriors in the land, the Cadwaladr Twins. Old She-dragons they might be, but that only made them more dangerous—and unstable.

"You coming, girl?"

"Yes," Ghleanna hissed, using her front claws to push herself all the way up. It took a moment for the cavern to stop spinning and another moment for the nausea to pass. But once they did, she was ready to at least get into the lake outside and bathe.

"What does Rhiannon want with me anyway?" she asked, heading outside with the twins right behind her, debating on whether to make a run for it.

"Unlike you, brat, we don't ask a bunch of questions."

"Our queen asks us to do something, we do it. That's our job."

"That's *your* job," Kennis insisted.

"Did we not train her well enough?"

"I hope that's not the case, Kyna. Hate to put her *back* through training."

Ghleanna winced, hearing the threat in those words loud and clear. "Won't be necessary," she muttered.

"Good. You were always one of our favorites, Ghleanna. We'd hate to have to beat you within an inch of your life because you've forgotten where you come from."

Kyna caught Ghleanna's forearm, made her look at her. "And there's no shame, girl. No shame in who you are, who your kin are, or who you want to be."

"And don't let anybody convince you different," Kennis finished. "You are special, Ghleanna. And some blokes—they can never handle that. While others . . ."

"While others what?"

"While others were born to be the sheathe to your sword—you just need to find that one, lass. Like we did."

"Like your Da did. But she can't do that if she stinks of ale and misery, Kennis."

"Not unless she wants a miserable bastard like herself, Kyna. And gods! Who'd want that?"

And Ghleanna, realizing the truth of that, headed toward the lake and prepared to meet with her queen.

Please don't hug me. Please don't hug me.

But she did. She did hug him. Right there in front of her entire court and, more importantly, in front of her consort. The most unpleasant of dragons, Bercelak the Great himself.

And Bram the Merciful, royal emissary for Queen Rhiannon of the House of Gwalchmai fab Gwyar, knew his queen did it on purpose. He knew she did it because she enjoyed torturing her mate, but she often failed to realize that she also, in the process, tortured poor Bram. Or perhaps she realized it but simply didn't care.

"Oh, Bram! You look so wonderful. Doesn't he look wonderful, Bercelak?"

Bram heard that growl of disapproval across the queen's chamber.

"Bercelak thinks you look wonderful, too," the queen lied. She patted Bram's shoulder and stepped away. "So my dearest Bram, are you ready for your most important of trips?"

"I am, my queen. I think nothing but good can come from this and I look forward to—"

"Yes, yes." She sat down on her throne, a bit of rock jutting from the cave wall. It never looked very comfortable to Bram, but the queen didn't seem to mind. "But I've been worrying about your safety."

"My safety? I'll be fine, Your Majesty."

"I've been hearing rumors. There are those who do not want this alliance to go through. They will try to stop you."

"Why? It's not Lightnings I go to see. The dragons of the Desert Lands have never been our enemies." He was simply ensuring that they would not side with those who were.

"Always so logical, my old friend. Logical and thoughtful and smart. But still . . . nothing is ever easy in the world of dragon politics, and you of all dragons should know that."

"Understood, my queen. And I promise you that I'll be quite care—"

"So I've arranged for your protection."

Uh-oh.

"Your Majesty, my contact in the Desert Lands is only expecting me. Not an entourage."

"An entourage sounds so large and daunting, and it's nothing of the sort. Just a few of my most trusted Dragonwarriors to ensure you make it safely to and from your destination."

"Dragonwarriors?" Gods, kill him now.

Which nightmare Dragonwarriors had this female dug up from the pits of hell to send him out with? Probably Bercelak's brothers. Or, even worse, Bercelak himself. The black dragon had never liked Bram due to Bram's apparent affliction to "thinking too much and lusting after my sister." And Bercelak was right, of course. About the thinking—and the lusting.

Ghleanna the Black, now the Decimator, had been Bram's unobtainable dream since he was a young dragon, barely even sixty winters. She'd stolen his heart from first glare when she'd slammed Bercelak's head into the wall and ordered him to, "Leave off the royal!", meaning Bram. Ghleanna had been in a recent battle, one of her first, and she'd gotten her first scar. A six-inch thing that cut across her collarbone. Bram had seen that scar and his mouth had dried up, his knees had gone weak, and he'd forgotten words. Not specific words, but *all* words. She'd rendered him temporarily mute.

But unlike Bercelak, Ghleanna barely noticed Bram after that, barely paid attention to him, barely remembered his name. He was the royal who sometimes visited her mother or her sister Maelona. The "thinkers" in the Cadwaladr Clan.

"And which warriors would that be, my queen? Anyone I know?"

The queen smiled—something that did not give Bram ease—and he heard a voice he knew so well say from behind him, "I can't believe you sent those mad bitches to fetch me, Bercelak. Do you not care for me at all?"

Bram briefly closed his eyes before looking at the female who now stood beside him. They eyed each other for a long moment until Ghleanna the Decimator sneered and demanded of her brother, "Babysitting? You dragged me all this way to be a babysitter to a weak-willed royal?"

"Thank you, Ghleanna," Bram murmured. "That was very nice."

"Nothing personal," she muttered back, her claw patting his shoulder. "Long night."

Long night? Looked more like a long century. Although he knew what it was that had one of the most decorated and feared captains of the last few centuries appearing as if she hadn't slept in years. Her hair, always short and well groomed, now reached her shoulders, the ends uneven. Her armor, always spit-shined and battle-ready, was now covered in dirt and dents and, if Bram wasn't mistaken, bits of some poor sod's brains. Even her battle axes, her favorite weapons as far back as Bram could recall, looked as if they had not been cleaned in months, the blade edges still encrusted in blood and bits of bone. No, this was not the Ghleanna he had known all these years. The Ghleanna he'd adored. More fool him.

"Oh?" Rhiannon asked Ghleanna. "Are you frightfully busy at the moment?"

"I know I'm too busy for this centaur sh—"

"Honestly, my queen," Bram cut in, "there's no call to involve Captain Ghleanna. I'm quite fine traveling on my own." In fact, he preferred it. This trip was too important for him to be distracted by the one female who still kept him up some nights. Sweating.

"Nonsense, Bram. I won't hear of it."

"Well, find someone else," Ghleanna told them all. "I didn't go through half-a-century of training and more than that of battles to end up the babysitter of Bram the Merciful."

Insulted, Bram snapped, "Would you like an actual blade to twist in my gut, Ghleanna?"

"It's nothing personal," she said again.

"Right. Nothing personal."

"What I find amusing," Rhiannon observed, ignoring them both, "is that you think I'm *asking* you to do this task, Ghleanna of the Cadwaladr Clan. After all this time being Captain of the Tenth Battalion, one would think you could tell an order from a request."

Ghleanna made a noise through her snout that sounded like an angry bull about to charge. "And one would think that a queen wouldn't waste the skill of her Dragonwarriors with centaur-shit tasks like babysitting!"

"Don't raise your voice to me, Cadwaladr! I am *not* one of your troops!"

"I can tell that because *they* don't waste my bloody time!"

"That is it!" Bercelak the Great roared, silencing both females. Black eyes, so much like his sister's, locked on the angry Captain. "Apologize, Ghleanna."

"Like hells I—"

"Apologize!" the consort's voice boomed across the cavern, every royal beside Bram making a hasty move for the exits. Ghleanna immediately lowered her gaze.

"I'm sorry if I offended you, my queen."

Rhiannon grinned. "Now, now, sister. We're all friends here." *We are?* "And I know you'll do this favor for me." The queen rose, walked down to Bram and, to his horror, patted his shoulder. "Bram means so much to me and to this court. We grew up together—and his safety is of the utmost importance. Do you think I would trust that with just anyone?" She laid her head on Bram's shoulder and Bram curled his claws into fists, desperate to move away from this crazed female. "Isn't Bram simply marvelous? The way he negotiates such important alliances and truces for me? Don't you simply adore him as much as I do?"

The queen's consort stood in front of Bram now, towering over him as most males of the Cadwaladr Clan did, and he glared at Bram with such loathing that all Bram wanted to do was scream out, "It's not me! I swear, it's not me!"

But before the terrifying bastard could remove parts of Bram that would definitely be missed, Ghleanna caught hold of her sibling's forearm and tugged, sighing loudly.

"Come, brother. Tell me what this all-important task is and why I, of all Dragonwarriors, must do it."

She dragged Bercelak from the cavern and Bram gazed at his old friend and now ruler of all Southland Dragons. And, with all honesty, he asked, "Why, Rhiannon? Why do you hate me so?"

"What is going on?" Ghleanna demanded of her brother once she'd found them a quiet alcove.

"How should I know? I mean what could Rhiannon see in that overthinking bastard? All he does is read all day and write papers. It's like his mind is a thousand miles away at all times. He's a talker that one, not a doer."

"I'm not talking about that, you git. I'm talking about what's going on that you think it's necessary for me to accompany the peacemaker anywhere. And it better be a good reason, brother. Or I'm likely to get cranky."

Bercelak took in a deep breath, trying to calm his desire to tear poor Bram wing from wing. Gods, the two of them would never be friends. "The royal is going into the Desert Lands to get us an alliance with the Sand Eaters." Their kind's nickname for the Sand Dragons of the Desert Lands.

"Why? We've had no problems with them before."

"And that royal"—and Bercelak sneered a bit—"wants to keep it that way. But I don't see why you'd have a problem babysitting—I thought you liked this one."

"I do. Bram's sweet." Sweeter than any other dragon she knew, which also made him the oddest dragon Ghleanna knew. "So is that it then? Rhiannon just needs me to make sure Bram gets there and back?"

"Actually your taking him was my idea."

Incredulous, Ghleanna asked, "Whatever the bloody hells for?" If anyone knew how ill-equipped Ghleanna was for babysitting duty, it was her brother. Even their own mother stopped allowing Ghleanna to babysit Bercelak after she'd dangled him over an active volcano, threatening to toss him in. And then there was that other time when she'd left Bercelak alone on a mountaintop when he still couldn't fly, but not before she told him, "It's not that Mum and Da don't love you—they just don't *want* you anymore. But I'm sure someone will come along who does."

Cruel perhaps, but he was such an arrogant little shit, even then, that she'd been unable to help herself. And her parents had eventually tracked down his sobbing, wailing ass and brought him home.

"Because," her brother replied, "I need someone I can count on. Until recently, you were the most reliable of us all. I sincerely hope that hasn't changed for good."

"Don't go there, brother."

"Over some male not worthy of you."

He went there!

"I will not speak of that," she growled and started to walk away. But her brother's tail wrapped around her throat and yanked her back. "Ack!"

"My sister," he said, his tail tightening around her neck so she had trouble breathing, "would not be so foolish as to let any male cause her to lose all that she has worked so hard for. *My* sister," he went on, ignoring Ghleanna's talons tearing at him, "would never let some idiot dragon convince her that her exemplary skills on the battlefield make her less than any other female." Bercelak began to slam her repeatedly into the cave floor like he used to when he'd gotten bigger and realized his sister had purposely tortured him for years. "And *my* sister would never, *ever* let some male who was never worthy of her in the first place, stop her from taking direct orders from her queen."

He slammed her to the ground one last time, the cave walls shaking, before he removed his tail. "That," he said softly, "is not what a sister of mine would do, correct?"

"You are a mean-hearted bastard!"

"But you already knew that about me, Ghleanna. You didn't think that would change simply because I found a mate, did you?"

Ghleanna stood, her claws kneading her bruised throat. "No. I really didn't."

Her brother placed his claw on her shoulder, ignoring the way she flinched. "I know he hurt you, Ghleanna—"

"No." She had to stop him. She couldn't hear anymore. "He didn't hurt me, Bercelak. He made a fool of me. In front of my kin—in front of my troops."

"And he did that because he's jealous."

She had to laugh. "Of what?"

"Of the fact that he could *never* take you in a fair fight. It eats at him that you're stronger than him, faster, definitely smarter, and worshipped by your troops. And instead of standing your ground, you let his centaur shit push you into hiding in your cave like some worthless human. Drinking yourself into a blind stupor and ignoring those who care for you. Like Mum and that bastard."

"You mean Da?"

"Call him what you like." Bercelak's perpetually scowling face softened a bit. "And, yes, sister, he's well aware that this is partially his doing."

"It's not really." And Ghleanna swiped at the tears sliding down her snout. "My own stupidity got me here."

"Then fix it, sister." He had both claws on her shoulders now. "Do this task for your queen with no questions. Bring a few of our kin with you. I hear things are winding down at Bolver Fields in the Southern Hills near the peacemaker's home. Addolgar is there. He'll be up for this trip, I think."

Ghleanna shook the rest of her pitiful tears off, pulled herself together. "Addolgar as well? You need both of us on this? Why?"

"Because, if that weak kitten of a dragon gets the Sand Dragon King to sign this alliance . . . it'll make Rhiannon one of the strongest monarchs in this region in the last millennium."

"Oh . . . that's why."

"There has to be someone else, Rhiannon. Anyone else."

"No one you'll be as safe with as Ghleanna."

Bram sighed and tried to think of how to carefully explain this to his dangerously unstable queen without insulting her or her recently acquired kin. At least now, though, they were in her privy chamber and away from the prying eyes and ears of her court.

"These are delicate negotiations, Rhiannon. The Sand Dragon King has to be handled with care. *Infinite* care."

"Och! These moody foreign royals. How do you tolerate such moodiness, my friend?"

Did she even listen to herself? Probably not.

"With patience," he answered. "And none of the Cadwaladrs are known for their patience."

Rhiannon's head tipped to the side, her blue eyes watching him. "But we are not speaking of the Cadwaladrs, are we, old friend? I sense that if we were speaking of any of Bercelak's other kin this wouldn't be such an issue. But we're not. We're speaking of Ghleanna."

Bram swallowed. "So?"

The queen began to circle Bram, the tip of her tail drawing little signs in the dirt floor as she moved. "Pretty, strong, defiant, difficult, and *scarred* Ghleanna."

"I know who she is, Rhiannon. I just don't see—"

"All those scars from all those battles, littering her body. Her long, strong body. Even her tail has scars—and an extra long . . . *tip.*"

"Stop."

"And when she gets angry, Bram . . . when she gets right up close and is threatening and vicious and cold; and you know in that second that you'll never meet someone as deadly as—"

"Please stop." Bram realized he was panting.

"We've been friends a long time, Bram. Do you really think I've forgotten?"

"I didn't think you'd noticed." No one else ever had—especially Ghleanna.

"Ghleanna is like the rest of her kin. Wonderful, but dense as thick marble."

"That's lovely, Rhiannon."

"I adore them all but you need to be more direct with them when you want something."

"She doesn't know I exist. She never has."

"Because you aren't direct with her. You're direct with everyone else, but once Ghleanna comes around you're suddenly a shy schoolboy."

"So? I should be like Feoras the Fighter instead?"

Rhiannon winced. "Heard about that, did you?"

"Everyone's heard about it because the bastard's *told* everyone."

"That annoying little rodent. I should have his veins removed." When Bram didn't say anything, Rhiannon noted, "No calls for mercy, peacemaker?"

"Not this time, no. And stop looking at me like that. I never like cruelty from anyone. So it's not as if I'm being particularly vicious here."

"It's endearing that you think not calling for mercy is vicious." Rhiannon waved all that away with her claw. "Look, when it comes to males, Ghleanna the Black doesn't know what she wants. So you'll have to show her."

"Show her?"

"It's the perfect time. She's absolutely *ripe* for the plucking."

Bram blinked. "What?"

"Vulnerable. That's the word. So it's the perfect time for a good, worthy dragon to swoop in and *get her.*"

"Rhiannon!"

"What? I'm only trying to help."

"That's not helpful. That's sneaky and deceitful."

She gave a soft snort. "Two words you're well acquainted with."

"Only when we're discussing politics. Ghleanna is not politics. She's . . . she's . . ."

"Scarred? Perfectly, perfectly scarred?"

"Stop, Rhiannon."

"So many scars," the viper whispered in Bram's ear. "All from the different weapons of those trying to kill her. She has a scar here"—her tail drew a long diagonal line across Bram's back—"from hip to shoulder where an ogre from the Dark Hills tried to cut her in half. He didn't succeed, though. And Ghleanna *slaughtered* their entire army. And when the healers sewed her up"—Rhiannon went on—"she insisted on being awake so that she'd fully understand that even a moment of being unaware had drastic consequences."

She pulled back slightly. "Why, Bram, you're shaking."

Because he was desperately trying to control his cock. It wouldn't do to get hard in front of his queen. No matter what the vision of Ghleanna getting her battle wounds tended did to him.

"You're cruel, Rhiannon. You were cruel when we were young—and you're cruel now."

"My mother was cruel, Lord Bram. I'm merely honest." She kissed his snout. "And don't ever say I'm not a good friend. I'm the best friend a dragon like you could hope for."

He turned slightly, both of them very close to each other, and smiled. "Best friend, my ass."

She laughed until that black snout pushed between them, forcing them apart, pitch black smoke streaming from the nostrils.

"Oh, hello, my love," Rhiannon said to her consort. "I was just giving Bram here a pep talk before he goes to face those difficult Sand Dragons. Wasn't I, Bram?"

"Uh . . . yes. She was."

"Now go with my blessing. And good luck to you."

Please don't hug me. Please don't hug me.

But she did.

Ghleanna waited outside the Queen's Privy Chamber, not surprised when she heard her brother's roar and the silver-haired royal slid-stumbled into the alcove, shoved there, no doubt by her intolerant kin.

"What were you thinking?" Ghleanna asked Bram without rancor. "Hugging her like that?"

"*I* didn't hug her. She hugged me!"

"Uh-huh."

A squeal came from the chamber and Rhiannon called out, "Bercelak! Put me down, you low-born bastard!" Although she didn't sound nearly as angry as she wanted to.

"We better go," Ghleanna offered, heading down the alcove.

"Yes, but—"

"No, Bercelak!" the queen cried out. "Not the collar! Not the chain! You bastard!"

"Stand there any longer, royal, and you'll get a visual you'll not forget for a very long while."

Bram rushed up behind her, his eyes focused on the ground, his silver scales nearly glowing from embarrassment.

"That was . . . awkward."

"Get used to it. Them two like to play their games." Ghleanna shrugged. "And who are we to stop them? If it makes them happy."

"I don't mind what they do together. I just hate it when they involve the rest of us."

"Then you shouldn't be hugging the queen."

"I didn't hug the bloody queen!"

"If you want to believe that."

Once out of the court, they headed to one of the exits that would lead them from Devenallt Mountain, the long-time Southland Dragon power stronghold and home to their reigning monarch.

"Look," Ghleanna continued, "all I'm saying is that you're my responsibility until this gets done. So perhaps you could not get me and yourself killed in the process. But especially me. I'm the most important."

"I'll do my best and yes, you heard sarcasm."

Ghleanna stopped and faced the royal she was tasked with protecting. He was taller than she, but so were her brothers, and she could take most of them in a fight. And she had, too.

"Listen well to me, Bram the Silver. You may be of royal blood, but I'm a Cadwaladr who's been given the task of keeping your peacemaking ass alive for the next few weeks, which means that until we return, you belong to *me*. So do us both a favor and don't piss me off. I'd hate to return to your beloved queen with only your head in tow, your body and that precious alliance you're so eager to have the Sand Eaters sign left back in the Desert Lands—both torn to shreds by *me*."

He glared at her for what felt like several minutes until the royal snapped, *"Damn that female, but she was right!"*

And when Bram the Merciful stormed off, muttering to himself, Ghleanna could only shake her head and follow, readying herself for a deadly long trip she was not looking forward to at all.

Chapter 2

Ghleanna stood outside Bram's home. She was allowing him time to pick up a few things before they got underway, and she was quite surprised.

"It's a castle."

"It is," he said, digging through his travel bag for who knew what while walking across the small courtyard. They'd shifted to human and put on clothes a few miles back and Ghleanna realized she'd forgotten how attractive Bram was as human. Actually . . . very attractive. Long silver hair framed his handsome face and brought out the deep blue of his eyes. His nose was flat and a little wide, making her want to poke at it with her finger; his lips full; his jaw square; and his hands and fingers long and elegant. He was as tall as Addolgar but not nearly as wide. It was clear he spent no long hours working with any weapon except the one he had attached to his shoulders, but he wasn't so thin that he looked emaciated or weak. There was some muscle there—very nice muscle.

"Why?" she asked, gazing up at the tower attached to the castle. It wasn't a large building and it was a bit rundown, but it could last through a battle or two as the spears embedded in the castle wall and the bit of damage done to the gate could attest.

"Why what?" Honestly, was the dragon listening to her at all?

"Why do you live in a castle?" She thought only her father did that, Ailean the Wicked even going so far as to raise his offspring in one.

"I work with as many humans as dragons." He tripped on his way through the doorway, but seemed to barely notice and she briefly wondered if he did it *every time* he walked through there. "And humans simply don't feel comfortable coming to a cave to discuss business of any kind."

They walked into the hall and Bram finally looked up from his bag.

"Charles?" he called out. "Are you here?"

A human ran in from the back somewhere.

"I'm here, my Lord. I'm here!"

"It's Bram, Charles. You can call me Bram."

"Of course, my Lord. Uh . . . my Lord Bram."

Bram sighed and she knew he'd immediately given up.

"I need my papers for the Alsandair trip."

"Yes, my Lord . . . uh . . . Lord Bram . . . uh . . ."

"And that book on etiquette of the Desert Lands. I should refresh my memory."

"Oy," Ghleanna finally cut in. "Don't bring a whole bloody library. I'll not be carrying all that bloody crap there and back."

"I think I can manage a few books and papers by myself, Captain."

"You better," she muttered.

Bram faced her. "Are you going to be this difficult the entire trip?"

"Probably."

"Lovely."

He motioned to a large table covered in papers and books; then she noticed that nearly every wall in the hall had floor-to-ceiling shelves filled with books and scrolls, but especially books. More books than she'd ever seen before in her life. She thought her mum had a lot—she didn't. And Ghleanna had a feeling there were even more books within the castle and the attached tower.

Gods, had he read all these books? Was it possible? He hadn't been alive for that long.

"You can sit there. I won't be long," he said while still searching through that blasted bag.

"Good. I want to meet with my brothers before the suns go down."

The dragon stopped, peered at her. "Whatever for?"

She frowned. Didn't they just have this conversation on the way here? "Because they're coming with us . . . to protect you? Remember?"

"Dammit, I'd put it out of my mind."

More like he'd hoped she'd changed hers. "It's better to be protected by five Cadwaladrs than just one."

"Perhaps, but your brothers hate me."

"Only Bercelak."

"No. I'm certain they *all* hate me."

"Don't be so full of yourself—my brothers barely know you exist."

Now he looked insulted. "So I'm meaningless?"

"To a Cadwaladr . . . yes."

"Then I'm so glad it's the Cadwaladrs protecting me."

And that sarcasm lashed across the room.

"You don't have to take it so personally. Most royals don't matter to us. So you don't *especially* not exist to us. You're just one of many royals that don't exist to us."

"Is any of that supposed to make me feel better?"

"Thought it might help."

"It didn't."

"I hope you don't always take things so personally. It'll be a long trip for us both if you do."

"Thanks so much for the warning." He dug through his travel bag again. "Blast and damnation! I can't find—"

"The terms of your proposed alliance agreement?" Charles asked, holding out a scroll to the royal.

"Oh," Bram said, taking the scroll. "There it is."

With a weary sigh, Ghleanna dropped into a chair and put her feet up on the table.

"Oh, my Lady!" Charles cried, horrified. "Please." He rushed to the table and carefully lifted Ghleanna's boot-shod feet so he could remove the books and papers from under them.

"Sorry, Charlie," Ghleanna said with a smile. "And you can call me Ghleanna. I'm not a royal like Bram over there."

"Of course, my Lady . . . uh . . . Lady Gh—I mean . . . uh . . ."

"Or just Captain. You can call me Captain."

Appearing heartily relieved at being able to use a title, Charles smiled and said, "Yes, Captain."

Once he'd cleaned off the area, he returned her feet to their proper place.

"There you go, Captain." He turned back to Bram. "I'll gather all you require, my Lord."

"Excellent."

Ghleanna waited until Charles had rushed off before she asked, "Does he know then? What we are?"

"He knows what I am—and I'm sure he's guessed about you. I simply don't have time to run around hiding that particular fact from my assistant." Bram leaned against the table and asked Ghleanna, "Now, what about your battalion?"

"What about them?"

"Can't a few of them accompany us?"

"Are we here again? My brothers do not hate you," she insisted.

"They don't exactly respect me either."

"They don't respect anyone but our mother."

"Well, I understand that. Your mother's amazing."

"I know." Amazing and smart enough not to be taken as a fool by any male. She'd made Ailean work for her love, and work he did. "And I'm nothing like her."

"You have her freckles."

"You mean these bloody dots on my face?" She swiped at her face with her hands.

"You can't rub them off, Ghleanna," Bram told her with a laugh.

"I know. I know. I just hate having them."

"I like them." And he smiled a little. Was he laughing at her?

"Yeah . . . well . . ." She lowered her hands, forcing herself not to act so self-conscious. "You don't have to live with them."

He continued to stare at her, making her nervous, when he finally observed, "You're letting your hair grow out."

"What? Oh." She refused to run her hands through her hair. "Haven't had much call lately to keep it short."

She shrugged and pulled out one of the blades she kept in her boot. "Guess I can do that now."

He caught hold of her hand. "What are you planning to do with that?"

"Cut my hair. You were the one complaining about it."

"I didn't complain."

"Then you dislike my hair when it's short?"

"That isn't what I meant either."

She threw up her hands. "Then what the bloody hells did you mean?"

The royal's blue eyes briefly flared before he closed them and let out a breath. "You do wear the scales off my hide."

She knew that—enjoyed doing it, too. And that was wrong, wasn't it?

"Charles!" he suddenly bellowed, and the human charged back into the hall a few moments later.

"Yes, my Lord . . . Bram . . . my Lord Bram . . . Lord—"

"Please take the Captain to one of the rooms so that she can freshen up." He wrestled the blade from her hand, making Ghleanna laugh. She hadn't laughed so in ages. It felt nice. "Perhaps you can also cut her hair. She prefers it short." He handed the blade to poor, confused Charles.

"Of course, my Lord . . . uh . . ."

"Do we have time for all that?" Ghleanna demanded.

"We do now." The royal turned his back on her, tossing over his shoulder, "I'll be in my study. Get me when she's done."

Ghleanna waited until the dragon was out of earshot. "Is he always so short of temper and patience?" she asked the servant.

"No, Captain. In fact, Lord Bram is considered the most patient and caring of beings in all the Southlands."

"Huh . . . must be me then."

Instead of trying to convince her that that was inaccurate, Charles pointed to an alcove that would lead to the tower. "This way, Captain."

Bram had nearly all he needed and was searching for some notes that he'd taken at the last Elder meeting he attended. A few additional codicils they wanted to add to the final alliance.

When he couldn't find them, Bram called out, "Charles!" and turned, only to come face to face with Ghleanna. How long she'd been standing behind him, Bram had no idea. But at least this was the Ghleanna he knew so well. Her chainmail had been cleaned and polished, a dark blue surcoat over that with her sword tied to her waist and her two battle axes strapped to her back. Her leather boots had been cleaned and buffed and her black hair cut back to its usual length right below her ears. She had her arms folded across her chest and her legs braced apart.

This . . . *this* was the Dragonwarrior he knew. The Decimator. Bram didn't realize how much he'd missed her until she'd been gone.

"That was quick," Bram said when he realized he was gazing at her like a lovesick schoolboy.

She blinked. "Quick? It's been four hours. Maybe a little more."

"Oh? Really?"

"Yeah. Really."

"Hadn't noticed," he muttered and walked around her to return to his desk. "We can go in a few minutes."

"If we leave now we won't get very far."

Bram sighed. "So we've already lost a day of travel?"

"You were the one who didn't want to be seen with me and my unruly hair."

"I never said that! And I don't see why we can't at least get started. I just need to find the blasted . . . Charles!"

Charles rushed in. "My Lord?"

"My notes from the last Elder meeting? I can't find them any—"

Charles pulled the scrolls out from the pile on the desk and held them out to Bram.

Bram took the scrolls and shoved them into his travel bag. "Thank you."

"Of course, my Lord . . . Lord Bram . . . uh . . ."

"I shouldn't be gone too long on this trip," he went on. "But if I am, don't worry. My sister will be checking in quite often."

"Very good sir."

Pulling the strap of his bag across his shoulder, Bram walked out of his study and headed for the front door.

"Don't forget," he informed Charles, "to pull together the research on the pirate attacks at the ports going up the coast. I'm supposed to meet with Duke Picton regarding that soon."

"I've already started, my Lord."

"Good. I'll need to deal with that when I get back." He stopped at the doorway leading to his small and very unkempt courtyard. He'd really have to get someone to clean it. He couldn't ask Charles to do it himself. Bram needed him on more important matters at the moment—and didn't he have a much bigger staff who handled these sorts of things? Maybe not . . .

Bram glanced around, then demanded, "Blast! Where is that female?"

"Right in front of you."

Bram nearly jumped out of his frail human skin when he realized that Ghleanna had gotten around him somehow.

"Don't do that."

"Don't do what?"

"Sneak around."

"Do you mean walk around? Because that's what I actually did. I usually crouch more when I sneak—and then I kill someone."

Deciding not to argue with her, Bram bid Charles farewell and left the castle.

"I guess we still have to pick up your brothers."

"We do."

"Where are they?"

"The Battle of Fychan."

"And how far away is that?" he asked Ghleanna. "Is it a long flight? Will we make it there tonight?"

They now stood outside his castle walls and Ghleanna gazed at him.

"What?" he asked, beginning to run out of patience.

Staring at him strangely, she said, "They're at the Bolver Fields. You know . . . the Battle of Fychan."

"Right. Right. You already said that. And I asked how far off is that?"

Her gaze narrowed a bit. "Really?"

"Really what?"

She took hold of his arm and headed west.

"Where are we going?" he asked. "We're not going to fly? Won't walking to a battlefield be a bit dangerous?" At least for him.

He asked questions but Ghleanna didn't answer. But when they were about a half-mile from his castle, she led him up a ridge that overlooked the valley beneath.

A valley filled with the dead and dying of what appeared to be a long-running battle.

"Right outside your door," she told him, staring at him with what could be either awe, pity, or disgust. "The Battle of Fychan has been outside your door for at least eight months. Everyone else in the nearby town as well as your servants, have abandoned the area except for you and poor Charles, who didn't want to leave your precious books and papers unattended. I do hope you pay that lad well."

"You know . . ." Bram gazed out over the battlefield. "Thought I heard some screams . . . a few times. But I've been so busy."

She released his arm and, while shaking her head, walked off down the hill and to the field below.

"Come on, peacemaker. Let's get my brothers. We can debate when we need to start later."

Morbidly embarrassed but not willing to admit it, Bram followed Ghleanna onto the battlefield.

Chapter 3

"Good gods, you look like cold shit."

Ghleanna gazed at her brother and again wondered why she hadn't smashed his bloody egg when she had the chance. Her mother would have eventually forgiven her.

"Thank you, brother. And you look fat and happy. Having an easy time of it here, are you?"

"Fat? *Fat?*" He speared the moaning human at his feet. "How dare you! My human form is in fighting trim, you callous cow."

"If you say so."

Addolgar glanced at the royal standing behind her. "Something's attached itself to you, sister." He shook the human remains off the spear he held. "Should I kill it for you?"

Ghleanna reached back and caught Bram's hand before he could walk off. She sensed him leaving and didn't really blame him, but still . . . he had to learn to toughen up. Then again, Addolgar did have a reputation among the royals as an intolerant bastard who'd kill without a second's thought or remorse. A reputation that, in some situations, was quite accurate.

"He's under my protection, Addolgar. So back off."

"He is?" He speared another human trying to crawl away. "Why?"

"I've been charged with getting him to the Desert Lands and back. Alive," she added so her brother was clear on this. "And a few of you lot are coming with me."

Addolgar glanced around the battlefield. The conflict seemed to have wound down and he appeared quite bored with it all. Her brother had done his damage and now there was nothing left to kill. Usually he'd return to his mate—unless she'd found her own battle to enjoy. It still amazed Ghleanna that instead of her brother finding a more sweet-natured female to complement his blackhearted and murderous nature, he'd taken to a dragoness with a worse reputation than his own. A dragoness even Ghleanna didn't challenge unless she had no choice.

"Might as well go with you. Nothing left to do here."

"Bored, are you?"

"Killed everything to be killed. There's nothing left but women and children—and they're no fun to kill. Even when they scream and beg for mercy."

Bram yanked his arm away from her so he could walk off, but she caught the strap of his travel bag and held it. Knowing how precious the thing was to him, she knew he wouldn't risk breaking it.

"Who is here with you?"

"A few of the younger ones. Cai, Hew, and Adain."

"What? None of my sisters are here?" She was unable to hide her disappointment.

"They headed into the west for some new battle. But I think we weak male Cadwaladrs can handle protecting one royal, sister."

"I guess you'll do."

"Gee. Thanks."

"Well, don't just stand there, you big ox. Go get them so we can be off."

"All right." He shoved the spear into her hands. "Kill the rest of this lot, would you? I'll be right back."

Once Addolgar walked away, the royal asked, "You really do hate me, don't you?"

"Don't be foolish. Of course, I don't." She began to work her way through the still-breathing humans at her feet, slamming the tip of the spear into a spot in their backs that would kill them quickly. There was no reason to prolong their suffering unless necessary. "Stop worrying. You'll be fine. And as long as you're under my protection, you have nothing to worry about."

She finished off the last human, pulled the spear from his back, planted the tip in the ground, and leaned against the staff. She smiled at the royal. "Now doesn't that make you feel better?"

Bram glanced at the bodies that surrounded them before answering, "Not really."

"These are my brothers," Addolgar said. "Cai the Green, Hew the Black, Adain the Yellow."

"It's gold, you bastard. I'm Adain the Gold."

"Yellow. Gold." Addolgar shrugged. "Who gives a centaur shit? Now," he said to Bram, "they ain't earned their names yet, but they ain't half bad. You'll be fine."

"Yes," Bram replied, "I feel safer already."

"Good!" Addolgar boomed, missing the sarcasm completely. "Now . . . where's Ghleanna?"

"She needed a few minutes alone," Bram told him.

"Went to take a piss, did she?"

Cai slammed his sizable fist into his older brother's shoulder. "Addolgar!"

"What?" And Bram saw that smirk. "It was just a question."

"Don't be such a bastard."

"Don't be such a suck-up," Addolgar shot back.

"Why is he a suck-up?" Hew asked. "Because he doesn't want you going on about our sister that way?"

"What way? All I asked was—"

"Shut it!" Adain snapped. "Blood and fire, you are such a bastard!"

"Fine. If the lot of you are going to get so girly about all this." He turned away from his brothers and winked at Bram. And Bram, for the first time, felt a little more at ease. Especially since it seemed Addolgar would spend more time torturing his siblings than bothering with Bram.

"There you are!" Addolgar announced when his sister approached them. "The royal here said you went off to take a piss."

"Don't involve me in this," Bram told him.

"Right," Ghleanna sighed. "That seems a very Bram thing to do. Announce that I'm off to take a piss. Next he'll tell you when I'm about to take a sh—"

"Can we just go?" Cai—thankfully—cut in.

Ghleanna sized the youngster up. "When did you get so girly?"

"So where are we taking him?" Addolgar asked.

"To the east," Bram explained. "The Port of Awbrey. There will be a boat there that will take us up the coast to the Alsandair ports. I'll meet my contact there."

"A boat?" Adain asked, frowning. "Why are you taking a boat? Why not just fly into the Desert Lands?"

"Flying into the Desert Lands would be seen as a sign of aggression by the Sand Dragons. And it's faster to go by sea than to walk.

"That far south," Ghleanna explained, "we've always traveled by foot unless escorted."

"Why not fly over the ocean then?"

Bram, Addolgar, and Ghleanna laughed outright at that.

"Gods," Bram observed, "they *are* young."

"What does that mean?"

"It means you've got much to learn about Sea Dragons," Ghleanna answered.

Addolgar explained, "If more than one or two dragons fly too far over the ocean, the Fins will definitely consider that a sign of aggression."

Hew asked Bram, "So you really can't make it on your own?" Bram could make it by himself easily, but he had his reasons for not flying over the ocean, alone or otherwise. Very good reasons. "Are you feeble in some way?"

"Babysitting the royal is Bercelak's idea." Ghleanna told them. "You going to disagree with *him,* brothers?" When her younger siblings didn't answer, she nodded. "That's what I thought."

"Do you have any fighting skills?" Hew pushed.

"I have a mighty flame."

The three younger brothers glanced at each other. "Don't we all?" Cai finally asked.

"Mine's stronger."

Cai shook his head. "Gods, that's pathetic."

Addolgar slapped Cai in the back of the head—ignoring his cry of pain—and asked, "Do you want to move out tonight, Ghleanna?"

"No. We leave at first light."

"That's fine. We can all camp here for the night."

"No need. We can stay at Lord Bram's castle."

Bram's entire body jerked. "They can?"

"Get your gear," she told her kin.

"Why are you doing this to me?" Bram demanded once Ghleanna's brothers had walked away. "Do you hate me so much?"

"You are the one who wants my brothers to like him."

"No, I don't. I couldn't care less if they like me or not."

"Well, they'll like you much better if they have a soft bed and warm food—or at least a cow or two—for the night. And what could it hurt?"

"What if they disturb my things? My papers." Bram began to panic. "My books!"

Ghleanna laughed. "And what, exactly, do you expect *my* kin to do to your precious books? If they notice your books at all, I'll be shocked." She stepped closer, surprising Bram, and brushed her hand against his shoulder. "I won't let my brothers harm your books or your papers."

"You promise?"

"I promise." She grinned, and it was a beautiful thing. "I'll take very good care of you, Bram the Merciful." Her grin grew wider. "Trust me."

Cai's big boots landed on the table, right on top of the peacemaker's important papers. So Ghleanna grabbed him by the ankles with one hand and flipped him back, Cai and the chair slamming to the hard earth-packed floor.

"Oy!" Cai demanded. "What was that for?"

"You keep your claws and your big, fat feet off Bram's books and papers."

Cai got to his feet and leaned down until they were eye to eye. "And if I don't?"

That's when Ghleanna head-butted her younger brother. Since he'd been asking for it and all. And it made her other brothers laugh. She did love making her brothers laugh.

"You mad cow!" Cai yelled, gripping his head.

"You'll do as I say, little brother, or that lump on your head will be the least of your problems. Now"—she looked at all her kin—"we're going to eat and sleep like civilized dragons and no one will start anything. Understood?"

When her brothers only grumbled in response, she cracked her knuckles for emphasis. "Understood?" she growled.

"Yeah, yeah," Addolgar quickly told her. "Understood."

"Good." She smiled and walked over to the royal, who stood a few feet away, watching her.

"See?" she asked. "I've got it all under control."

"You head-butted your brother," Bram noted.

"Aye."

"Your brother."

"Sometimes it's the only way to get through to them. And it's kind of fun," she admitted. "Me and Addolgar do it to each other all the time. Since we were hatchlings. Used to drive our Mum insane."

"I can imagine."

"Don't worry about us." Ghleanna motioned him away with her hands. "I've got control of this lot and I can see that you're desperate to go and do something important with your books."

"I should stay. I've been told enough I'm a horrible host. Great peacemaker—horrible host."

"You don't need to be a host with me or my kin. We can take care of ourselves."

"You sure you don't mind?"

"I'd tell you if I did. Go on."

"All right. But just a few minutes. I just need to write a few letters. I won't be long. I'll be back before you know it."

"Sure. No problem." Ghleanna watched the royal rush off to his study. "Won't be seeing him for hours."

"So can we put our feet up on his things *now?*" Hew asked from behind her.

"No, you lazy git! And don't test my patience. Head like granite, I have," Ghleanna reminded him, pointing at her forehead. "Just like our dear Da."

* * *

Bram signed the last letter he needed to finish and leaned back in his chair, stretching his fingers to loosen them up. That's when he saw Ghleanna sitting in the chair across from him.

"Hello. Is dinner ready?"

One corner of her mouth quirked up on one side, but she didn't answer.

"What?"

"Four hours."

"Four hours what? Four hours until dinner?"

"Four hours until the suns come up."

"What?" Bram pushed his chair back and strode to the window. He looked outside and winced, realizing when he'd first sat down it had still been light out. Now it was pitch black. Even the moon was gone.

"I got up for some water and realized you were still in here. How are you going to travel all day without any sleep?"

"I'll be fine," he promised.

"We've eaten. My brothers argued over who'd get to bathe in that big tub first." She grinned. "I won that."

"Another head-butt?"

"There's no shame in the head-butt. If it works it works. They all went to bed hours ago. Charles said you shouldn't be much longer . . . I think Charles lied to me."

"It's not his fault. He always reminds me of the time and I just get . . . lost."

"That's all right. I find it endearing."

"You do? Most females have found it rude and intolerable."

"Stuck up, prissy asses, if you ask me."

Bram laughed. "I've never heard 'stuck up prissy asses' before."

"Because I just came up with it. Look, it's not like you're at the pub, feeling up the bargirls. You're doing important work."

"You think what I do is important?"

"Definitely. Because when your precious truces and alliances are broken, war breaks out." Her grin was wide, showing all her teeth. "And then *my* important work begins." She stood and walked over to him. "We need you peacemakers. Without you, there'd be no reason for war, now would there?"

"It's nice to know how integral my job is to your happiness."

"And my career! Don't move up the ranks of Dragonwarrior without a war to fight, enemies to kill. So thank you, peaceful dragon, for being ever so helpful."

"It's my pleasure, warmongering female."

They laughed and she caught his hand. "Now off to bed with you. You need at least a few hours if you hope to make it through the day." She pulled him out of his study and led him down the hall. "Addolgar's a tyrant when traveling. He likes to go and go and go. The quicker the better for him."

"Is that my shirt you're wearing?"

"I needed something to wear. Charles practically fainted earlier today when I got naked in front of him. These humans . . . so ridiculous about their own bodies."

But what did she expect when her body looked so . . . astounding. Long legs stretched out from under his shirt, while a plump ass moved seductively under the plain cotton. Then they were walking up the stairs and Bram realized she wore no underthings. Gods, the female was torturing him. What had he ever done to deserve such torture?

She stopped in front of his room. "This is your room, yes?"

"It is."

"I could tell when I walked past. All the books."

"I read a lot."

"Don't have to defend yourself to me. My cave is filled

with weapons. Same thing." She released his hand and gestured him inside. "Need help getting undressed?"

Bram faced her. "Yes. Yes, I do."

"I was joking."

"I'm not." He lifted his hands. "They're weak from writing."

"Bed. Sleep. I'll see you in the morning."

"You shouldn't offer if you're not going to deliver, Captain."

"Yeah, yeah. Like I've never heard that before." She walked away but returned. "Thanks, by the way."

"For what?"

"Letting my brothers stay. I know you'd rather have yourself impaled, but . . . I appreciate it."

"No problem. Although I don't know if I'd let them in when you're not here."

"That's probably a good idea." She winked and walked off.

And unable to help himself, Bram followed her out into the hallway, watching that perfect plump ass move down the corridor until she reached her bedroom and stepped inside, closing the door behind her.

Bram blew out a breath and wondered about going down there and knocking.

"You haven't gotten to bed yet?"

Bram gritted his teeth—*all of them sneak!*—and said, "I was about to, Captain Addolgar."

"Just call me Addolgar." The big oaf stood beside Bram now, staring off down the hall. "My sister . . . you think she's pretty, yeah?"

Unsure where this was going, and a little terrified, Bram answered, "Uh . . . yes. Your sister is very attractive. A handsome woman and a"—*enticing? No. Don't say that*—"a beautiful dragoness."

Addolgar faced Bram, the two staring at each other. Addolgar was nearly the same height as he, perhaps an inch or two taller, but he was much, much wider. Among most, human or dragon, Bram never considered himself small. But when he was around the Cadwaladrs . . . Honestly, did the adults perform spells to make their offspring so unnaturally large?

The dragon gazed down at Bram for several long seconds—*Am I shrinking? Why does it feel like I'm shrinking?*—then grunted at him and walked off.

"Get some sleep," Addolgar called back. "We got a long trip tomorrow and we need to make a stop."

"A stop? I don't have time for a—"

The dragon halted at his door and stared back at Bram until Bram said, "Good. A stop. Can't wait."

Another grunt and then he was gone, closing the door behind him.

And that's when Bram knew he'd be lucky if he made it back from this trip alive.

Chapter 4

For six dragons to leave for a time, there was an awful lot going on. She'd seen military campaigns start with less activity.

"Charles!" she heard Bram call from his study. "Have you seen the—"

"Have it, m'Lord."

"Good. Good."

"Are we leaving?" Addolgar demanded. "The suns are nearly up."

"Give him another minute."

"I'm running out of patience."

"I can see that, brother. Everyone within a league can see that."

Bram stalked through the hall, followed by poor Charles, who was desperately trying to keep up with his long strides.

"You remember everything, Charles?"

"Yes, sir. It'll be taken care of by the time you get back."

"Good. Good." Bram stopped in front of them. "Why are we just standing around? We need to be off."

Ghleanna slapped her hand against Addolgar's chest before her brother could rip poor Bram's arms off.

"We're ready whenever you are, Lord Bram."

"All right then. Let's go, let's go." He motioned them out and followed behind. They walked past the gates and Bram stopped.

"What are your cousins doing here?" Bram asked her.

"The troops are moving out from Bolver Fields and they have a tendency to pillage everything in their wake. My cousins will ensure that no one touches your castle or, more importantly, poor Charles. And I really think you should give him more money. He earns it."

Bram turned toward her, gazing into her face. "Thank you, Ghleanna. That was very thoughtful."

Ghleanna had rarely had anyone thank her before, so she didn't know what to say and ended up staring after Bram long after he'd walked off.

"What if we get hungry?" one of her cousins asked.

"Cows. In the field." She pointed a finger at them. "But you leave the human inside *alone*. He's not to be eaten. Do you understand?"

"But what if we're *really* hungry?"

And by the time she'd pulled her axe, her cousins had already charged back inside the gates, laughing the entire time.

They didn't make their first stop until late morning, proving Ghleanna right about Addolgar. He was a tyrant about travel. But Bram was unclear why they'd come *here*. Gods, he hoped it wasn't to round up more blasted Cadwaladrs.

"What are we doing here, Addolgar?" Ghleanna demanded once her talons touched the ground.

"You know why. Did you think you could leave the Southlands without coming here first?"

"As a matter of fact, I did," she snapped back.

"Well, you can't. An hour here. A bit of food. And then we'll be on our way."

"But—"

"No arguments, annoying female!"

Ghleanna stamped her back claw. "Worthless bastard!"

"Whiny harpie!"

"This is your parents' home."

The siblings faced Bram and Addolgar asked, "How'd ya know that?"

Bram gazed at them all. "I used to visit. Quite often. Even stayed here for a while."

"You did?"

With a sigh, he walked off until he could comfortably shift and put on clothes. Once he'd done that, he headed toward Ailean the Wicked's castle. Eventually, Ghleanna caught up to him. She'd shifted and changed into clothes as well.

"*I* remember you visiting."

"Remarkable. Since you were rarely here back then."

"But when I was here, I remember you. You were always chatting with my father."

"I came to him for advice quite often. He was a great help to me when I was first starting out."

Ghleanna slowed to a stop. "My father?"

"Your father," he said while he kept walking.

She caught up with him again. "*My* father helped you with that . . . that thing you do?"

"Yes. Your father helped me with that peacemaking thing I do that keeps you happily killing for a living."

She caught his arm and brought him up short. "He helped you do what?"

"Many things."

"What things?"

"Different things."

"Like what?"

"Things."

"Now you're pissing me off."

"Then my goal's been obtained!"

Frustrated but, it seemed, unwilling to beat the answer out of him, Ghleanna stomped her foot as she'd stomped her back claw earlier and said, "Tell me!"

"No. I will tell you nothing. It's between me and your father."

"What's between you?"

Bram shrugged. "Things."

Laughing, she tugged at his arm as Addolgar walked up behind them.

"Would you two pack it in. I want to—"

Addolgar's body lifted and flew into a nearby tree. Sent there by very strong arms and a total disregard for acceptable father-son boundaries.

"Still not paying attention, boy!" Ailean the Wicked bellowed good naturedly. For an older dragon, he still had a healthy set of lungs.

"You mad bastard!"

"And watch your mouth, boy," Ailean ordered.

The three youngest siblings stood beside their embarrassed older brother, laughing. Until another dragon crept up behind them, unseen, and slammed his shield into them, sending Cai and Adain flying and Hew screaming like a little girl in surprise.

"Weak!" Ailean bellowed. "The whole lot of you." He suddenly pointed at Ghleanna. "Except her. Except my beautiful daughter who saw me all the way over there."

"You saw him?" Addolgar snarled, dragging himself to his feet. "And you didn't warn me?"

"I was talking to—"

"Bram!" Ailean held his arm out and Bram gripped it.

"Ailean. How are you?"

"Fine, boy. Fine. Notice you didn't jump either." He glared at Hew. "Unlike some others."

"Weak," the older dragon with the shield said. "All your sons, brother. Weak as newborn babies."

"Uncle Arranz!" Ghleanna ran over to the older dragon and threw herself into his open arms. "It's been ages."

"It has." He put her down, looked her over. "You look good. Solid. Like your mother."

"Why are you here?" Ailean asked Bram. "I thought you were on your way to Alsandair."

"I thought Ghleanna should see Mum before we left," Addolgar explained, while he brushed dirt and leaves off his clothes. "I heard from her last night." Being able to talk to each other with their minds was the way immediate kin kept in touch. Very important when having to communicate with parents or siblings when a long distance off, but also a way for some kin to nag. Something that Bram was sure annoyed Ghleanna—at least at the moment.

"I'm glad she did." Ailean looked at his daughter. "She was worried about you."

"I'm fine."

"Tell her that then, so she'll stop pacing the floors."

Ghleanna's mother wrapped her arms around her daughter and held her tight. Ghleanna closed her eyes and buried her nose against her mum's neck. She loved her mother's scent. It always made her think of home, made her feel safe—and very loved.

"Are you all right?"

"I'm fine, Mum. Really." Ghleanna pulled away and saw the tears in her mother's eyes. "Oh, Mum. Please don't cry. I'm fine."

"I know. I know." Her mother wiped at her eyes, smiled. "You know how worried I get, though. About all of you. I'm just glad you stopped by."

"Can't stay long, though. Just an hour or two."

"You can eat, though, can't you?"

"Food!" her brothers cheered, pushing past her and going into the castle they'd been raised in.

"How long are you going to be on the road with that lot?"

"Too long," Ghleanna told her mum and they laughed.

"Lady Shalin."

Her mother's smile was warm. "Bram!" He leaned down and hugged Shalin the Innocent, Tamer of Ailean. "Oh, Bram. I'm so happy to see you. How are you doing?"

"I'm fine, my Lady."

"Well come in, come in. There's enough food for all of you." She took their hands and pulled them into the hall. Like a pack of ravenous beasts, her brothers had already descended on the food that had been put out.

"Like wild dogs," Ghleanna murmured.

"Not really," Bram murmured back. "Wild dogs have more manners."

He smiled and, out of politeness only, Ghleanna smiled in return. Unfortunately, though, her mother caught her smiling and Ghleanna saw those gold eyes widen, her nostrils flare.

"Talk to me about your plans, Bram," Ailean said as he walked into the hall. "Come back to the war room."

"You have a war room?"

"Don't you?"

Ghleanna waited until Bram and her father had walked off—while she tried not to notice her father taking the time to pinch her mother's hip . . . weren't they too old for this sort of thing?—before she turned to her mother and said, "Stop it."

"Stop what?"

"You know exactly what I mean, Mum. And you're going to stop right now."

Ghleanna started to head to the table, ready to fight her way through her brothers for a scrap of bread, but her mother yanked her back.

"Why not?"

"You must be joking."

"What's wrong with him?"

"Nothing. He's just . . . just . . ."

"Just what?"

"A peacemaker." And she'd dropped her voice to a whisper. "What would *I* do with a peacemaker?"

"The same thing I did with a whore." And Shalin the Innocent sounded highly superior at the moment. "Made him mine."

"I have no intention of making Bram the *Merciful* anything. Mine, yours, or ours."

"Foolish girl! Right in your face. Right there. And has been . . . for years! Yet you continue to ignore what's right before you, then you whine—"

"I do no such thing."

"—about worthless scum like Feoras."

"Mum . . ."

"Fine. Fine. Don't listen to your mother who is never wrong. See how far you get." Then she lifted the hem of her skirt and flounced away. Her mother was an excellent flouncer. A skill Ghleanna had thankfully never learned. Instead she *stomped* like a proper warrior and threw Hew and Cai away from the table and head-butted Adain so she could get some food.

"This is excellent, Bram. Excellent work."

"Thank you. I've been slaving over it for months."

"Rhiannon give you a lot of changes?"

Bram shrugged and Ailean laughed, leaning back in his chair. "I wouldn't worry about it. You're handling her well. Just stay clear of the boy."

"I try. She won't let me. I think she's trying to get me killed."

"She's using you to make her mate jealous. I'm sure she doesn't want you dead. Although if it happens, I'm not sure she'd lose any sleep over it. But that's Rhiannon and that's what you get dealing with monarchs, which is why I don't."

He tapped the parchment Bram had given him. "But this, Bram . . . this will get you killed. You do understand that? There are royals who don't want Rhiannon any more powerful than she already is."

"But how would killing me stop this? Delay it perhaps but—"

"Your death would make Rhiannon look weak and that will make her even more of a target. Besides, do you think anyone has your skill, Bram? To get dragons of all stripes to meet and agree on terms." Ailean lowered his head. "Do I need to remind you of exactly how good you are at what you do, boy?"

"No, sir."

"Good. But I am glad my Ghleanna is traveling with you. You need her protection."

"It's too blatant," Bram admitted, knowing Ailean would understand. "I was trying to keep this quiet. Trying to make it seem . . . of no consequence. But with a good number of your brood *escorting* me around the Southlands, it's obvious this alliance will change things."

"It was already obvious to those who'd give a centaur shit anyway. Trust me, Bram. You're better off with my girl watching out for you. She's a solid choice by Bercelak. And her and Addolgar together? A mighty force. Let them protect you. At this point, there can be no subtle."

Bram relaxed back in his wood chair. "I guess you're right."

"Don't worry, son. What you're doing is right. That's all you need to know."

"Thank you, Ailean."

"Any time. And feel free to visit more. Perhaps when this is all over." Ailean handed the parchment to Bram and stood. "I've missed you. So has Shalin."

Bram stood and lifted his gaze up to see the giant blue dragon in human form. "I've missed you both as well. And when this is all done, I might take you up on that visit."

"Good. And you can bring Ghleanna with you."

Bram slammed the war room door shut before Ailean could walk through it. "Don't start this again."

"And don't you be a fool. You going to let her get away?"

"She doesn't even notice me, Ailean. She forgets I exist on this planet."

"And you forget *everyone* exists on this planet. When you're working. That's how it is with my girl. When Ghleanna works, she forgets everything but her troops and who her enemy is. Honestly, Bram, the pair of you were made for each other."

"I'm not the problem."

"If you don't go after what you want, lad, you definitely *are* the problem."

Frustrated—and knowing Ailean was right—Bram yanked the door open. "Can we just go please?"

"You were the one who stopped *me*."

As promised, the stay was short and within the hour, Ghleanna was hugging her mum good-bye.

"You're crying again, Mum."

"Because I'll miss you." She pulled away from Ghleanna

and reached up so she could hug Addolgar. "I'll miss all of you."

"Mum, all we gotta do is babysit this one." Addolgar said as he pointed at Bram. "Easy job."

Bram sighed. "Yes. I do adore being equated to a human child."

After saying good-bye to her sons, Shalin returned to Ghleanna. They gazed at each other for a long moment.

"I love you, Mum."

"And I you, my daughter." They hugged again and then Ghleanna quickly turned away before she started to blubber like her mother. But she came face to chest with her father.

"And do I get nothing?" His voice lowered a bit. "Will I be paying for my past forever with you, my Ghleanna?"

Ghleanna looked up at her father. Gods, she adored that face. But still . . . "You do make it so very hard to be your daughter."

"But worth it, yes?"

"Some days, Da . . . I really don't know."

She walked around him and tried to ignore the hurt she heard in his voice when he whispered, "Good-bye, little one."

Ghleanna walked through the gates that surrounded her family home and toward the clearing where they could take off.

"You all right?" Bram asked her, his long stride matching hers.

"Aye."

"You know, your father—"

"I don't want to talk about it."

"—he adores you like the suns."

Ghleanna stopped abruptly, spun to face him. "Did my mother tell you that?"

"No. He did."

"When? Today?"

"Once, years ago when I'd stopped by to discuss some strategy with a difficult Duke who'd decided dragons needed to be hunted by his army—"

"Why didn't you just kill the Duke and his army?"

"Which was why I spoke to your father, but that's neither here nor there. Anyway, you walked in, slammed a blood-covered axe on the table and said, 'Thanks for the axe, Da. Worked like a charm.' Then you walked back out and he sighed and said with great pride, 'I adore that girl like the suns.' Then we went back to our conversation—with that blood-covered axe sitting there the entire time." Bram gazed off. "I tried not to take it as an unspoken threat."

Ghleanna shook her head a little. "Is that really true?"

"I lie when I have to, Ghleanna. Like when I tell people our queen is utterly sane or that 'No. Of course Bercelak would never kill your offspring while you slept.' But on something like this? That is not something I'd lie about."

"You don't understand. I am judged by my father's past deeds because, as usual, he didn't think past his cock. I am Ailean the *Slag's* daughter, after all, which to many means I'm no more than a slag myself."

"You are judged by your father's past because you allow yourself to be. Because you allow yourself to feel shame for the life *he* decided to live. How is that Ailean's fault? Perhaps you should accept him as he is—the way he's accepted you."

"Know so much about my family, do you, royal?"

"Well . . . I did *live* with your parents for a year while I studied alchemy under your mother."

Ghleanna frowned. "You did? When was that . . . well, don't walk off mad! It was an innocent question!"

Chapter 5

They flew the rest of the day and late into the night until they reached the outskirts of the city of Baynham. Instead of sleeping outside, though, they all decided to go into town, get some warm food and soft beds.

But it had been someone's brilliant idea for them all to stay in the pub for the night and share a single room with several beds. There was just one problem—the Cadwaladr males' ability to snore in a way that suggested very loud temple construction.

It wasn't even that Bram was a light sleeper. He wasn't. Far from it, having slept through all manner of things during the time he traveled the length and breadth of the Southlands for several years. But four Cadwaladr males in one room? That was too much even for him.

They didn't even snore in unison, but instead created a wall of sound that surrounded him so that Bram could never hope to find sleep anytime soon. After many hours of trying, he finally gave up, pulled on his boots, and slipped out of the room. Once he closed the door behind him, he let out a deep sigh of relief that the thick wood at least blocked a bit of the noise those dragons could make.

"Making a run for it?"

Ghleanna sat on the stairs that led to the next floor of rooms. She had one of her axes in her lap and was sharpening the blade.

"No offense to you, Ghleanna, but that noise—"

"I know. I know. Why did you think I offered to take first watch? Hew's the worst of the lot, though, with Addolgar a close second."

He motioned to the steps. "Mind if I join you or are you still mad at me for what I said earlier?"

Ghleanna hadn't spoken to him since they'd left her father's lands, and Bram knew he should have stayed out of it—but he couldn't. Her rage at her father was unwarranted and for some reason none of her kin would tell her so.

In answer to Bram's question, however, Ghleanna simply moved over a bit and placed her axe on the landing behind her.

Bram sat down beside her, and asked, "Too close?"

"Not so's I mind."

Bram nodded and stared straight ahead. "Any trouble so far tonight?" he asked when the silence began to choke him to death.

"Nay. Quiet as a tomb."

"Do you think a watch is necessary?"

"If my brother Bercelak is worried for your safety—it's better to err on the side of caution."

They sat in silence for a few more minutes until Bram asked, "Is that what taking first watch entails? Sitting around, sharpening your weapons . . . and waiting?"

"Mostly."

"No books to read?"

"Don't need any."

"No one to talk to?"

"Too much chatter gets on my nerves."

"Do you ever find yourself wishing for an attack of some kind to help with the boredom?"

"Not really."

Bram gazed at her. "You truly are a soldier, aren't you?"

"Me mum used to say I came out of my egg saluting and already in formation. Not sure I believe her, though."

Bram chuckled. "I adore your mother. One of the kindest dragons I've ever known."

"Aye. That she is."

"And skilled with the written word as well."

Ghleanna shrugged. "Wouldn't know. Not much of a reader."

"Well, tell me, because there's always been some debate among my friends and I, and your mother won't admit anything one way or the other—did your mother help your father write those books of his?"

Bram, finally enjoying their late-night conversation, thought it was an innocent enough question—until the tip of one of Ghleanna's blades pressed against his throat, her black eyes angry as she glared at him.

Apparently not an innocent question at all.

Seething with rage, Ghleanna hissed, "You dare bring up those books to me, royal?" The series of books that had chronicled her father's sexual escapades before he met Shalin—the damn things were still bestsellers. "Do you think I won't cut your throat and leave you bleeding out on these steps like a cow used for sacrifice? Do you think Rhiannon can protect you from *me?*"

His gaze on hers, his voice steady, the royal stated, "I meant no offense, Captain. Although I don't know why you'd be so offended."

"Of course you wouldn't," she snapped back. "The daughter of a whore's just a whore herself, right? You want to think I'm no more choosey about my bedmates than my father—fine. But don't you *dare* bring my mother into it. She's the purest thing my father's had in his life and I'll not have you sully it with your—"

"Wait." He was remarkably calm considering the fact that she had her favorite blade to his human throat—opening a main artery was a sure way to kill a dragon in human form. "I don't think we understand each other."

"We understand each other quite well. No wonder you've been so bloody nice to me. You're no better than the rest. Be nice to me, talk sweet to me, tell me my father adores me, then get me on my back or my knees, so you can run around telling everyone how you fucked the slag's daughter. Isn't that it, royal?"

"Ghleanna," he began slowly, speaking to her as if she were a very slow child, and she knew some centaur-shit soothing words would leave his mouth. He was well known throughout the kingdom for his ability to talk himself out of any situation. Yet she had to say . . . she was curious to see where he'd go. "I know that your father—and especially your mother—did not write the books you speak of. From what I understand, they were written without Ailean's knowledge or consent. Those are not the books I meant."

Ghleanna frowned. "Then what are you talking about?"

"The book your father wrote about handling close-quarter combat with Lightnings. Another about fighting human legions in open battlefields with no trees or mountains for cover. And there's another on tactical maneuvers in the Western Mountains when fighting the barbarian tribes. He dedicated that one to you because of your work there a few decades back before you received your captain's rank. But my favorite is about his peacekeeping efforts in the Outerplains between humans and dragons. He had some brilliant suggestions on how to use what he did there with all humans in the Southlands to ease negotiations. Of course, a lot of dragons think it's a scandalous and outrageous book because his insane suggestions included things like not eating humans, not destroying their villages, not stomping on them for fun. Your father has some very unorthodox ideas," Bram finished with a smile.

Yet when Ghleanna could only gawk at him, the hand with the blade sitting limply in her lap, Bram asked, "You did know your father had written books on philosophy and war tactics, didn't you?"

As a matter of fact . . . no! She didn't know. She'd had no clue. Her father? Writing books? Even with her mother's help . . . her father barely read! Not that he was stupid. Far from it. But he'd always been so busy raising his offspring and teaching them how to protect themselves—mostly against him and his two brothers—that he'd never bothered to share his philosophy on anything other than what they should do the next time he and Uncle Arranz tossed their human forms off the roof.

"Gods, Ghleanna, you didn't know, did you?" Bram asked, sounding appalled. She knew the peacemaker's family was very close and very . . . cultured. They probably sat around a dinner of roasted oxen and discussed world events. When her family got together, there was mostly just drinking and arguing, arguing and drinking. She loved it, though. Still . . . Bram would know if his father had written any books. And he would have read them. Bragged about them. Ghleanna, as much as she loved her father, also resented him because he hadn't seemed to be able to keep his blasted cock in his pants before he'd taken her mother as his mate. A reputation that had haunted her since she was of an age to take lovers.

Yet Ghleanna was still ashamed she hadn't known something so important about her own father. "No. I didn't."

"He never told you?"

"No. But he did teach me how to use two axes at once to disembowel someone in seconds."

"Well . . . I'm sure that's quite helpful, too."

She slid her blade back into her boot. "I wonder why he didn't tell us."

"Maybe he thought . . ."

"Thought what?"

Bram shrugged. "Maybe that you wouldn't care."

"Of course I would." Ghleanna reached over and wiped the bit of blood away from Bram's throat where the tip of her blade had dug in a little too deep. "He's my father. No matter what, I love the old bastard."

"Aye," Bram said with a sweet smile. "I can see that."

She planted her elbow on her knee and rested her chin on her raised fist. "Now I feel bad."

"Why?"

"Because I should have known. I should have cared enough to find out."

"And when would you have done that, I wonder? During the Battle of Hoesgyn or perhaps the Battle of Prothero in the Medus Mountains? Or maybe during the Battle of—"

"All right. All right. I get your point." She gave a short laugh. "You certainly are Lord Know-It-All this evening, aren't you?"

"Only when necessary. Otherwise I try not to let my brilliance overshadow my giving and loving nature."

"Do you know that you're not nearly as arrogant as most of my family?"

"Actually . . . I do know."

She gazed at him. "I'm so sorry I thought . . ."

"The worst of me?" he guessed.

"Something like that." She rubbed her hands across her face. "It's been a very long few months. And not very good ones, I'm afraid."

"Want to tell me about it? I'm a very good listener."

"Tell you? So you can feel sorry for me, too?"

"Ghleanna, you just had a blade to my throat. There are limits to my mercifulness I'm afraid."

That made her smile. A little. "I'm afraid there's not much to tell really. I usually spend my time in battle. Dragons have few wars, but humans fight all the time. When one battle ended, there was always another. Another fight. Another war." She briefly closed her eyes. "But one time . . . this one time in a very long decade, I . . ." She cracked her neck. "I took a chance."

"You loved him," Bram said, so quietly she almost didn't hear him.

She shook her head. "Gods, no. I didn't love him. I *don't* love him. I'm ashamed to say I was just lonely. And stupid. Very, very stupid."

"We all make mistakes, Ghleanna. The point is not to dwell on them."

"Easy enough for you. You probably never make mistakes. When you fart, I bet rainbows shoot out your ass."

"That is far from the truth," he said around a laugh. "I've made my share of mistakes. Especially with females."

"Like what?"

"Apparently I'm easily distracted—"

"You are."

"I don't need your help in listing my mistakes, Captain."

"It's not a mistake. You have a lot on your mind. One just needs to be aware of it so you can be . . . managed."

"You manage me?"

"Quite well. And is that it? Being distracted because your brilliant brain is constantly turning isn't much of a mistake."

"I'm always involved in my precious books and papers."

"Not a mistake."

"And I spend more time doing things for the reigning queen than I do for anyone else in my life."

She blew out a breath. "Still waiting on those mistakes."

"Isn't being a distractible dullard who's never around mistake enough?"

"Not to me. Sounds like you're just very busy. You simply need to find someone who can handle that. Who respects your space without crowding you. Probably someone who has a job of her own so you don't become her job. That's where you probably get into problems, peacemaker. You need an independent female who's not threatened by all the work you're doing."

The royal blinked. "You mean someone like you?"

She shrugged. "Sure. If you like, I can introduce you to a few of my cousins. I'm suggesting my cousins rather than my sisters because you don't want to have to go through the gauntlet that is my brothers. It's not fair to any dragon." She raised her gaze, found the dragon staring at her, eyes narrowed a bit. "What? Are my cousins not good enough for you? Because they're not of royal blood? Don't be such a snob, Bram the Merciful."

With a sigh, the dragon stood. "On that note, I guess I'll go back to bed. *Try* to get some sleep."

Ghleanna pulled a key from the top of her boot. "Here."

"What's this?"

"I reserved the room across the hall for myself but you can use it. See if you can get some sleep in there."

Bram took the key from her. "Are you sure?"

"We have a long day of walking tomorrow. Many of the nearby towns are too dangerous to fly over. Plus you didn't get much sleep last night. So go," she insisted. "It's fine."

"What about you?"

"Addolgar will be up soon enough to take my place."

"But where will you sleep?"

She looked over her shoulder at him and said, "In the room with you. Unless you snore."

And that's when she saw it. When he was dragon, his

scales just shined a bit more. But when he was human—his face turned red.

"Wh-What?" he stammered. "No. No. I don't snore."

"Then I don't see a problem. Do you?"

"No, no. That's fine. I'll leave it unlocked. Good-night." Then he went into the room and closed the door.

Grinning, Ghleanna went back to sharpening her weapons.

Bram entered the simple room and sighed in relief. Had she noticed his sudden panic? And lust? No. No. He doubted that. She didn't notice. She never noticed anything about him, including his attempt not to be overeager about the pair of them sharing a room.

Nay. She hadn't noticed a thing.

Bram stepped into the room and smiled. Quiet. Lovely, lovely quiet. Without bothering to remove his clothes, he fell face first on the bed and tried to push thoughts of Ghleanna from his mind.

Didn't work, though. She was right there. Like always. Driving him mad.

And then there was Feoras. She hadn't said his name but Bram knew whom she'd been speaking of. Feoras the Fighter. So named because he always fought to find a way not to have to do anything. Always looking for the easy way 'round. The easy way to earn gold, move up the ranks, whatever. Honestly, his name should be Feoras the Jealous. He wanted to be where Ghleanna was but he didn't want to work for it. Not like she had. The constant training; battles with humans as human so she could hone her skills; taking any dangerous, sure-not-to-survive assignment that came her way. No. Feoras wasn't willing to do that. But he'd still wanted to be a Captain. A Dragonwarrior Captain who received all the best assignments, led the most important battles. When that didn't pan out, he'd fucked Ghleanna instead.

Then ran around telling *everyone*. Including many of her soldiers in the Tenth Battalion, hoping to turn them against her. Ghleanna had been mortified and had disappeared for months.

But what she still didn't know was that her troops had not taken kindly to what Feoras had done. They'd not taken kindly to it at all. And they'd gone after him like rabid dogs after a bone. Last Bram had heard, Feoras was still on the run, hiding out somewhere in the Creese Mountains. And Bram hadn't said a word to Ghleanna about it, because he'd hoped that Feoras would be tracked down and killed in short order so that it wouldn't matter. It wasn't very merciful, but as he'd told Ghleanna—his mercy only stretched so far.

Then again, everyone learned that about him eventually.

Ghleanna finished sharpening the blades of her axes, her sword, and her knives. By the time she slid the last blade into her boot, the door to the bedroom her brothers slept in opened—followed by a nightmarish amount of snoring—and closed.

Yawning and rubbing his face with his hands, Addolgar dropped onto the stair right beneath Ghleanna. Unlike Bram, he'd never be able to sit next to her without his shoulders forcing her into the wall.

"Anything?" he asked around a yawn.

"Nope. Quiet."

"Get some sleep. We have a few hours before the suns rise. I can take it from here."

"You sure?"

"Aye. Go, sister. Because nothing is worse in the morning than you without enough sleep. Cranky cow that you are."

"Thank you so much for that. The love of my kin simply overwhelms me."

Addolgar motioned her away with a flick of his hand and Ghleanna walked up to the room she'd put the royal in.

"Oy," her brother whispered. "What are you doing?"

"Sleeping with the royal. It's just for a few hours."

Her brother grinned. "Saucy wench."

"I just mean I'm staying in the same room, you dirty bastard." She pointed at the room her younger brothers slept in. "You can't expect me to put up with that for the next few hours?"

"No, no. I really can't."

Ghleanna stepped inside and closed the door behind her.

The royal slept fully clothed on his stomach, his long silver hair reaching down his back, his head resting on his crossed arms. And, except for his breathing, he was silent.

No. She'd not be sleeping in her brothers' room this night. Not when she could sleep in wonderful silence without having to make herself deaf first with one of her blades.

Ghleanna carefully placed her two axes and her sword on the wood chest at the foot of the bed—she still had blades strategically placed in her boots and inside her chainmail shirt and leggings should something need to be killed during the night—and eased onto the mattress beside Bram. He didn't even move or wake up and she realized how exhausted he must be.

Once she was stretched out on her back, one arm behind her head, the other at her side, Ghleanna let out a luxurious sigh. Now she'd be able to sleep like a baby.

That is until Bram wrapped one arm around her waist and pulled her in tight against his body. Ghleanna froze. Was he awake? She didn't think so.

She tried to remove his hand from her waist, but he only gripped her tighter. Then he moved closer, pushing into her side, resting his head on her shoulder, his face turned toward hers. His eyes were still closed and his breathing normal. He was asleep but . . . still. He was awfully affectionate while he slept.

"Bram?" she whispered, loath to wake him up, but . . . *still.* "Bram."

He moved around a bit, sighed out, "More oil. Bring me more oil so we can see all those delicious scars."

Good gods, what was he going on about? Or maybe she didn't want to know.

Deciding there were worse ways she could be spending the night—like in a room with her brothers—Ghleanna stopped worrying and went to sleep.

It was the first good sleep she'd had without the help of ale in six bloody months.

Chapter 6

"Wake up!" a voice boomed, shocking Bram into wake-fulness. "The two suns are nearly up and we must face the day!"

"Shut up, Addolgar," another, sweeter voice said from beside him.

"Don't have all day, sister. We need to get on the road. Many miles to go."

"I am quite aware. Now *piss off!*"

"Suit yourself."

The door slammed shut and the body that sweet voice belonged to burrowed in deeper beside Bram.

"Uh . . . Ghleanna?"

"Just another five minutes," she softly begged. "Just another five."

But in less than five minutes—more like ten seconds—Ghleanna jerked away from him, wide dark eyes gawking.

"What are you—" she began.

But Bram quickly cut in, "I was here first."

"You . . . oh. You were." She closed her eyes, shook her head. "You got a bit clingy when I stretched out last night."

"Did I?" Bram sat up, ran his hand through his hair. "Sorry about that."

"No need to apologize. And you weren't . . . I mean, your hands didn't go . . . I mean . . ." She let out another breath. "You were quite proper is what I mean to say."

"Good. Good." He threw his legs over the side of the bed. "Then we can forget it ever happened."

"Right. Good idea. It never happened. We were both just . . . tired."

"And all that snoring."

"Right! The snoring. How could anyone expect us to sleep with that lot snoring away? We *had* to sleep together. It was necessary."

"Although," Bram admitted after a moment, "it was quite lovely, wasn't it?"

"Aye," she replied, her voice soft. "It was."

"Thank you for that."

"And thank you. That's the best I've slept in—"

The door swung open again, cutting off Ghleanna's words. "Oy!" Cai yelled into the hallway. "Addolgar did see 'em in bed together! Who knew the little bastard had it in him?"

Hew stuck his head in. "They still have their clothes on. What's the point of being human if you're going to do it with your clothes on? Playing with the flesh is the best part."

"Maybe they got dressed quick."

"Nah. I bet they just slept." Hew shook his head. "Boring."

"Not everyone's like you, Hew. Running around, fucking anything that moves."

"Let's go!" Adain yelled from out in the hallway. "I want to eat!"

The door slammed shut and Bram closed his eyes, trying to remember that this would all be over soon enough.

"That was a bit awkward," Ghleanna sighed.

"Of course it wasn't. We're dragons. We don't have all those weak sensibilities like humans." He waved toward the door. "That was nothing."

"Come on, you two whores!" Addolgar bellowed from the hallway, most likely waking up the entire building, and if not, the brothers' laughter probably did the trick. "It's time to eat! Let's move, move, move!"

"Okay," Bram told her. "Now *that* was awkward."

After a quick morning meal in the pub, they'd gotten on the road as the two suns rose, heading toward the ocean and the port where they'd meet the boat that would take them into the Desert Lands. As they walked, Ghleanna kept thinking about what had happened that morning. Waking up in Bram's arms—even fully clothed—had been . . . strange. Mostly because she'd been so comfortable. She'd never been that comfortable in a male's arms before.

Maybe it was because the royal seemed so non-threatening. He was Bram the Merciful, after all. He never ate humans and was always running around trying to create alliances and truces with their kingdom's enemies. He'd never been in a battle in his life and hadn't even noticed the one right outside his own castle gates.

He was definitely not the kind of dragon she ever saw herself with. As a warrior from a warrior clan, she'd always been with other warriors. Then again, she'd rarely stayed the night and when she did, she never slept in those warriors' arms. And Ghleanna was even less comfortable with human males.

But Bram . . .

She shook her head, confused. Annoyed. But surprisingly refreshed, as if she'd had a full twelve hours of sleep.

"You all right, sister?" Addolgar asked her after a few hours on the road. "You've been very quiet today."

"Aye. I'm fine, brother."

"Is it the royal?" he asked, his voice low so only she could hear. "Should I break him in half for you?"

Ghleanna smiled. She'd always been very close to Addolgar. They'd spent a lot of time together killing things in battle and weren't very far apart in age. And it always warmed her heart how protective he was of her, although she was often the last one who needed that protection.

"No. That's not necessary."

"If it becomes necessary, you simply say the word." They walked on for a bit and Addolgar added, "He's not terribly weak, though."

"What?"

"The royal. He's not too weak, I don't think. And he doesn't *look* weak. His human body's not very large but it probably helps him blend in more with the humans. And as dragon he's a tolerable, *average* size."

"Your point?"

Her brother shrugged. "Maybe you should see all that's in front of you rather than just a small piece. I wanted a She-dragon tiny and soft, like a kitten. And yet my mate is everything but. And I adore that about her."

Ghleanna sighed. "I don't know what's going on with you and Mum, but it is a very sweet thought, brother. Still, I think I may be too much She-dragon for our peacemaker. What kind of do-gooder like him would tolerate how many times a year I go out and kill things for sport and profit? I'm rarely home and when I am home, I'm usually recovering from battle wounds and working with one of our blacksmiths on new weapons I want to try out."

"You give him too little credit, I think. Besides"—Addolgar leaned down and whispered in her ear—"when he doesn't think you're looking, he stares at your scars."

What Bram had muttered in his sleep the previous evening came back to her, but she brushed it away and said, "All that proves is he's odd."

"Not at all. I know that look. Me mate has it for me when I get home fresh from a battle. He *likes* those scars, Ghleanna. He likes them a lot."

Aye. Crazy. Every one of her kin was absolutely stark raving mad.

Bram was digging through his travel bag and walking, trying not to trip on anything, when he realized that he was surrounded by Ghleanna's younger brothers.

He slowed to a stop. "Is there something you lot—"

"No, no. Keep moving." Adain shoved Bram forward while Cai and Hew nervously looked back at Ghleanna and Addolgar. "You, uh . . . you like our sister, yeah?"

What in holy hells was going on with everyone?

"Sorry?"

"You," Adain pushed, "like our sister. That's what Addolgar says."

"Well, I don't see—"

"All we want to say is that if you want to, you know, take a run at her—we won't rip your arms and legs off."

"Take a run—"

"Our sisters call it the Gauntlet. Most blokes aren't good enough for 'em, you see."

"Human or dragon," Hew added. "Don't matter. They're mostly idiots."

"But you're not bad," Adain confided. "And the females like the pretty ones."

"I don't—"

"Look, all we're saying is that if you want a shot at her, we won't stop you. The last bastard she was with—he hurt her."

Cai whispered, "She don't like to admit it, though."

"Right, but *you,* you're supposed to be real nice. Feeble maybe, but nice."

"I am *not*—"

"So maybe you can take her out sometime. Or buy her something a female would like. Flowers or whatever."

"And," Hew insisted, "tell her she's beautiful."

"She *is* beautiful."

"Yeah. Tell her just like that. Like you mean it."

Bram stopped walking. "I do mean—"

"Good, good." Adain patted his shoulder. "We'll leave you to it then."

The brothers walked off and Bram, confused and becoming more and more terrified by Ghleanna's kin, went back to digging through his bag. And that's when he finally heard it. A bird. A crow specifically. Cawing.

Bram looked over at the trees on the other side of the beach they walked on. The crow cawed again, his wings spread out wide from his body.

"What is it?" Ghleanna asked him.

"Someone's following us."

"Aye. We know."

Surprised, Bram again looked at the brothers. Although they were still talking, they all had their hands on the closest weapon.

"You're not going to panic on me and run, are you, royal?"

"My, you do have a high opinion of me, Ghleanna. It's very heartwarming."

She laughed and shook her head. "No insult meant. Simply wanted to be sure I didn't need to chain you to me."

"To stop me from running away? Not necessary." Bram gave her a small smile. "However, if you find other reasons to chain me to you, feel free."

Ghleanna stumbled a bit. "Wait. What?"

But before Bram could elaborate on his request—in detail—Hew yelled out, "The trees!"

The Cadwaladrs moved in unison and with purpose, all of them surrounding Bram, their shields up and locked together, their weapons ready to strike.

"Watch your right, Hew!" Addolgar yelled out. "Look to the trees, Cai. Adain, send a call out. See if any of our kin are nearby. Tell them where we are."

"I don't see anything."

"All you need to know," Ghleanna reminded Cai, "is that Addolgar and Hew did. Now shut the fuck up and hold formation!"

Then there was silence. A painful, bloated silence that had Bram panting lightly so that when he needed his flame, he could unleash it as he'd been trained to do since hatching.

They waited, the moment growing more and more tense, but not once did any of the Cadwaladrs move. Not once did they even flinch. Even the younger ones who, according to Cadwaladr Code were still too young and untrained to be on their own.

And, just when he thought perhaps Cai had been right and there was nothing for Addolgar or Hew to see, a dragon in full armor dropped right in front of them, the beach and trees around them shaking.

"*Shift!*" Ghleanna yelled and Bram shifted to his natural form at the same time the Cadwaladrs did. It was all that kept him from being crushed to death, too.

"Shields!" Addolgar yelled and with a slam against the ground, their shields changed from human-sized to a size fit for enormous warrior dragons. "Weapons!" Another slam, this time to the base of their weapons, which had the deadly implements expanding in size. He knew that the Cadwaladrs had some special blacksmith among them, but gods, what a creation.

"Ghleanna!" Addolgar ordered, "Protect the royal!"

And as soon as Addolgar's words left his snout, the first strike came.

With the open sea to their backs, Ghleanna felt relatively sure the traitors—because that's how she thought of them—would be coming from one direction. They could try to come at them from the sea but they'd be quickly seen and dealt with by the Fins.

No. Approaching by land was safer and quicker. Besides . . . there were many of them. She counted at least twenty. And all of them trained soldiers of Rhiannon's army. Soldiers Ghleanna had fought with, drunk with, raided small towns with. And yet, without a word, they were striking at the Cadwaladrs and the peacemaker.

For that betrayal alone, Ghleanna would make sure this beach would soon be called Red Sands.

The traitors advanced and Addolgar raised his lance. "Steady on, Cadwaladrs. Steady."

The first traitor, a youngster who only recently got his Corporal armor, struck first, his impatience being his undoing as so often happened with those young warriors not trained by other Cadwaladrs.

Addolgar saw the opening and struck, his lance piercing right under the forearm—a major artery. The young warrior's screams echoed out and the rest of the traitors attacked.

Ghleanna moved back, pushing the royal with her rear. He didn't speak but she didn't feel him shaking or trying to fly away in a panic. Good. She didn't have time to track the fool down if he fled.

Her brothers fought bravely but, when more traitors came, they were forced to break formation. They did their best to keep their enemies away from Ghleanna and Bram, yet it was impossible to do it without risking their own lives. She wouldn't have that.

When several went for Cai, Ghleanna used her battle axe to strike them down. Cutting one from shoulder to hip and the other from one leg to the other. Once she'd finished them off, she stepped back again to shield the royal.

"There are more, Ghleanna," Bram told her, not once raising his voice. Never showing fear. "Coming from the north."

She nodded. "Cai! Hew! North!"

When her two younger brothers turned, shields and weapons raised, Ghleanna sensed another dragon landing to the right of her and the royal.

She spun, pulling back her axe to strike, but she froze at the last second, her shock making her foolish and causing her to stop in mid-swing.

"Feoras?" she asked, unable to hide the emotion she felt at the sight of him.

The green dragon grinned wide—and slammed his sword into her chest. The last thing that went through her mind was that the only reason he'd missed her heart was because the royal behind her had pulled her to the side at the last second.

The peacemaker is much faster than I thought . . .

Bram released a blast of flame that sent Feoras the Fighter—now Feoras the Traitor when Bram was done telling this tale—and a group of soldiers several hundred feet away from them. Bram hadn't merely been bragging when he said his flame was mighty. It was a family truth. As if their flame compensated for their lack of weapons skill. With no more than two fiery blasts, Bram could wipe out an entire village.

"Addolgar!" Bram called out. Ghleanna was in his arms, blood pouring from her wound.

Her brother cut another dragon down before looking over his shoulder.

"Gods!"

"It was Feoras!" Bram motioned to the dragon, who still hadn't managed to get back on his claws, his head having struck the ground hard when he'd landed.

Addolgar snarled, ready to go after the one who'd cut down his beloved sister. But then more dragons landed around them.

"Take her!" he ordered Bram.

Bram looked around. All he saw were trees and ocean. The next port was several leagues away. And with him carrying Ghleanna—they'd never stand a chance. "Where?"

"Anywhere! Just go!"

"But—"

"She's dying, royal!"

Bram looked down at the She-dragon in his arms and realized that Addolgar spoke truly. Blood pumped from her chest in big gouts.

"Take her! Help her!" Addolgar killed two dragons in front of him by running them through with one thrust of his spear. "We'll do what we can to hold them off." He glanced back at Bram one more time. "Help my sister. Please."

Bram nodded and took another quick look around, his gaze finally settling on the ocean. It was the last place he wanted to go. The place he swore he'd never return to.

Yet he had no choice but to risk it. So Bram grabbed firm hold of Ghleanna and took to the skies, moving over the ocean. He heard the shouts of those trying to capture him. They were coming after him but Bram kept going until he was far enough out and high enough.

"Ghleanna? Can you hear me?"

"Aye." But she sounded weak.

"Take in a deep breath. The deepest breath you can. Then hold it."

He felt her take in several breaths, but it was not easy with her losing so much blood. When he knew she'd done what she could and that she now held her breath, Bram tightened his hold on her—and flipped them both over.

A few of the soldiers were near now. Only a few feet away, but they never expected Bram to suddenly flip over—nor to suddenly race toward the ocean beneath them.

"Stop him!" someone yelled from the shore. "Stop him before he reaches the water. *Stop him!*"

Unwilling to stop until he was made to, Bram kept going, glad for his lighter weight, knowing it allowed him to move faster than the bigger dragons.

He neared the blue water, was right there when he heard Addolgar bellow, *"What the hells is he doing?"*

It was the last thing Bram heard before he hit the water, dragging Ghleanna down with him. Down and down, deep into the ocean.

A few dragons followed him in. Foolish dragons. Or they didn't know what the older, more experienced ones did.

For as he kept going, the others behind him, those who ruled these waters, shot past him, their weapons out, their shark-like fangs bared. They ripped past Bram, the webs between their talons and the bright colored fin that cut down their back giving them unholy speed, while their gills allowed them to breathe.

Bram kept going until more dragons surrounded him. Older soldier Fins who'd patrolled these waters for quite some time. They looked at the wounded She-dragon in Bram's arms and then at Bram.

It was Bram they recognized.

Understanding that their visitors were quickly running out of oxygen, the Sea Dragons separated the pair. A Fin wrapped his forearms around Bram while another did the same to Ghleanna. Then they used their underwater speed to whisk the visitors deeper in the ocean—and the caves beneath. To the Empress of the Sea Dragon Empire.

And the gods knew . . . that conniving bitch was ten times worse than Rhiannon could even dream of being.

Chapter 7

Bram used his forearms to brace his body, his talons pressing into the packed earth of the cave floor, and he spewed seawater from his burning lungs. He sensed much activity around him but he paid it little mind. He was too busy trying to get his bearings.

Confused, he lifted his head to try to see where he was but his eyes stung and his hair was in his face.

"Breathe, my Lord," someone gently told him, patting his back. "You're safe now."

He recognized that voice, but from where? "Kleitos?"

"Good memory, old friend."

"Where . . . ?" Feeling his lungs had cleared, Bram sat back and pushed the wet hair from his eyes. That's when he saw Ghleanna. She lay on her back, with several dragons surrounding her. "No."

He tried to get up, to go to her, but Kleitos quickly pulled him back. "Let them do their work, Bram. You can't help her now."

Shaking his head, Bram tried desperately to remember what had happened. "We were set upon," he said out loud.

"Betrayed." He frowned, pressing his talons to his forehead. "They were trying to stop me."

"Who, old friend? Who was trying to stop you?"

The thought was just out of reach, so Bram did what he always did—he reached for his travel bag. It was a Magickal item designed to survive all flames, including the ones from his shifting. But the bag was no longer on him. His gaze, suddenly clear, shot across the cavern and he saw several dragons going through it.

He stood but Kleitos grabbed his forearm, held him back.

That's when everything became terribly, ridiculously clear.

"Get your claws off me, Kleitos."

"Now, now, old friend—"

"We are *not* old friends, you deceitful bastard."

Kleitos's smile was wide, revealing those shark-like fangs. It had taken years, nearly a decade for Bram to stop having nightmares about those bloody fangs. "I know we're not friends, but it worked for a time, didn't it?"

Bram tried again to pull his forearm away.

"Now, now, my Lord. Don't make such a fuss. I'm sure we can be reasonable about all this, wouldn't you agree?"

Annoyed more than he'd been in an age, Bram slammed his head into Kleitos's the way he'd seen Ghleanna do to Cai.

"What the hells was that?" Kleitos cried out, holding his head.

"You deserved it."

"Barbarians," Kleitos accused him. "All the Land Dwellers are nothing but barbarians!"

"That is enough, Kleitos," a female voice ordered and nearly every male in the chamber dropped to a knee in supplication. Bram, however, merely bowed his head.

"My Lord Bram."

"Empress Helena."

The dragoness circled him. "You do look the worse for

wear," she told him, her claw brushing his shoulder. "What have you been up to?"

"I'm sorry to have dropped in like this, Empress. But I really had no choice. I was set upon and—"

"Yes, yes. The ones who followed you were slain by my soldiers. They were foolish to follow you down here." She stopped in front of him, green-blue eyes looking him over. "Foolish for *you* to come back. I let you go once, Land Dweller. Who is to say I'll feel so kindly toward you a second time?"

"It was not my first choice to come here, Empress, but to be quite honest . . . I really didn't have another option."

"And that?" she asked, pointing at Ghleanna with a dark green claw.

"She is with me and helped save my life. I'll do what I have to to protect her."

"Will you now?" The Empress moved closer. Her scales, like the scales of her people, fascinated Bram because they constantly changed colors the way the sea around them changed colors. Swirling from blue to dark green to light pink to another shade of blue. It was a beautiful sight to behold—when you felt confident they wouldn't kill you for sport. "That's very interesting."

She moved away, heading out of the cavern. "Keep them both alive," Helena tossed over her shoulder. "At least until I change my mind."

"It must be your lucky day," Kleitos observed once Helena and her entourage had left. "Bram of the Land Dwellers."

Sneering, Bram jerked his head a little and the bastard quickly scrambled away, hiding behind a few soldiers.

"Barbarians," the Fin hissed. "All of you."

And why would Bram argue with him?

* * *

Ghleanna knew someone was sitting on her chest. Someone extremely heavy. Addolgar? He'd done it before. He'd tried to smother her once with a buffalo.

But when Ghleanna forced her eyes open, all she saw were some strange looking dragons standing around her. All with scales in varying shades of green, blue, and yellow; and long braided hair that constantly shifted color whenever the light changed around them. And fins. Rather than horns on their heads, as any *true* dragon had, this lot had fins.

Fins? What kind of dragon had . . . ?

Gods. Sea Dragons. Sea Dragons were surrounding her. Why? Were they trying to kill her? Or, even worse . . . experiment on her? The Fins had been known to do that sort of thing. They considered themselves intellectuals and superior to all other dragon species—the way all the other dragons considered themselves superior to each other. But where those on land were content to kill each other in battle, the Fins tended to avoid conflict. But those who strayed too far into their watery territory might be used to test out the Fins' many potions and poisons and all manner of terrible things.

Moments from unleashing her flame to remove the Fins from her presence, a familiar and welcome face leaned over her. "It's all right, Ghleanna. They're here to help you. Just relax. Sleep." Without her making one move, Bram had known what she was planning and had eased her discomfort. Such a useful dragon, that one. And so very cute.

"Sssh. Sleep." He stroked her hair with his talons. "Shut your eyes and sleep."

And, feeling much safer, that's what Ghleanna did.

It had taken much work from not only the surgeons but the Empress's personal wizard guild to save Ghleanna's life. While the wizards kept her heart beating and her brain functioning, the surgeons had worked quickly to repair her lungs and the damaged artery caused by that traitor's weapon.

And for that, Bram would make sure Feoras paid dearly, for Bram's mercy only went so far.

Now he sat beside Ghleanna's prone form and held her claw in his, waiting for her to wake. But he was anxious and with good reason. When he'd seen Kleitos scurry from the cave, smiling and giggling like a child, Bram knew no good could come of it.

It had been a few decades since Bram had been in the underwater lairs of the Fins, and it had been under very different circumstances. Circumstances he had no intention of repeating. This time, however, he was no hatchling of a dragon. And this time he had so much more to protect. But he wasn't talking about bloody truces or alliances.

"You dare," Helena's voice softly demanded from behind him, "bring *that* here? Into my court?"

Getting to his claws, exhaustion making him much slower than usual, Bram said to the monarch, "I do not understand, Empress."

"That," she said again, pointing at a still-unconscious Ghleanna. "You brought *that* here. Abusing my good nature"—*her good what?*—"and risking my subjects."

"I still don't understand—"

"A Cadwaladr!" she bellowed. "You brought a Cadwaladr into my palace!"

Shit.

"Kleitos said you called her Ghleanna. Is that Ghleanna the *Decimator?* Sister of that bastard Bercelak?"

"Empress—"

"No! I don't want to hear it!" She pointed her talon at Ghleanna and ordered her royal guard to, "Kill it. Before it awakes and destroys us all."

"No."

The Empress's eyes narrowed on Bram. "Did you say no to *me?*"

"I did and I apologize, but no one touches Ghleanna. We are unarmed and unable to fight, asking for your protection. So to kill us now—"

"But you didn't give me all the facts. You simply brought that fighting dog into our midst like it was a harmless puppy."

"She is wounded and has much healing to do. I don't see what kind of threat—"

"She's a Cadwaladr. Don't pretend you don't know what that means, peacemaker."

"Aye. She's a Cadwaladr. And my protector and my friend. Not only that, she's directly tied to the Royal House of Gwalchmai fab Gwyar. Harm her, Empress, and Queen Rhiannon will not stop until your vast ocean is nothing but a boiling pot of Sea Dragon stew."

"Like her mother then, is your young queen?"

"Actually," he sighed, "no. She's nothing like her mother, which means she won't hesitate to do what she can to destroy you should you harm Ghleanna. I assure you, you'll not have the same inaction you experienced with Adienna."

"Is the Cadwaladr her pet?"

"No. She's Rhiannon's sister by mating. That bastard Bercelak, as you called him, is Rhiannon's consort. And as we both know, my Lord Bercelak forgives nothing. Harm his sister and I won't be responsible for what he does. And trust me when I say . . . he'll do *something.*"

"So I'm supposed to allow this low-born creature to wander around here among us? Untethered, unmonitored?"

"Ghleanna owes her life to you. Like all Cadwaladrs she takes that debt very seriously. As do I."

"Which means what? Exactly?"

"It means I never forget those who've helped me."

"Is that right?" The Empress's eyes narrowed, her mind calculating as always. "Still . . . we can't take the chance."

She motioned to Kleitos and he stepped toward Ghleanna's prone body, a blade in his hand.

"Take another step"—Bram warned, stopping Kleitos in his tracks—"and I'll flay the scales from your bones."

One of the guard's placed the tip of his pike against Bram's throat and Bram moved his gaze to Helena. "Do you really think I'd let this piece of metal stop me?"

"Interesting," she murmured, and Bram realized too late it was a test. She didn't want to challenge Rhiannon—who did?—but she wanted to see how protective Bram was toward Ghleanna. How much she could possibly use his protectiveness to her own ends.

Annoyed with himself, Bram looked away and that's when he saw that Ghleanna's eyes were open and staring at Kleitos who, at the moment, was blissfully unaware of her.

He could have warned Kleitos; it would have been the merciful thing to do . . .

Yet it was much more entertaining to watch Ghleanna raise her claw, slap the blade from Kleitos's hand, pull back, and punch him directly in the snout. And she broke something in that snout. Something important.

Roaring in pain, Kleitos stumbled back, both claws around his damaged appendage, tears leaking from his eyes.

The Empress, now standing behind another contingent of guards who'd moved in to protect her the way Ghleanna and her kin had moved in to protect Bram, observed, "I see your pet needs a leash, peacemaker."

"Forgive her, Empress. She's still unwell. Not in her right mind."

Helena stepped around her guards and whispered, "You can stop smiling, Bram. I'm sure Kleitos got the message." She smirked and motioned to one of her guards. "Fetch Euthalia."

The guard ran off and Helena studied Ghleanna, who'd passed out once more. "So many scars." She shuddered in distaste. "An abused pet it seems." She gritted her fangs. "Kleitos. Honestly. Stop all that blubbering."

A few minutes later a sorceress arrived. "You called for me, Empress?"

"Do you have what we discussed earlier, Euthalia?"

"Aye, my mistress." She held a large gold ring in her hand.

"Excellent. Put it on her."

"Empress—" Bram began but Helena cut him off with a slash of her front claw and he was forced to watch while the sorceress stepped beside Ghleanna and fastened the ring around her throat.

And while they all silently observed, the ring grew smaller and smaller—as Ghleanna shifted to human. When it was over, Ghleanna was in her human form with a gold collar around her throat. A collar that would keep her in her human form for as long as Helena wanted.

"Is this really necessary?"

"Either this, Bram the Merciful, or I allow my guards to cut her Land Dweller throat and I take my chances with your queen—and you. Your choice."

Bram had no option but to nod. "The collar, Empress."

"That's what I thought."

Helena headed toward the exit. "Take him and his pet to one of the rooms we keep for human visitors," she ordered her servants. "They can be human together."

Then she was gone.

"I wish she'd allowed me to cut the Low Born's throat," Kleitos told him, copious amounts of blood leaking from his nostrils, his entire snout slightly off. He slithered closer to Bram and hissed, "I would have enjoyed watching the life drain from your barbarian whore."

That's when Bram headbutted the bastard again. You know . . . on principle.

"Owwww! *Why do you keep doing that?*"

Chapter 8

Ghleanna awoke with a snarl and demanded, "Why am I human?"

"Calm yourself or you're likely to open your wound again." Bram stood next to her. He was also in human form, dressed in a plain cotton shirt, black breeches, and black boots. They were in a rather large bedroom with a closed door. She'd guess it was locked.

"Answer me." And her voice sounded weak to her own ears. "Why am I human?"

"Why do you think?" He sat down on the bed. "Because you're a much bigger threat when you're dragon."

"When last I woke, some Fin was standing over me with a blade."

"Aye. You handled him, though."

"Good." Ghleanna tried to sit up, but she was too weak to do it on her own and Bram wouldn't let her. With his hands against her shoulders, he gently eased her back to the bed. "Relax, Ghleanna. You're not going anywhere until that wound heals."

She panted from even that small exertion but she hated

feeling like this. Like she couldn't defend them both if need be.

"You look exhausted," she told him. "Have you not slept at all?"

"Not much. But that's all right."

"Where are we, Bram?"

"Palace of the Sea Dragon Empress Helena."

"I thought an Emperor ruled the Fins."

"He did—until his untimely death. Now it's Helena's empire to rule. And, unfortunately, Helena has heard about you, I'm afraid, or at least your kin. Hence your current human form."

Bram reached over and brushed her neck with the tips of his fingers. That's when Ghleanna realized something was on her. She touched her throat, felt the metal around it.

"A collar? They put a collar on me?"

"It's a sorcerer's tool that's keeping you human. It'll be removed when we leave. Is it uncomfortable?"

"Not really. But it annoys me to know it's there." Ghleanna closed her eyes in disgust. "But no less than I deserve. I've fucked this all up royally."

"What are you talking about?"

"This." She glanced around the room. "This is all my doing. Because I was weak and stupid."

"How the hells can you blame yourself for any of this?"

"Who else should I blame?"

"Gods, I don't know . . . the *traitors* who set upon us perhaps?"

"I should have listened to Rhiannon. I should have insisted on more warriors."

"None of us took this seriously except Bercelak and Rhiannon. And even they never thought there would be such an attack."

Ghleanna let out a breath. "But *I* should have known."

"Why you?"

"Because I'm smarter than all of you when it comes to general evilness and trickery. There are Elders who have many Dragonwarriors and soldiers in their debt for one reason or another. If they wanted to stop you from making this trip, they're the lot who could do it. I should have remembered that and planned accordingly. But I was too busy feeling sorry for myself and trying to recover from that bloody hangover."

"There were forces greater than you or I who were busy trying to stop us, Ghleanna. I realize that now. Those who will never accept Rhiannon as rightful queen. To stop me, to have me killed, would reflect very poorly on her and her young reign. Now here." He slipped a hand under her shoulders, lifted her a bit, and placed a cup against her lips. "It's water. Drink it."

"Sea water?"

"Is this a time to joke?"

Who said she was joking?

She sipped from the cup Bram held, relieved it was clean drinking water.

When she pushed the cup away, she asked the question that she dreaded the answer to—yet she had to know, "My brothers?"

"It sounds as if they're alive and well."

"Sounds?"

"Warriors matching your brothers' descriptions were spotted on the beach chopping the limbs and wings off the surviving traitors. Needless to say the Fins who spotted them did not stick around to verify it was your kin."

"I need to know, Bram."

"I know you do. But you're still weak and the Empress's sorceress guild has protections up. You'll never be able to contact them on your own."

"Unless you want my brothers coming down here and ripping this place apart—"

"I didn't say we wouldn't try." And gods, he sounded so exhausted. "But you'll need my help."

"Right now, peacemaker? I need you more than I've ever needed anyone. And I'm sorry if I sound like I'm threatening. I'm not. It's just my brothers . . ."

"I know well." His smile was sweet. "And I understand more than you can ever realize." He slipped long, strong fingers into her hand. "So we'll do this together, yes?"

Ghleanna nodded and she felt power flow from Bram and into her, giving her the temporary strength she needed to force her way through the barriers the Fins had protecting this place so she could contact her blood-related kin with her mind.

Sister. Thank the gods. Addolgar's relief at realizing Ghleanna still lived was palatable, zipping through her like a bright wave. That's when her first tear fell.

Addolgar . . . the others?

Ease yourself, sister. They're fine. But tell me you're all right.

I'm fine, brother. Healing but fine. Are all the traitors dead?

No. And she could feel her brother's anger even at this great distance. *Feoras and quite a few others escaped while we killed their comrades. Seems loyalty is in short supply these days.*

Good. Then I can kill Feoras myself.

We're coming for you, Ghleanna.

No! You'll be outnumbered and underwater has never been our best battleground.

I'll not leave you to die among the Fins.

I have no intention of dying anytime soon, brother. Call to the Cadwaladrs. Get them ready for battle.

Those who aren't already here are headed this way.

Good. Wait to hear from me. But do not, under any circumstances, come down here to fetch me. Understand?

Ghleanna—

Understand?

Aye. No need to bark so. I hear you just fine.

Then I won't need to repeat myself.

After a moment, Addolgar asked, *The royal?*

With me. Alive.

Her brother grunted. *Good. I owe that bastard an ale. Hate to have it over his funeral pyre.*

That's very sweet, brother.

Go, sister. Rest.

I will. But send a few of the cousins over to Bram's parents' cave and his sister's. It's best we watch out for them as well until Feoras has been dealt with. But tell them nothing. Leave that to Bram.

I'll take care of it. Now get some rest, sister. The Cadwaladrs will be ready when you need us to be.

Ghleanna ended the communication with her brother and relaxed back into the mattress. Through tears of relief, she looked at Bram and told him, "All who betrayed us will die."

Bram nodded and kissed the back of her hand. "And I'd expect no more and no less."

Bram jerked awake, confused about where he was, his gaze searching the room. It wasn't until he saw Ghleanna asleep in the bed, the fur covering her only up to her waist, that he remembered.

He didn't know how the Fins did it. Lived under the ocean's surface in the outcrop of caves they'd discovered eons ago. Bram couldn't tell if it was morning or night. Had the suns come out or was it raining? Was it chilly or warm?

He felt trapped in this place and he hated it. And although he could sneak out anytime he wanted—the guards barely noticed him and allowed him to leave the room as he pleased—he knew he wouldn't go, which was why Helena allowed him the freedom of her palace. She knew he wouldn't leave without Ghleanna.

He let his gaze rest on the She-dragon and again thanked the gods for saving her. She was healing quite well and was looking stronger with each passing hour. Aye, the wizards and surgeons had done a good job. But lack of skill, talent, and knowledge had never been a problem for the Fins. They were, in fact, well regarded for their knowledge on a vast wealth of subjects. No, the true weakness of the Fins was their arrogance.

Something that said a lot considering all dragons were arrogant to some degree. As a race they simply couldn't help themselves. But even with their arrogance, most of them knew they couldn't separate themselves from the world around them and still function. They needed humans, they needed other breeds of dragons, they needed the gods . . . they needed everything life had to offer. Yet the Fins felt they were above all that. They didn't need anything but their brilliance and their ability to live under the vast ocean.

"Do you never rest, peacemaker?"

Bram blinked, realizing Ghleanna was awake and had been watching him. He'd been so busy letting his eyes rove over her exposed body, he'd failed to notice.

"I've slept some."

"Just some?"

"It's not easy to relax."

"Worried the Empress will change her mind?"

"She's been known to."

Ghleanna started to push herself up and Bram came to her side, slipped his arm around her, and helped her until she could lean her back against the headboard. He brought the fur covering up until it covered her chest.

She glanced down and back at him. "Something wrong with me tits?"

"No. They're perfect. That's the problem."

She smiled. "I didn't know I was such a distraction."

"Then you are remarkably unobservant."

Laughing, she patted the bed. "Sit with me before I get sleepy again."

Bram did, sitting on the edge of the bed. A very respectable distance.

"Here," Ghleanna pushed. "Stretch out next to me."

He thought about arguing but realized he didn't want to. He hated being respectable all the time. Especially since most dragons weren't, so why was he?

To Ghleanna's surprise, Bram got on the bed beside her. He stayed on top of the fur and kept his boots on, but that was all right. She wasn't sure he could handle it if she told him to strip naked.

"I have one question for you, Bram. And I want you to be honest with me."

"Of course."

"Are you in danger here? Should we be getting you out?"

Bram gazed at her. "You think I'd leave you?"

"My assignment was to get you to Alsandair and back— alive. If something happened to me along the way . . . well, that's the price one pays when a soldier."

"Unless I know you're safe, there won't be an alliance."

"But—"

"I'm not leaving you, Ghleanna. And we can argue about that until you pass out from exhaustion or you can just let it go so we can sit here and relax instead. Staring at that blue-green wall."

"Is that algae?"

"It's a design motif."

"And you lost me."

"We Land Dwellers don't have many motifs, so that's understandable."

She glanced around their very nice jail cell. "Are we really under water?"

"Yes. We really are."

"But we're not *in* water at the moment, right? You know, by some Magickal means that could suddenly go away and I end up drowning?"

"The Fins have gills but they are descended from land dragons. Although they don't like to admit that. Ever. This palace was designed for the Land Dwellers they once were and the human pets they keep now."

"But the walls won't suddenly come crashing in from the force of water, will they?"

"After a millennia? Doubtful."

"So we're safe?"

"We're safe."

"You're sure?"

"I'm sure, Ghleanna."

"Then why do I feel like the walls are closing in?"

"It's panic."

"I don't panic, Bram."

"You do now." He put his arm around her shoulders and gently pulled her close, careful of her wound. "Close your eyes, Ghleanna."

"So I won't know I'm drowning?"

"You're not drowning. You're fine. Close your eyes." She did, appalled she was acting so weak, but unable to stop the fear that was coursing through her. "Now breathe. Deep breath in, deep breath out."

She followed Bram's instruction. It helped. But she began to think his stroking of her hair might be helping more.

"You've been here before, haven't you?" she asked when she felt calm again.

"I have."

She wanted to push him for more, but now that the panic was gone, she was getting tired very quickly.

"It's all right, Ghleanna. Sleep. Your body needs it."

"I'm getting better."

"I know." She felt something brush against her forehead and she realized Bram had kissed her. She wanted to ask him to do it again, but she was just so sleepy . . .

Bram eased Ghleanna down into the bed again and brushed her hair off her face. Her color was back on her human form and she was getting stronger. He eased the fur back a bit and studied her wound. It was healing nicely.

Good.

There was a knock at the door, and Bram pulled the fur up to Ghleanna's chin and said, "Come."

The door was pushed open and Kleitos walked in. As human.

Bram smiled, enjoying the knot that could clearly be seen on Kleitos's pasty white forehead and the obvious destruction of his nose. "How's the head, old friend?"

The slithering bastard snarled a bit, then said, "The Empress requests your presence."

"Why?"

"Don't ask questions, Land Dweller. Just come along. I promise your pet will be perfectly safe."

Bram glanced at Ghleanna one last time, unsure of what waited for him outside this room.

He walked to the door and stopped, glaring down at Kleitos. "She better be safe."

"Or what? What will the peacemaking Land Dweller do?"

Bram jerked a little and Kleitos slammed back into the door, trying to get away from him. And to think Bram had at one time been afraid of this dragon.

Bram walked out and let Helena's guards lead him to their Empress.

Chapter 9

Ghleanna woke up with a Fin standing over her. Again.

"Good. You're awake." He handed something to a young assistant behind him. "I've taken out the stitches. You've healed up incredibly well."

Glancing around, Ghleanna sat up. "Where's Bram?"

"Who?"

"My companion. The Silver."

"With the Empress, I think. I'm sure he'll be back soon." The Fin motioned his assistant away. "Now, I know you're feeling stronger, but don't let that fool you. You still need some time to recuperate. But I doubt you'll be indisposed for long." He gestured to her. "You're quite the specimen. Built like a sturdy building. Are all your Low Born females like you?"

"You've begun to annoy me."

"Sorry, sorry." He smiled and it suddenly struck her that he was in his human form. Perhaps that was for ease of treating her. "Drink lots of fluids. Water. A little wine. Eat well but nothing too heavy. I've tied your left arm down to ensure you don't move it around too much. The outside of the wound has healed up but I don't want to take the chance you'll rip something internally. Although if having your arm tied down irritates you when you sleep, and if you're not a flailer, untie it when you go to bed. Understand?"

"I do."

"Good. Good." He nodded his head and walked out, closing the door behind him. She didn't hear it lock.

Ghleanna sat up and threw her legs over the edge. She stood and quickly sat back down again. The room spun, and she closed her eyes, waiting for everything to stop. When it did, she blew out a breath and slowly got to her feet. Slowly being the key. Once she was up, she found a long cotton shirt that looked like it belonged to Bram. She put it on and went to the door. She carefully eased it open and, after a quick glance around, she stepped outside.

Ghleanna's mouth dropped open as her gaze swept everything around her. This floor of rooms was just one of many. A rotunda built into the rock wall of the cave, with rotundas above and below that went miles in either direction. She leaned over a steel railing and gawked at all she could see. And she knew without being told that this was just a wing of the Empress's palace. A place they kept their human "pets."

No. She wasn't a big fan of the Fins, but she could appreciate their engineering skills because this was amazing.

Ghleanna turned and saw the two dragons guarding her door. The two *sleeping* dragons. Her first thought was that they were lazy but then she wondered if they'd been on duty since her arrival. She knew a few commanders who did that at home. They'd get so caught up in whatever they were doing that they'd forget the little things. For instance, that dragons can't stay awake all day, every day until your hostage leaves your custody.

About to return to her bed—even if she were completely healed, she wouldn't be making a run for it without Bram—Ghleanna heard someone call out, "My Lord General!"

She looked over and saw a large dragon stop at the end of a hallway and turn to face whoever had called him.

Realizing how the sleeping Fins would look—and having been in the same position more than once when left on duty too long—Ghleanna went to the guards and lifted the eyelid of one, then the other.

"Get up," she said low. "Your commander is coming." She gestured with her free arm. "Get up, get up, get up!"

They did, scrambling to their claws and standing at attention just as the General made his way down to her room.

"What's she doing out here?" the General demanded.

"I'm looking for my companion." Not much of a lie. "Where is he?"

"I have no idea. But I want you back in your room."

"Just admit it." She walked up to him, leaned her head all the way back so she could see that far up. "You're afraid I'm going to take you on. Right now. Just like this." She held up her one fist. "Let's go, General. Let me show you my skills."

The General chuckled and shook his massive head. "Get some rest, Land Dweller. Perhaps, when you're feeling better, we'll have that challenge. Until then . . ."

"Your fear amuses me, General." She grinned and headed back to her room.

The General moved on and one of the soldiers let out a breath. "Thanks for that."

"No problem. But if you've been here for more than a day, you need a break. Have someone else take watch as soon as you can manage it. Besides—" she shrugged and headed inside her room—"it's not like I'm going anywhere at the moment."

"You sent for me, Empress?"

"I did, Bram. Please." She motioned him closer. And he was surprised to find Helena in her human form, her bright blue dress glittering in the glowing light coming from the walls. "What do you think?" she asked when he stood beside her.

"It's beautiful, my Lady."

They stood on a landing that overlooked an enormous hot spring.

"Would you like to try it out?"

"No thank you, my Lady."

"And why is that?"

"Because I'll never be able to relax while I'm in it."

"Because of Kleitos?"

"Because of all of you."

The Empress smiled. "I do like your honesty. You know, Bram, when I sent you off the last time I truly never thought to see you again. And I *never* expected to see my lover return—but you did as you promised. You got him released."

"I did. But I haven't seen him since my arrival. Is he—"

"I had him executed," she told him flatly. "For treason, a few years back." She shrugged, not appearing remotely fazed by that. "Long story. Anyway," she went on, "I'm relying on your innate nature now."

"I don't under—"

"A truce, peacemaker."

"With me?"

"With Rhiannon."

Bram blinked. "Rhiannon *who?*"

"Your queen."

"The one you called wide ass?"

"One time. Gods that viper forgets nothing!"

"If you want my honesty, Empress, there is no way—"

"Make it happen."

"Rhiannon will—"

"You're not hearing me, peacemaker." Helena stepped closer to Bram. "You will get me a truce. I want it and you'll get it for me."

"I can't force Queen Rhiannon to do anything."

"You can persuade her. You're very good at that."

"Yes, but—"

"And I am trying so *very* hard to keep your low-born pet safe. Yet Chancellor Kleitos *loathes* her. I have him on a tight leash, but . . ." Helena briefly pursed her lips. "What if that leash slipped from my grasp?"

Bram clenched his jaw, but said nothing.

"I'm sure you remember your time with Kleitos, yes? I'm sure I need not remind you."

"No, my Lady. You need not remind me."

"Excellent. Then you'll promise me, yes? A truce. A *favorable* truce with your queen."

"Aye. I promise."

"Excellent," she said again. "Excellent." Then Helena walked off, leaving Bram to stare off across the cavern, rage and hatred making him unable to move for quite some time.

Ghleanna waited up as long as she could manage, hoping to see Bram before she fell asleep. Human servants came in, bringing her food and a tub so she could bathe. She'd done that and eaten—but still Bram had not returned.

And while she'd debated whether she should go out and track him down—she'd fallen asleep. Yet now she sensed Bram's return, and knew he stood over her—staring.

Ghleanna opened her eyes and gazed up at him.

"What's wrong?"

"I didn't think it was possible—but this situation has managed to get worse."

"But you're so calm," she observed.

"That's usually when you can tell everything has gone to shit."

"I'll make sure to remember that." Ghleanna struggled to get up with one arm. She'd left the other tied down because she'd fallen asleep before she could take off the binding. "Perhaps it's not as bad as you think."

Bram caught her around the waist and lifted her until she was sitting up.

"I rarely blow things out of proportion, Ghleanna. When stakes are this high, I simply don't have the luxury."

Ghleanna leaned forward and caught Bram's hand. She winced a bit from the pain, and he said, "I should leave you to sleep."

"Like all the hells you will." She tugged. "Come. Sit beside me."

He did, stretching his long legs out on top of the fur.

"Now talk to me, Bram. What has you so worried?"

"She wants me to build a truce."

"A truce? Between . . ." When Bram didn't answer, "The Fins—and us?" Bram nodded. "She wants a truce with Rhiannon?" Ghleanna laughed. "Good luck to her then. Rhiannon hates her."

"And Helena her." Bram's voice was cold, his gaze across the room. She could see that he was drawing in on himself. Protecting himself for some reason. She didn't think it was anything she'd done, and he created truces every day. Why should this one bother him? "But her subjects tire of their limits. They want to travel farther inland and, in return, we'll be able to use the seas. Especially during wartime."

Ghleanna instantly saw the benefit of that. The thought of moving up the Northern Coasts and striking at the Lightnings almost made her tingle.

"That seems reasonable."

"I am a peacemaker, Ghleanna. Not a miracle worker. Rhiannon will never agree to a truce with Helena. Never."

Ghleanna winced. "Because of that wide ass comment? When Rhiannon took the throne?"

"It was said Helena's exact words were, 'I can't believe that wide-ass cow now rules the Southlands.'"

"And after Rhiannon heard that, Bercelak's, 'I love your wide ass' . . . not really helpful." Ghleanna waved all that away. "No matter. Simply tell Helena no."

Bram didn't move. He didn't speak. And yet Ghleanna could feel him recoil. Not from her, but from everything else.

Ghleanna pushed the fur off and got to her knees beside Bram. "What aren't you telling me, Bram?"

"Nothing you need to know."

"Are you protecting me?"

"You're still healing. You need rest—not tales of the past."

Fed up and worried for her friend—she didn't remember ever seeing him like this before—Ghleanna straddled Bram's lap.

He blinked hard, brought quickly back into the moment. "What are you doing?"

Ghleanna tugged off the cotton material that held down her arm and had covered her breasts.

"Ghleanna—"

"Look at me, Bram."

He smiled a little. "I can hardly look away."

"I meant look at my *eyes,* you pervy bastard." She laughed and said, "Now hear me well. I am no weak female who cannot handle hard news. I am a Cadwaladr." And her back automatically straightened, her chin lifted. "And we are in this together, you and I. For good and bad. So tell me what you've been hiding from me."

Bram closed his eyes, his breathing deepened. The walls of this place were closing in on him as they'd done to her.

Ghleanna lifted Bram's hand and pressed it to the wound on her chest.

"We're bound together, Bram. Nothing can ever change that. Nothing ever will."

"Understand, it is not shame that stops me from telling you the truth, Ghleanna. It's fear . . ."

His words faded out, his gaze on hers, and Ghleanna's brow peaked. "You fear what I might do."

"As you said . . . you *are* a Cadwaladr."

She appeared so insulted, Bram almost felt bad for what he'd said. But she always demanded honesty. So honesty was what she would get.

"Don't look at me like that," he argued. "It's not as if I'm pulling this concern out of my ass."

She gave a little snort. "You might have a point."

"I just need to know—"

"I won't touch her. The Empress. At least not without orders from you or someone who outranks me. There. Happy?"

"Fair enough." Bram took in a breath, watched his forefinger ease across the scar of her recent injury. He focused on that so he could let the words flow.

"Many years ago. I was lured here."

"By the Empress," Ghleanna guessed.

"She wasn't the Empress then, but yes. By Helena. I was young and she was . . . beautiful, and it never occurred to me that I was being used. Once I was here, they sent word to Adienna that they had one of her royals and they wanted her to return the Fin who had gone past the port towns and been captured by Adienna's troops."

"Adienna didn't bargain."

"No. She didn't."

"Then why did we not hear of this? This is the sort of thing the Cadwaladrs excel at. We should have been sent to fetch you."

"It was Adienna's decision to do nothing."

Ghleanna leaned back, her scowl dark and dangerous, her voice flat. "She left you here?"

"Aye."

"So what did you do?"

"I bargained my own way out. It wasn't easy. I learned to enjoy fish. All kinds of fish. And, in time, they eventually let me go."

"It couldn't have been that easy."

"It wasn't."

Ghleanna cupped his jaw in her hand. "They hurt you."

"Yes. Some scales were removed to send to the queen. But that didn't help."

"But there was more, wasn't there?"

"The Emperor's chancellor decided to make me his personal project. I'm still not sure why."

"He enjoyed your pain. I've known blokes like that. They're never for the quick kill. Not if they don't have to."

"Chancellor Kleitos does like his pain. And he enjoyed mine."

"But you got out."

"I did. The Fin Adienna had in her dungeons was Helena's lover. When Adienna wouldn't release him, Helena came to me."

"Because she thought her *hostage* would help?"

Bram chuckled. "No. She came to me to complain. I'm in chains, missing scales—bleeding quite profusely. And she's complaining."

"How's that funny?"

"You had to be there." He shrugged. "She complained and I listened, pretended I cared, pretended I empathized."

"Then you manipulated her?"

"No. I persuaded. And promised I could get her lover out."

"And she released you?"

"She had no choice. Her father would no longer help and Adienna wouldn't bargain. Killing me would only ensure her lover's death."

"So she let you go."

"She let me go."

"And, of course, you returned home and called for revenge."

"No. I secured the release of her lover."

"Why, Bram?"

"Because I'd given my word."

"I'd call you a fool except that I'm sure it is the very reason you're now the most trusted dragon in the Southlands. Which I'm sure is why she's asking you to get this truce for her now. You helped her before . . ."

"More fool I."

"You survived, Bram. Without anyone's help." Ghleanna's head tipped to the side and she studied him. "It couldn't have been easy for you to come back here." When Bram only stared at her, "And yet you did. You came here to save me."

"It was the only place I could think of at the time."

She stroked his cheek. "Gods, I owe you more than I realized."

"No. You owe me nothing."

"Bram—"

"Haven't you realized yet?" he asked, frustrated. Because the gods knew he didn't want her pity. "I'd do anything to keep you safe? Anything at all?"

"I was to be protecting *you*, royal."

"We'd run out of options."

Ghleanna framed Bram's face with both her hands, her dark eyes focused on his mouth. He didn't know what he'd said to prompt this, but he watched her lean in, his breath halting in his lungs as her lips neared his.

But then there was that damn knock at the door.

Bram closed his eyes. Why? Why were the gods torturing him?

"What?" he snarled.

Kleitos in human form walked in. "I am sorry to interrupt, Lord Bram. But the Empress has requested your presence at the Senate."

"Of course she does," he muttered.

"Sorry, my Lord?"

"I said I'll be there in a minute. Now go."

"Of course, my Lord. I'll be right outside."

Kleitos slinked away, closing the door behind him.

"That was him, wasn't it?" Ghleanna demanded after a moment.

"That was who?"

"The one who tortured you. The one who hurt you."

"How do you know that?"

"Because you're never rude to anyone. Even my idiot brothers. Not only that but I could feel it in your body. The way you tensed. It was him."

"Ghleanna—"

Ghleanna scrambled off Bram's lap naked, and stalked across the room. She yanked the door open and Kleitos quickly pulled back.

"Really, Kleitos?" Bram asked, slipping off the bed. "Listening at the door? Isn't that beneath even you?"

"Oh, no, my Lord. I was doing nothing of the kind. Surely you—owwww!"

Ghleanna had rammed her head into Kleitos's with all the force she could muster.

"You barbarian whore!"

That's when Ghleanna hauled back and punched the Fin, most likely re-breaking his nose.

Kleitos scurried away and Ghleanna followed.

"I'm going to enjoy removing your skin, lizard."

Bram caught Ghleanna around the waist before she could get her hands around Kleitos's throat. He picked her up and carried her back into their room, slamming the door with his foot.

"You promised!" he roared, shoving her away.

"I promised I wouldn't touch the Empress. Didn't say anything about him!"

And damn her, but she was right.

Ghleanna itched to go back outside and finish what she'd started.

Imagining Bram as a young dragon, not even a full-grown adult, trapped in a dungeon and at the mercy of that slithering pond scum had her blood boiling.

She'd been alone like that before, but her kin had come quick enough. And she knew they would. She knew that none of her kin would leave her to die. But they were warriors, trackers, blacksmiths, pit fighters. Bram's kin were cultured royals who relied on their queen for protection—and she'd failed them. Adienna had left their son and her loyal subject to the whims of the enemy.

And no one had suffered for it. Not Adienna. Not the Empress nor her father. And not Bram's torturer. Unsurprisingly that stuck in her craw most of all.

"You're right. You did only promise to leave Helena be. But now I'm asking you to do the same for Kleitos."

"I'll not make that promise, peacemaker."

"He's chancellor, Ghleanna."

"I don't care."

"Do you wish to get out of here alive?"

"Of course I—"

"Then I want you to leave him be. Do you understand?"

She looked off.

"Ghleanna . . ."

"Yes," she hissed. "I understand."

"Good. I need to go." He frowned at her chest. "Your wound is irritated."

"It'll be fine."

"Yes, but—"

"It'll be fine!"

Bram stepped back, raised his hands, palms out. "I'll see you later then."

He turned but Ghleanna caught his arm.

"Ghleanna, I have to go."

"I know. It's just . . ."

"Just what?"

Ghleanna raised herself onto her toes and pressed her mouth against his, her hands sliding into his hair, fingers digging into his scalp.

Bram caught hold of her waist and she thought he meant to push her away. But he pulled her close, held her tight, and slipped his tongue into her mouth.

Her human body heated, her nipples hardened, her sex became wet. It was all instantly there. And instantly perfect. But then Ghleanna was falling, everything around her spinning.

Bram caught her in his arms. "Ghleanna?"

"I'm all right."

"I'll send for the surgeons."

"No, no. Just bed. I'm just tired." He didn't look like he believed her. "Don't question me, royal. Just take me to the bed and go to your meeting."

Bram picked her up in his arms and carried her to the bed. With infinite care, he placed her on it, then covered her with the fur.

"Get some sleep. We'll talk more later."

Talk? As far as Ghleanna was concerned they were long past talking. But the peacemaker was skittish. Best not to spook him.

She nodded. "Later then."

Ghleanna watched him walk out, the door closing behind him, and her mind turned.

For the first time in six months, she wasn't thinking of her own misery. She was thinking of others—and how to make their misery *worse*.

Chapter 10

When Bram didn't return for several hours, Ghleanna got up again and found some leggings that fit her.

She opened the door—still unlocked—and walked out into the hallway. There were new guards at her door. They turned, facing each other, and slammed the butt end of their pikes into the ground.

"My Lady—"

"It's Captain."

"Captain."

"Why are you human?" she asked.

"Orders, Captain."

That was good enough. They probably didn't get an explanation and knew better than to ask for one. "I'm hungry. Any food around?"

"We can have the servants bring you—"

Ghleanna waved that away. "Not in the mood for servants. I need to move around a bit. Or am I still under arrest or whatever you're calling it?"

"No, Captain. We are merely here as protection for an honored guest."

Ghleanna blinked. "Honored guest? Wasn't it just a few

days ago that I was the horrifying Low Born that had to be kept human?"

"They still want you human, Captain, but you've been given leave to walk where you'd like."

So the Empress was sucking up—interesting.

Ghleanna started off, but eventually came to a stop. "And you're to follow me everywhere?" she asked the guards right behind her.

"Yes, Captain."

Good. Even better. "Well, what're your names then?"

"Anatolios, Captain. This is Demetrius."

"Anatolios. Demetrius. Does the Empress feed her guards and soldiers well?"

"She does, Captain."

"Good. Take me to where you eat."

The arguing turned out to be quite monumental. Full of passion and eloquence.

And yet . . . it was also a phenomenal waste of time.

These senators, the representatives of the Fin populace, were arguing the logic of a truce with the Southland Land Dwellers. A very good discussion to have for any ruling body—except that these senators did not rule. They had no power except that which their monarch allowed them. And Helena, like her father before her, allowed very little.

But she enjoyed the arguing, enjoyed sitting on her throne and watching all of them go at it like wolves after a deer carcass, only to overrule them when they were done.

Even more annoying—she wanted Bram to be a witness to her power. As if he cared. As if any of this mattered when he could still feel Ghleanna's skin under his fingers. Still taste her on his lips.

At the moment, that was all that mattered to him.

Bram.

Bram blinked, glanced around. Helena smiled at him.

Br-amm.

That sing-song voice. But . . . but that was impossible. Absolutely impossible. Only immediate kin could communicate with each other among dragon kind. He'd already been in touch with his parents and sister. He'd only told them that he was safe and caring for a wounded Ghleanna. He had *not* told them where he was caring for her. He knew how they would take it and he didn't want them to worry.

So they wouldn't contact him unless it was urgent—and this female voice was not his mother's or his sister's.

Br-ammmmm.

Good gods.

There you are, my little ray of sunshine!

Rhiannon? How are you . . . why are you . . . what is happening?

Calm down, Bram. Calm down.

But how?

My witch skills have advanced quite a lot lately. Soon I'll be able to create a space so we can talk directly to each other. Won't that be fun?

Actually . . . no!

Rhiannon giggled. *Oh, Bram. Just so cute!*

Ghleanna ate the cooked and seasoned fish and let the soldiers in the hall stare at her. Almost all of them were in human form—orders from their Empress, according to Anatolios. The royal was sucking up to Bram by sucking up to Ghleanna. That slut.

But Ghleanna would not worry about any of that now. She had other things to deal with.

"All right," she said loudly, so the entire hall could hear her. And they all tensed a little, watching her closely as she pushed her seat back, stood, and sat down on the long table, her feet in her chair.

"What do you want to know about me?"

"What makes you think we want to know *anything* about you, Land Dweller?" a Fin from the back of the hall asked.

"Because I killed Grimhild the Vile. The Lightning warlord."

"That's a load of—"

"I tore him open from bowel to throat. I wear his horns on my battle helm and his scales are hammered into my shield. His teeth are a decorative necklace I wear at family gatherings."

Another Fin stepped forward. "And what makes you think we'd believe that?" He stepped as close as he dared, appearing tough to his comrades, but still out of arm's length. At least he was out of arm's length for dragons who'd rarely fought as human before. "What makes you think that we'll believe a little twat like you brought down Grimhild the Vile?"

Ghleanna slammed her foot down, breaking the wood chair into pieces. She picked up a leg and swung it. The soldier, unprepared, tried to block the blow with his arm, but Ghleanna spun, changed her trajectory, and sent him flying back twenty feet or so.

Biting pain hit her at the site of her recent wound, but she ignored it. Convincing herself she felt no pain, she tapped the chair leg against the palm of her hand and said, "Grimhild called me a twat, too."

She smiled. A little. "So . . . would you lot like to hear how I brought the big bastard down?"

Why, Rhiannon, are you in my head?
First my question . . . are you all right?

And that's what was different between Rhiannon and the old queen. Rhiannon actually gave a shit about her subjects.

I am perfectly well, Rhiannon. And Ghleanna is healing.

Good. Bercelak . . . he never says it, but he adores his sister. As do you, I think.

As do I . . . you know.

A soft laugh. *My dear, sweet Bram. But . . . that female. The Empress. What does she want from you?*

I don't know—

Don't lie to me, peacemaker. You wouldn't be alive if she didn't want something.

Why did he bother trying to hide anything from Rhiannon?

She wants a truce.

With me?

Aye. She's quite . . . adamant about it. I can try to put her off until Ghleanna is at full strength but—

No, no. See what her terms are.

My Lady?

I am not my mother, peacemaker. I can be reasonable. It's a new time for us all. A new time of hope and of change and of—

You want access to the coast so you can attack the Lightnings, don't you?

And it is time for those barbarian Lightnings to bow down before me.

You want me to arrange peace with one breed so that you can destroy another?

Get me my truce, peacemaker. Make me a happy monarch.

And then—Rhiannon was gone.

Ghleanna walked out of the army dining hall, Anatolios and Demetrius behind her.

"You do eat well," she told them.

"Aye." Anatolios was a little more talkative than Demetrius.

"You must have good representation in your Senate."

"Representation?"

Ghleanna slowed and stopped. She faced the two soldiers. "You do have representation? For the army? Older, ranking warriors who speak for you, ensure that you're all fairly treated and compensated for risking your lives?"

"The Empress's rule is absolute, as Chancellor Kleitos has pointed out to the rank and file many, *many* times."

"Huh." Ghleanna again headed toward her room. "That's interesting."

Bram eased into the room, trying to be quiet since Ghleanna was asleep. He placed notes he'd made for the truce on the small desk against the wall and debated whether to go back to work or not.

"Come to bed."

Startled, he turned. Ghleanna still had her eyes closed but she held her hand out to him.

"I should—"

"If you say work, I'm going to get nasty. Bed. Now." She opened one eye. "It's not like we haven't slept together before."

Bram sat at the edge of the bed and removed his boots. "At least this time your brothers won't be storming in to wake us up and calling us whores." He dropped the last boot and asked, "Or will they?"

"Not that I'm aware." She moved over and Bram got into the bed fully clothed. Ghleanna didn't complain, for which he was grateful. He knew he couldn't handle being naked around a naked Ghleanna. Not right now.

"Should you be sleeping on your side?" he asked. "And why isn't your arm tied down?"

"Don't harass me," she barked back, sounding adorably cranky half-asleep. "The surgeon says I only need to wear it during the day. I think he fears I'll start swinging a sword before I'm fully healed." That was probably because Bram had told the surgeon she might do that and did he have a way to keep her from doing so. But Bram wouldn't mention that. Why cause problems when there were none?

"What if you flail wildly in your sleep? Then what?"

"You'll get hit in the face and my wound will be the least of your worries. Now can we both get some rest?"

He relaxed on his side, facing Ghleanna. Her eyes were once again closed, her breathing even. She was asleep once more.

Bram didn't know how things would be once they left here. Once they were free again, heading to Alsandair to finish what they'd started. But Bram knew what he wanted. He wanted Ghleanna and, as Rhiannon had accurately guessed, he'd wanted her for a very long time. Whether Ghleanna felt the same or not, however, he really didn't know.

But when she reached out in her sleep and cupped his jaw in her hand, he felt a definite sense of hope.

Chapter 11

"Fruit."

Bram opened his eyes and stared at the big shiny fruit held up before him. "Yes, it is."

"Plus bread and cheese. Hungry?"

Bram sat up, but immediately frowned. "Why is the area around your wound bruised?"

Ghleanna shrugged and bit into a big piece of bread.

"What aren't you telling me?"

"Nothing. Eat."

Bram glanced down at himself. "I'm . . . naked."

Ghleanna nodded, bit into a juicy piece of fruit.

"And when did that happen?"

"No idea." She held out another piece of fruit. "Must say, though . . . I do like you naked."

He took the treat from her hand. "Thank you. For the fruit and the compliment."

"You're welcome."

They ate in silence for a while, Bram busy trying not to stare. Gods, she was beautiful.

"Do you have much work to do today?" she asked.

"I'm afraid so. I heard from Rhiannon." When Ghleanna

frowned, he added, "Something to do with her increasing powers. Which are, I must admit, becoming daunting."

"She'd been held back a lifetime because of her mother. She has much time to make up for."

"I guess."

"I wouldn't worry. Rhiannon's grandmother had that level of power and she managed it fine."

"And Bercelak's there for balance. A rational thought in the chaos of Rhiannon's mind." Ghleanna raised a brow at that and Bram shrugged. "I've never doubted the good your brother brings to our young queen's reign. I merely wish they wouldn't stick me in the middle of whatever they like doing. It's off-putting."

"Then you shouldn't keep hugging her."

"It's not me!"

Ghleanna laughed, bit into another fruit, and Bram noted, "You have your appetite back."

"Had I ever lost it?"

"It was definitely diminished for a while there."

Ghleanna stared at him for a moment. "You were very worried about me, weren't you?"

"Sword through the chest," he said. "That may be normal for your kin, but not mine."

"You and your lot—sit around drinking wine and discussing important things, I bet."

"You'd be wrong. We sit around, drink wine, and argue. A lot."

"Argue? You?"

"Raised to argue. Both my parents are lawmakers, and no Dragon Law is created without much discussion, debate, and arguing. Sometimes a fist fight, but those are rare—and never very impressive. Almost sad."

Ghleanna shook her head. "And all your kind do it? Argue, I mean."

"My mother can find reason to argue about a grain of

sand. And my father doesn't think a meal is complete unless someone proclaims, 'That's the most ridiculous thing I've ever heard! Where's your proof to that statement?' I don't mind so much now." He sighed. "It was a little overwhelming, though, when I was only eight winters. My wings hadn't even unfurled."

"Me and mine . . . we argue. But to back up your statement Cadwaladrs just need to be willing to take a claw to the face. Or a shield."

"Aye. I remember that."

Ghleanna blinked, frowning. "You were at our dinners?"

There was a pause and then Bram demanded, "Was I *entirely* invisible to you?"

"Well . . . not entirely."

Deciding it was time to get to work, Bram began to get up. But Ghleanna caught his arm, her laughter annoying him even more.

"I'm teasing," she said, pulling him back. "I swear."

"Isn't it bad enough I assumed you'd always ignored me? Now I find out I was just invisible to you."

"That's not true." She put the tray of half-eaten food on the floor before taking his hands in hers. "I noticed you, Bram."

"Don't lie."

"I'm not. But you were a bit younger than me."

"Only by half a century or so."

"And I thought you liked my sister."

"Maelona?"

"Yes. Maelona. Pretty, shy, insecure, scar-free Maelona. *That* Maelona."

And she sounded wonderfully jealous.

"And you can stop smirking," Ghleanna told him.

"I'm not."

"Liar." But he was an adorably cute liar. "Look, I just never thought—"

"I was good enough?"

Aghast, Ghleanna said, "That's not true!"

"It is." Bram stretched out on his side. "All the Cadwaladrs are the same."

"All the same what?"

"Snobs. You're all snobs."

Ghleanna's mouth fell open.

"Don't look at me like that."

"*We* are snobs?"

"Snobs. Big snobs. If one can't handle a sword or an axe—not worthy."

"That's not true."

"It is true. And what does your brother call me? The thinker? As if it's a disease. An ailment I need to be cured of."

"You can't listen to Bercelak. He's a mean bastard and he treats everyone as if they have ailments in need of cure."

"Snobs."

"We are not. We're not of royal blood."

"Snobs."

"We're just poor warriors."

"Who are snobs. It's all right, though." He reached over and patted her hand. "You don't know any better."

"You condescending—"

"Now, now. No need to get nasty." He smiled. "I like you despite your snobbery."

"Do you?"

"You don't know?" He caught her hand, held it. "Really?"

"I know I'm not an easy She-dragon to . . . not fear."

"I'm not afraid of you, Ghleanna. I've never been afraid of you. To be quite honest . . . I think you're amazing. I always have. Since the first time you ignored me."

"I didn't ignore you then." She stretched out on her side,

the two of them facing each other. "And I can assure you that I'm *not* ignoring you now."

Ghleanna bit her lip and asked, "So when do you have to work on your precious truce?"

Bram reached for her, his hand slipping behind the back of her neck. "Not for days."

"Don't you mean hours?"

He tugged her close, their lips almost touching. "No, Ghleanna, I mean days. Minimum. I've been waiting a very long time to—"

"My Lord Bram?" a voice from outside the door said.

Bram fell back on the bed. "This isn't happening. This can't be happening."

And that's when that Lord Kleitos idiot opened the door without invitation. He grinned when he saw the pair naked and nearly entwined on the bed.

"So very sorry to interrupt, my Lord, but the Empress asks for your *immediate* attendance."

"Right."

Kleitos stood there, the silence in the room stretching, until he pushed, "*Now*, my Lord."

And that's when Ghleanna charged off the bed and tackled the Fin into the far wall. She clasped her hand around his throat and squeezed. She felt water begin to pour from his skin and she warned, "I'll snap your neck before you'll have a chance to shift."

Kleitos settled back and Ghleanna explained, "Lord Bram will be along when he's dressed and ready. *You* will no longer just walk into this room without invitation. And, if you can manage it, stop slithering around. I find it nauseating."

Ghleanna pulled Kleitos away from the wall and pushed him out the door and onto the walkway. "Now tell your Empress that Lord Bram will be there shortly."

She released him and Kleitos rubbed his neck, glaring at the two guards outside her door.

"And you do nothing?" he demanded.

Demetrius shrugged. "Our orders are quite specific, Chancellor—"

"Never mind!"

Kleitos stormed off and Ghleanna cracked her neck. "Slithering bastard," she muttered, before heading back into her room.

As she passed the two guards, Anatolios winked at her.

Ghleanna closed the bedroom door, but the bed was empty. It wasn't a large room, so she had no idea where Bram could have gone.

Ghleanna walked around the bed, stopped, and placed her hands on her hips.

"Bram the Merciful! Stop laughing and get off the floor. The Empress awaits!"

She released him and Kleitos rubbed his neck, glaring at

Chapter 12

Ghleanna had just finished pulling her shirt over her head when the bedroom door opened and the ruling monarch of the Fins walked through—without even a knock!

Even Rhiannon didn't do that.

"Oh. I thought Bram would be here."

Helena knew damn well Bram wasn't here because she'd been the one to order him to some ridiculous Senate meeting or whatever, but the royal wanted to play games. The kind of games many She-dragons played. She-dragons other than Ghleanna.

"He's in a Senate meeting, I think."

"That doesn't start for another hour at least," Helena stated.

Then why did she order him to the Senate right away? Or was that demand simply Kleitos being a twat? Probably both.

Fighting a sigh, "Perhaps the library then. But is there something I can do for you, my Lady?"

"No, no. I just need to talk to him. Do you know which library?"

Ghleanna dropped her boots on the floor and sat on the

edge of the bed so she could tug them on with her free hand. Bram had insisted on tying her arm down before leaving her. "There's more than one?"

The Empress sighed and began to move about the room. "Are you enjoying your stay with us?"

"I'm glad I'm healing. Glad I'm breathing. So I guess I'm enjoying it."

"I'm having most everyone stay in their human form. Just for you."

Ghleanna fell back on the bed and lifted her leg up in the air, the boot half on and half off. She struggled to tug the tight leather on while trying to have this ridiculous conversation.

"That's quite nice of you, my Lady. But it's not necessary. I can hold me own in whatever form I'm in."

"Really?"

Once she had the boot on, Ghleanna sat up. She grinned, shrugged. "It's a skill. I am a Cadwaladr after all . . . my Lady."

The Empress stepped closer. "So you and Bram . . . you're very close?"

"We are."

"But you have no claim on him, yes?"

"No. I have no claim on him." Ghleanna held the other boot in her hand and looked up at Helena. "But I haven't had him tortured and beaten either, which kind of puts me in the lead . . . don't you think, my Lady?"

Those strange-colored eyes narrowed, that back straightened, "Excellent point. Then again my father doesn't have an entire forest of books on his past conquests. My, my, you must be proud," she sneered. "Being the daughter of Ailean the Slag."

A few months ago, the Empress's head would have been ripped off and thrown against the wall, but not only had Ghleanna had a sword shoved into her chest by an ex-lover—

something that often changed one's perspective on the little things—but with all this time on her claws she had been thinking a lot about Bram's words to her right after they'd left her parents' castle. Her father's life, his past, was not her own.

Not only that, but her father wrote books, was highly respected by the royal peacemaker, and had taught all his offspring to protect themselves in *any* given situation. Even Maelona had her skills. A whore Ailean may have been, but a loving, caring whore who adored his offspring and mate. Who adored Ghleanna. A daughter who'd refused to forgive him his past indiscretions. That is until now.

Now she'd be damned if she'd let some little prissy tail make her feel shame over anything. Those days were over for her. Long over.

"That's very true, my Lady. Then again, according to what I've heard and my mother's general satisfaction, I'm guessing Ailean the Wicked is an awesome—"

"Yes," the Empress cut in. "I see your point." She also clearly saw that Ghleanna wouldn't be goaded. "Why don't I leave you to finish dressing."

"Yes, my Lady."

Helena walked out and Anatolios, who still had the watch, stuck his head in. "You all right?"

"Aye. That one's only as scary as you let her be." Ghleanna held up her boot. "Could you help me with this?"

Eight hours of absolutely nothing but more arguing. Not even effective arguing but just ridiculous arguing because the final say on any matter was Helena's. Yet she sat back and enjoyed the angry arguing of her Elders, senators, and other sycophants. Bram didn't know if any of these dragons was aware that Helena already had her mind made up, or if they knew but decided to argue for her amusement despite that.

And, because she enjoyed spreading the misery around even more, she'd insisted on Bram being in attendance, even going so far as to track him down in the library where he was working diligently on her blasted truce.

Finally, the Empress called a halt to the day's discussion. "We'll meet tomorrow to explore this further."

Bram stood and stretched his back. "Why do you let them think they have a say?" he had to ask, when the others had filed out. "Isn't that just cruel?" And a waste of his bloody time.

"Not cruel at all. It's good to let your subjects think they have some control over their lives, otherwise they get a bit unruly. I loathe unruly, don't you?"

"Never thought much about it." He began to organize his scrolls. "I'm going to see if I can get more work done. If you'll excuse me, my Lady."

"Aren't you going to thank me?" she asked.

"Thank you?"

"For being nice. I've insisted everyone be human for the time being. So your little Low Born won't feel so tiny and insecure." The Empress smiled. "Wasn't that nice of me?"

Huh. Bram just thought the Empress wanted to try on her overabundance of gowns. "Aye, Empress. Very . . . nice."

"I have to say you're looking much better these days, Bram."

"Thank you."

"And you've really . . . come into your own."

Bram didn't answer; he simply picked up his scrolls.

"My Lord Bram?"

"Yes?" he asked.

"I was just thinking that since you'll be here for a while, perhaps we can . . ." she reached out and stroked his arm.

Before she could go on, Bram felt it was important to point out that, "If you think I've forgotten how I was tortured and beaten when I was here the first time . . . I haven't."

Helena folded her arms over her chest, a little sneer on her lips. "Going to hold that against me, are you?"

Bram decided retreat was his best option, so he headed back to the room he shared with Ghleanna.

But before he could make his escape, the Empress tossed at him, "I've heard that your Low Born has gotten rather chummy with the other soldiers."

Bram stopped. He knew that Helena was a conniving, vicious sea-viper, but he couldn't help the swell of jealousy he immediately felt.

"The soldiers do seem to like her. I'm guessing she's very friendly when you're away." The Empress eased around him, smiling sweetly. "I'm sure she's more comfortable with them. Her own kind and all that."

"She is *my* kind, my Lady. Remember? Barbarian Land Dwellers. That's us."

Bram bowed his head and walked out. He made it to the room he shared with Ghleanna, but when he walked in, he found her gone.

Bram tossed his travel bag and papers into a corner and stalked out of the room and onto the walkway. The guards were gone as well. He headed back the way he'd come, trying to catch a glimpse of Ghleanna somewhere.

The Empress's palace was a marvel of Sea Dragon engineering built inside a vast series of underwater caves. Air breathers could easily survive inside its ocean-colored stone walls for centuries. They had access to fresh lake and river water, and fresh air from the land above. How the Fins managed to get it all down here, Bram didn't know. And he didn't even think to ask, he was so concerned with finding Ghleanna.

Bram heard a roar down a long hallway, watched large-sized Fins heading in that direction. He recognized them as soldiers. His eyes narrowed and he followed, pushing through the dragons until he reached a chamber. Two Sea Dragons in human form battled against each other with spears while their comrades stood around them in a circle and cheered them on.

And, sitting on top of a boulder was Ghleanna. She wore another long shirt and dark blue leggings and her arm was still tied down under her shirt. Not surprisingly, she cheered right along with the other warriors—when she wasn't stopping to chat with the generals who stood around her in their dragon form.

One male slammed another onto his back by using the staff of his spear and Ghleanna called out, "No, no, no!" She held her free arm out and—to Bram's astonishment—one of the generals hauled her off the boulder and carefully placed her on the ground.

"You keep fighting like that, lad," she admonished, "and you'll be on your back a lot when you're human."

She waited until the dragon was on his feet. "You're not paying attention to the way he's coming at you," she instructed. "You're so busy staring at the tip, you miss the way his body's moving. Human bodies hide nothing, but that spear tip can change on you in a second and you won't have a chance to get out of its way." She shrugged and lightly patted where she'd been stabbed by that sword. "Take my word on it." The Fins laughed and she went on. "But if you pay closer attention to your opponent, you can watch what *he* does, and he'll show you which way he's going. I know very few human soldiers or dragons who don't signal their move long before they make it. You just have to watch for it. Understand?"

The soldier nodded and Ghleanna slapped his shoulder, which didn't seem to offend him. "Good. Good. But don't worry. You're doing well. Just need more training is all. I'm betting *all of you* need more training to fight as human." She flicked her hand. "So get to work."

The Fins went back to sparring and Ghleanna saw Bram and walked to his side.

"Hello there."

"I leave you alone for a few—"

"I was bored. What did you expect me to do? Sit on my ass and count the algae on the walls."

"That's a design motif."

"And again you lost me."

"You should be in our room, Ghleanna."

"You mean hiding? Why? I didn't do anything wrong."

"Not hiding. Resting."

"I'm fine."

"You took a sword to the chest!"

The room grew silent and Ghleanna rolled her eyes. "If you're going to make a big deal out of it."

"You all right, Captain?" one of the soldiers asked.

"I'm fine. Going to take a rest. You lot keep up the work. I'll check in later."

She walked out and Bram realized that the soldiers were now all staring at him. "It's for her own good," he insisted. "She needs her rest."

There was some grunting and they all turned away from him.

Letting out a frustrated growl, he followed Ghleanna.

"Do you enjoy doing that?" Bram demanded once he'd closed their bedroom door.

"Enjoy doing what?"

"Turning those soldiers against me?"

"What are you talking about?"

"A few days ago, they didn't even know of my existence. Ten minutes with you"—he threw his hands up—"and they all hate me."

"You're mad. I was doing nothing but talking to them." She lowered her voice, "Do you know they have absolutely no say and no representatives in their own government? That sea cow rules it all!"

"I know. That's why I need you to leave the soldiers alone. Stop talking to them."

"I don't see why that upsets you so. You're arranging a truce anyway, so they won't be our enemies for long." She walked up to him, leaned in close, and whispered against his ear, "Besides, it gives me a chance to find out how they fight on land and in the sea. You know . . . in case your truce falls apart and I and my kin need to kill them all."

She leaned back and smiled, sure she'd made her point.

"You're bloody mad," he said, shaking his head and gawking at her. "All of you. Every damn Cadwaladr in this world is bloody mad except your mother and your sister Maelona."

"What are you bringing my sister up for?"

"Because I'm relatively certain she wouldn't be running around after getting a sword through the chest, trying to teach Fin soldiers new fighting techniques."

"That's because she doesn't know any fighting techniques. But if you think so highly of her, I'm sure I can arrange a proper introduction between you two."

Bram glared at her for a few seconds before he reminded her, "Besides *living* with your kin, I also attended school with Maelona for years. When I returned to your parents' home it was usually as Maelona's guest."

"Oh."

"Tell me, was there *ever* a time when you noticed me? Or did I not exist for you at all?"

"That's not fair."

He dismissed her with a wave of his hand. "Forget it. I'm tired and I need sleep."

"So you're just walking away?"

"Looks that way."

"Bram—"

He growled at her—growled!—and reached over his shoulders to gather up his cotton shirt and pull it over his head. He shook out his silver hair, tossed the shirt onto a chair, and dived face first onto the bed.

"This conversation isn't over, peacemaker."

"Yes it is," he said into the fur covering. "I'm tired of being reminded how little I've ever meant to you."

"You're acting like a hatchling."

He lifted his arm from the bed, raised his hand, and gestured at her with two of his fingers.

Ghleanna's mouth dropped open. "You rude bastard!"

"Sleeping!" he yelled into the bed.

So unbelievably pissed, Ghleanna paced around the room for nearly a whole minute until she yelled, "This discussion is not done!"

Snarling—at her!—Bram pushed himself off the bed and stormed over to her. "What, Ghleanna? What is it you just have to say now? At this moment?"

"Kiss me."

He took a step back. "What? Why?"

She had absolutely no clue! "Because I said so."

"No."

"Are you going to tell me you don't want to?"

"Maybe I don't."

"Liar!"

"I don't need this." He headed to the door.

"Scared, are you?"

Bram stopped. "What?"

"I asked if you're scared. Frightened. Like a little mouse."

Bram again faced her. "The only thing that scares me is how Rhiannon uses me to torture your brother, because he's a murdering bastard."

Ghleanna walked across the room and stood in front of Bram. "Then kiss me if you have the—"

Before she could even finish her challenge, Bram had slipped his hand behind Ghleanna's neck and yanked her in until their toes touched. But he only stared into her eyes, not making any further move.

"What are you waiting for, peacemaker?" she asked, a little breathless.

"I'm waiting until *I* am ready."

"So I'll be waiting until the end of time for you to do something so simple?"

"There is nothing simple about you, Captain Ghleanna. And let no one convince you otherwise."

Bram couldn't believe Ghleanna. Such a maddening cow! And the worst part was that he'd wanted to kiss her for half a century at least! Now he had her but he was so mad at her he couldn't see straight. And, if he were to be honest with himself, he was incredibly jealous. She was so comfortable with other soldiers, how could he ever hope to get close to her when they had so very little in common? When he'd dropped down on the bed, he'd figured it was over. His obsession for her. His quiet waiting. Waiting for her to notice him. And if all this wasn't over, he'd make it over. He had to. How else was he going to live the next few centuries without her if he didn't?

But he should have known. Ghleanna would never allow herself to be ignored. To be pushed aside. Not the Captain of the Dragon Queen's Tenth Battalion.

And yet who was Bram? The peacemaker. The merciful one. The one who didn't eat humans passing him on the road just because he'd missed his morning meal.

So, was he really going to let his peace-loving and, at times, non-violent nature stop him? Him? Bram the Merciful?

He, who had traveled all over the Southlands, Outer-plains, and Desert Lands, on foot. As human.

He, who'd escaped the Sea Dragon Emperor's dungeons with all his parts intact and wits about him?

He, who'd managed to not only survive Queen Adienna's reign but the takeover of her daughter?

That dragon wasn't going to take the kiss that was being offered to him because Ghleanna didn't know what she had right in front of her.

He was many things, but Bram the Merciful was not a fool.

With his hand still gripping the back of Ghleanna's neck, Bram leaned in, tilted his head to the side, and placed his lips against hers. He pressed his tongue to her mouth, stroked her lips until she opened to him. He pressed further, allowed his tongue to slip inside and he tasted what waited there. Gods, so wet and warm, he could almost taste the flame burning inside her.

Ghleanna slid the fingers of her free hand into his hair, leaning her body into his naked chest. He could feel her nipples harden under the soft cotton of her shirt, feel her pulse race under his fingertips.

And he knew in that moment that he would never be over Ghleanna. Not ever.

Ghleanna gripped the silver strands of Bram's hair in her fist and melted against his body as she'd never done before with any male.

Good gods, this dragon had a mighty kiss. Yet what she found fascinating was how slowly he took it all. His lips easing around hers; his tongue lazily dipping in, swirling. The dragon took his time and she appreciated that. It was a rarity with most males, she'd found. Especially in her world, where everything was about moving fast and getting things done. Even fucking. Even a kiss.

Deciding to follow her instincts, Ghleanna pulled her hand away and lowered it to Bram's groin. She reached for his cock, ready to play with it through his leggings and then play with it without them. But he caught her hand, held it.

"No." He stepped away from her, looked around the small room. Ghleanna tried to pull her hand away, but he wouldn't release her. Instead, he yanked her over to a desk tucked into a corner. He pushed her up on it, keeping her legs dangling. He gripped her leggings and yanked them off her body. She wore nothing underneath since she'd had nothing to put on and Bram stood there for several moments, his hand gliding up her thighs, brushing against her pussy, stroking it with his fingers.

Ghleanna reached for him again with her free arm, but Bram said, "No."

And then she understood.

She placed her hand against the desk, palm flat against the wood. Her free arm kept her propped up so she could watch, but otherwise she relaxed back and let Bram take the lead. Because for once . . . she didn't have to.

Chapter 13

Bram slipped a finger inside Ghleanna and watched her. She stared back, panting, her bottom lip catching between her teeth.

Gods, she was so hot . . . and wet. He couldn't believe she was already wet. From arguing with him.

He turned his finger, curling the tip and rubbing a little spot inside her. He watched her, enjoying the way her back arched, listened to the groan she let loose.

"I should leave you alone," he murmured while he slipped another finger inside her, continued to play with her. "You need your rest. You're still healing."

"Don't you dare stop."

Bram grinned and pulled his fingers out of her. "But I have to stop."

Ghleanna groaned again, but this time there was real frustration.

"I'm fine," she told him. "I swear. I feel great."

"You sure?"

"I'm sure. I am *extremely* sure."

"Lie back, Ghleanna." She did. "Close your eyes."

She lifted her head. "Why?"

"Because I told you to."

Her eyes narrowed a bit and Bram was certain she was going to argue with him, but she again stretched out on the desk and closed her eyes.

"Now do me a favor," he murmured. "Just relax."

And exactly how was she to relax? But she kept her eyes closed and waited.

"You aren't breathing, Ghleanna."

"I'm not?"

"No. But you should."

"Of course, of course." She forced herself to breath and continued to wait. Thankfully, she didn't have to wait long. She felt Bram's mouth press against the inside of her thigh, teeth grazing the skin. She shuddered and tried to spread her legs wider but he held her legs in his arms, and he was controlling how far she could open or close them.

The thought made her shudder.

"Are you in pain?" he asked, his breath—but not his mouth—brushing her pussy.

"What? No. No. I'm fine. Really. Fine."

"Just checking. We don't want any relapses."

"There won't be." And she knew she was begging. "I promise."

"Good."

Ghleanna still had her eyes closed, was still stretched out on the desk. Then she felt Bram's mouth pressing against her, his tongue sliding inside her. And, as he'd done with that kiss, he took his time, rushed nothing. He used long, sweeping strokes of his tongue to carefully lick out her pussy. She moaned, unable to stay still on the desk, her body writhing underneath his mouth.

She should have known, shouldn't she? That he'd have this talent. That Bram would know how to bring tears to her

eyes and pleasure to her body. He'd be as careful and determined with her as he was with everything else in his life.

Ghleanna gripped the back of Bram's head, her fingers
digging into his hair.

"Bram," she begged through her panting. "Bram . . .
please."

He didn't reply but his finger returned, pushing up inside
her, twisting and turning until it found that spot he'd discovered earlier. Ghleanna choked out a gasp, her body beginning to shake, her legs fighting to close. But Bram never lost
control. Not of her, not of the situation. Without moving her
from that spot, he twisted her around and tore her apart until
Ghleanna came hard, her fist shoved in her mouth to stifle
her scream since she had no intention of entertaining every
Fin within hearing range.

When the climax had passed through her, Bram was moving up her body, kissing and licking his way across her flesh,
spending extra time on her scars. Maybe Addolgar had been
right—Bram did seem to enjoy her scars.

His lips moved over her throat, past the gold collar she
wore until he slid over her jaw and took her mouth. Ruthless.
There was no other word for the way he kissed her. There
was nothing merciful in that kiss. He must keep his merciful
side for every place *but* his bed.

And she had to admit—she really liked that about him.

Bram felt the way Ghleanna kissed him and he knew she
wanted him. And the gods knew he wanted her. He wanted
to be inside her so badly. But giving her pleasure by enjoying
her pussy was vastly different from fucking her. He couldn't
fuck her. Not until she was better . . . right?

Making up his mind, he pulled back but Ghleanna came
with him, her free arm around his shoulders, her chest lifting
from the desk.

"What are you doing?" she demanded.

"Leaving you alone." He took a breath, tried to steady his legs. "You're wounded and it would be wrong to—"

She tore off the material keeping her arm tied to her body and reached for him.

"Ghleanna, what are you—"

"Don't leave me like this, Bram. Please."

"But—"

She licked his throat, nipped his chin. "You *can't* leave me like this," she whispered.

"I can," he reminded her. "I should."

"Please don't." She kissed him again and by the gods her tongue was talented. "We both know that once won't be enough for me," she reminded him when she pulled away. And it was true. She-dragons were demanding of their lovers, why should Ghleanna be any different?

"And if I hurt you?"

"You won't." She grinned. "I'm incredibly sturdy. It's in the bloodline."

She reached down and gripped his cock through his leggings and they both gasped, her hand stroking the length of him.

Bram began panting, his legs shaking. He caught her hand, held it.

"Evil vixen," he accused her.

"I do what I must to get what I want. Perhaps you can punish me for my evil ways . . . later. But for now . . ."

Bram pushed his leggings down until his cock sprang free. Then he gripped Ghleanna by her hips and dragged her ass to the very edge of the desk. Still holding her tight, he brought her close until he could push inside her, his cock hard and demanding. One good shove and he was there, both of them stopping, mouths open, their breathing shallow as they gazed at each other in unabashed amazement.

He had never imagined she would feel like this. So hot and wet and, gods, so tight!

Ghleanna brought her hands up, stroked his jaw, his neck and Bram kissed her. He pulled her tighter against him until he was buried balls deep. Until he knew nothing would be getting between them anytime soon.

Ghleanna surprised herself with a squeak. A sound she'd never made before. But she'd been unable to help herself once Bram filled her. She shuddered around him, kissed him harder and nearly wept when he began to move inside her. His strokes long, powerful, and as always it seemed, in complete control.

Knowing that for once she didn't have to do anything but enjoy the ride was a rather heady experience for her. All day, every day, Ghleanna planned and plotted and executed. She led three hundred dragons into battle whenever they were called by their queen and every decision she made affected the lives of those dragons. But for once . . . for once she didn't have to do anything. She didn't have to think, question, or kill. She just had to enjoy. And enjoy she did.

Bram still had tight hold of her hips when he began to take her harder, faster. And she didn't mind. Did her wound hurt? A bit. But it was nothing she couldn't handle. Nothing she wouldn't risk to experience the best bloody fuck of her entire life.

She came hard, her body stiffening in Bram's arms, her cry of pleasure caught in her throat. She wrapped her arms around his shoulders and let the climax rip through her. When she gave that last gasp, Bram laid her back out on the desk and then he was pounding inside her, taking her brutally until he came, his body shaking over hers, his head dropping between her breasts.

Ghleanna stroked Bram's hair and let out a soul-deep breath. They didn't speak. Perhaps there was nothing to say. Instead, after a few minutes, Bram picked her up and stumbled to the bed, dropping them both onto it. He pressed his hand to her wound and she patted it. As she'd predicted, the wound had not opened. She had not been further damaged. She was fine. More than fine in fact.

He stayed inside her, managing to get off his leggings and boots without moving away from her.

Once Bram was completely naked, he began kissing her neck, her jaw, her mouth, and slowly, taking his time, he began to thrust inside her again. This time, she knew, would again be on his very controlled terms.

And she had no problem with that.

Chapter 14

Bram woke and he knew Ghleanna was already awake too. He knew because he felt her sucking his cock into her mouth. She was under the fur cover, but he opened his eyes and watched as the fur rose and fell while she manipulated his cock the way she manipulated her damn battle axes.

One hand reached back and he gripped the headboard. Gods, her mouth! Her beautiful, wonderful mouth. Everything about Ghleanna was wonderful, beautiful, amazing, perfect . . . absolutely perfect. Perfect, perfect—

"I have been waiting over an hour for—" The Empress of all Sea Dragons in this region halted to a stop after walking into Bram and Ghleanna's room unannounced.

Helena stopped. Ghleanna, however . . .

Helena's mouth opened, closed, opened again. Then she rolled her eyes and snapped, "When you two cretins are done molesting each other, we are waiting for the next draft of your truce proposal, peacemaker. *And I don't like to wait!*"

With Ghleanna turning him inside out, all Bram could manage was a, "Uh-huh" along with a thumbs-up.

Disgusted, Helena spun on her heel and stormed out, slamming the door behind her.

"Barbarians!" he heard Helena yell from the hallway. "Every Land Dweller is a bloody barbarian!"

If she said anything after that, Bram didn't hear it. He couldn't hear anything over the roar of the rushing wave in his head as his body bowed and he came in Ghleanna's mouth. She sucked and licked until she'd milked him dry and then she crawled back out from under the covers, licked her lips, and grinned at him.

"Did I hear something?" she asked, cheeky cow that she was. "A little earlier?"

Bram caught hold of her face between his hands and held her in place while he kissed her, tasting himself on her lips, knowing she'd taken all of him in.

"You are *such* a naughty She-dragon," he laughingly accused her while he pushed her back on the bed. "What am I going to do with such a naughty She-dragon?"

Bram had left her alone so he could finish that stupid truce. And feeling remarkably well, Ghleanna headed back to the soldier's training room. When she entered, the soldiers stepped back, bowed their heads in respect.

"Captain Ghleanna."

"Captain."

"Lady Captain."

Ghleanna grinned. Oh, yes. She had all sorts of things to keep her busy until Bram was done.

She picked up a battle axe, gave it a few practice swings, feeling complete with a weapon back in her hand, then asked the roomful of soldier dragons, "Who's first then?"

While the senators argued and debated about issues they had absolutely *no* control over—why did he need to be here again?—Bram stared off across the chamber and wondered when this would all be over so he could get back to Ghleanna. Get back *inside* Ghleanna.

They'd only spent a few hours together in the big scheme of things, but gods! That female. She turned out to be everything he'd ever dreamed of. In bed and out. And not everyone fucked well while human—but she did. A good thing since it was one of his favorite pastimes.

"So," the Empress asked over the shouting of the senators, "you and the Cadwaladr?"

Bram looked up at the dais she sat upon and replied, "Aye."

"Shocking. I thought you'd find someone more . . . feminine."

She smirked and returned her attention to the arguing senators but Bram asked, "Why?"

"What?"

"Why?"

"Why what?"

"Why did you think that?"

Her eyes widened a bit and the Empress stammered, "Well, you are so . . . and she is so . . . and the two of you together are so . . ." She gazed at Bram a moment, forced a smile and a laugh and said, "Oh, nothing!"

Bram had focused on the arguing senators again when one of the royal pages rushed into the chamber. He stood in front of the Empress until she motioned him closer. He whispered something in her ear. And, while Bram watched, her pale human skin turned bright red with rage. Helena jumped to her feet and rushed from the chamber, her entourage scrambling to catch up with her.

Bram gazed at the page. "I'm sensing this isn't good."

The page shook his head. "No, sir. It's not."

* * *

Ghleanna was sitting on the bed, trying to pull off her boots, when the door slammed open. She looked up, expecting a foolish Kleitos—but it was the Empress.

"You," the royal snarled. "*You* did this."

"I did what, my Lady?"

"Don't lie to me, barbarian!"

Slowly Ghleanna stood, and she towered over the monarch. "I don't appreciate being called a liar by you or anyone else, my Lady. I'm not one of your subjects."

The Empress didn't let Ghleanna's size overwhelm her. Far from it. "But you could easily become one of my victims, Cadwaladr. You're in *my* territory."

"Aye. I am. But I have what you *need*, my Lady."

"Ghleanna."

Ghleanna heard Bram's voice, but she didn't move her gaze from Helena's until the Empress sniffed and stormed out, taking her suffering entourage with her. Gods, to do nothing all day but follow that viper around. Like a form of hell.

Bram closed the door once they were alone and that's when he asked, "Do you want us to die here, among the Fins? Is that your purpose, Captain? To get us both killed?"

"No."

"Ghleanna . . ."

"It all happened so fast," she explained. "One minute I was showing them how to fight with a battle axe and the next"—she shrugged—"revolution."

Bram walked over to the bed and sat down. "Don't use that word. Not if you want us to live through the night."

Ghleanna sat on the edge of the bed. "The soldiers have no representation in her court. No one watching out for them. And no say in decisions that affect them directly. How is that fair?"

"Fair? Captain, we are hundreds and hundreds of miles under the ocean and at the whim of a dictator."

"A dictator not nearly as powerful as her father. A dictator who needs her army, who needs our queen. A dictator whose tiny head I could easily crush between my big, meaty hands." She smiled. "A dictator who needs you. And now . . . she needs me."

"But why? Why do you want her to need you?"

Ghleanna leaned in, kissed Bram once, twice. "My reasons are my own." She kissed him again. "But for now"—another kiss—"we're going to let her stew." And another.

"And while she's stewing whatever will we do to fill the time?"

Ghleanna climbed into Bram's lap, facing him. She put her arms around his shoulders and said, "Fucking, my Lord. We'll be fucking."

"Well . . . if we must."

Laughing, Ghleanna nipped his throat. "We must, my Lord. We must."

Chapter 15

Bram held Ghleanna's hips, pulling her in tighter, gripping her hard with his hands while she gripped him hard with her pussy.

Sweating and gasping, the pair rolled, Bram on top once again.

He dragged his tongue along the new scar Ghleanna had where the sword had torn through scale and flesh and bone.

Ghleanna's legs wrapped around his hips, her head thrown back and Bram buried himself inside her body again and again.

She groaned, loud and long, her body shaking beneath his as she came hard, his name a whisper on her lips.

Bram, grateful she'd climaxed because he was unsure he could hold on much longer, held Ghleanna against him as he came hard inside her.

Blindly, he lifted his head from her neck and sought her mouth, found it. They kissed, their tongues sliding, teasing, tasting—enjoying. And they'd been enjoying each other for hours.

Too bad nothing wonderful could last forever.

The bedroom door flew open.

"Are you two still at it?" the Empress snarled. "My empire is falling apart and you two are swallowing each other's tongues—and other body parts?"

Bram pulled out of the kiss and asked, "Is there a problem, Empress?"

"You damn well know there's a problem. She"—and the Empress pointed right at Ghleanna—"has turned my soldiers against me. Her death is mine for the betrayal."

Bram kindly suggested, "It seems a foolhardy move since she is the only one who currently has control of your soldiers, my Lady."

"I should have killed her when I had the chance."

"But it's too late for that now. We have to deal with what we have. Here. At this moment."

Pointing at the door, the Empress ordered, "Get out, peacemaker."

"Empress, I don't think it's—"

"Pull your cock out of her cunt and *get out.*"

Ghleanna pressed her hand against Bram's chest. "It's all right."

He gazed at her a moment. "You sure?"

"Positive. Besides, you need to finish that truce."

He did need to finish it. The quicker the better.

Once Bram was gone, Ghleanna sat up. She didn't get dressed, didn't wipe the sweat from her body or Bram's seed from her pussy.

Instead, she smiled and said, "My Lady."

"You've turned my soldiers against me."

"Hardly. They just want what's fair."

"I decide what's fair."

"Every strong monarch I've known has understood that their soldiers are their life's blood. Deny that at your peril."

"What do you want, Land Dweller?"

"What your soldiers want. Representation for them in your Senate—and for your Senate to have some actual power in your empire."

"I am the one who rules here. As my father did before me."

"Isn't he dead now?" Ghleanna asked. "By poison, I think."

Cold blue-green eyes locked on Ghleanna. "That's never been proven."

Ghleanna chuckled. "Of course. But imagine how loyal your soldiers will be to you if you do this? Who would dare risk their wrath by angering you, knowing you have several legions at your back? And, of course, I can help you with this."

The royal smirked. "And what will that cost me, I wonder?"

"Not much, my Lady," Ghleanna told her. "Not much at all."

Chapter 16

The gold collar was removed from Ghleanna's throat and Bram watched her shift back to her natural form. She shook out her hair and wings and unleashed a nice bout of flame at the cave ceiling—something else that had been denied her by Helena's yoke.

"Good gods," Helena muttered to the sorceress who had placed and then removed the collar from Ghleanna. "Even her bloody scales have scars."

"Beautiful, isn't she?" Bram asked with a smile.

"Land Dweller," she sneered.

Ghleanna put on armor given to her by the soldiers. It was quite . . . elaborate and spoke of how they felt about her.

Her battle axes were tied to her back and her sword to her side.

"Excellent," Helena said, prodding. She couldn't wait to see the back of them. "So you're off."

"We are." Bram faced the Empress. "Thank you for everything, my Lady."

"You're very welcome, Bram the Merciful. Good and *safe* travels to you." She looked over at Ghleanna. "And to you, Captain."

"Thank you, my Lady."

She didn't mention the truce because she didn't have to. She knew Bram would keep his end of the bargain. It was a tragic flaw in his nature.

The Empress motioned her entourage to leave and Kleitos took the opportunity to slither over to Bram.

"Good-bye, old friend."

"Shut up."

The Fin sneered and turned to Ghleanna. "And good-bye to you, Captain."

She gazed at the Fin. "And to you, Chancellor Kleitos."

Bram turned, thinking they were done with all the formalities when he saw a flash of steel. He spun back around as Ghleanna's sword rammed into Kleitos's gut.

"Ghleanna!"

Gods, what had she done? What had she done?

Ghleanna twisted her sword, and Kleitos dropped to his knees. She pressed her back claw to his chest and shoved him off her blade. The Fin dropped to the ground, his insides pouring out from the hole Ghleanna had made.

Yet Bram began to notice something—no one did anything. Nothing. Not to him, not to Ghleanna. There was no shock, no confusion, no outrage.

Ghleanna wiped off her blade and put it back into its sheath. She walked to the Empress, and stopped, briefly bowing her head. "Empress."

"Captain."

Completely confused, Bram followed Ghleanna to the tunnel they'd take back to the surface. "Ghleanna?"

She stopped, faced him. "Did you really think I'd let Kleitos live? After what he did to you?" She raised a brow. "Really?"

"I told you that Kleitos was not to be touched. You said you understood."

"And I did. I understood that you wanted me to leave Kleitos be. I never said I would. Never agreed to that."

"Gods," he sighed in awe, "my father will *adore* you."

Catching his tail with hers, Ghleanna tugged. "Come, peacemaker. My kin awaits."

Chapter 17

Bram landed on the ledge and waited for Ghleanna. She landed beside him.

"So Helena agreed?" he asked.

"She hated Kleitos and so did most of her army. Plus he firmly represented her father's reign. Getting rid of him was a favor she was more than happy to allow."

"And?"

"And?"

"You don't like Helena, Captain. You'd do her no favors unless it was in your best interest."

She shrugged. "Well, I wanted Kleitos dead and . . ."

"And you still have the loyalty of her army, in case she ever tries to cross us. And you'll most likely have that loyalty for a very long time after the rights you've won them."

"Perhaps."

Bram grinned. "And if you'd been completely wrong? Miscalculated even the tiniest bit?"

"I'd have let you fix it." She nuzzled his snout with her own. "Now let's get out of here."

Good plan. He was done with the memories of this place.

He'd faced it again, and had conquered it—again. But there'd be no nightmares this time.

"Come. This way."

Another mile to the surface they went, cutting tree roots that were in their way until they reached the mouth of the cavern. It was brilliantly hidden behind a close-by hill and together they maneuvered around it and headed toward the ocean.

But suddenly Ghleanna stopped.

Lifting her face, she gazed up, past the trees of the surrounding forest, at the two suns. "I didn't realize how much I would miss them until they were gone from my sight for so long."

"I don't know how the Fins do it," he admitted. "Living under there without the suns. The moon. It's not like our caves, is it? Where fresh air and freedom are just a short walk or flight away. And the short time we were down there, I began to feel . . ."

"I know. Me, too."

Ghleanna caught Bram's claw and tugged, her eagerness clear. "Let's go. My kin wait for me on the beach."

They walked until they reached the edge of the forest, but Bram stopped and gazed out. "How long do you think they've been standing there like that?"

He watched Ghleanna smile at the backs of her kin. They all stood on the beach, looking like statues, staring out at the ocean, waiting for Ghleanna to appear. She'd originally told Addolgar she'd be coming from the ocean because she hadn't known there was another exit. One that placed them directly on land.

"Hours. Perhaps a couple of days."

"And how much longer—"

"Days. Weeks. Eventually, though, they'd take turns. One

bunch would have first watch and then another bunch would have second . . . that's just how they are. How *we* are."

"Amazing."

Ghleanna put a talon to her snout, then crept up behind the group of warriors. The number had substantially increased from the original group who'd been escorting Bram and he suddenly began to worry that he'd have all these Cadwaladrs escorting him into the Desert Lands.

Uh-oh.

Once Ghleanna was right behind her kin, she screamed. Like a wild banshee.

And her kin screamed in return, spinning around, raising weapons and shields.

"Did you lot miss me?" Ghleanna asked with a smile.

"You mad cow!" Addolgar yelled, shoving her with his shield. "That was about to be the second time you got a sword in the chest!"

"As if you've *ever* been that fast, brother."

Then they were hugging and Bram knew nearly everything was as it should be.

Ghleanna accepted hugs, shoves, punches, and hair yanks for what they were. Familial affection—the Cadwaladr way. A way she'd missed so much.

"But you're all right, yeah?" Hew pushed. "You sure you're all right?"

"I'm fine." She held her forearms away from her body. "Look at me. Better than ever. Them Fins have good surgeons, they do."

"Thank the gods for that," Kyna said. "Isn't that right, Kennis?"

"It is. For them. 'Cause if they hadn't sent our girl back to us—"

"—we'd have grown gills and gone down there ourselves

to their watery pit to tear the scales from their flesh and those bloody fins from their backs."

Ahhh. Nothing like the true love and caring of the Cadwaladr Twins.

It was all as she'd expected and she was damn grateful for her kin. But what Ghleanna hadn't expected . . .

"The Twins would have been the least of the Fins' problem if they hadn't sent my girl back to me alive and well."

Eyes wide, Ghleanna faced her father. He was in his battle armor, weapons strapped to him and ready. He hadn't left her mother in ages to go into battle. He left that "to me brats."

"Da?"

"I'm so glad you're home, girl. So glad you're safe."

Ghleanna swallowed past the lump in her throat before she threw herself into her father's arms. Let them all say what they would about Ailean the Wicked—none of it mattered. His heart was as big as any ocean and the love he had for his offspring as mighty and strong as any mountain.

"I'm glad, too, Da. And what I said to you before—"

"It's forgotten, Ghleanna. Don't even think about it." He pulled back. Smiled at her. "Understand?"

"Aye."

"Good. And Bercelak's sorry he couldn't be here—"

"He can't leave Rhiannon when we have traitors in our midst."

"—but he said you'd understand." Ailean gazed down at his daughter and Ghleanna saw in that one look how proud he was of her. "Now, what do we do next? Escort you and our Bram to the Sand Eaters? Or take you back to Rhiannon first?"

"First Feoras dies."

As one, all the Cadwaladrs faced the forest behind them . . . and Bram the Merciful.

Frowning, Kyna asked, "What was that?"

"Feoras dies," Bram repeated.

"And why is that then?"

Bram walked toward them, his reliable traveling bag around his shoulder. "Because he betrayed the throne, betrayed our queen, tried to stop an important alliance that I'm sure he'll try to stop again and, most importantly . . ." Bram stood in front of Ghleanna now, his claw brushing along her jaw. ". . . he tried to kill my Ghleanna. For that offense alone he dies."

Cai rested his elbow on Ghleanna's shoulder and asked, "But ain't you the merciful one?"

"I am." And, with his gaze never leaving Ghleanna's, "But there are limits to my mercifulness, I'm afraid."

Chapter 18

Ghleanna waited for Feoras about five miles from where Rhiannon had tracked the bastard down. The queen's skills had, as Bram had said, gotten mighty. It seemed she could track nearly any dragon she wanted without ever leaving Devenallt Mountain unless the fugitive had the protection of a witch as strong as she. And Rhiannon had tracked Feoras here, not more than fifteen miles from where he'd tried to kill Ghleanna.

As Bram had said, Feoras and the rest of the soldiers he'd bribed, were waiting for Bram to return so they could finish the job that had been started.

And here Bram was, relaxing next to a tree, still in his dragon form, quietly scratching away on some parchment. Did he ever pay attention to anything going on around him that wasn't on a piece of paper or in a bloody book? She doubted it. But he seemed to have complete faith in her. He still trusted her to protect him and that was all she needed to know.

She heard Feoras and his soldiers moving through the trees. They were quiet enough but Ghleanna knew what to listen for. The flutter of a leaf, the warning of a bird . . . the slither of a tail.

Feoras came around a boulder, but he stopped when he saw Ghleanna standing there. He reared back in surprise, golden eyes blinking wide.

"Ghleanna?"

"Feoras."

"I . . ." His gaze shifted and he saw Bram leaning against that tree, still writing—and blatantly ignoring him.

"You . . . ?" she pushed when he stopped speaking. "You . . . what? Thought I was dead?"

Feoras focused on her again. "I knew you wouldn't go down that easy." He leered. "You never did . . . go down easy."

"Not unless I want to." She moved forward, pulling out her axes, holding one in each claw. "I am going to stop you here."

"You're going to try." Soldiers moved out of the trees, some stopping and staring at her, also seemingly shocked to see her alive. If she survived this, her name would be legendary. "You going to take us all on? Are you into that now?"

"Your disrespect to Captain Ghleanna," Bram said from his tree, his voice soft, "offends me."

"Does it now?" Feoras said with a laugh. "Oh, well. Don't want to offend Bram the Merciful. He might bore us to death with his vast knowledge of *nothing*." Feoras sauntered closer but not close enough to Ghleanna's axes. "So, Mercy . . . you seem quite attached to the fair Captain. Tell me, did you two get close while she was trying to survive the wound I gave her?"

Bram continued to scribble away on his parchment. "We did. Very close. In fact—" he finally looked up from his papers but he gazed at Ghleanna—"I love her. Have for years."

"Gods!" Feoras laughed. "Are you really that desperate, friend? Because the honest truth is, when it comes to getting under a Cadwaladr wench's tail, the last thing you need to do is tell them you love them." He eyed Ghleanna and she couldn't believe she'd ever found him attractive. "That's how it is for all of them, but especially Ailean's offspring. All whores . . . just like their father."

Ghleanna had heard it all before but, unlike her sisters, she never knew how to let it roll off her scales like rainwater. But that was before, wasn't it? When she actually gave a centaur shit what other dragons thought. Now, however, she realized what her kin had been trying to tell her was true—she was a mighty She-dragon who could do better than Feoras the Traitor. A sad, jealous lizard not worthy of her time or her drunken whining. That being said, she also had no intention of letting Feoras goad her into a rash move. There was a plan, and she intended to stick with it.

But when Bram unleashed an explosion of flame that rammed into Feoras and half his soldiers, sending them flying back through the trees, decimating part of the forest in the process while setting fire to another part . . . she had to admit she was surprised. And rather impressed.

"What?" Bram asked her when she could only gawk at him. "I thought you wanted them over in that clearing so they were surrounded by your kin."

"I . . . I did. It's just I thought you were going to run and let them give chase. Not set the entire forest on fire."

"I don't run for anybody. I wouldn't worry about the forest." He glanced up at the sky. "It looks like it might rain. Besides, I warned you . . . my flame is mighty."

"I thought you were embellishing."

"I don't embellish."

"I see that now."

They stepped through a wall of flames and into the clearing as Feoras and his fellow traitors got to their claws.

Feoras was angry now. Bram could see that. Because it was one thing to be bested by a fellow Dragonwarrior, even a female, but by a politician? No. He wasn't having that.

More traitors landed in the clearing.

"They weren't there," one of the soldiers told Feoras, before his eyes locked on Ghleanna in surprise.

"Where are they, Ghleanna?" Feoras demanded. "We've been watching that kin of yours for days, knowing they'd lead us to the politician. And we both know they won't leave you to fight alone with just this one by your side."

"They're waiting," she told him.

"For what?"

"For me to kill you."

That's when Ghleanna threw the first battle axe. But Feoras was fast. He quickly stepped aside, and the axe hit the dragon behind him in the chest—killing him instantly.

"Bitch," Feoras snarled.

"Come on, Feoras." She swung her second axe in an arch. The flat of it slapping hard into the middle of her claw. "Let's finish this."

He roared and charged her and Ghleanna flew at him. They met, collided, and spun. When they landed, Ghleanna pulled away first and swung her axe. Feoras ducked, moved around her. She quickly turned, lifted her weapon, and blocked the sword aimed at her back.

More dragons surrounded Bram, but these were friends not foes.

"This has been coming," Addolgar remarked while he watched. He'd never intervene in his sister's fight unless her death was imminent. That was the Cadwaladr way.

"Aye," Bram answered. "It has."

"Were you two all right down there? With them Fins?"

"Aye. Quite all right. The Empress wants a truce with Rhiannon and her army came to worship Ghleanna."

Addolgar shook his head. "How does the cranky cow

manage to do that? A few days with her—and they're ready to follow my sister into hell."

Feoras slammed his fist into Ghleanna's snout, sending her tripping back. But she stayed on her claws and struck again.

"What about you, peacemaker?" Addolgar asked.

Without taking his eyes off Ghleanna, "What about me?"

"Would you follow my sister into hell?"

"Wherever her soul goes, mine will follow." Bram let himself briefly glance at Addolgar. "She means everything to me. But you already knew that."

"Yeah. We already knew. The whole lot of us. But you're so damn polite, we figured you needed a push." He gestured at the growing number of watching dragons. "We never expected all this, though."

"Nor I. Not for an alliance."

"An alliance in writing. With dragons of the Desert Lands. You make that happen, and Rhiannon becomes the strongest dragon monarch in the last six centuries."

When Bram only blinked, Addolgar added, "I'm not stupid, royal. No matter what you've heard."

Ghleanna blocked another blow from Feoras's sword. Spun, brought her axe down, and when he blocked it, brought her tail around and slammed the tip of it into a weak spot under his arm.

Feoras roared in pain and yanked his body away from her. He stumbled a few feet ahead of her, bringing his arm down to stop the flow of blood.

Ghleanna turned on her talons, swung her axe and imbedded it into Feoras's spine.

The dragon whimpered, his body tensed. Ghleanna yanked out her axe and walked around him. Feoras dropped to his knees, gazing up at her once she stood in front of him.

She held out her free claw to Addolgar and he tossed his own axe to her. Ghleanna caught it, held it.

"Don't, Ghleanna," Feoras begged. "Please. Don't."

Ghleanna stared at the dragon for a moment. "I never loved you at all," she murmured. "I know that now.

"Of course—" Ghleanna hefted both axes—"that makes this so much easier."

She brought both axes together, not stopping until the blades met in the middle of Feoras's neck. The dragon's head popped off clean, landing on the ground at Ghleanna's claws while blood shot out and covered his comrades.

She stepped back and slowly looked over the other warriors and soldiers who were waiting. Waiting for their next orders. Their next decision. Ghleanna gave it to them.

"Death to all traitors!"

Her kin roared in agreement before descending on Feoras's foolish sycophants. She walked through the slaughter and over to Bram. He, again, leaned against a tree—waiting for her. And beside him stood her father.

"You off then, Da?" she asked.

"Aye. Too old for all this killing." And to prove that, her father turned and brought his axe down on the head of a traitor that had gotten too close. Spun once more and cut off the legs of another.

He faced them again. "Need to get back to my rocking chair and some hot tea."

"Clearly." Ghleanna hugged her father. "Tell Mum I'm fine and when this is all done, I'll be back to see her."

"You better. She will track you down if you don't." Ailean smiled at Bram. "Take good care of her, royal. She means the world to me."

"I will, sir."

Her father walked off and Ghleanna looked at Bram.

"That—" and he motioned to the pieces of Feoras's body— "was a bit showy."

"I like to give the lads a bit of a show. It's good for morale."

He leaned down, pressed his snout against hers. They held like that a moment and then he told her, "You have more killing to do."

"And I thought you'd try to stop me."

"My mercy has never extended to traitors, Ghleanna."

She stepped away from him, twisting her axes in both hands. "Then I'll get to work."

"Good. Because when we're done here, we still have a contact to meet in Alsandair."

"Overachiever," she accused him with a grin, before she turned and killed every traitor in her path.

Chapter 19

The Sand Dragon King's first born son and his entourage of fifty, a count that did not include his battalion of warrior dragons, gazed down at Rhiannon for several minutes. He said nothing as he watched the queen, then sniffed and turned from her.

Bercelak had his sword out and almost embedded in the Prince's back but the black dragon was taken down by at least four of his brothers and three of his sisters.

"I'll sign," the Prince said, sounding more bored than he'd been on the trip—which was no small feat. He represented his father on this, the king refusing to sign anything until he or someone he trusted had met with the new queen. So instead of Bram getting the signature he needed and returning to Rhiannon with alliance in claw, he'd been forced to bring the Prince and his entourage back to the queen's court. It would have been an intolerable and long trip, too, if not for Ghleanna.

Bram held up the parchment and handed him a quill. The Prince scratched off his signature and walked out, his entourage and guards following.

Ghleanna motioned to several of her cousins, "Escort them to the Borderlands. Keep 'em safe until they cross."

Once the Prince had left her court, Rhiannon snarled, "The arrogance!"

"He is the Dragon King's first born and heir to his throne," Bram reminded her.

"A throne of *sand*. As if that's anything to brag about." Rhiannon closed her eyes and roared, "Bercelak! Would you leave your brothers and sisters alone!"

"They started it!"

Rhiannon opened her eyes and smiled at Bram. "So my Lord Bram, it seems there are traitors in my midst."

"Aye, my queen."

"Did you get any names from Feoras?"

"Well . . ."

"I took his head before we had the chance," Ghleanna admitted.

"Honestly!" Rhiannon shook her head. "Just like your brother. Kill first, ask questions of the corpse later. Well . . . I guess I'll just have every Elder interrogated until someone admits his involvement—"

"Or," Bram quickly cut in, "I could do a quiet inquiry into the matter. Perhaps I can find more accurate information than torture can provide."

"Did I say torture? I don't remember saying torture. But your mercy, as always, leads the way. So you have my permission."

"Thank you, Majesty. And the truce?"

"Truce?"

"The one you wanted with Empress Helena?"

"The squid? Oh, yes. Yes." Although Ghleanna knew the

conniving cow forgot nothing. "Leave the documents with Elder Margh."

"Very well, my queen."

"And thank you, Lord Bram, for all your excellent work and sacrifice."

"I'm at your service and the service of your throne."

She smirked. "I know." Rhiannon glanced at the alliance document the Sand Dragon had signed. "But I must say that when Bercelak and I have *our* offspring, we will never allow them to be as arrogant as that!"

Ghleanna passed one quick glance to Bram before they both replied, "Uh-huh."

Please don't hug me. Please don't hug me.

But she did. And now Bram had *two* sets of black eyes glaring at him.

Finally, he said out loud, "It's not me! I swear!"

Rhiannon laughed and leaned back from Bram. "So cute! Isn't he cute, Bercelak?"

"No."

"Bercelak's only teasing."

"No, I'm not."

And then Ghleanna was there, prying Rhiannon's forearms from around Bram's shoulders.

"Back off, she-viper! This one's mine. You've got yours. Now you're stuck with him!"

"Oy!" Bercelak bellowed.

Bram pulled Ghleanna away from the one Dragonwitch who could turn her blood to acid. "Everyone just calm down. There's no point in—"

"And what the hells is going on with you and my sister?" Bercelak demanded.

"Uh . . ."

Ghleanna stepped between Bram and her brother.

"I wouldn't challenge him if I were you, Bercelak."

The greatest Dragonwarrior snorted. "Is that right?"

"He's got skills."

"What skills?"

"He's a right good head-butter. You should see what he did with the Fins."

Good gods, had the female gone mad?

Bercelak moved in. "Their heads are soft—like pudding. Not like mine. Hard as granite."

That's when Ghleanna said, "Addolgar says his head is harder than yours."

"That's 'cause it is," Addolgar happily tossed in.

"Centaur shit."

"Come on then, brother. Try me."

Bercelak refocused his attention on his brother and Ghleanna grabbed Bram's claw and dragged him out of the throne room.

"Wait . . . are they really going to—"

"Head butt each other until one passes out or dies of blood on the brain? Yep. They really are."

"And they protect our queen and lands. How reassuring."

"You'll get used to it."

"Ghleanna." And Bram stopped, bringing her up short.

"What is it?"

"I'm a dragon. I naturally assume I always get what I want. But there are no guarantees with you, I'm afraid."

She grinned. "Are you asking me now what you should have asked me a fortnight ago when we were lounging in the Sand Dragon King's salt springs?"

"Well, I couldn't rightly ask with your brothers, sisters, and cousins constantly popping in to stare at us and say, 'You two ain't done yet? What exactly are you doing in there anyway?'"

"Good point. But you are asking me now?"

"I am."

"To be your mate?"

"I am."

"Because you love me as I love you?"

"Aye."

"Because you can't imagine your life without me?"

Bram cupped Ghleanna's jaw with his claw, stroked a talon across her scales, and in a heartfelt whisper replied, "Aye."

That's when Ghleanna crossed her forearms over her chest and demanded, "Are you going to keep hugging that Rhiannon?"

"But it's not me!"

Epilogue

"Bram?"

Bram looked up from his work and smiled. "You're back quick."

His mate shook her head. "We've been gone eighteen months battling bloody Lightnings."

"Oh." He pointed at the document he worked on. "This is the truce for that. If it makes you feel—"

"It doesn't."

Oh, well. Best not to dwell, and changing the subject was always a good way to go. "Did you know they insisted I add a clause just for your nephew? What exactly was Gwenvael doing in the north?"

"You really don't want to know." She came around his chair and dropped into his lap. "Just wished you'd been there to calm that situation down."

"Or you could stop bringing Gwenvael with you *any-where*."

"That's our next option. At least not until he has a mate who can control his whorish ass. He's beginning to rival my father!"

"Beginning?"

"Och! Let's not speak of it." She kissed him and Bram held her tight.

"Have you gotten any sleep since I left?" she asked while Bram kissed a new scar on her throat.

"Why go to bed when you're not there?"

"Well, I'm back for a while."

"Is it just you?" And Bram was already leaning in to kiss her again.

"Hello, Da."

Bram's eldest slammed his blood-and-gore encrusted battle axe onto the table—on top of Bram's books and papers. "I'm starvin'. Any food?"

"Well—"

"Da." His second oldest, a dragoness who looked just like her mother, unloaded a battalion's worth of weapons onto the table—on top of his books and papers. "Any food? I'm starvin'."

"I just asked," her brother remarked.

"Are you saying I can't ask?"

"I didn't say you couldn't ask, you whiny little cow."

Two more of his offspring stormed in, dropping into chairs and putting their feet up on the table—all on top of his damn papers!

"You really want more offspring?" he had to ask Ghleanna as he always asked at moments like this.

"Just three more. Maybe four. Addolgar already has six!"

"Well, I'm not trying to keep up with your siblings, Captain! And do you think we can teach the next lot better manners?"

"They'll still be Cadwaladrs, luv."

"Guess that's a no then."

"Oy!" Ghleanna barked at the lounging dragons. "Get your hooves off the table and put your weapons away like I bloody taught ya!"

Grumbling as they liked to do, his offspring did what they

were ordered. They'd learned early not to question their mother's directives. Not if they, to quote Ghleanna, "Know what's good for them."

"Look at this mess they left," Ghleanna complained. "Charles!"

"He's out researching something for me and his name is Jonathan. Charles has been gone from this life for ages."

"I know. But I still miss him," she sighed. "Bang up job he did."

"Jonathan will be gone for a few days." He kissed her neck. "Perhaps the offspring can go to the pub tonight. For a few hours."

Ghleanna laughed and put her arms around Bram's shoulders. "I'm sure that'll be hard to do. You know how pious they all are."

Bram buried his nose against her neck, breathed in deep. "Gods, female. You smell like blood and death."

Ghleanna smiled. *Honestly, this dragon.* "I'd be insulted, peacemaker, and hurt, if I couldn't feel your cock trying to burrow its way through me chainmail."

"You've always known what you do to me, Ghleanna. Especially when you come back from battle with all your new scars and still covered in the blood and gore of our enemies. There's only so much a dragon can take!"

"All right. All right. Calm yourself. You barely notice when I'm gone and then you're all over me when I'm here."

"It's how I get through our time apart. It's worked so far. Now kiss me again."

She did, melting at the way his tongue delved deeper, his fingers stroking her shoulders and back. He'd do the same when he got her naked, but then he'd be slower. Lingering over every part of her. It made it worth coming back to a bloody castle rather than a cave.

"We're hungry."

Ghleanna glared across the table at her youngest male offspring and the rest of the brats standing beside him. "Then go get a cow."

"You're not going to feed us? What kind of mother are you?"

"One that can separate your legs from the rest of ya!"

"Or," Bram cut in, "you can go to the pub. We'll meet you there later."

Her youngest daughter shrugged. "Ain't got no money, do we?"

"I don't understand. Why aren't you pillaging like the rest of your kin?"

"It was the Northlands, Da. Ain't nothin' to pillage but the crows in the trees."

"And snow," their eldest added. "Lots and lots of snow."

Bram motioned to his study. "You know where I keep the gold coin."

As if on fire, their offspring made a desperate run for their father's study, climbing over the table and fighting each other through the door. It wasn't pretty.

"Ghleanna—"

"You tolerate them because you love me," she quickly reminded him.

"Gods, I do love you. I even love that lot. Crazed, murdering scum that they are."

"They are cute. And already making their names. And . . ."

"And?" Bram pushed.

"I was promoted to General."

Bram's smile was real and so very warm.

He hugged her tight. "My beautiful, beautiful mate. I'm so proud of you."

She knew that. Reveled in it. "And believe it or not—I got my rank directly from Bercelak."

"How the hells did you manage that?"

"No idea. And you know how he is. If we're Cadwaladrs, we gotta kill twice as many as other Dragonwarriors before that tight-lipped bastard will even grunt in our direction."

"Still a ray of sunshine, is he?"

Ghleanna laughed until their brats tore past them again on their way out the castle doors.

"Off to the ale," she muttered.

"And leaving us alone."

"Aye. That they have." She pressed her forehead against her mate's. "Gods, I've missed you, peacemaker. Those bloody cold nights fighting those damn Lightnings. And all I wanted was to get home to you."

"You are, Ghleanna. You are home. And I've never been happier."

Don't miss Erin Kellison's SHADOWMAN,
in stores now!

GHOSTS

They haunt the halls of the Segue Institute, terrifying the
living, refusing to cross over. But one soul is driven by a
very different force.

LOVE

It survives even death. And Kathleen O'Brien swore she
would return to those she was forced to leave too soon.

SHADOWMAN

He broke every rule to have her in life; now he will defy the
angels to find her in death.

THE GATE

Forging it is his single hope of being reunited with his
beloved, but through it an abomination enters the world.
Leaving a trail of blood and violence, the devil hunts her
too. Pursued through realms of bright fantasy and dark
reality, Kathleen is about to be taken . . .

"Fans of dark drama will be captivated by this intense new
series."—*Romantic Times*

"Powerful and fast-paced . . . a riveting read."
—*New York Times* bestselling author Nina Bangs